Compton Mackenzie

Carnival

JOHN MURRAY

First published in Great Britain in 1912

This paperback edition first published in 2012 by John Murray (Publishers)
An Hachette UK Company

1

© The Society of Authors 1912, 1951

A CIP catalogue record for this title is available from the British Library

ISBN 978-1-84854-770-4
E-book ISBN 978-1-84854-771-1

Typeset in Sabon by Hewer Text UK Ltd, Edinburgh

Printed and bound by Clays Ltd, St Ives plc

John Murray policy is to use papers that are natural, renewable
and recyclable products and made from wood grown in sustainable forests.
The logging and manufacturing processes are expected to conform to
the environmental regulations of the country of origin.

John Murray (Publishers)
338 Euston Road
London NW1 3BH

www.johnmurray.co.uk

'Put out the light, and then — put out the light.'

Foreword

In the autumn of 1907, having had a play produced at Edinburgh that spring and a slim book of poems published that October, I went to spend the winter at Cury, half-way between Helston and the Lizard. One afternoon a farmer of my acquaintance asked me to come to tea and meet his wife whom he had just wooed and married in the course of a brief visit to London.

'Do 'ee know the Leicester Lounge?' he asked.

The Leicester Lounge was a raffish bar at the corner of Leicester Square, looking down Coventry Street, where to-day stands Peter Robinson's shop.

'I do indeed,' I told him.

'Well, I took a fancy to one of the barmaids there and after I'd argued with her for a bit she married me. She's down home along now.'

So I went to tea, and in the kitchen of that farmhouse a quarter of a mile inland from a wild coast was sitting a young woman in her late twenties with an elaborate peroxide coiffure beneath which a pink-powdered face gazed in bewilderment at its surroundings while the sea-wind rattled the windows and moaned in the chimneys.

The bride was obviously embarrassed by my visit and I was aware of such a profound mental distress that I could never bring myself to intrude upon it again. Yet the memory of that inappropriate figure in that farmhouse kitchen haunted my fancy, and I made up my mind to write a play one day in an attempt to provide an explanation for the state of mind which led a barmaid in the Leicester Lounge to marry a dour Cornish farmer after a week's wooing.

Meanwhile, I spent the next six months in writing my first novel, and the next three years in finding a publisher for it. I made a vow I would not attempt so much as a short story until *The Passionate Elopement* was published.

In the late summer of 1910, H. G. Pélissier of the Follies offered me the job of writing the words to his music for a revue at the Alhambra called *All Change Here*; the words having been written, I was asked to turn the *corps de ballet* into a revue chorus and find girls in it able to sing trios and quartets. Few young authors can have been blessed with such an opportunity as those wonderful girls gave me to reach the heart of London. I still hear from some of them and I gratefully set on record that the foundation of my pile of books, over seventy volumes high now, was laid by those girls at the Alhambra forty years ago.

One afternoon I came out from a long rehearsal during which I leaned back in the dim, empty stalls, watching the *corps de ballet* flit like gay ghosts about the shadows of the stage. I came out just before the shutting in of a rainy autumn dusk and noticed an inquisitive figure waiting by the stage door. He was not unlike my Cornish farmer of three years ago as he stood there to eye the girls hurrying home to rest before the evening performance, and suddenly

I fancied one of them, gay and lovable, transported by circumstance to a storm-beaten farmhouse. The story of *Carnival* began to take shape in my imagination.

My first novel *The Passionate Elopement* was published on January 17th, 1911, my twenty-eighth birthday, and on the next day I sat down to write my second novel, the original title for which was *London Pride*. However, a play with that name was announced and I had to find another. *Columbine* was the next choice and finally that gave way to *Carnival*.

The first dozen chapters of the book were written at 36 Church Row, Hampstead, where my wife and I had taken the Muirhead Bones' flat for six months. Then in the spring we went back to the house in Phillack opposite Hayle in St. Ives' Bay where we were now living, and the rest of the book was written there with many interruptions by the work I was doing for the Follies. I finished *Carnival* at about three o'clock of a wild January morning. Martin Secker, my publisher, was lying asleep on a sofa. The fire had flickered out. I punched him hard and shouted: 'I've finished. Shall I read you the last chapter?' He heard it, and said: 'Thank God, it's finished.' He had reason for gratitude because the book was due to be published in a fortnight, and the printers were waiting for the final copy.

Carnival was published on January 17th, 1912, and although it was dismissed by the *Times Literary Supplement* in a few frigid lines among the 'also ran' novels of that week, which in those days was a really serious set-back for a young author, the rest of the reviews with very few exceptions were generous. J. M. Barrie sent me a heartening letter. Yeats, much to my surprise, gravely approved of the book. Henry James, while insisting that my heroine lacked the heroic stature for so elaborate a treatment, declared the book was in the tradition of those French romances like *Vie de Bohême*, 'all roses and sweet champagne and young love'.

'And lest you should be hurt by what I have said about your heroine, let me hasten to add that I should say the same of Flaubert's *Madame Bovary*.'

Gerald du Maurier suggested that I should make a play of *Carnival* for him, but Frank Curzon, under whose management he was, objected to Maurice Avery's being off the stage for the whole of the third act, and as I could not see a remedy for this I missed the great pleasure of writing a part for an actor I much admired.

That summer an enquiry came from William A. Brady, whose wife, Miss Grace George, had decided she would like to play the part of Jenny Pearl. So in September 1912 I sailed for the United States and a dramatized version was produced at the Garrick Theatre, Toronto, in November. Miss Grace George has been the only actress on the stage or in the films who has come near to my own idea of Jenny Pearl.

In 1915 *Carnival* was filmed for the first time. In 1922 I made another dramatic version under the title *Columbine*, Matheson Lang having used *Carnival* as a title for a melodrama he had adapted from the Italian. *Columbine* was first played at Nottingham, and later at the Prince's Theatre in London. In 1929 Eric Maschwitz made a remarkable radio version of the book which in its original form played from 9.30 p.m. to midnight, and was revived several times in a ninety-minute version made by Val Gielgud. That collaboration with Val Gielgud and Eric Maschwitz was among the most enjoyable experiences of my life. In 1931 a second film version was made with the stupid title *Dance Little Lady*. I declined to see a performance. In 1945 a third film was made, which kept the title *Carnival* but little else of the book I had written thirty years before. I refused to see a performance of this, but I did catch an unavoidable glimpse of a trailer of the film in Hong Kong and congratulated myself on that refusal.

A short opera was made of *Carnival* for the B.B.C., and in the spring of 1951 I read an abridged version of it for the 'Book at Bedtime'.

The book has been published in various editions by some eight publishers and the total sales in Britain and America were over half a million when it went out of print during the last war. It has been translated twice into French, and into several other languages.

I was tempted in correcting this new edition for press to make alterations to suit the lessons I have learnt in writing during the last forty years, but I resisted the impulse. Long ago I told Henry James that when I came back from the First World War I intended to rewrite *Carnival*.

He held up his hands in a wide gesture of dismay.

'You alarm . . . you . . . appal me with such news,' he declared, his large smooth face momentarily puckered with genuine distress. 'I once wasted ten . . . indeed, twelve precious years in foolishly supposing that in the light of experience I could grope my way toward a more . . .

toward that always elusive . . . in short that I could add yet something to what, when it was written, I had given all that I could give at that time. Renounce this preposterous ambition of yours, my dear boy. You have been granted the boon which above all a novelist should beg for himself. You have been granted that boon with a generosity beyond that accorded to any of your young contemporaries. You fling the ball up against the wall and it rebounds immediately into your hands. Whereas I . . .', he looked round that room in the Chelsea flat from the windows of which one saw the river shimmering through a filigree of boughs now almost bare of leaves, 'whereas I fling the ball against the wall, whence it rebounds not into my hands, but on to the next wall and from that wall to the next.' He followed with apprehensive glance the flight of that ghastly ball round the room. 'Until,' he concluded, 'at last it falls to the ground and dribbles very, very slowly toward my feet, and I, all my old bones aching, stoop, and most laboriously pick it up.'

Some critics have maintained that *Carnival* breaks in two with the marriage of Jenny Pearl to Zachary Trewhella. They may be right, but in as much as the original conception of the book was inspired by the strange scene in that Cornish farmhouse when I met the perplexed bride from the Leicester Lounge, I have never been able to see the marriage of Jenny as a break. That is a natural prejudice, and fondness for the book that made his name may be forgiven to any writer.

COMPTON MACKENZIE, 1951

Contents

I

Birth of Columbine

All day long over the grey Islington street, October casting
pearly mists had turned the sun to silver and made London
a city of meditation whose tumbled roofs and parapets
and glancing spires appeared serene and baseless as in a
lake's tranquillity.

The traffic, muted by the glory of a fine autumn day,
marched, it seemed, more slowly and to a sound of
heavier drums. Like mountain echoes street cries haunted
the burnished air, while a muffin-man, abroad too
early for the season, swung his bell intermittently with
a pastoral sound. Even the milk-cart, heard in the next
street, provoked the imagination of distant armour. The
houses seemed to acquire from the grey and silver web of
October enchantment a mysterious immensity. There was
no feeling of stressful humanity even in the myriad sounds
that in a sheen of beauty floated about the day. The sun
went down behind roofs and left the sky plumed with rosy
feathers. There was a cold grey minute before dusk came
stealing in richly and profoundly blue: then night sprang
upon the street, and through the darkness an equinoctial
wind swept moaning.

Along the gutters the brown leaves danced: the tall plane tree at the end of the street would not be motionless until December should freeze the black branches in diapery against a sombre sky. Along the gutters the leaves whispered and ran and shivered and leaped, while the gas-jets flapped in pale lamps.

There was no starshine on the night Jenny Raeburn was born, only a perpetual sound of leaves dancing and the footsteps of people going home.

Mrs. Raeburn had not been very conscious of the day's calm beauty. Her travail had been long: the reward scarcely apprehended. Already two elder children had closed upon her the gates of youth, and she was inclined to resent the expense of so much pain for an additional tie. There was not much to make the great adventure of childbirth endurable. The transitory amazement of a few relatives was a meagre consolation for the doubts and agonies of nine slow months. But the muslin curtains, tied back with raffish pink bows, had really worried her most of all. Something was wrong with them: their dinginess or want of symmetry annoyed her.

With one of those rare efforts towards imaginative comprehension which the sight of pain arouses in dull and stolid men, her husband had enquired, when he came back from work, whether there was anything he could do.

'Those curtains,' she had murmured.

'Don't you get worrying yourself about curtains,' he had replied. 'You've got something better to do than aggravate yourself with curtains. The curtains is all right.'

Wearily she had turned her face to the sad-coloured

wall-paper. Wearily she had transferred her discontent to the absence of one of the small brass knobs at the foot of the bed.

'And that knob. You never remember to get a new one.'

'Now it's knobs!' he had exclaimed, wondering at the foolishness of a woman's mind in the shadows of coming events. 'Don't you bother your head about knobs neither. Try and get a bit of sleep or something, do.'

With this exhortation he had retired from the darkening room to wander round the house, lighting various jets of gas, turning them down to the faintest blue glimmer, and hoping all the while that one of his wife's sisters would not emerge from the country at the rumour of the baby's arrival in order to force her advice upon a powerless household.

Edith and Alfred, his two elder children, had been carried off by the other aunt to her residence in Barnsbury, whence in three weeks they would be brought back to home and twilight speculations upon the arrival of a little brother or sister. In parenthesis, he hoped it would not be twins. They would be so difficult to explain, and the chaps in the shop would laugh. The midwife came down to boil some milk and make final arrangements. The presence of this ample lady disturbed him. The gale rattling the windows of the kitchen did not provide any feeling of fire-light snugness, but rather made his thoughts more restless, was even so insistent as to carry them on its wings, weak formless thoughts, to the end of Hagworth Street, where the bar of the Masonic Arms spread a wider and more cheerful illumination than was to be found in the harried kitchen of Number Seventeen. So Charlie Raeburn went out to spend time and money in piloting several friends across the shallows of Mr. Gladstone's mind.

Upstairs Mrs. Raeburn, left alone, again contemplated the annoying curtains; though by now they were scarcely visible against the gloom outside. She dragged herself off the bed and moving across to the window stood there, rubbing the muslin between her fingers. She remained for a while thus, peering at the backs of the houses opposite that, small though they really were, loomed with menace in the lonely dusk. Shadows of women at work, always at work, went to and fro upon the blinds. There were muffled sounds of children crying, the occasional splash of emptied pails, and against the last glimmer of sunset the smoke of chimneys blown furiously outwards. To complete the air of sadness and desolation the faded leaf of a dried-up geranium was lisping against the window-pane. She gave up fingering the muslin curtains and came back to the middle of the room, wondering vaguely when the next bout of pain was due and why the 'woman' didn't come upstairs and make her comfortable. There were matches on the toilet-table; so she lit a candle whose light gave every piece of ugly furniture a shadow and made the room ghostly and unfamiliar. Presently she held the light beside her face and stared at herself in the glass, and thought how pretty she still looked and, flushed by the fever, how young.

She experienced a sensation of fading personality. She seemed actually to be losing herself. Eyes, bright with excitement, glittered back from the mirror, and suddenly there came upon her overwhelmingly the fear of death.

And if she died, would anybody pity her, or would she lie forgotten always after the momentary tribute of white chrysanthemums? Death, death, she found herself saying over to the tune of a clock ticking in the passage. But she had no desire to die. Christmas was near with its shop-lit excursions and mistletoe and merriment. Why should she die? No, she would fight hard. A girl or a boy? What did it matter? Nothing mattered. Perhaps a girl would be nicer, and she should be called Rose. And yet, on second thoughts, when you came to think of it, Rose was a cold sort of a name and Rosie was common. Why not call her Jenny? That was better – with, perhaps, Pearl or Ruby to follow, when its extravagance would pass unnoticed. A girl should always have two names. But Jenny was the sweeter. Nevertheless, it would be as well to support so homely a name with a really ladylike one – something out of the ordinary.

Why had she married Charlie? All her relatives said she had married beneath her. Father had been a butcher – a prosperous man – and even he, in the family tradition, had not been considered good enough for her mother who was a chemist's daughter. Yet, she, Florence Unwin, had married a joiner. Why *had* she married Charlie? Looking back over the seven years of their married life, she could not remember a time when she had loved him as she had dreamed of love, in the airy room over the busy shop, as she had dreamed of love staring through the sunny window away beyond the Angel, beyond the great London skies. Charlie was so stupid, so dull; moreover, though not a drunkard, he was fond of half-pints and smelt of sawdust and furniture polish. Her sisters never liked, never would like him. She had smirched the great tradition of respect-ability. What would her grandfather the chemist have said? That dignified old man in brown velvet coat, treated always with deference even by her father, the jolly hand-some butcher? Florence Unwin married to a joiner – a man unable to afford to keep his house free from the inevitable lodger who owned the best bedroom, the bedroom that by right should have been hers. She had disgraced the family and for no high motive of passion – and once she was young and pretty. And still young, after all, and still pretty. She was only thirty-three now. Why had she married at all? But then her sisters did give themselves airs, and the jolly, handsome butcher had enjoyed too well and too often those drives to Jack Straw's Castle on fine Sunday afternoons under the rolling Hampstead clouds, had left little enough when he died, and Charlie came along, and perhaps even marriage with him had been less intolerable than existence among the frozen sitting-rooms of her two sisters, drapers' wives though they both were.

And the aunts, those three severe women? She might, perhaps, have lived with them when the jolly, handsome butcher died, with them in their house at Clapton, with them eternally dusting innumerable china ornaments and correcting elusive mats. The invitation had been extended, but was forbidding as a mourning-card or the melan-choly visit of an insurance agent with his gossip of death. Death? Was she going to die?

It did not matter. The pain was growing more acute. She dragged herself to the door and called down to the midwife, called two or three times.

There was no answer except from the clock with its whisper of Death and Death. Where was the woman? Where was Charlie? She called again. Then she remembered through what seemed years of grinding agony that the street door was slammed some time ago. Charlie must have gone out. With the woman? Had he run away from her? Was she, the wife, for ever abandoned? Was there no life in all the world to reach her solitude? The house was fearfully, unnaturally silent. She reached up to the cold gas bracket, and the light flared up without adding a ray of cheerfulness to the creaking passage. Higher still she turned it until it sang towards the ceiling, a thin geyser of flame. The chequers upon the oil-cloth became blurred as tears of self-pity welled up in her eyes. She was deserted, and in pain.

Her mind sailed off along morbid channels to the grim populations of hysteria. She experienced the merely nervous sensation of many black beetles running at liberty around the empty kitchen. It was a visualization of tingling nerves, and, fostered by the weakening influence of labour pains, it extended beyond the mere thought to the endowment of a mental picture with powerful and malign purpose so that, after a moment or two, she came to imagining that between her and the world outside black beetles were creating an impassable barrier.

Could Charlie and the woman really have run away? She called again and peered over the flimsy balustrade down to the ground floor. Or was the woman lying in the kitchen drunk? Lying there, incapable of action, among the black beetles? She called again: 'Mrs. Nightman! Mrs. Nightman!'

How dry her hands were, how parched her tongue; and her eyes, how they burned.

Was she actually dying? Was this engulfing silence the beginning of death? What was death?

And what was that? What were those three tall, black figures moving along the narrow passage downstairs? What were they, so solemn and tall and silent, moving with inexorable steps higher and higher?

'Mrs. Nightman, Mrs. Nightman!' she shrieked, and stumbled in agony of body and horror of mind back to the flickering bedroom, back to the bed.

And then there was light and a murmur of voices, saying: 'We have come to see how you are feeling, Florence,' and sitting by her bed she recognized the three aunts from Clapton in their bugles and cameos and glittering bonnets.

There was a man, too, whom she had only just time to realize was the doctor, not the undertaker, before she was aware that the final effort of her tortured body was being made without assistance from her own will or courage.

She waved away the sympathizers. She was glad to see the doctor and Mrs. Nightman herding them from the room, like gaunt black sheep; but they came back again as inquisitive animals will when, after what seemed a thousand thousand years of pain, she could hear something crying and the trickle of water and the singing of a kettle.

Perhaps it was Aunt Fanny who said: 'It's a dear little girl.'

The doctor nodded, and Mrs. Raeburn stirred and with wide eyes gazed at her baby.

'It is Jenny, after all,' she murmured; then wished for the warmth of a new-born child against her breast.

II

Fairies at the Christening

A fortnight after the birth of Jenny, her three great-aunts, black and stately as ever, paid a second visit to the mother.

'And how is Florrie?' enquired Aunt Alice.

'Going on fine,' said Florrie.

'And what is the baby to be called?' asked Aunt Fanny.

'Jenny, and perhaps Pearl as well.'

'Jenny?'

'Pearl?'

'Jenny Pearl?'

The three aunts disapproved the choice with combined interrogation.

'We were thinking,' announced Aunt Alice, 'your aunts were thinking, Florrie, that since we have a good deal of room at Carminia House—'

'It would be a capital plan for the baby to live with us,' went on Aunt Mary.

'For since our father died' (old Frederick Horner the chemist had been under a laudatory stone slab at Kensal Green for a quarter of a century), 'there has been room and to spare at Carminia House,' said Aunt Fanny.

'The baby would be well brought up,' Aunt Alice declared.

'Very well brought up, and sent to a genteel academy for young – ladies.' The break before the last word was due to Miss Horner's momentary but distinctly perceptible criticism of the unladylike bedroom where her niece lay suckling her baby girl.

'We should not want her at once, of course,' Aunt Fanny explained. 'We should not expect to be able to look after her properly – though I believe there are now many Infant Foods very highly recommended even by doctors.'

Perhaps it was the pride of chemical ancestry that sustained Miss Frances Horner through the indelicacy of the last admission. But old maids' flesh was weak, and the carmine suffusing her waxen cheeks drove the eldest sister into an attempt to cover her confusion by adding that she for one was glad in these days of neglected duties to see a mother nursing her own child.

'We feel,' she went on, 'that the arrival of a little girl shows very clearly that the Almighty intended us to adopt her. Had it – had she proved to be a boy, we should have made no suggestions about her except, perhaps, that her name should be Frederick after our father the chymist.'

'With possibly Philip as a second name,' Miss Mary Horner put in.

'Philip?' her sisters asked.

And now Miss Mary blushed, whether on account of a breach of sisterly etiquette or whether for some guilty memory of a long-withered affection, was never discovered by her elders or anyone else either.

'Philip?' her sisters repeated.

'It is a very respectable name,' said Miss Mary

apologetically, and for the life of her could only recall Philip of Spain, whose admirable qualities were not enough marked to justify her in breaking in upon Miss Horner's continuation of the discussion.

'Feeling as we do,' the latter said, 'that a divine providence has given a girl-child to the world on account of our earnest prayers, we think we have a certain right to give our advice, to urge that you, my dear Florence, should allow us the opportunity of regulating her education and securing her future. We enjoy between us a comfortable little sum of money, half of which we propose to set aside for the child. The rest has already been promised to the Reverend Williams to be applied as he shall think fit.'

'Like an ointment, I suppose,' said Florrie.

'Like an ointment? Like what ointment?'

'You seem to think that money will cure everything – if it's applied. But who's going to look after Jenny if you die? Because,' she went on before they had time to answer, 'Jenny isn't going to be applied to the Reverend Williams. She isn't going to mope all day with Bibles as big as tramcars stuck on her knees. No, thank you, Aunt Alice, Jenny'll stay with her mother.'

'Then you won't allow us to adopt her?' snapped Miss Horner, sitting up so straight in the cane-bottomed chair that it creaked again and again.

'I don't think,' Aunt Fanny put in, 'that you are quite old enough to understand the temptations of a young girl?'

'Aren't I?' said Florence. 'I think I know a sight more about 'em than you do, Aunt Fanny. I am a mother, when all's said and done.'

'But have you got salvation?' asked Miss Horner.

'I don't see what salvation and all that's got to do with my Jenny,' Mrs. Raeburn argued.

'But you would like her to be sure of everlasting happiness?' enquired Miss Fanny mildly, amazed at her niece's obstinacy.

'I'd like her to be a good girl, yes.'

'But how can she be good till she has found the Lord? We're none of us good,' declared Miss Mary, 'till we have been washed in the blood of the Lamb.'

'I quite believe you're in earnest, Aunt Alice,' declared Mrs. Raeburn. 'In earnest and anxious to do well by Jenny, but I don't hold and never did hold with cooping children up. Poor little things!'

'There wouldn't be any cooping up. As a child of grace, she would often go out walking with her aunts, and sometimes, perhaps, be allowed to carry the tracts.'

Mrs. Raeburn looked down in the round blue eyes of Jenny.

'Perhaps you'd like her to jump to glory with a tambourine?' she said.

'Jump to glory with a tambourine?' echoed Miss Horner.

'Or bang the ears off of Satan with a blaring drum? Or go squalling up aloft with them saucy Salvation hussies?'

The austere old ladies were deeply shocked by the levity of their niece's enquiries.

Sincerely happy, sincerely good, they were unable to understand anyone not burning to feel at home in the whitewashed chapel which to them was an abode of murmurous peace. They wanted everybody to recognize with glad familiarity every text that decorated the bleak walls with an assurance of heavenly joys. Their quiet encounters with spiritual facts had nothing in common with those misguided folk who were escorted by brass bands along the shining road to God. They were happy in the exclusiveness of their religion not from any conscious want of charity, but from the exaltation aroused by the privilege of divine intimacy and the joyful sense of being favourites in heavenly places. The Rev. Josiah Williams, for all his liver-coloured complexion and clayey nose, was to them a celestial ambassador. His profuse outpourings of prayer took them higher than any skylark with its quivering wings. His turgid discourses, where every metaphor seemed to have escaped from a Store's price-list, were to them more fruitful of imaginative results than any poet's song. His grave visits, when he seemed always to be either washing his hands or wiping his boots, left in the hearts of the three old maids memories more roseate than any sunset of the Apennines. Therefore, when Mrs. Raeburn demanded to know if they were anxious for Jenny to jump to glory with a tambourine, the religious economy of the three Miss Horners was upset. On consideration, even jumping to glory without a tambourine struck them as an indelicate method of reaching Paradise.

'And wherever did you get the notion of adopting Jenny?' continued the niece. 'For I'm sure I never suggested any such thing.'

'We got the notion from above, Florence,' explained Miss Fanny. 'It was a direct command from our Heavenly Father. I had a vision.'

'Your Aunt Fanny,' proclaimed the elder sister, 'dreamed she was nursing a white rabbit. Now we have not eaten rabbits since on an occasion when the Reverend Williams was taking a little supper with us, we unfortunately had a bad one – a high one. There had been nothing to suggest rabbits, let alone white rabbits, to your Aunt Fanny. So I said: "Florence is going to have a baby. It must be a warning." We consulted the Reverend Williams who said it was very remarkable, and must mean the Almighty was calling upon us as He called upon the infant Samuel. We enquired first if either of your sisters was going to have a baby also. Caroline Threadgale wrote an extremely rude letter and Mabel Purkiss was even ruder. So, evidently it is the will of God that we should adopt your baby girl. We prayed to Him to make it a little girl because we are more familiar with little girls, never having had a brother and our father having died a good while ago now. Well, it is a girl. So plainly, oh, my dear niece, can't you see how plainly God commands you to obey Him?'

Then Miss Horner stood up and looked so tall and severe that her niece was frightened for a moment, and half expected to see the flutter of an angel's wing over the foot of the bedstead. She nerved herself, however, to resist the will of Heaven.

'Dreaming of rabbits hasn't got nothing to do with babies. I forget what it does mean – burglars or something, but not babies, and you shan't have Jenny.'

'Think, my dear niece, before you refuse,' Miss Horner remonstrated. 'Think before you condemn your child to everlasting damnation; for nothing but the gates of Hell can come from denying the Heavenly Will. Think of your child growing up in wickedness and idle places, growing old in ignorance and contempt of God. Think of her dancing along the broad ways of Beelzebub, eating of the fruit of the forbidden tree, kissing and waltzing and making love and theatre-going and riding outside omnibuses. Think of her journeying from vanity unto vanity and becoming a prey to evil and lascivious men. Remember the wily serpent who is waiting for her. Give her to us that she may be washed in the blood of the Lamb and, crying Hallelujah, may have a harp in the Kingdom of Heaven.

'If you reject us,' the old lady went on, her marble face taking on the lively hues of passion, her eyes on fire with the greatness of her message, 'you reject God. Your daughter will go by ways you know not of; she will be lost in the mazes of destruction, she will fall in the pit of sin. She will be trampled under foot on the Day of Judgment, and be flung for ever into wailing and gnashing of teeth. Her going out and coming in will be perilous. Her path will be set with snares of the giant of Iniquity. Listen to us, my dear niece, lest your child become a daughter of pleasure, a perpetual desire to the evil-minded. Give her to us that we may keep her where neither moth nor rust doth corrupt, and no thieves break in and steal.'

The old lady, exhausted by the force of her prophecy, sank down into the chair and, elated by the splendours of the divine wrath, seemed indeed to be a noble and fervid messenger from God.

In Mrs. Raeburn, however, these denunciations wakened a feeling of resentment.

'Here,' she cried, 'are you cursing my Jenny?'

'We are warning you.'

'Well, don't sit nodding there like three crows; your cursing will come to nothing, because you don't know nothing about London, nor about life, nor about nothing. What's the good of joring about the way to Heaven when you don't know the way to Liverpool Street without asking a policeman? I say Jenny shall be happy. I say she shall be jolly and merry and laugh whenever she wants to, bless her, and never come to no harm with her mother to look after her. She shan't be a Plain Jane and No Nonsense with her hair screwed back like a broom, but she shall be Jenny sweet and handsome with lips made for kissing and eyes that will sparkle and shine like six o'clock of a summer morning.'

Mrs. Raeburn was sitting up in bed holding high the unconscious infant.

'And she *shall* be happy, d'ye hear? And you shan't have her, so get out, and don't wag your bonnets at my Jenny.'

The three aunts looked at each other.

'I see the footprints of Satan in this room,' said Miss Horner.

'Not a bit of it,' contradicted her niece. 'It's your own muddy feet.'

Outside, a German band seduced from hibernation by St. Luke's summer played the March of the Priests from *Athalie*, not always in perfect tune; and soon a jaded omnibus with the nodding bonnets of the three Miss Horners jogged slowly back to Clapton.

When the old ladies withdrew from the dingy bedroom

the swish and rustle of their occupation, Mrs. Raeburn was at first relieved, afterwards indignant, finally somewhat anxious.

Could this strawberry-coloured piece of womanhood beside her really be liable to such a life of danger and temptation and destruction? Could this wide-eyed stolidity ever become a spark to set men's hearts afire? Would those soft uncrumpling hands know some day love's fever? No, no, her Jenny should be a home-bird — always a home-bird, and marry some nice young chap who could afford to give her a comfortable house where she could smile at children of her own, when the three old aunts had mouldered away like dry sticks of lavender. All that babble of flames and hell was due to religion gone mad, to extravagant perusal of brass-bound bibles, to sour virginity. With some perception of human weakness, Mrs. Raeburn began to realize that her aunts' heads were full of heated imaginations because they had never possessed an outlet in youth. The fierce adventures of passion had been withheld from them, and now in old age they were playing with fires that should have been extinguished long ago. Fancy living with those terrible old women at Clapton, hearing nothing but whispers of hell-fire. All that talk of looking after Jenny's soul was just telling the tale. There must be some scheme behind it all. Perhaps they wanted to save money in a servant, and thought to bring on Jenny by degrees to a condition of undignified utility.

Mrs. Raeburn was by no means a harsh judge of human nature, but her aunts having arrived at an unpropitious moment she could not see their offer from a reasonable standpoint. Moreover, she had the proud woman's invariable suspicion of a gift; withal, there was a certain cynicism which made her say 'presents weren't given for nothing in this world.' Anyway, she decided, they were gone, and a good riddance, and she wouldn't ask them to Hagworth Street again in a hurry. The problem of getting in a woman to help now arose. Mrs. Nightman was off to-morrow; Alf and Ede would be back in a week; and Charlie's breakfast must be attended to. Mrs. Nightman informed her she knew where a likely girl of fifteen was to be found – a child warranted to be willing and clean and truthful. To-morrow, Mrs. Raeburn settled, this paragon must be interviewed.

To-morrow dawned, and in the wake of sunrise came the paragon. She still wore the dresses of childhood, but paid toll to responsibleness by screwing up her mouse-coloured hair to the likeness of a cockle-shell, adding thereby, in her mother's estimation, eighteen months, in her own, ten years to her age. She was a plum-faced child with glazed cheeks. The paragon was just an ordinary old little girl, pitched into life with a pair of ill-fitting boots, a pinafore and half a dozen hairpins. But she would do. Wait a minute. Was she inclined to loll or mouch? No. Was she bound to tilt a perambulator? No. Must she read light fiction when crossing a road? She didn't like reading.

Mrs. Raeburn decided more than ever that she would do.

Was she good at washing unwilling children? She washed many brothers and sisters with yellow soap and dried them thoroughly every Saturday night. Did she want the place? Mother would be glad if she got it. What was her name? Ruby. Mrs. Raeburn thanked goodness she had abandoned Ruby as a possible suffix to Jenny. Her surname? O'Connor. Irish? She didn't know. Yes, she should have a week's trial.

So the paragon became a part of the household as integral as the furniture and almost as ugly, and, as she grew older, almost as unnecessarily decorated. Alfie, the young Tartar, tried to break her in by severe usage, but succumbed to the paragon's complete imperviousness. Edie was too young to regard her as anything but an audience for long and baseless fits of weeping.

The two children were brought back by Aunt Mabel from her house at Barnsbury, where they had sojourned during the birth of their sister.

'Careful, now, Alfie,' adjured his aunt, as he stumped upstairs to greet his mother. 'Don't you get making a noise, you naughty boy.'

Fortified by half-unveiled pieces of toffee, Alfred and Edith were scooped into the room by Mrs. Purkiss, who had renounced the cash-desk for the day in order to nod elaborate smiles at Jenny, in order to say 'catchee-catchee' to Jenny, in order to congratulate her sister Florence. 'Isn't she a little dear? Oh, Florrie, she is a little love. Oh, look, Alfie, there's a lovely little baby. Kiss little Cissie. Kiss her, Alfie.'

'What is it?' demanded the latter bluntly.

'A dear little sister. Oh she is a little duck. And if she isn't laughing! Well, there! did you ever?'

Alfie looked at Edie to observe how she received the raptures of admiration. Edie unluckily dropped her toffee at this crisis of judgment, and began to cry.

'Lost your toffee, you silly girl?' asked Aunt Mabel, stepping back to rescue it and crushing it to atoms in the attempt. Edie cried all the louder, and Alfie, being commanded to soothe her by surrendering a share of his own piece, began to cry too. And then the baby cried and Mrs. Raeburn said:

'Don't you wish you had your hands full, Mabe?' Whereupon Mabe looked very wise and put a finger to her lips.

'What, really?' said Mrs. Raeburn.

'In May, if all goes according,' her sister replied.

'What's Bill say?'

'Oh, he's quite delighted. Goes out with himself all the time now.'

The paragon came in to carry off Edie and Alfie to the consolations of the kitchen.

'You can give him the rolling-pin, Ruby. Only see he doesn't get banging about with it and knock nothing over: and put Edie in her chair.'

'Kiss your dear little sister, Alfie.' Reconciled to the loss of his toffee by the prospect of playing with the rolling-pin, Alfie was lifted up by Aunt Mabel to affix sweetened pledges of piety to his mother and Jenny.

'Why's my mummy in bed?'

'Because she isn't very well.'

'Will she be well to-morrow?'

'Yes.'

'And the next day?'

'Very likely.'

'And for ever an' dever?'

20

'Now that'll do with questions, Mr. Knowall,' inter-rupted his mother. 'Pop off with Ruby, like a good boy'; and Alfie popped off, even justifying the comparison with the standard of merit until half-way downstairs, when he kicked the O'Connor's ankle, and was told he was a young spiteful and no mistake. Edie, on second thoughts, had been considered safer in the custody of her mother and aunt who, having discussed the technical side of Jenny's arrival, concentrated ultimately upon the moral aspects of bringing up children.

'You see, what I say is the mother's the proper one to know what's best for her own child,' declared Mrs. Raeburn.

'That's quite right.'

'I know you're a marvel for chapel—'

'Not the same as Aunt Alice.'

'Weslean, isn't it?'

'Ours is. Theirs is Primitive Methodist.'

'Oh, well, it's all the same.'

'Pardon me, it's a very different pair of shoes. Halfway to Church of England, you might say, ours is.'

'Yes, but you don't hold with humbugging kids about with prayer-meetings noon and night. You remember what father used to say? He didn't hold with it, and you couldn't meet a nicer man than father, so jolly as he always was.'

'But he didn't leave any money,' Mrs. Purkiss pointed out.

'And I don't blame him for one. He enjoyed himself, and I don't suppose he saw the inside of a hymn-book all his life, and mother, you come to think of it, mother wasn't out of the way religious, not like them sisters of hers.'

'She used to go to chapel.'

'Yes, when it was fine, but when it was wet, not she. "This isn't a new bonnet morning," she used to say.'

'And it didn't do the business any good, either, her being so unregular,' said Mrs. Purkiss. 'Regular chapel-going looks respectable and customers like it, more perhaps in drapering than in butchering, but that's not to say as you ought to have given them Jenny.'

'Well, you don't think I did wrong?'

'No, I don't. I think you acted all for the best, and I'd have done the same thing myself. I was *very* off-handed with 'em when they came buzzing round me. What did Charlie say?'

'Oh, Charlie,' replied Mrs. Raeburn. 'Well, there, you know what Charlie is.'

'I do, and though he's your husband and my brother-in-law, I don't like him.'

'Charlie's all right.'

'He may be, but he acts all wrong. But there, he's your husband, not mine.'

They made a curious contrast, the two sisters, as they chattered on. Mrs. Purkiss was by about two years the senior of Florence, and so far childless. She had married Mr. William Purkiss, a draper of no great importance to drapery, but still quite comfortably off and, being thrifty and unspeculative, a safe match. Moreover, Caroline the eldest had also married a draper – Mr. James Threadgale of Galton in Hampshire, and Mabel could not resist the temptation to establish herself upon an exactly equal footing with her sister. Mabel Purkiss was tall and thin, a kindly woman in most ways, but, according to Charlie, blooming stuck-up. He couldn't put up with her at no price, he asserted. On the present occasion she was carrying out her reputation for stuck-uppishness by wearing a hard-featured dress of electric blue, and her inconspicuous breast was piped after the fashion of a hussar.

'Too much of it altogether,' said critical Charlie that night. 'I'm glad I haven't got to walk down the Holloway Road with that. And that bonnet. Come off! Why, it would make a Frenchman laugh.'

Mrs. Raeburn was softer and plumper and shorter than her sister. She had a rosy complexion, and eyes as bright as a bird's. She had too the merriest laugh in the world till Jenny grew older and made it sound almost mirthless beside her own. It was this capacity for laughter which made her resent the aunts' attempt to capture Jenny for melancholy.

Although, before the child's birth, she had not been particularly enthusiastic about its arrival, the baby already possessed a personality so compelling that the mother esteemed her above both the elder children, not because she was the last born, but because she genuinely felt the world was the richer by her baby. If she had been asked to express this conviction in words, she would have been at a loss. She would have been embarrassed and self-conscious, sure that you were laughing at her. She did venture once to ask Mabel if she thought Jenny prettier than the other two; but Mabel laughed indulgently and Mrs. Raeburn could not bring herself to enlarge upon the point.

She wished somehow that her mother could have lived

to see Jenny, and her father, too. Of this desire she was not aware when Alfie and Edie arrived. She felt positive her father would have considered Jenny full of life. Paradoxically enough for a butcher, Mr. Unwin had admired life more than anything else. Perhaps Mrs. Raeburn experienced an elation akin to that felt of old by wayside nymphs who bore children to Apollo and other divine philanderers. She knew that, however uneventful the rest of her life might be, in achieving Jenny she had done something comparable to her dreams as a girl in the sunny Islington window that looked away down to the Angel. She could not help feeling a subtle pity for her elder sister, whose firstborn was due in May. Boy or girl, it would be a putty statuette beside her Jenny. The latter was alive. How amazingly she was conscious of that vitality in the darkness, when she felt the baby against her breast.

Her own eyes were bright, but Jenny's eyes were stars that made her own look like pennies beside them. Such fancies she found herself weaving, lying awake in the night-time.

III

Dawn Shadows

Jenny reached the age of two years and a few months without surprising her relatives by any prodigious feats of intelligence or wickedness. But in Hagworth Street there was not much leisure to regard the progress of babyhood. There was no time for more than physical comparisons with other children. It would be pleasant to pretend that Jenny gazed at the stars, clapping a welcome to Cassiopea and singing to the Pleiades; but as a matter of fact it was not very easy to regard the heavens from the kitchen window of Number Seventeen. It would be pleasant to say that flowers were a joy to her from the beginning, but very few flowers came to Hagworth Street – groundsel for the canary sometimes, and plantains, but not much else. The main interest of Jenny's earliest days lay rather with her mother than herself.

The visit of the three old aunts roused Mrs. Raeburn to express her imagination at first, but gradually assumed a commonplace character as the months rolled by without another visit, and as Jenny with a chair pushed before her learned to walk rather earlier than most children, but showed no other sign of suffering or benefiting by that grim intervention. Perhaps, when she pushed her wooden guide so quickly along the landing that chair and child bumped together down every stair, her mother was inclined to think she was lucky not to be killed. Anyway, she said so to the child who was shrieking on the mat in the hall; and in after years Jenny could remember the painful incident. Indeed, that and a backward splash into the washtub on the first occasion of wearing a frock of damson velveteen were the only events of her earliest life that impressed themselves at all sharply or completely upon her mind. Through time's distorted haze she could also vaguely recall an adventure with treacle when, egged on by Alfie, she had explored the darkness of an inset cupboard and wedged the stolen tin of golden syrup so tightly round her silvery curls that Alfie had shouted for help. The sensation of the sticky substance trickling down her face in numerous thin streams remained with her always.

People were only realized in portions. For example, Ruby O'Connor existed as a rough red hand descending upon her suddenly in the midst of baby enjoyments. Alfie and Edie were two noises acquiring with greater nearness the character of predatory birds. That is to say in Jenny's mind the intimate approach of either always announced loss or interruption of a pleasure. Her father she first apprehended as a pair of legs forming a gigantic archway, vast as the Colossus of Rhodes must have loomed to the triremes of the Confederacy. Better than kisses or admonitions she remembered her mother's skirt whether as support or sanctuary. The rest of mankind she did not at all distinguish from trees walking. She was better able to

26

conceive a smile than a face, but the realization of either largely depended upon its association with the handkerchief of 'peep-bo.'

Seventeen Hagworth Street was familiar first of all through the step of the front door which she was invariably commanded to mind. She did not grasp its propinquity from the perambulator, for, when lifted out of the latter and told to run in to mother, it was only the step which assured her of the vast shadowy place of warmth and familiar smells in which she spent most of her existence. Of the smells the best remembered in after-life was that of warm blankets before the kitchen fire. Her only approach to an idea of property rested in the security of a slice of bread and butter that could be devoured slowly without wakening Alfie's cupidity. On the other hand, when jam was added, the slice must be gobbled not from greediness, but for fear of losing it. This applied also to the incidental booty of stray chocolates or paints. Her notion of territory was confined to places where she could sit or lie at ease. The patchwork hearthrug which provided warmth, softness, something to tug at and, sometimes, pieces of coal to chew, was probably her earliest conception of home, and perhaps her first disillusionment was due to a volatile spark burning her cheek. Bed struck her less as a prelude to the oblivion of sleep than as a spot where she was not worried about sucking her thumb. Perhaps her first emotion of mere sensuousness was the delicious anticipation of thumb-sucking as Ruby O'Connor propelled her upstairs with the knee, a sensuousness that was only very slightly ruffled by the thought of soap and

27

flannelette. Suspicion was born when once she was given a spoonful of jam whose melting sweetness disclosed a clammy sediment of grey powder, so that ever afterwards the offer of a spoon meant kicks and yells, dribbles and clenched resistance. Her first deception lay in pretending to be asleep when she was actually awake, as animals counterfeit death to avoid disturbance. Whether, however, she had any idea of being what she was not is unlikely, as she did not yet possess a notion of being. Probably 'peep-bo' when first practised by herself helped to formulate an embryonic egoism.

The birth of light on summer mornings kindled a sense of wonder, when she realized that light did not depend on human agency. Later on dawn was connected in her mind with the suddenly jerky movement of the nightlight's luminous reflection upon the ceiling, at which she would stare for hours in meditative content. This movement was always followed by the splutter and hiss of the drowning wick, and her first feeling of nocturnal terror was experienced when once these symptoms occurred and were followed, not by morning light, but by darkness. Then she shrieked, not because she feared anything in the darkness yet, but because she could not understand it.

The sensations of this Islington baby may have resembled those of a full-grown Carib or Hottentot in their simple acceptance of primary facts, in a desire for synthetic representation which distinguishes an unsophisticated audience of plays, in that odd passion for accuracy whose breach upsets a habit, whose observance confirms dogs, children and savages in their hold upon life.

As was natural for one more usually occupied with effects than causes, Jenny took delight in coloured chalks and beads, and probably a vivid scarlet pélisse first awoke her dormant sense of beauty. The appearance of this vestment was more important than its purpose, but the tying on of her 'ta-ta' – at first a frilled bonnet, later on a rakish Tam o' Shanter – was clapped as the herald of drowsy glidings in cool airs. She would sit in the perambulator, staring solemnly at Ruby and only opening her eyes a little wider when she was bumped down to take a crossing and up to regain the pavement. Passers-by, who leaned over to admire her, gained no more appreciation than a puzzled blink, less than was vouchsafed to the sudden shadow of a bird's flight across her vision.

Then came hot summer days and a sailor hat which enrolled her in the crew of H.M.S. Goliath. This hat she disliked on account of the elastic which Alfie loved to catch hold of and let go with a smacking sound that hurt her chin dreadfully; and sometimes in tugging at it she would herself let it slip so that it caught her nose like a whip.

These slow promenades up and down the shady side of Hagworth Street were very pleasant; although the inevitable buckling of the strap began to impede her ideas of freedom, so much so in time that it became a duty to herself to wriggle as much as possible before she let Ruby fasten it round her waist. Perhaps the first real struggle for self-expression happened on a muddy day when she discovered that by letting her podgy hand droop over the edge of the perambulator, the palm of it could be exquisitely tickled by the slow and moist revolutions of the wheel. Ruby instantly forbade this. Jenny declined to obey the command. Ruby leaned over and slapped the offending hand. Jenny shrieked and kicked. Edie fell down and became involved with the wheels of the perambulator. Alfie knelt by a drain to pretend he was fishing. Jenny screamed louder and louder. An errand-boy looked on. An old lady rebuked the flustered Ruby. The rabbit-skin rug palpitated with angry little feet. Ruby put up the hood and tightened the strap round Jenny, making her more furious than ever. It came on to rain. It came on to blow. It was altogether a thoroughly unsatisfactory morning.

'I'll learn you, Miss Artful, when I gets you home. You will have your own way, will you? Young Alfie, come out of the gutter, you naughty boy. I'll tell your father. Get up, do, Edie.'

At last they reached Number Seventeen. Summoned by yells, Mrs. Raeburn came to the door.

'Whatever have you been doing to the children, Ruby?'

'Lor', mum, they've been that naughty, I haven't known if I was on my head or my heels.'

The interfering old lady came up at this moment.

'That girl of yours was beating your baby disgracefully.'

'No, I never,' declared Ruby.

'I shall report you to the Society for the Prevention of Cruelty to Children.'

'That's right, Mother Longnose, you'll do a lot,' said Ruby, whose Irish ancestry was flooding her cheeks.

'Were you whipping Jenny?' enquired Mrs. Raeburn.

'I slapped her wrist.'

'What for?'

'Because she wouldn't keep her hands off of the wheel. I told her not to, but she would go on.'

'I shall report you all,' announced the old lady.

This irritated Mrs. Raeburn, who replied that she would report the old lady as a wandering lunatic. Jenny's right to act as she wished was in the balance. The old lady, like many another before, ruined freedom's cause by untimely propaganda. Mrs. Racburn plucked her daughter from the perambulator, shook her severely and said: 'You bad, naughty girl,' several times in succession. Jenny paused for a moment in surprise, then burst into yells louder by far than she had ever achieved before, and was carried into the house out of reach of sympathy.

From that moment she was alert to combat authority. From that moment to the end of her days, life could offer her nothing more hateful than attempted repression. That this struggle over the wheel of a perambulator endowed her with a consciousness of her own personality, it would be hard to assert positively, but it is significant that about this age (two years and eight months) she no longer always spoke of herself as Jenny, but sometimes took the first personal pronoun. Also, about this age, she began to imagine that people were laughing at her and, being taken by her mother into a shop on one occasion, set up a commotion of tears because she insisted the ladies behind the counter were laughing at her, when really the poor ladies were trying to be particularly pleasant. When Jenny was three, another baby came to Hagworth Street – dark-eyed, puny and wan-looking. Jenny was put on the bed beside her.

'This is May,' said her mother.

'I love May,' said Jenny.

'Very much, do you love her?'

'Jenny loves May. I love May. May is Jenny's dolly.'

And from that moment, notwithstanding the temporary interruptions of many passionate quarrels, Jenny made that dark-eyed little sister one of the great facts in her life. This was well for May, because, as she grew older, she grew into a hunchback.

Two more years went by of daily walks and insignificant adventures. Jenny was five. Alfie and Edie were now stalwart scholars who rushed off in the mornings, the former armed, according to the season, with chestnuts, pegtops or bags of marbles, the latter full of whispers and giggles, always one of a bunch of other girls distinguishable only by dress. About this time Jenny came to the conclusion she did not want to be a girl any longer. But the bedrock of sexual differences puzzled her: obviously one vital quality of boyishness was the right to wear breeches. Jenny took off her petticoats and stalked about the kitchen.

'You rude thing!' said Ruby, shocked by the exhibition.

'I'm not a rude thing,' Jenny declared; 'I'm being a boy.'

'And wherever is your petticoats?'

'I frowed 'em away,' said Jenny; 'I'm a boy.'

'You're a rude little girl.'

'I'm not a girl. I won't be a girl. I want to be a boy.' Jenny darted for the street, encountering by the gate the outraged blushes of Edie and her bunch of secretive companions.

'Did you ever?' said the ripest. 'Look at Ede's sister.'

Boys opposite began to 'holler.' Alfie appeared bent double in an effort to secure a Blood Alley. He lost at once the marble and the respect of his schoolfellows. His confusion was terrible. His sister skirtless before the public eye! Young Jenny making him look like a fool!

'Go on in, you little devil,' he shouted. He ground his teeth.

'Go on in!'

Ruby was by this time in pursuit of the rebel. Mrs. Raeburn had been warned and was already at the gate. Alfie, haunted by a thousand mocking eyes, fled to his room and wept tears of shame. Edie broke away from her friends and stood, breathing very fast, in petrified anticipation. Jenny was led indoors and up to bed.

'Why can't I be a boy?' she moaned.

'Well, there's a sauce!' said Ruby. 'However on earth can you be a boy when you've been made a girl?'

'But I don't want to be a girl.'

'Well, you've got to be and that's all about it. You'll be fidgeting for the moon next. Besides, if you go trapesing round half-dressed, the policeman'll have you.'

Jenny had heard of the powers of the policeman for a long time. Those guardians of order stood for her as sinister, inhuman figures, always ready to spring on little girls and carry them off to unknown places. She was never taught to regard them as kindly defenders on whom one could rely in emergencies, but looked upon them with all the suspicion of a dog for a uniform. Their large quiescence and their habit of looming unexpectedly round corners shed a cloud upon the sunniest moment. They were images of vengeance at whose approach even boys huddled together shamefaced.

Mrs. Raeburn came upstairs to interview her discontented daughter.

'Don't you ever do any such a thing again. Behaving like a tomboy!'

'Why mayn't I be a boy?'

'Because you're a girl.'

'Who said so?'

'God.'

'Who's God?'

'That's neither here nor there.'

God was another shadow upon enjoyment. He was not to be found by pillar-boxes. He did not lurk in archways, it is true. He was apparently not a policeman, but something bigger, even, than a policeman. She had seen his picture – old and irritable among clouds.

'Why did God say so?'

'Because He knows best.'

'But I want to be a boy.'

'Would you like me to cut off all your curls?'

'No–o–o.'

'Well, if you want to be a boy, off they'll have to come. Don't make any mistake about that – every one, and I'll give them to May. Then you'll be a sight.'

'Am I a girl because I'm pretty?'

'Yes.'

'Is that what girls are for?'

'Yes.'

This adventure made Jenny much older because it set

34

her imagination working, or rather it made her imagination concentrate. Reasons and causes began to float nebulously before her mind. She began to ask questions. Gone was the placid acceptance of facts. Gone was the stolid life of babyhood. Darkness no longer terrified her because it was not light, but because it was populated with inhabitants both dismal and ill-minded. At first these shapes were undefined, mere cloudy visualizations of Ruby's vague threats. Bogymen existed in cupboards and other places of secluded darkness, but without any appearance capable of making a pictorial impression. It was a Punch and Judy Show that first endowed the night with visible and malicious shadows.

The sound of the drum boomed from the far end of Hagworth Street. The continual reiteration of the pipes' short phrase of melody summoned boys and girls from every area. The miniature theatre stood up tall in a mystery of curtains. Row after row of children was formed, row upon row waited patiently till the showman left off his two instruments and gave the word to begin. Down below, ineffably magical, sounded the squeaking voice of Punch. Up he came, swinging his little legs across the sill, up he came in a glory of red and yellow, and a jingle of bells. Jenny gazed spellbound from her place in the very front row. She laughed gaily at this world of long noses and squeaking merriment, of awkward, yet incredibly agile movement. She turned round to see how the bigger children behind enjoyed it all and fidgeted from one foot to the other in an ecstasy of appreciation. She laughed when Punch hit Judy, she laughed louder still when he threw the baby into the street. She gloried in his discomfiture of the melancholy showman with squeaky wit. He was a wonderful fellow, this Punch; always victorious with stick and tongue. His defeat of the beadle was magnificent, his treatment of Jim Crow a triumph of strategy. To be sure, he was no match for Joey the clown. But lived there the mortal who could have contended successfully with such a jovial and active and indefatigable assailant?

Jenny was beginning to see the world with new eyes. The kitchen of Number Seventeen became a dull place; the street meant more to her than ever now with the possibility of meeting in reality this enchanted company, to whom obedience, repression, good-behaviour were just so many jokes to be laughed out of existence. How much superior to Jenny's house was Punch's house. How delicious it would be to bury dogs in coffins. But the clown! After all, he could have turned even Jenny's house into one long surprise. He summed up all Jenny's ideas of enjoyment. She heard Ruby behind her commenting upon his actions as 'owdacious.' The same unsympathetic tyrant had often called her 'owdacious,' and here, before her dancing deep eyes, was audacity made manifest. How she longed to be actually of this merriment, not merely a spectator at the back of whose mind bed loomed as the dull but inevitable climax of all delight.

Then came the episode of the hangman, and the quavering note of fear in Punch's voice found a responsive echo in her own.

'He's going to be hanged,' said Ruby gloatingly.

Jenny began to feel uneasy. Even in this irresponsible world, there was unpleasantness in the background.

Then came the ghost – a terrifying figure. And then came a green dragon with cruel, snapping jaws – even more terrifying, but most terrifying of all was Ruby's answer to her whispered enquiry:

'Why was all that?'

'Because Punch was a bad, wicked man.'

The street so crudely painted on the back of the puppet-show took on suddenly a strange and uninviting emptiness, seemed to stand out behind the figures with a horrid likeness to Hagworth Street, to Hagworth Street in a bad dream devoid of friendly faces. Was a green dragon the end of pleasure? It was all very disconcerting.

The play was over; the halfpennies had been gathered in. The lamplighter was coming round, and through the dusk the noise of pipes and drum slowly grew faint in the distance with a melancholy foreboding of finality.

Jenny's brain was buzzing with a multitude of self-contradictory impressions. For once in a way she was glad to hold tightly on to Ruby's rough red hand. For once, she did not mind the warts. But the conversation between Ruby and another big girl on the way home was not encouraging.

'And she was found in an area with her throat cut open in a stream of blood, and the man as did it got away and ain't been caught yet.'

'There's been a lot of these murders lately,' said Ruby.

'Hundreds,' corroborated her friend.

'Every night,' added Ruby, 'sometimes two.'

'I've been afraid to sleep alone. You can hear the paper boys calling of 'em out.'

True enough, that very night, Jenny, lying awake, heard down the street cries gradually coming nearer in colloquial announcement of sudden death, in hoarse revelations of blood and disaster.

'Could I be murdered?' she asked next day.

'Of course you could,' was Ruby's cheerful reply. 'Especially if you ain't a good girl.'

Jenny went over in her mind the drama of Punch and Judy. Murder meant being knocked on the head with a stick and thrown out of the window.

That night again the cries went surging up and down the street. Details of mutilation floated in through the foggy air till the flickering night-light showed peeping hangmen in every dim corner. Jenny covered herself with the blankets and pressed hot sleepless eyelids to her eyes, hoping to distract herself from the contemplation of horror by the gay wheels of dazzling colours which such an action always produces. The wheels appeared, but presently turned to the similitude of blood-red spots. She opened her eyes again. The room seemed monstrously large. Edie was beside her. She shook her sleeping sister.

'Wake up, oh, Edie, do wake up!'

'Whatever is it, you great nuisance?'

In the far distance 'Another Horrible Murder in Whitechapel' answered Edie's question, and Jenny began to scream.

IV

The Ancient Mischief

There was nothing to counterbalance the terrors of childhood in Hagworth Street. Outside the hope of one day
being able to do as she liked, Jenny had no ideals. Worse,
she had no fairyland. Soon she would be given at school a
bald narrative of Cinderella or Red Riding Hood, where
every word above a monosyllable would be divided in such
a way that hyphens would always seem of greater importance than elves.

And where was the Sunday-school with its angels of
watchfulness and fiery saints? To tell the truth, Jenny was
not much impressed by the occasional visits she paid to the
Sunday-school. The little teacher was earnest, but unimaginative and incapable of stirring the collective mind of her
class. In reedy accents she piped of morality and sniffed
her way through a Cockney rendering of the Sermon on
the Mount. In her blue serge skirt and blue flannel blouse
and over-feathered hat she led many hymns to Almighty
God and corrected offences against cleanliness, manners,
harmony and common sense in accents whose echoes of
immortality were lost in a maze of adenoids. Sunday-
school did not extend Jenny's outlook. She gained more

from Ruby's account of mean and sordid crimes, for, with all their inherently vicious effect, they did provide her with some sort of vehicle for concentration. They did give her, however wrong and distorted, a conception of life, whereas Sunday-school gave her nothing except boredom and an hour's leg-swinging.

About this time Jenny's greatest joy was music, and in connection with this an incident occurred which, though she never remembered it herself, had yet such a tremendous importance in some of its side-issues as to deserve record.

It was a fine day in early summer. All the morning, Jenny, on account of household duties, had been kept indoors and, some impulse of freedom stirring in her young heart, she slipped out alone into the sunlit street. Somewhere close at hand a piano-organ was playing the Intermezzo from *Cavalleria* and the child tripped towards the sound. Soon she came upon the player and stood, finger in mouth, abashed for a moment, but the Italian beamed at her – an honest smile of welcome, for she was obviously no bringer of pence. Wooed by his friendliness, Jenny began to dance in perfect time, marking with little feet the slow rhythm of the tune.

In scarlet serge dress and cap of scarlet stockinet, she danced to the tinsel melody. Unhampered by anything save the need for self-expression, she expressed the joyousness of a London morning as her feet took the paving-stones all dappled and flecked with shadows of the tall plane tree at the end of Hagworth Street. She was a dainty child with silvery curls and almond eyes where laughter rippled in a blue so deep you would have vowed they were brown. The scarlet of her dress, through long use, had taken on the soft texture of a pastel.

Picture her then dancing alone in the quiet Islington street to this faded tune of Italy, as presently down the street that seemed stained with the warmth of alien suns shuffled an old man. He stopped to regard the dancing child over the crook of his ebony walking-stick.

'Aren't you Mrs. Raeburn's little girl?' he asked.

Jenny melted into shyness, lost nearly all her beauty and became bunched and ordinary for a moment.

'Yes,' she whispered.

'Humph!' grunted the old man, and solemnly presented the organ-grinder with a halfpenny.

Ruby O'Connor's voice rang down the street.

'Come back direckly, you limb!' she called. Jenny looked irresolute, but presently decided to obey.

That same evening the old man tapped at the kitchen door.

'Come in,' said Mrs. Raeburn. 'Is that you, Mr. Vergoe? Something gone wrong with your gas again? I do wish Charlie would remember to mend it.'

'No, there's nothing the matter with the gas,' explained the lodger, for Mr. Vergoe was the lodger of Number Seventeen. 'Only I think that child of yours'll make a dancer some day.'

'Make a what?' said the mother.

'A dancer. I was watching her this morning. Wonderful notion of time. You ought to have her trained, so to speak.'

'My good gracious, whatever for?'

41

'The stage, of course.'

'No, thank *you*. I don't want none of my children gadding round theatres.'

'But you like a good play yourself?'

'That's quite another kettle of fish. Thank you all the same, Mr. Vergoe, Jenny'll not go on to the stage.'

'You're making a great mistake,' he insisted. 'And I suppose I know something about dancing, or ought to, as it were.'

'I have my own ideas what's good for Jenny.'

'But isn't she going to have a say in the matter, so to speak?'

'My dear man, she isn't seven yet.'

'None too early to start dancing.'

'I'd rather not, thank you, and please don't start putting fancies in the child's head.'

'Of course, I shouldn't. Of course not. That isn't to be thought of.'

But the very next day Mr. Walter Vergoe invited Jenny to come and see some pretty picture-books, and Jenny, with much finger and pinafore sucking and buried cheeks, followed him through the door near which she had always been commanded not to loiter.

'Come in, my dear, and look at Mr. Vergoe's pretty pictures. Don't be shy. Here's a bag of lollipops,' he said, holding up a pennyworth of bullseyes.

On the jolly June morning the room where the old clown had elected to spend his frequently postponed retirement was exceedingly pleasant. The sun streamed in through the big bay-window: the sparrows cheeped and twittered

42

outside, and on the window-sill a box of round-faced pansies danced in the merry June breeze. The walls were hung with silhouettes of the great dead and tinsel pictures of bygone dramas and harlequinades and tragedies. There were daguerreotypes of beauties in crinolines, of ruddy-cheeked actors and apple-faced old actresses. There was a pinchbeck crown and sceptre hung below a small-sword with guard of cut steel. There were framed letters and testimonials on paper gradually rusting, written with ink that was every day losing more and more of its ancient blackness. There were steel engravings of this or that pillared Theatre Royal, stuck round with menus of long-digested suppers; and on the mantelpiece was a row of champagne corks whose glad explosions happened years ago. There was a rosewood piano whose ivory keys were the colour of coffee, whose fretwork displayed a pleated silk that once was crimson as wine. But the most remarkable thing in the room was a clown's dress hanging below a wreath of sausages from a hook on the door. It used, in the days of the clown's activity, to hang thus in his dressing-room, and when he came out of the stage door for the last time and went home to stewed tripe and cockles with two old friends, he took the dress with him in a brown-paper parcel and hung it up after supper. It confronted him now like a disembodied joy whose race was over. Rheumatic were the knees that once upon a time were bent in the wide laugh of welcome, while in the corner a red-hot poker's vermilion fire was harmless for evermore. Dreaming on winter eves near Christmas time, Mr. Vergoe would think of those ample pockets that once held inexhaustible supplies of crackers. Dreaming on winter eves by the fireside, he would hear out of the past the laughter of children and the flutter of the foot-lights, and would murmur to himself in whistling accents: 'Here we are again.'

There he was again, indeed, an old man by a dying fire, sitting among the ashes of burnt-out jollities.

But on the morning of Jenny's visit the clown was very much awake. For all Mrs. Raeburn's exhortations not to put fancies in the child's head, Mr. Vergoe was very sure in his own mind of Jenny's ultimate destiny. He was not concerned with the propriety of Clapton aunts, with the respectability of drapers' wives. He was not haunted by the severe ghost of Frederick Horner the chemist. As he watched Jenny dancing to the sugared melodies of *Cavalleria*, he beheld an artist in the making: that was enough for Mr. Vergoe. He owed no obligations to anything except Art, and no responsibleness to anybody except the public.

'Here's a lot of pretty things, ain't there, my dear?'

'Yes,' Jenny agreed, with eyes buried deep in a scarlet sleeve.

'Come along now and sit on this chair which belonged, so they say, so they told me in Red Lion Passage where I bought it, to the great Joseph Grimaldi. But then, you never heard of Grimaldi. Ah, well, he must have been a very wonderful clown by all accounts, though I never saw him myself. Perhaps you don't even know what a clown is? Do you? What's a clown, my dear?'

'I dunno.'

44

'Well, he's a figure of fun, so to speak, a clown is. He's a cove dressed all in white with a white face.'

'Was it a clown in Punch and Judy?'

'That's right. That's it. My stars and garters, if you ain't a knowing one. Well, I was a clown once.'

'When you was a little boy?'

'No, when I was a man, as you might say.'

'Are clowns good?' enquired Jenny.

'Good as gold – so to speak – good as gold, clowns are. A bit high-spirited when they come on in the Harlequinade, but all in good part. I suppose, taking him all round, you wouldn't find a better fellow than a clown. Only a bit high-spirited, I'd have you understand. "Oh, what a lark," that's their motto, as it were.'

Ensconced in the great Grimaldi's chair, Jenny regarded the ancient Mischief with wondering glances and, as she sucked one of his lollipops, thoroughly approved of him.

'Look at this pretty lady,' he said, placing before her a coloured print of some famous Columbine of the past.

'Why is she on her toes?' asked Jenny.

'Light as a fairy, she was,' commented Mr. Vergoe, with a bouquet of admiration in his voice.

'Is she trying to reach on to the mantelpiece?' Jenny wanted to know.

'My stars and garters, she's not! She's dancing – toe-dancing, as they call it.'

'I don't dance like that,' said Jenny.

'Of course you don't, but you could with practice. With practice, I wouldn't say as you mightn't be as light as a pancake, so to speak.'

45

'I can stand on my toes,' declared Jenny proudly.

'Can you now?' said Mr. Vergoe admiringly.

'To reach fings off of the table.'

'Ah, but then you'd be holding on to it, eh? Tight as wax, you'd be holding on to it. That won't do, that won't. You must be able to dance all over the room on your toes.'

'Can you?'

'Not now, my dear, not now. I could once, though. But I never cared for playing Harlequin.'

'Eh?'

'That's a fellow you haven't met yet.'

'Is he good?'

'Good – in a manner of speaking – but an awkward sort of a laddie with his sabre and all. But no malice at bottom, I'm sure of that.'

'Can I be a C'mbine?'

'Why not?' exclaimed the old man. 'Why not?' and he thumped the table to mark the question's emphasis.

Jenny became very thoughtful and wished she had a petticoat all silver and pink like the pretty lady on her toes.

'Would I be pretty?' she asked at length.

'Wonderfully pretty, I should say.'

'Would all the people say – "pretty Jenny"?'

'No more that wouldn't surprise me,' declared Mr. Vergoe.

'Would I be good?'

The old man looked puzzled.

'There's nothing against it,' he affirmed. 'Nothing, in a manner of speaking; but there, what some call good, others don't, and I can't say as I've troubled much which

46

way it was, so to speak, as long as they was good pals and jolly companions every one.'

'What's pals?'

'Ah, there you've put your finger on it – as it were – what's a pal? Well, I should say he was a hearty fellow – in a manner of speaking – a fellow as would come down handsome on Treasury night when you hadn't paid your landlady the week before. A pal wouldn't ever crab your business, wouldn't stare too hard if you happened to use his grease. A pal wouldn't let you sleep over the train-call on a Sunday morning. A pal wouldn't make love to your girl on a wet, foggy afternoon in Blackburn or Warrington. What's pals? Pals are fellows who stand on the prompt side of life – so to speak – and stick there to the Ring Down.'

All of which may or may not be an excellent definition of 'paliness,' but left Jenny, if possible, more completely ignorant of the meaning of a pal than she was when Mr. Vergoe set out to answer her enquiry.

'What's pals?' she reiterated therefore.

'Not quite clear in your little head yet – as it were – well, I should say, we're pals, me and you.'

'Are pals good?'

'The best. The very very best. Now you just listen to me for a minute. My granddaughter, Miss Lilli Vergoe that is, she's wonderfully fond of the old man, that is your humble. Now next time she comes round to see him, I'll send up the call-boy – as it might be.'

Hereupon Mr. Vergoe closed his left eye, put his fore-finger very close to the other eye and shook it knowingly several times.

47

'Now you'd better get on or there'll be a stage wait, and get back to ma as quick as you like.'

Jenny prepared to obey.

'Wait a minute, though, wait a minute,' and the old man fumbled in a drawer from which at last he extracted a cracker. 'See that? That's a cracker, that is. Sometimes one or two used to get hidden in my pockets on last nights, and – well, I used to keep 'em as a recollection of good times, so to speak. This one was Bristol, not so very long ago neither. Now you hook on to that end and I'll hook on to this and when I say "three" pull as hard as you like.' The antagonists faced each other. The cracker came in half with the larger portion in Jenny's hand, but the powder had long ago lost all power of report. Age and damp had subdued its ferocity.

'A wrong 'un,' muttered the old man regretfully. 'Too bad, too bad! Well, accidents will happen – as it were. Come along, open your half.'

Jenny produced a compact cylinder of mauve paper.

'Is it a sweet?' she wondered.

'No, it's a cap. By gum, it's a cap. Don't tear it. Steady! Careful does it!'

Mr. Vergoe was tremendously excited by the prospect. At last between them they unrolled a gilded paper crown which he placed round Jenny's curls.

'There you are,' he observed proudly. 'Fairy Queen as large as life and twice as natural. Now all you want is a wand with a gold star on the end of it, and there's nothing you couldn't do, in a manner of speaking. Now pop off to ma and show her your crown.' He held her for a moment

48

up to the glass, in which Jenny regarded herself with a new interest, and when he set her down again she went out of the room with the careful step of one who has imagined greatness.

Downstairs she was greeted by her mother with exclamations of astonishment.

'Whatever have you got on your head?'

'A crown.'

'Who gave it you, for heaven's sake?'

'The lodger.'

'Mr. Vergoe?'

Jenny nodded.

'I may wear it, mayn't I, mother?'

'Yes, I suppose so,' said Mrs. Raeburn grudgingly. 'But don't get putting it in your mouth.'

'There's a Miss Vain,' said Ruby.

'I'm not.'

'Peacocks like looking-glasses,' nagged Ruby.

'I isn't a peacock. I'se a queen.'

'There's a sauce! Whoever heard!' commented Ruby.

The clown's sentimental and pleasantly rhetorical descriptions had no direct influence on the child's mind. But when his granddaughter, Miss Lilli Vergoe, all chiffon and ostrich plumes, took her upon a *peau de soie* lap, and clasped her rosy cheeks to a Frangipani breast, Jenny thought she had never experienced any sensation half so delicious. Amid the heavy glooms and fusty smells of the old house in Hagworth Street, Miss Lilli Vergoe blossomed like an exotic flower, or rather, in Jenny's own simile, like lather. Her china-blue eyes were amazingly attractive. Her

49

honey-coloured hair and Dresden cheeks fascinated the impressionable child with all the wonder of an expensive doll. There was no part of her that was not soft and beautiful to stroke. She woke in Jenny a cooing affection such as had never been by her bestowed upon a living soul.

Moreover, what Mr. Vergoe talked about, Lilli showed her how to achieve; so that, unknown to Mrs. Raeburn, Jenny slowly acquired that ambition for public appreciation which makes the actress. Terpsichore herself, carrying credentials from Apollo, would not have been a more powerful mistress than Lilli Vergoe, a second-line girl in the Corps de Ballet of the Orient Palace of Varieties. Under her tuition Jenny learned a hundred airs and graces which, when re-enacted in the kitchen of Number Seventeen, either caused a command to cease fidgeting or an invitation to look at the comical child.

She learned, too, more than mere airs and graces. She was grounded very thoroughly in primary technique, so that, as time went on, she could step passably well upon her toes and achieve the 'splits' and 'strides' and 'handsprings' of a more acrobatic mode.

Therefore, though in the September just before her seventh birthday Mrs. Raeburn decided it was time to begin Jenny's education, it is obvious that Jenny's education was really begun on the sunlit morning when Mr. Vergoe saw her dancing to a sugared melody from *Cavalleria*.

School, however, meant for Jenny not so much the acquirement of elementary knowledge, the ability to distinguish a cow from a sheep, as an opportunity to exhibit more satisfactorily attainments she had developed from the instigation of Miss Lilli Vergoe. Neither her mother nor Ruby nor Alfie nor Edie nor anyone in the household had been a perfect audience. Her schoolfellows, on the other hand, marvelled with delighted respect at her Pas Seuls upon the asphalt playground of the board school and clapped and jumped their praise.

Jenny had no idea of the stage at present. She had never yet been inside a theatre, and was still far from any conception of art as a profession. It merely happened that she could dance, that dancing pleased her and, less important, that it made her popular with innumerable little girls of her own age and even older.

By some instinct of advisable concealment she kept this habit of publicity a secret from her family. Edie, to be sure, was aware of it and warned her once or twice of the immorality of showing-off: but Edie was too indolent to go into the matter more deeply and too conscious of her own comparative greatness through seniority to spend much time in the guardianship of a younger sister.

So for a year Jenny practised and became daily more proficient, and danced every morning to school.

V

Pretty Apples in Eden

Shortly after her eighth birthday Jenny was puzzled by an incident which, with its uneasy suggestions, led her to postulate to herself for the first time that mere escape from childhood did not finally solve the problem of existence.

She had long been aware of the incomplete affection between her parents, that is to say, she always regarded her father as something that seemed like herself or a chair to be perpetually in her mother's way.

She had no feeling of awe towards Mr. Charles Raeburn, but rather looked upon him as a more extensive counterpart of Alfie, both prone to many deeds of mischief. She had no conception of her father as a bread-winner; her mother was so plainly the head of the house.

In the early morning her father vanished to work and only came back just before bedtime to eat a large tea like Alfie, in the course of which he was reprimanded and pushed about and ordered, like Alfie, to behave himself. To be sure, he had liberty of egress at a later hour, for once when in the midst of nocturnal fears she had rushed in the last breath of a dream along the landing to her mother's room, she saw him coming rosily up the stairs. He made no attempt to justify his late arrival with tales of goblin accidents as Alfie was wont to do. He did not ascribe the cracked egg appearance of his bowler hat to the onset of a baker's barrow. He seemed so far indifferent to the unfinished look of his clothes as not to bother to lay the blame on the butcher's boy. Her mother merely said:

'Oh, it's you?'

To which Mr. Raeburn replied:

'Yes, Flo, it's me,' and began to sing 'Ta-ra-ra-boom-de-ay.'

Even Ruby O'Connor who, in earlier days at Hagworth Street, used to quell Alfie with terrible threats of a father's vengeance, gave them up as ineffective; for the bland and cheerful Charlie, losing the while not a morsel of blandness or cheerfulness, was fast becoming an object of contemptuous toleration in his own house. He was a weak and unsuccessful man, fond of half-pints and tales of his own prowess, with little to recommend him to his family except an undeniable gift of humorous description. Yet, even with this, he possessed no imagination. He was accustomed to treat the world as he would have treated a spaniel. 'Poor old world,' he would say in pitying intention; 'poor old world.' He would pat the universe on its august head as a pedagogue slaps a miniature globe in the schoolroom. He never expected anything from the world, which was just as well, for he certainly never received very much. To his wife's occasional enquiry of amazed indignation: 'Why ever did I come to marry you?' he would answer:

'I don't know, Flos. Because you wanted to, I reckon.'

53

'I never wanted to,' she would protest.

'Well, you didn't,' he would say. 'Some people acts funny.'

'That's quite right.'

Hers was the last word: his, however, the pint of four ale that drowned it.

Jenny at this stage in her life was naturally incapable of grasping the fact of her mother throwing herself away in matrimony; but she was able to ponder the queer result that however much her mother might be annoyed by Charlie, she did not seem able to get rid of him.

Alfie, with his noise and clumping boots, was an equally unpleasant appendage to her life, but for Alfie she was responsible. In whatever way children came about, it was not to be supposed they happened involuntarily like bedtime or showers of rain. Moreover, mystery hung heavy over their arrival. Edie and Alfie would giggle in corners, look at each other with oddly lighted eyes and blush when certain subjects arose in conversation. Human agency was implied, and all that talk of strawberry-beds and cabbage leaves so much trickery. Alfie, bad habits and all, was due to her father and mother being married.

But why be married when Alfies were the result? Why not close the door against her father and be rid of him? And take somebody else in exchange? Who was there? Nobody.

One foggy afternoon early in January, Jenny came back from school to the smell of a good cigar. She did not know it was a good cigar, but the perfume hung about the dark hall of Number Seventeen with a strange richness never associated in her mind with the smell of her father's smoke. She was conscious, too, from the carefully closed doors both of the parlour and the kitchen, that company was present. The voice of a polite conscience warned her not to bang about, not to shout 'Is tea ready, mother?' but rather to tread discreetly the little distance to the kitchen and there to await developments. If Alfie and Edie were already arrived by a punctual chance, she would learn from them the manner and kind of company hid in the parlour.

The kitchen was empty. No tea was laid. Over her stole an extraordinary sensation of misgiving. She felt as if she were standing at the foot of a ladder, watching Alfie about some mischievous business.

Presently Ruby returned from the scullery, like a sudden draught.

'However did you get in so quiet?' asked the newcomer. Then Jenny remembered the street door had been open.

'Who's in along of mother?'

'That's right. Be nosy.'

'Tell us, Rube.'

'I can't tell what I don't know.'

'But you do know,' persisted Jenny; 'so tell us.'

'D'you think we all wants to poke in where we isn't wanted, like you, Miss Meddlesome? How should I know?'

'Well, I told you yesterday what teacher called Edie, so tell us, Rube; you might tell us.'

'There isn't nothing to tell, you great inquisitive monkey,' Ruby declared.

Then there was a sound in the hall of a man's voice, a rich voice that suited somehow the odour of the cigar. Jenny longed to peep round the kitchen door at the visitor, but she was afraid that Ruby would carry on about it. A moment or two's conversation and the street door slammed, and when her mother came back to the kitchen, Jenny was afraid to ask bluntly:

'Who was that?'

Instead she announced:

'We did sewing this afternoon. Teacher said I sewed well.'

'You sew on with your tea,' said Mrs. Raeburn. 'And wherever can Edie and Alfie have got to?'

A week or two afterwards Jenny returned to the same smell of cigar, the same impression of a rich and unusual visitor, but this time the parlour door gaped to a dark and cold interior, and when Jenny followed Ruby into the kitchen he was there, a large florid man with a big cigar and heavy moustache and a fur coat open to a snowy collar and shining tie-pin.

'And this is Jenny, is it?' he said in the cigar voice. Jenny kissed him much as she would have kissed the walrus he slightly resembled; then she retreated, finger in mouth, backwards until she bumped against the table by which she leaned to look at the stranger much as she would have looked at a walrus.

Her father came in after a while, and his wife said:

'Mr. Timpany.'

'Eh?' said Charlie.

'Mr. Timpany, a friend of father's.'

'Oh,' said Charlie. 'Pleased to meet you,' with which he retired to a chair in a dusky corner and was silent for a long time. At last he asked:

'Have you been to Paris, Mr. . . . Tippery? Thrippenny, I should say.'

'Timpany, Charlie. I wish you'd listen. Have you got cloth ears? Of course he's been to Paris, and, for gracious, don't you start your stories. One would think to hear you talk as you were the only man on earth as had ever been further than Islington.'

'I was in Paris once some years back – on business,' Charlie remarked. 'I think Paris is a knock-out, as towns go. Not but what I like London better. Only you see more life in Paris,' and he relapsed into silence, until finally Mr. Timpany said he must be going.

'Who's he?' demanded Mr. Raeburn when his wife came back from escorting her visitor to the door.

'I told you once – a friend of father's.'

'Ikey sort of bloke. He hasn't made a mistake coming here, has he? I thought it was the Duke of Devonshire when I see him sitting there.'

'You are an ignorant man,' declared Mrs. Raeburn. 'Don't you know a gentleman when you see one? Even if you have lost your own shop and got to go to work every morning like a common navvy, you can tell a gentleman still.'

'Are you bringing any more dukes or markisses home to tea?' asked Charlie. 'Because let me know next time and I'll put on a clean pair of socks.'

Mrs. Raeburn did not bring any more dukes or

57

marquises home to tea; but Mr. Timpany came very often, and Charlie took to returning from work very punctually, and though he was always very polite to Mr. Timpany when he was there, he was very rude indeed about him when he was gone, and Jenny used to think how funny it was to wait until Mr. Timpany's departure before he began to make a fuss.

Vaguely she felt her father was afraid to say much. She could understand his fear, because Mr. Timpany was very large and strong, so large and strong that even her mother spoke gently and always seemed anxious to please him. And looking at the pair side by side, her father appeared quite small – her father whom she had long regarded as largeness personified.

One day Jenny came home late from school and found her parents in the middle of a furious argument.

'I ain't going to have him here,' Charlie was saying. 'Not no more, not again, the dirty hound!'

'You dare say that, you vulgar beast.'

'I shall say just whatever I please. You're struck on him, that's what you are, you soft idiot. You're potty on him.'

'I'm no such thing,' declared Mrs. Raeburn. 'Nice thing that a friend of father's can't come and have a cup of tea without your carrying on like a mad thing.'

'Not so much "cup of tea," Mrs. Raeburn. It's not the tea I minds. It's while the kettle's boiling as I objecks to.'

'You're drunk,' said the wife scornfully.

'And it's — lucky I am drunk. You're enough to make a fellow drunk with your la-di-da behaviour. Why, God help me, Florrie, you've been powdering your face. Let me get hold of the—. I'll learn him to come mucking round another man's wife.'

'You'll do a lot, Mr. Big,' said his wife, folding her arms.

'Yes, I would, you— !'

'Nice language for children to hear from their father!'

'And who else is they going to hear it from except their father? Him? Nice example you sets, bringing home a great— in a fur coat to hang round you and paw and maul you about. All right, Mrs. Nice, let him come here again, and, strike me, I'll . . .'

'You'll do a lot,' said Mrs. Raeburn; then, in a sudden access of rage, she picked up a new broom which had just arrived and banged it down on Charlie's head. For a moment he was too much dazed to do anything, for another moment he seemed inclined to strike her in turn; but drink and laziness had long ago worn out his power of execution. So he got up and went across to the door. There he paused to survey his domestic hearth.

'And some soppy idiots actually advises you to get married. Tut-tut.'

With which scornful reminiscence of bygone persuasion he went out.

On the very next day Mr. Timpany came to tea for the last time. Mrs. Raeburn had told her husband it was to be the last time, for he did not put in an appearance. Ruby had gone out by permission. May was secured by a fortified nursery-chair. Alfie was away on some twilight adventure of bells and string. Edie was immersed in a neighbouring basement with two friends, a plate of jam, and the cordial teasing of the friends' brother, young Bert; and Jenny, urged on by a passionate inquisitiveness, crept along the passage and listened to the following conversation:

'You're wasted here, Flo, wasted – a fine woman like you is absolutely wasted. Why won't you come away with me? Come away to-night, I'll always be good to you.'

'The children,' said their mother.

'They'll get on all right by themselves. Bring the little one – what's her name, with fair hair and dark eyes?'

'Jenny.'

'Yes, Jenny. Bring her with you. I don't mind.'

'It wouldn't be fair to her. She'd never have a chance.'

'Rubbish! She'd have more chance in a cosy little house of your own than stuck in this rat's hole. You'd have a slap-up time, Flo. A nice little Ralli car, if you're fond of horses, and – oh, come along, come now. I want you.'

'No; I've fixed myself up. I was done with life when I married Charlie, and I'm fixed up.'

'You're in a cage here,' he argued.

'Yes; but I've got my nest in it,' she said.

'Then it's goodbye?'

'Goodbye.'

'I'm damned if I can understand why you won't come. I'd be jolly good to you.'

'Goodbye.'

'You're a cold woman, aren't you?'

'Am I?'

'I think you are.'

'It doesn't always do to show one's feelings.'

'You're a regular icicle.'

'Perhaps,' whispered Mrs. Raeburn.

Jenny stole back to the kitchen greatly puzzled. Whether the florid Mr. Timpany kissed Mrs. Raeburn before he went out to look for the hansom cab that was to jingle him out of her life is not known; but she waved to him once as she saw him look round under a lamp-post, for Jenny had crept back and was standing beside her when she did so.

'You come on in, you naughty girl,' said Mrs. Raeburn, drowning love in a copper bubbling with clothes.

'Would you like that man better than father?' Jenny enquired presently, pausing in the erection of a tower of bricks for the benefit of May, who watched with sombre eyes the quivering feat of architecture.

'What do you mean?' said Mrs. Raeburn sharply.

'Would you like father to go away and never, never come back here along of us ever again and always have that man?'

'Of course, I shouldn't, you silly child.'

'I would.'

'You would?'

'Yes,' said Jenny; 'he smelt nice.'

'Ah, miss, when you're married, you're married.'

'Could I be married?'

'When you grow up. Of course.'

'Could I have little boys and girls?'

'Of course you could if you was married.'

'Could I have lots and lots?'

'More than you bargain for, I dare say,' declared her mother.

'Did you marry to have a little girl like me?'

'Perhaps.'

Encouraged by her mother's unusual amenity to questions, Jenny went on:

'Did you really, though?'

'For that and other reasons.'

'Were you glad when you saw me first?'

'Very glad.'

'Did I come in by the door?'

'Yes.'

'Who brought me?'

'The doctor.'

'Did he ring the bell?'

'Yes.'

'Did father know I was coming?'

'Yes.'

'Was I a present from father?'

'Yes.'

'Would you like that gentleman to give you a present?'

'What do you mean?'

'Would you like him to give you a lil girl like me?'

'Not at all; and you stop asking questions, Mrs. Chatter.'

Her mother was suddenly aware of Jenny's cross-examinations, which she had been answering mechanically, her thoughts far away with a florid man in a jingling hansom cab. Jenny was conscious of her dreaming and knew in her sly baby heart that her mother was in a weak mood. But it was too good to last long enough for Jenny to find out all she wanted to know.

'Why don't you send father away and have that gentleman as a lodger?'

'I told you once; don't keep on.'

'But why don't you?'

'Because I don't want to.'

In bed that night Jenny lay awake and tried to understand the conversation in the parlour. At present her intelligence could only grasp effect. Analysis had not yet entered her mind.

She saw in pictures on the ceiling her mother and the rich strange gentleman. She saw her father watching. She saw them all three as primitive folks see tragedies, dimly aware of great events but powerless to extract any logical sequence. Lying awake, she planned pleasant surprises, planned to bring back Mr. Timpany and banish her father. It was like the dreams of Christmas time, when one lay awake and thought of presents. She remembered how pleased her mother had professed herself by the gift of a thimble achieved on Jenny's side by a great parsimony in sweets. The gentleman had offered a cosy house. At once she visualized it with lights in every window and the delicious smell that is wafted up from the gratings of bakers' shops. But what was a Ralli cart? Something to do with riding? And Jenny was to come too and share in all this. He had said so distinctly. If he gave mother a house, why should he not give her a doll's house such as Edie boasted of in the house of a friend, such as Edie had promised to show her some day? She began to feel a budding resentment against her mother for saying 'No' to all these delights, a resentment comparable with her emotions not so long ago when her mother refused to let her go for a ride on an omnibus with Mr. Vergoe.

63

Good things came along very seldom, and when they did come, grown-up people always spoilt them. Only the other day Ruby had promised to celebrate May's birthday by a sprat supper, when May was to be allowed to sit up and watch the household commemorate her nativity, sucking emptily the while a rubber teat. Squashed, of course, this plan too. Life, as Jenny lay awake, seemed made up of small repressions. Life was a series of hopes held out and baffled desires, of unjust disappointments and aspirations unreasonably neglected. She lay there, a mite in flowing time, sensible only of having no free will.

Why couldn't she grow up all of a sudden and do as she liked? But then grown-up people, whom she always regarded as entirely at liberty, did not seem to be able to do as they liked. Her mother had said 'No, thank you' to a cosy house, just as she was taught to say 'No, thank you' to old gentlemen who offered her pennies to turn somer-saults over railings – surely a harmless way of getting money. But her mother had not wanted to say 'No, thank you.' That Jenny recognized as a fact, although if she had been asked why, she would have had nothing approaching a reason.

'I will do as I like,' Jenny vowed to herself. 'I will, I will. I won't be told.' Here she bit the sheet in rage at her powerlessness. Desire for action was stirring strongly in her now. 'Why can't I grow up all at once? Why must I be a little girl? Why can't I be like a kitten?' Kittens had become cats within Jenny's experience.

'I will be disobedient. I will be disobedient. I won't be stopped.' Suddenly a curious sensation seized her of not

64

being there at all. She bit the bedclothes again. Then she sat up in bed and looked at her petticoats hanging over the chair. She was there, after all; and she fell asleep with wilful ambitions dancing lightly through the gay simplicities of her child's brain, and as she lay there with tightly closed determined lips, her mother with shaded candle looked down at her and wondered whether, after all, she and Jenny would not have been better off under the rich-voiced, cigar-haunted protection of Mr. Timpany.

And then Mrs. Raeburn went to bed and fell asleep to the snoring of Charlie, just as truly unsatisfied as most of the women in this world.

Only Charlie was all right. He had spent a royal evening in bragging to a circle of pipe-armed friends of his firmness and virility at a moment of conjugal stress.

And outside the cold January stars were reflected in the puddles of Hagworth Street.

VI

Shepherd's Calendar

It was unlikely that Jenny's dancing could always be kept a secret. The day came at last when her mother, in passing the playground of the school, looked over the railings and saw her daughter's legs above a semicircle of applauding children. Mrs. Raeburn was more than shocked: she was profoundly alarmed. The visit of the aunts rose up before her like a ghost from the heart of forgotten years. They had faded into a gradual and secure insignificance, only momentarily displaced by the death of Aunt Fanny. But the other two lived on in Carminia House like skeletons of an outraged morality.

Something must be done about this dancing craze. Something must be done to check the first signs of a prophecy fulfilled. She thought of Barnsbury; but Mrs. Purkiss had now two pasty-faced boys of her own, and was no longer willing to act as deputy-mother to the children of her sister. Something must certainly be done about Jenny's wilfulness.

'How dare you go making such an exhibition of yourself?' she demanded, when Jenny came home. 'How dare you, you naughty girl?'

Jenny made no reply but an obstinate frown.

'You dare sulk and I'll give you a good hiding.'

The teacher was written to; was warned of Jenny's wild inclinations. The teacher, a fish-like woman in a plaid skirt, remonstrated with her pupil.

'Nice little girls,' she asserted, 'don't kick their legs up in the air.'

The class was forbidden to encourage the dancer; a mountain was made of a molehill; Jenny was raised to the giddy pinnacle of heroism. She wore about her the blazing glories of a martyr; she began to be conscious of possessing an exceptional personality, for there had never been such a fuss over any other girl's misdemeanour. She began to feel more acutely the injustice of grown-up repression. She tried defiance and danced again in the playground, but learned that humanity's prime characteristic is cowardice; perceived with Aristotle that man is a political animal, a hunter in packs. She thought the school would support her justifiable rebellion, but, alas, the school deserted her. Heroine she might be in corner conferences. Heroine she might be in linked promenades; but when her feelings were crystallized in action, the other girls thought of themselves. They applauded her intentions, but shrank from the prominence of the visible result. Jenny abandoned society. The germ of cynicism was planted in her soul. She came to despise her fellows. In scarlet cloak she travelled solitary to school, and hated everybody.

The immediate and obvious result of this self-imposed isolation was her heightened importance in the eyes of the boys. One by one they approached her with offers of escort, with tribute from sticky pockets. Little by little she became attached to their top-spinning, marble-flicking journeys to and from school; gradually she was admitted to the more intimate fellowship of outlawry. She found that, in association with boys, she could prosecute her quarrel with the world. With them she wandered far afield from Hagworth Street; with them she tripped along on many a marauding expedition. For them she acted as decoy, as scout against policemen. With them she rang the bells of half a street at a run. With them she broke the windows of empty houses; climbed ladders and explored roofs and manipulated halfpennies stuck with wax to the pavingstones. She was queen of the robbers' camp on a tin-sprinkled waste of building-land. She acquired a fine contempt of girls, and wished more than ever she had been fortunate enough to be born a boy. She became Moll Cutpurse in porcelain miniature and tinkled out oaths that were the merest elfin blasphemy. Even Alfie condescended not merely to take notice of her, but also sometimes to make use of her activity. She looked back with wonder to the time when she had regarded her brother with a shrinking distaste. He became her standard of behaviour. She saw his point of view when nobody else could, as on the occasion when he asked Edie if she dared him to hit her on the head with the bar of iron he was swinging, and when Edie, having in duty bound dared, found herself with a large cut on the forehead. Alfie, finding other boys admired it, encouraged her dancing; and they used to flock round the organs while Jenny learned step-dancing from big, rough girls who were always to be found in the middle of the music.

One day, however, Mrs. Raeburn and Mrs. Purkiss, coming back together from a spring hat foray, walked right into one of Jenny's performances, and there was a heart-beating moment of suspense not improved by the big, rough girls' free use of 'lip.' Mrs. Raeburn might have endured the shame of it alone, but the company of her sister upset her power of dealing with an awkward situation. If in the past she had been inclined to compare Percy and Claude, her pasty-faced nephews, unfavourably with her own children, on the present occasion their mother drained the cup of revenge to the dregs.

With Jenny between them, the two sisters walked back to Hagworth Street.

'It isn't as if it was just showing her legs,' said Mrs. Purkiss. 'That's bad enough, but I happened to notice she had a hole in her stocking.' . . .

'And those great, common girls she was hollering with. Wherever on earth can she have picked up with them? Some of Charlie's friends, I suppose.' . . .

'It seems funny that Alfie shouldn't have more shame than go letting his sister make such a sight of herself, but there, I suppose Alfie takes after his father.' . . .

'All I'm thankful for is that Bill wasn't with us, he being a man as anything like that upsets for a week. He never did have what you might call a good liver, and anything unpleasant turns his bile all the wrong way. Only last week, when Miss Knibbs, our first assistant, sent an outsize in combinations to a customer who's *very* particular about any remark being passed about her stoutness, Bill was sick half of the night.' . . .

'I can't think why you don't send her away to Carrie's. The country would do her good and Carrie's got no children of her own. I'd like to have her myself, only I'm afraid she'd be such a bad example to Percy and Claude.'

Mrs. Raeburn was silent. Vulnerable through Jenny's lapse from modesty, she had no sting for her nephews.

After tea, Mrs. Purkiss remonstrated with Jenny in the parlour.

'Aren't you ashamed of yourself, miss?'

'No.'

'Wouldn't you be sorry if I told your cousins?'

'I don't care.'

'Don't care'll come to the gallows.'

'I *don't* care.'

'You're a bad, obstinate girl.'

'You're not my mother.'

'No, I'm very glad I'm not your poor mother. *My* little boys don't go playing about in the streets making sights of themselves.'

'They always are sights.'

'How dare you say any such thing?'

'They're all over with spots,' persisted Jenny, lowering.

Mrs. Purkiss boxed her ears. The child, with a cry of fury, sprang towards her aunt and bit her wrist. The latter fell back on to the horsehair sofa, screaming as she bumped up in the air again from the unused springs.

'Whatever is the matter?' cried Mrs. Raeburn hurriedly arriving from the kitchen.

'Oh, the little tiger-cat!' groaned Aunt Mabel. 'Bit my hand, she did, like some uncultivated beast.'

'Out of the room and up to bed, you,' said Mrs. Raeburn sternly.

Jenny retreated with head erect.

In the passage Alfie accosted her.

'What's the row?'

'She hit me and I bit her.'

'Good job,' came the laconic rejoinder.

Finally it was settled that Jenny should spend a year with Mrs. Threadgale at Galton. It was laid on the shoulders of Hampshire to curb her haughtiness. It remained to be seen how far country sights and sounds would civilize her rudeness.

Having made up her mind to banish the child, Mrs. Raeburn began at once to regret the decision. With all her disobedience, Jenny was still the favourite. 'She was such a character,' in her mother's words; and her gay dark eyes and silvery curls would be missed in Hagworth Street. But the day of departure came along. A four-wheeler threw a shadow on the door. There were kisses and handkerchiefs and last injunctions and all the paraphernalia of separation. Jenny was bundled in. Mrs. Raeburn followed.

'Now mind, Ruby,' cried the latter from the window, 'don't you let May get putting nothing in her mouth, and see Mr. Raeburn has his tea comfortable, and, Alfie, you dare misbehave while I'm away. Goodbye, all.'

It was a fine May morning with sunlight everywhere, sparkling on the river as they crossed Waterloo Bridge, glittering on the windows and even lending a ray of beauty to the cavernous cruel entrance to Waterloo Station. The latter wore its eternal air of chestnut-brown excitement. Never had Jenny been bumped about so much. Never had it seemed so impossible to achieve the right train. But at last they steamed out on the way to the country, past long lines of squalid houses with occasional glimpses of the river, past the hundred platforms of Clapham Junction, past Surbiton with its flannelled loiterers and vivid tulips. Into the pines and heather in a new compartment which smelt of varnish and old ladies' black dresses went Jenny and her mother. The former hated the old ladies with their baskets and disapproving glances.

'Why do all the people stare at me?' she whispered.

'Pay no attention, hold your tongue, and look out of the window,' commanded Mrs. Raeburn.

At last the train drew up at Galton along a grey gravel platform that smelt fresh and flowery after the railway carriage. There was lilac in bloom and red hawthorn, and a pile of tin trunks, and, when the train had puffed on, Jenny could hear birdsong everywhere.

While the two sisters embraced, the little girl surveyed her new aunt. She was more like her mother than Aunt Mabel. Nicer altogether than Aunt Mabel, though she disliked the flavour of veil that was mingled with the kisses of welcome.

'They'll wheel the luggage along on a barrow,' said Aunt Caroline. 'It's not far where we live.'

They turned into the wide country street with its amber sunlight and sound of footsteps, and very soon arrived before the shop of James Threadgale, Draper and

Haberdasher. Jenny hoped they would go in through the shop itself, but Mrs. Threadgale opened a door at the side and took them upstairs to a big airy parlour that seemed to Jenny's first glance all sunbeams and lace. Having been afforded a glimpse of Paradise, they were taken downstairs again into the back parlour which would have been very dull, had it not looked out on to a green garden sloping down to a small stream.

Uncle James, with pale square face and quiet voice, came in from the shop to greet them. Jenny thought he talked funny with his broad Hampshire vowels. Ethel the maid came in too, with her peach-bloom cheeks and creamy neck and dewy crimson mouth. Jenny compared her with 'our Rube,' greatly to our Rube's disadvantage.

Mrs. Raeburn stayed a week and Jenny said goodbye without any feeling of home-sickness. She liked her new uncle and aunt. There were no pasty-faced cousins and Ethel was *very* nice. She was not sent to the National School. Such a course would have been derogatory to Mr. and Mrs. Threadgale's social position. So she went to a funny old school at the top of the town kept by an old lady called Miss Wilberforce – a dear old lady with white caps and pale blue ribbons and a big pair of tortoise-shell spectacles. The school was a little grey house with three gables and diamond lattices and a door studded with great nails over which was an inscription that said, 'Mrs. Wilberforce's School, 1828.'

In the class-room on one side was heard a perpetual humming of bees among the wallflowers in the front garden, and through the windows on the far side which looked away over the open country floated the distant tinkle of sheep-bells. All along one side hung rows of cloaks and hats, and all over the other walls hung pictures of sheep and cows and dogs and angels and turnips and wheat and barley and Negroes and Red Indians: there were also bunches of dried grasses and glass cases full of butterflies and birds' eggs and fossils, and along the window-sills were pots of geraniums. On her desk Miss Wilberforce had an enormous cane which she never used, and a bowl of bluebells or wild flowers of the season and a big ink-horn and quill pens and books and papers which fluttered about the room on a windy day. There was a dunce's stool with a fool's-cap beside it, and a blackboard full of the simplest little addition sums. All the children's desks were chipped and carved and inked with the initials of bygone scholars, and all the forms were slippery with the fidgetings of innumerable little girls. About the air of the warm murmurous schoolroom hung the traditions of a dead system of education.

Jenny learned to dance and sew; to recite Cowper's *Winter Walk* after Miss Wilberforce, who was never called 'teacher,' but always 'ma'am'; to deliver trite observations upon the nature of common animals such as 'The dog is a sagacious beast,' 'The sheep is the friend of man,' and to acquire a slight acquaintance with uncommon animals such as the quagga, the yak and the ichneumon, because they won through their initials an undeserved prominence in the alphabet. She learned that Roman Catholics worshipped images and, incidentally, the toe of the Pope, and wondered vaguely if the latter were a dancer. She was

74

told homely tales about Samuel and Elijah. She was given a glazed Bible which smelt of oil-cloth, and advised to read it every morning and every evening without any selection of suitable passages. She learned a hymn called 'Now the day is over,' which always produced an emotion of exquisite melancholy. She was awarded a diminutive plot of ground and given a penny packet of nasturtium seeds to sow, but, being told by another girl that they were good to eat, she ate them instead and her garden was a failure.

There were delightful half-holiday rambles over the countryside when she, still in her scarlet serge, and half a dozen girls and boys danced along the lanes picking flowers and playing games with chanted refrains like Green Gravel and Queen of Barbary. She made friends with farmers' lads and learned to climb trees and call poultry and find ducks' eggs. Hay-making time came on when she was allowed to ride on the great swinging loads right into the setting sun, it seemed. She used to lie on her back, lulled by the sounds of eventide, and watch the midges glinting on the air of a golden world.

She slept in a funny little flowery room next to her uncle and aunt, and she used to lie awake in the slow summer twilights, sniffing in the delicious odour of pinks in full bloom below her window. Sometimes she would lean out of the window and weave fancies round the bubbling stream beyond the grass till the moon came up from behind a hop-garden and threw tree-shadows all over the room. Below her sill she could pick great crimson roses that looked like bunches of black velvet in the moonlight, and in the morning she used to suck the honey from the sweet starry flowers of the jasmine that flung its green fountains over the kitchen porch.

Summer went on; the hay was cut, and in the swimming July heat she used to play in the meadows till her face grew freckled as the inside of a cowslip. Now was the time when she could wear foxglove blooms on every finger. Now was the time to watch the rabbits scampering by the wood's edge in the warm dusk. The corn turned golden, and there were expeditions for wild raspberries. The corn was cut, and blackberry time arrived, bringing her mother, who was pleased to see how well Jenny looked and went back to Hagworth Street with a great bunch of fat purple dahlias.

In October there was nutting – best of all the new delights, perhaps – when she wandered through the hazel coppices and shook the smooth boughs until the ripe nuts pattered down on the damp woodland earth. Nutting was no roadside adventure. She really penetrated into the heart of the woods and with her companions would peep out half-affrighted by the lisp of the October leaves along the glades, half-afraid of the giant beeches with their bare grey branches twisted to the likeness of faces and figures. She and her playmates would peep out from the hazel coppice and dart across the mossy way out of the keeper's eye, and lose themselves in the dense covert and point with breathless whisper to a squirrel or scurrying dormouse. Home again in the silvery mists or moaning winds, home again with bags of nuts slung across shoulders to await the long winter evenings and fireside pleasures.

Jenny was allowed to celebrate her ninth birthday by a

glorious tea-party in the kitchen, when little girls in clean pinafores and little boys in clean collars stumped along the flagged passage and sat down to tea and munched buns and presented Jenny with dolls' tea-services and pop-guns and Michaelmas daisies with stalks warm from the tight clasp of warm hands.

She grew up to love her Aunt Carrie, and Uncle James with the voice and thin, damp hair.

Winter went by to the ticking of clocks and patter of rain. But there was snow after Christmas and uproarious snow-balling and slides in Galton High Street. There was always a fine crackling fire in the kitchen and a sleek tabby cat, and copper kettles singing on the hob. There was Ethel's love-affair with the grocer's assistant to talk and giggle over amid the tinkle and clatter of washing up the tea-things.

And then in March Mrs. Threadgale caught cold, and died quite suddenly; and Jenny put some white violets on her grave and wore a black dress and went home to Islington.

The effect of this wonderful visit was not much more permanent than the surprise of a new picture-book. Galton had meant not so much a succession of revelations as a volley of sensations. She was sad at leaving the country; she missed the affection of her uncle and aunt. She missed the easy sway she had wielded over everybody at Galton. But she had very little experience to carry back to Hagworth Street. One would like to say she carried the memory of that childish wondertime right through her restless life, but actually, she never remembered much about it. It soon became merely a vague interval between two long similarities of existence, like a break in a row of houses that does not admit one to anything more than an added space of sky. She never communed with elves or, like young Blake, saw God's forehead pressed against the window-pane. Jenny was no mystic of nature, and the roar of humanity would always move her more than the singing of waves and forest leaves.

Her great hold upon life was the desire of dancing. This she had fostered on many a level stretch of sward, with daisy chains hung all about her. She had danced with damson-stained mouth like a young Bacchante. She had danced while her companions made arches and hoops of slender willow-stems. She had danced the moon up and the sun down; and once, when the summer dusk was like wine cooled by woodland airs, when a nightingale throbbed in every roadside tree and glow-worms spangled the grass, she had taken a spray of eglantine and led an inspired band of childish revellers down into the twinkling lamplight of Galton.

Yet this wonderful year became a date in her chronicle chiefly because age or sunlight or wind tarnished her silver curls to that uncertain tint which is, unjustly to mice, always called mouse-coloured; so that her arrival at Number Seventeen was greeted by a chorus of disapproval.

'Good gracious!' cried Mrs. Raeburn, when she saw her. 'Will you only look at her hair?'

'What's gone with it?' asked Jenny.

'Why, what a terrible colour. No colour at all, you might say. I feel quite disgusted.'

'Perhaps she won't be quite such a Miss Vain now,' Ruby put in.

Jenny was discouraged. The London spring was trying after Galton, and one day, a month or two after she came back, she felt horribly ill, and her face was flushed.

'The child's ill,' said Mrs. Raeburn.

'Ill? Nonsense!' argued Charlie. 'Why, look at her colour. Ill? Whoever heard? Never saw no one look better in my life. Look how bright her eyes is.'

'You ignorant man,' said his wife, and sent for the doctor.

The doctor said it was scarlet fever, and Jenny was taken away in blankets to the hospital. She felt afraid at first in the long quiet ward with all the rows of nurses and palms and thin beds from which heads suddenly popped up.

'Do you think you'll go to heaven when you die?' the charge-nurse whispered to Jenny as she tucked her in.

'I don't care where I go,' said Jenny; 'as long as there isn't any castor-oil.'

As she lay waiting to get better and watched the lilac buds breaking into flower outside the big windows, she could not help wishing she were in Galton again, although in a way she liked the peace and regularity of hospital life. It amused her to have breakfast at half-past five and lunch at nine. The latter she laughed at all the time she was in hospital. Her convalescence was an exceptionally long one, but she had two jolly weeks before she left, when she could run about and help to carry the meals to the other patients. She danced once or twice then for the benefit of the ward and was glad that everybody clapped her so loudly. She cried when she left in August to go home to her family. But soon they all went to Clacton-on-Sea and enjoyed themselves.

Jenny was growing more and more impatient of restraint and had many quarrels with her mother – one particularly violent, over the probability of rain during a country walk, when Mrs. Raeburn's umbrella blew inside-out and Jenny lost her shoe in a nettle-bed and declined to rescue it, and made an exhibition of her mother by limping home through the mud with only one shoe.

'Time you went back to school, my lady,' said Mrs. Raeburn.

The board school was tiresome after the dame's school at the top of Galton town, after the petting of hospital nurses and the sun-burnt joys of Clacton. Jenny became atrociously naughty. She stamped and kicked and sulked and disobeyed and provoked the mistresses, one after another, to write indignant letters home to her mother. She was rebellious and spiteful and altogether a type of what a little girl ought not to be.

What was to be done with her?

VII

Ambition Wakes

The great event came about because Mrs. Raeburn, in return for similar favours in the past, went to superintend the behaviour of pasty-faced Claude and Percy so that her sister could spend a fortnight with a brother-in-law lately elected to the Urban Council of an important town in Suffolk. So, with some misgivings on the side of his wife, Charlie was left in charge of 17 Hagworth Street.

One day Mr. Vergoe came downstairs to ask his landlord if he would let Jenny and Alfie and Edie accompany him to the pantomime of Aladdin at the Grand Theatre. Charlie saw no harm in it, and the party was arranged. It appeared that Miss Lilli Vergoe had been temporarily released from the second line of girls at the Orient Palace of Varieties in order to make one of a quartette of acrobatic dancers in the pantomime. In the circumstances, her grandfather considered himself bound to attend at least one performance, although he felt rather like a mute at his own obsequies.

It was a clear winter's evening when they set out, a rosy-cheeked, chattering, skipping party. Mr. Vergoe, wrapped in a muffler almost as wide as a curtain, walked in the middle. Jenny held his hand. Edie jigged on the inside, and Alfie, to whom had been entrusted the great responsibility of the tickets, walked along the extreme edge of the kerb, occasionally jolting down with excitement into the frozen gutter. They hurried along the wide raised pavement that led up to the theatre. They hurried past the golden windows of shops still gay with the aftermath of Christmas. They hurried faster and faster till presently the great front of the theatre appeared in sight, when they all huddled together for a wild dash across the crowded thoroughfare. Ragged boys accosted them, trying to sell old programmes. Knowing men enquired if they wanted the shortest way to the pit.

'No, thank you,' said Mr. Vergoe proudly. 'We have seats in the dress circle.'

The knowing men looked very respectful and moved aside from the welded plutocracy of Edie, Alfie, Jenny and Mr. Vergoe. Fat women with baskets of fat oranges tried to tempt them by offering three at once, but Mr. Vergoe declined. Oranges would not be polite in the dress circle.

In the vestibule Alfie was commanded to produce the tickets. There was a terrible moment of suspense while Alfie, nearly as crimson as the plush all round him, dug down into one pocket after another. Were the tickets lost? Edie and Jenny looked daggers. No; there they were. Row A, numbers 7, 8, 9, and 10. 'Upstairs, please,' said a magnificent gentleman in black and gold. 'This way, please,' said a fuzzy-haired attendant. The children walked over the thick carpet in awed silence. A glass door swung open. They were in the auditorium of the Grand

Theatre, Islington, in the very front row, by all that was fortunate; and, having bestowed their hats and coats beneath the elegant and comfortable tip-up chairs, they hung over the red-plush ledge of the circle and gazed down into what seemed the whole of the population of London. The orchestra had not yet come in. Down in the pit the people were laughing and talking. Up in the gallery they were laughing and talking. Babies were crying: mothers were comforting them. Everybody down below seemed to be eating oranges or buns or chocolate. Alfie let his programme flutter down, and Jenny nearly burst into tears because she thought they would all be turned out of the theatre in consequence.

The whole of the vast audience was there for enjoyment. Enjoyment was in the air like a great thrill of electricity. What could be more magnificent than the huge drop curtain, with its rich landscape and lightly clothed inhabitants? What could be more exciting than the entrance, one by one, of the amazingly self-possessed musicians?

The orchestra was tuning up. The conductor appeared to the welcoming taps of fiddle-bows. One breathless moment as he held aloft his baton and looked round at his attentive company, then all together the fiddles and the drums and the flutes and the cornets, the groaning double-bass and the 'cello and the clarinets and the little piccolo and the big bassoon and the complicated French horns and the trombones and the triangle (perhaps the best-enjoyed instrument of all) and the stupendous cymbals started off with the overture of the Christmas pantomime of the Grand Theatre, Islington.

Could it be borne, this enthusiastic overture? Was it not almost too much for children, this lilting announcement of mirth and beauty? Would not Jenny presently fall headforemost into the pit? Would not Alfie be bound to break the seat by his perpetual leaps into the air? Would not Edie explode in her anxiety simultaneously to correct Jenny, devour bullseyes and see more of a mysterious figure that kept peering through a little square hole in the corner of the proscenium?

The orchestra stopped for a moment. A bell had rung, shrill and pregnant with great events. Green lights appeared, and red lights: there was hardly a sound in the house. Was anything the matter?

'They're just ringing up,' said Mr. Vergoe.

Slowly the rich landscape and lightly clothed inhabitants vanished into the roof.

'Oh!' exclaimed Jenny.

'Hush!' whispered Edie.

'My gosh!' said Alfie.

A weird melody began. Demons leaped maliciously round a cauldron. Green demons and red demons danced with pitchforks. The cauldron bubbled and steamed. There was a crash from the cymbals. A figure sprang from the cauldron, alighting on the boards with a loud 'ha-ha.' Evil deeds were afoot and desperate dialogue of good and ill.

The scene changed to a Chinese market-place. There were comic policemen, comic laundrywomen. There was the Princess Balroubadour in a palanquin more beautiful than the very best lampshade of the Hagworth Street parlour. There was the splendidly debonair Aladdin. There

84

was the excruciatingly funny Widow Twankey. There was the Emperor with bass voice and moustaches trailing to the ground to be continually trodden on by humorists of every size and sort.

It would be impossible to relate every scene. It was like existence in a precious stone, so much sparkle and colour was everywhere. The cave was wonderful. The journey to the Enchanted Palace through Cloudland was amazing. Then there were gilded tables, heaped with gigantic fruits, that rose from the very ground itself. There was the devilishly cunning Abanazar. There were songs and dances and tinsel and movement and jingles and processions and laughter and gongs and lanterns and painted umbrellas and magic doors and an exhaustingly funny bathing scene with real water. There was the active and slippery Genius of the Lamp, the lithe and agile Genius of the Ring, who ran right round the ledge of the circle and slid down a golden pillar back on to the stage amid thunders of applause.

To Jenny perhaps the most real excitement of all was the appearance of her darling Lilli, first in gold and blue and then in white and then in black, and finally in a dress that must have been stolen from the very heart of a rainbow, such scintillating streams of colour flickered and gleamed and radiated from its silken folds.

How gloriously golden looked her hair, how splendidly crimson her lips, how nobly brilliant were her eyes. And how she danced, first on one leg, then on the other; then upside down and inside out, and over one girl and under another. How the people clapped her and how pleased she looked, and how Jenny waved to her till Alfie and

Edie simultaneously suppressed such an uncontrolled and conspicuous display of feelings. Then there was the transformation scene, which actually surpassed all that had gone before, with its bouquets of giant roses turning into fairies, with its clouds and lace and golden rocks and jewels and silver trees and view of magic oceans and snowy mountains and gaudy birds.

Suddenly crimson lights flared. There was a jovial shout from somewhere, and 'Here we are again!' cried Joey, as round and round to 'Ring a ring o' roses' galloped Clown and Pantaloon and Harlequin and Columbine. Jenny looked shyly up into Mr. Vergoe's face and could just see tears glittering in his eyes.

Down came the front cloth of the Harlequinade with shops and mischievous boys and everlastingly mocked policemen and absent-minded nursemaids and swaggering soldiers. Inspiring were the feats achieved by the Clown, wild were the transformations and substitutions effected by the trim and ubiquitous Harlequin. But what Jenny loved most were the fairy entrances of Columbine, as like a pink feather she danced before the footlights and in and out of the shops. Oh, to be a Columbine, she thought, to dance in silver and pink down Hagworth Street with a thousand eyes to admire her, a thousand hands to acclaim the beautiful vision.

It came to an end, the pantomime of Aladdin. It came to an end with the Clown's shower of crackers. Triumph of triumphs, Jenny actually caught one.

'You and me will pull it,' she whispered to Mr. Vergoe, clasping his hand in childish love.

It came to an end, the pantomime of Aladdin; and

home they went again to Hagworth Street. Home they went, all three children's hearts afire with the potential magic of every street corner. Home they went, talking and laughing and interrupting and imitating and recalling, while Mr. Vergoe thought of old days. How quiet and dark Hagworth Street seemed when they reached it.

But it was very delightful to rush in past Ruby and turn somersaults all the way to the kitchen. It was very delightful to stand in a knot round their father and tell him the whole story and recount each separate splendour, while he and Mr. Vergoe sipped a glass of Mr. Vergoe's warm whisky with a slice of lemon added. It was good fun to disconcert Ruby by tripping her up. It was fine to seize the poker and chase her all round the kitchen.

The bedtime of this never-to-be-forgotten evening came at last. Jenny and Edie lay awake and traced in the ceiling shadows startling similarities to the action of the Harlequinade. Edie fell asleep, but Jenny still lay awake, her heart going pitter-pat with a big resolve, her breath coming in little gasps with the birth of a new ambition. She must go on the stage. She must dance for all the world to gaze at her. She would. She would. She must. What a world it was, this wonderful world of the stage – an existence of colour and scent and movement and admiration.

The oilcloth of Hagworth Street seemed more than usually cold and dreary on the following day. Alfie, too, was in a very despondent mood, having fallen deeply in love with Miss Letty Lightbody, who had played the part of Pekoe, Aladdin's friend and confidant. An air of staleness permeated everything for a week. Then Mrs. Raeburn came back from Barnsbury, and Jenny raised the question of going on the stage.

The former was very angry with her husband for allowing the visit to the pantomime. Mr. Vergoe tried to take the blame, but Mrs. Raeburn was determined the brunt of the storm should fall on Charlie. Jenny was ordered to give up all ideas of the stage. School-time came round again and the would-be dancer behaved more atrociously than ever. She was the despair of her mistresses, and at home she would sit by the fire sulking. She began to grow thin, and her mother began to wonder whether, after all, it would not be wiser to let her have her own way. She went upstairs to consult Mr. Vergoe.

'You'll make a big mistake,' he assured her, 'if you keep her from what she's set her heart on, so to speak. She has it in her too. A proper little dancer she'll make.'

Mrs. Raeburn was still loth to give in. She had a dread of putting temptation in the child's path. She did not know how to decide, while Jenny continued to sulk, to be more and more unmanageable, to fret and pine and grow thinner and thinner.

'Where could she go and learn this dancing?' the bewildered mother asked.

'Madame Aldavini's,' said the old clown. 'That's where my granddaughter learnt.'

It was a profession after all, thought Mrs. Raeburn. What else would Jenny do? Go into service? Somehow she could not picture her in a parlourmaid's cap and apron. Well, why not the stage, if it had got to be? She discussed the project with her sister Mabel, who was horrified.

'A ballet-girl? Are you mad, Florence? Why, what a disgrace. Whatever would Bill say? An actress? Better put her on the streets at once.'

Mrs. Raeburn could not make up her mind.

'If any daughter of yours goes play-acting,' went on Mrs. Purkiss, 'I can't allow her to come to tea with my Percy and my Claude any more, and that's all about it.'

'Jenny doesn't think going to tea with her cousins anything to wave flags over.'

'Pig-headed, that's what you are, Florence. All the years you've been a sister of mine, I've known you for a pig-headed woman. It doesn't matter whether you're ill or well, right or wrong, no one mustn't advise you. That's how you come to marry Charlie.'

The opposition of Mrs. Purkiss inclined her sister to give way before Jenny's desire. It only needed a little more family interference, and the child would be taken straight off to Madame Aldavini's School for Dancing.

Miss Horner supplied it; two or three days after this a letter came from Clapton, written in a quavering hand crossed and recrossed on thin crackling paper deeply edged in black.

CARMINIA HOUSE,
February 20th.

Dear Florence,

My niece Mabel writes to tell us you intend to make your little girl an actress. This news has been a great shock to me. You must not forget that she is a granddaughter of Frederick Horner the Chymist. She must not be a harlot given over to paint and powder. God is jealous of the safety of His lambs. This plan of dancing is a snare of Satan. You should read the Word, my dear niece. You will read of young maidens who danced before the Ark of the Covenant in the joy of the Lord, but that is not to say your little girl should dance for lewdness and gold when she might be singing the sweet songs of Salvation and joining in the holy mirth of the children of Israel. If you had let us adopt her, this desire would not have come. We do not let the Devil into our house. You will be the cause of my death, niece, with your wicked intentions. I am an old woman very near to Emmanuel. This great sin must not be.

Your loving aunt,
Alice Horner

P.S. I am in bed, but with the warmer weather I shall come to see you, my dear niece, and warn you again. A.H.

'Good thing she is in bed,' commented Mrs. Raeburn as she finished reading her aunt's letter.

'What's all this about Jenny going for a dancer?' asked Charlie that evening.

'Whatever has it got to do with you, I should like to know?' said his wife.

'Well, I am her father, when all's said and done. Aren't I?'

'And a nice example to a child. I suppose somebody's got to look after you when I die.'

'I expect the old man will die first. I've been feeling very poorly this year.'

'First I've heard of it.'

'Why, only last night my finger was hurting something chronic.'

'Show me.'

'Be careful.' Mr. Raeburn offered the sick finger for his wife's inspection.

'I can't see anything.'

'There, blessed if I'm not showing of you the wrong hand.'

'You must have been shocking bad.'

'Well, it's better now.'

'That's enough of you and your fingers. Why shouldn't Jenny be a dancer?' persisted Mrs. Raeburn.

'Don't go blaring it all over the neighbourhood, anyhow, and don't give me the blame for it if anything goes wrong.'

'Look here, Charlie, when I married you, I hadn't got nothing better to do, had I?'

Charlie shook his head in sarcastic astonishment.

'Yes,' went on Mrs. Raeburn. 'You can wag your great silly head, but I'm not going to have my Jenny marrying *any*body. She's going to be able to say "No, thank you," to a sight of young chaps. And if I can't look after her sharp when she's at the theatre, I can't look after her anywhere else, that's very certain.'

'Well, I call it rank nonsense – rank nonsense, that's what I call it, and don't you turn round on me and say I put it into her head. What theatre's she going to?'

'You silly man, she's got to learn first.'

'Learn what?'

'Learn dancing – at a school.'

'Learn dancing. You're all barmy. If she's got to learn dancing, what's the sense in her going for an actress?'

91

'You had to learn carpentering, didn't you?'

'Of course, but that's very different to dancing. Anybody can dance – some better than others; but *learn* dancing, well, there, the ideas some women gets in their heads, it's against all nature.'

'Have you finished? Because I've got my washing to see to. You go and talk it over at the Arms. I reckon they've got more patience than me.'

Jenny was in bed when her mother told her she should become a pupil of Madame Aldavini.

'Aren't you glad?' she asked, as her daughter made no observation.

'Yes; it's all right,' said Jenny, coldly it seemed.

'You are a comical child.'

'Shall I go to-morrow?'

'We'll see.'

Mrs. Raeburn thought to herself as she left the room, how strange children were; and, having settled Jenny's future, she began to worry about May, who was just then showing symptoms of a weak spine, and lay awake half the night thinking of her children.

VIII

Ambition Looks in the Glass

On Mr. Vergoe's recommendation, Madame Aldavini granted an interview to Mrs. Raeburn and her daughter, and the old clown was to accompany them on the difficult occasion.

It was a warm April day when they set out, with a sky like the matrix of turquoise. The jagged purple clouds were so high that all felt the outside of an omnibus was the only place on such a day. Mrs. Raeburn and Jenny sat in front and Mr. Vergoe sat immediately behind them, pointing out every object of interest on the route. At least, he pointed out everything until they reached Sadlers Wells Theatre, when reminiscences of Sadlers Wells occupied the rest of the journey. They swung along Rosebery Avenue and into Theobald's Road and pulled up at last by Southampton Row. Then they walked through a maze of narrow streets to Madame Aldavini's school in Great Queen Street. No longer can it be found: whatever ghosts of dead coryphées haunt the portals must spend a draughty purgatory in the very middle of Kingsway.

It was a tall grey Georgian house, with flat windows and narrow sills and a suitable cornice of dancing Loves and Graces over the door, which had a large brass plate engraved with 'School of Dancing' and more bells beside it than Jenny had ever seen beside one door in her life. She thought what games could be played with Great Queen Street and its inhabitants, if it were in Islington and all the houses had as many bells. Mr. Vergoe pressed a button labelled 'Aldavini,' and presently they were walking along a dark dusty passage into a little panelled room with a large desk and pictures of dancers in every imaginable kind of costume. At the desk sat Madame Aldavini herself in a dress of tawny satin. Jenny thought she looked like an organ-woman, with her dark wrinkled face and glittering black eyes.

'And how is Mr. Vergoe?' she enquired.

'How are *you*, Madame?' he replied, with great deference.

'I am very well, thank you.'

Mrs. Raeburn was presented and dropped her umbrella in embarrassment, making Jenny feel very much ashamed of her mother and wish she were alone with Mr. Vergoe. Then she herself was introduced, and as Madame Aldavini fixed her with a piercing eye, Jenny felt so shy that she was only able to murmur incoherent politeness to the floor.

The dancing-mistress got up from her desk and looked critically at the proposed pupil.

'You think the child will make a dancer?' she said, turning sharply to Mrs. Raeburn.

'Oh, well, really I – well, she's always jigging about, if that's anything to go by.'

Madame Aldavini gave a contemptuous sniff.

'I think she will make a very good dancer,' Mr. Vergoe put in.

'You've seen her?'

'Many times,' he said. 'In fact, this visit is due to me – in a manner of speaking.'

'Come, we'll see what she can do,' said the mistress, and led the way out of the little room along a glass-covered arcade into the dancing-room.

The latter was probably a Georgian ballroom with fine proportions and Italian ceiling. A portion of it was curtained off for the pupils to change into practice dress, and all the way round the walls was a rail for toe-dancing. At the far end was a dais with a big arm-chair and a piano, over which a large oil painting of some bygone ballet at the Théâtre de l'Opéra in Paris, and also an engraving of Taglioni signed affectionately by that great Prima Ballerina Assoluta.

Madame Aldavini rang a bell, and presently Miss Carron, her pianist and assistant teacher, came in. Miss Carron was a Frenchwoman, who had lived so long in London that she spoke English better than French, except in moments of great anger, when her native tongue returned to her with an added force of expression from such long periods of quiescence.

'What tune do you like, miss?' enquired Madame. 'What is her name? Jenny? *Si*, I have no Jenny at present.'

But the would-be dancer had no tune by name.

'Play the what's it called from what's its name,' suggested Mr. Vergoe, to help matters along.

'*Hein?*' Miss Carron exclaimed sharply.

95

'The – you know – the – the – well, anyway it goes like this,' and he hummed the opening bars of the Intermezzo from *Cavalleria*.

'Ah!' said Miss Carron. 'But that's no tune to dance to. You want something to show off the twiddly-bits.'

'Play the Intermezzo,' commanded Madame Aldavini.

Miss Carron began, but Jenny could only wriggle in a shame-faced way and was too shy to start.

'You great stupid,' said her mother.

'One, two, three, off,' said Mr. Vergoe.

'You are frightened, yes? Timid? Come, I shall not eat you,' declared Madame.

At last the novice produced a few steps.

'Enough,' said Madame. 'I take her. She will come once a week for the first year, twice a week for the second year, three times a week the third year and every day – how old is she?'

'Ten.'

'Every day when she is thirteen.'

The ampler details of Jenny's apprenticeship were settled in the little panelled-room, while Jenny listened to wonderful instructions about stockings and shoes and skirts. When it was all over, the three visitors walked out of the grey house, where Jenny was to spend so many hours of childhood, into Great Queen Street and an April shower sprinkling the pavement with large preliminary drops. Mr. Vergoe insisted on standing tea at a shop in Holborn for the luck of the adventure. Jenny's first chocolate éclair probably made a more abiding impression on her mind than the first meeting with Madame Aldavini.

So Jenny became a dancer and went, under her mother's escort, to Great Queen Street once a week for a year.

The pupils of Madame Aldavini all wore pink tarlatan skirts, black stockings clocked with pink, and black jerseys with a large pink A worked on the front. There were about twenty girls in Jenny's class, who all had lockers and pegs of their own in the anteroom curtained off by black velvet draperies. Fat theatrical managers with diamond rings and buttonholes sometimes used to sit beside Madame and watch the pupils. She sat on the dais, whence the glittering black eyes in her keen face could follow the dancers everywhere. Jenny used to think the mistress was like a black note of the piano come to life. There was something so clean and polished and clear-cut about Madame. Her eyes, she used to think, were like black currants. Madame's feet in black satin shoes were restless all the while beneath her petticoats; but she never let them appear, so that the children should have no assistance beyond the long pole with which she used to mark the beat on the floor and sometimes on the shoulders of a refractory dancer.

Two years rolled by, and Jenny was able to go alone now. She was considered one of Madame Aldavini's best pupils, and several managers wanted her for fairy parts; but Mrs. Raeburn always refused, and Madame Aldavini, because she thought that Jenny might be spoilt by too premature a first appearance, did not try persuasion.

As might have been expected, the instant that Jenny had her own way and was fairly set on the road to the gratification of her wishes, she began to be lazy. She was so far a natural dancer that nearly every step came very easily to her. This facility was fatal; for unless she learned at once, she would not take the trouble to learn at all. Madame used to write home to Hagworth Street complaints of her indolence, and Mrs. Raeburn used to threaten to take her away from the school. Then for a very short time Jenny would work really hard.

At thirteen she went every day to the dancing school, and at thirteen Jenny had deliciously slim legs and a figure as lithe as a hazel wand. Her almond eyes were of some fantastic shade of sapphire-blue with deep grey twilights in them and sea-green laughters. They were extraordinary eyes whose underlids always closed first. Her curls never won back the silver they lost in the country; but her complexion had the bloom and delicate texture of a La France rose, although in summer her straight little nose was freckled like a bird's egg. Her hands were long and white, her lips very crimson and tralucent; but the under-lip protruded slightly, and bad temper gave it a vicious look. Her teeth were small, white and glossy as a cat's. She cast a powerful enchantment over all the other girls, so that when, from tomboy loiterings and mischievous escorts, she arrived late for class, they would all run round for her with shoes and petticoats and stockings, like little slaves. Laughingly, she would let them wait upon her and wonder very seldom why she was the only girl so highly favoured. She had a sharp tongue and no patience for the giggles and enlaced arms of girlhood. She had no whispered secrets to communicate. She never put out a finger to help her companions, although sometimes she would prompt the next girl through a difficult step. She was entirely indifferent to their adoration. As if the blood of queens ran in her veins, she accepted homage naturally. Perhaps it was some boyish quality of debonair assurance in Jenny that made the rest of them disinclined to find any fault in her. She seemed as though she ought to be spoilt, and if, like most spoilt children, she was unpleasant at home, she was charming abroad. Her main idea of amusement was to be 'off with the boys,' by whom she was treated as an equal. There was no sentiment about her, and an attempted kiss would have provoked spitfire rage. There was something of Atalanta about her, and in Hellas Artemis would have claimed her running by the thyme-scented borders of Calydon.

Madame Aldavini, with some disapproval, watched her progress. She was not satisfied with her pupil and determined to bring her down to the hard facts of the future. Jenny was called up for a solo lesson. These solo lessons, when Madame used to show the steps by making her fingers dance on her knees, were dreaded by everybody.

'Come along now,' she said, and hummed an old ballet melody, tapping her fingers the while.

Jenny started off well enough, but lost herself presently in trying to follow those quick fingers.

'Again, foolish one,' cried the mistress. 'Again, I say. Well can you do it if you like.'

'I can't,' declared Jenny sulkily. 'It's too difficult.'

Madame Aldavini seized her long pole and brandished it fiercely.

'Again, self-willed baby, again.'

Jenny, with half a screwed-up eye on the pole, made

a second attempt: the pole promptly swung round and caught her on the right shoulder. She began to cry and stamp.

'I can't do it, I can't do it.'

'You will do it. You shall do it.'

Once more Jenny started and this time succeeded so well that it was only at the very end of the new step that Madame angrily pushed the pole between her pretty ankles, rattling it from side to side to show her contempt of Jenny's obstinacy.

'For it is obstinacy,' she declared. 'It is not stupidity. Bah! well can you do it, if you like.'

So Madame conquered in the end with her long pole and her sharp tongue, and Jenny learned the new and difficult step.

'Listen to me,' said the former. 'Do you not wish to become a Prima Ballerina?'

'Yes,' murmured Jenny, the sooner to be out of Madame's reach, and back with the boys in Islington.

'You have not the banal smile of the *danseuse* who takes her strength from her teeth. You have not the fat forearm or dreadful wrist of those idiots who take their strength from them, and, thanks to me, you might even become a Prima Ballerina Assoluta.'

The words of an old comic song about a girl called Di who hailed from Utah and became a Prima Ballerina Assoluta returned with its jingling tune to Jenny's head while Madame was talking.

'Whistle not while I talk, inattentive one,' cried her mistress, banging the pole down with a thump.

'Have you dreams of success, of bouquets and sables and your own carriage? Look around you, lazy one. Look at the great Taglioni whom emperors and kings applauded. Yet you, miserable child, you can only now make one "cut." Why do you come here unless you have ambition to succeed, to be *maîtresse* of your art, to sweep through the stage door with silk dresses? Do I choose you from the others to dance to me, unless I wish your fortune – eh? If, after this, you work not, I finish with you. I let you go your own pig-headed way.'

Jenny did work for a while, and even persevered and practised so diligently as to be able to do a double cut and a fairly high beat, sweeping all the cups and saucers off the kitchen table as she did so. But when she had achieved this accomplishment, how much nearer was she to a public appearance, a triumphant success? What was the use of practising difficult steps for the eyes of Ruby? What was the use of holding on to the handle of the kitchen door and putting one leg straight up till her toes twinkled over the top of it? Ruby only said, 'You unnatural thing,' or drew her breath in through ridged teeth in horrified amazement. What was the good of slaving all day? It was better to enjoy oneself by standing on the step of young Willie Hopkins' new bicycle and floating round Highbury Barn with curls and petticoats flying, and peals of wild laughter. It was much more pleasant to shock old ladies by puffing the smoke of cigarettes before them, or to play Follow my Leader over the corrugated-iron roof of an omnibus depôt.

Sometimes she took to playing truant for wind-blown

afternoons by Highgate Ponds in the company of boys, and always made the same excuse to Madame of being wanted at home until Madame grew suspicious and wrote to Mrs. Raeburn.

Her mother asked why Jenny had not gone to her dancing-lesson, and where she had been.

'I *was* there,' vowed Jenny. 'Madame can't have noticed me.'

So Mrs. Raeburn wrote and explained the mistake, and Jenny managed with great anxiety to obtain possession of the letter, ostensibly in order to post it, but really in order to tear it to a hundred pieces round the corner.

She was naturally a truthful child, but the long restraint of childhood had to be mitigated somehow, and lying to those in authority was no sacrifice of her egoism, the basis of all essential truthfulness. With her contemporaries she was always proudly, indeed painfully frank.

This waiting to grow up was unendurable. Everybody else was emancipated except herself. Ruby went away to be married – a source of much speculation to Jenny, who could not understand anybody desiring to live in a state of such corporeal intimacy with Ruby.

'I'm positive he doesn't know she snores' said Jenny to her mother.

'Well, what's it got to do with you?'

What, indeed, had anything to do with her? It was shocking how utterly unimportant she was to Hagworth Street.

Edie had gone away to learn dressmaking, and Alfie had vanished into some Midland town to learn something else, and occupying his room there was another lodger whom she liked. Then one day he came into the kitchen in a queer brown suit and said he was 'off to the Front.'

'Gone for a soldier?' said her father, when he heard of it. 'Good lord! some people don't know when they're well off, and that's a fact.'

There was nobody to enflame Jenny with the burning splendours of patriotism. It became merely a matter of clothes, like everything else. She gathered it was the correct thing to wear khaki ties, sometimes with scarlet for the soldiers or blue for the sailors. It was also not outrageous to wear a Union Jack waistcoat. But any conception of a small nation fighting inch by inch for their sun-parched country, of a great nation sacrificing even its sense of humour to consolidate an empire and avenge a disgrace, was entirely outside her imaginative experience.

What had it got to do with her?

There was nobody to implant ideals of citizenship or try to show her relation to the rest of mankind. Her education at the board school was mechanical: the mistresses were like mental coffee-grinders who having absorbed a certain number of hard facts roasted by somebody else, distributed them in a more easily assimilated form. They tried to give children the primary technique of knowledge, but without any suggestion about the manner of application. She had enough common sense to grasp the ultimate value of drearily reiterated practice steps in dancing. She perceived that they were laying the foundation of something better. It was only her own impatience which nullified some of the practical results of much academic instruction. Of her intellectual education the foundations were not visible at all. The teachers were building on sand a house which would topple over as soon as she was released from attendance at school. Jenny was a sufferer from the period of transition through which educational theories were passing, and might have been better off under the old system of picturesque misapprehensions of truth, or even with no deliberate education at all. It is important to understand the stark emptiness of Jenny's mind now and for a long while afterwards. Life was a dragging, weary affair unless she was being amused. There had been no mental adventures since, flashing and glorious, the idea of dancing came furiously through the night as she lay awake thinking of the pantomime. The fault was not hers. She was the victim of sterile imaginations. Her soul was bleak and cold as the life of man in the days before Prometheus stole fire from heaven.

If it had not been for May, Jenny would have been even less satisfactory than she was. But May with her bird-like gaiety – not obstreperous like a blackbird's, but sweet and inconspicuous as the song of a goldfinch dipping through the air above apple-orchards, May with her easy acceptance of physical deformity, shamed her out of mere idle discontent. Jenny would talk to her of the dancing-school till May knew every girl's peculiarity.

'She's funny, my sister. She's a caution is young May. Poor kid, a shame about her back.'

They quarrelled, of course, over trifles, but May was the only person to whom Jenny would behave as if she were sorry for anything she had done or said. She never admitted her penitence in words to anybody on earth. It was a pleasure to Mrs. Raeburn, this fondness of Jenny for May, and once in a rare moment of confidence she told the elder child that she depended on her to look after May when she herself was gone.

'With her poor little back she won't ever be able to earn her living – not properly, and when you're on the stage and getting good money, you mustn't leave May out in the cold.'

Here was something vital, a tangible appeal, not a sentiment broadly expressed without obvious application like the culminating line of a hymn. Here was a reason, and Jenny clung fast to it as a wrecked seafarer will clutch at samphire, unconscious of anything save greenery and blessed land. People were not accustomed to give Jenny reasons. When she had one, usually self-evolved, she held fast to it, nor cared a jot about its possible insecurity. Reasons were infrequent bits of greenery to one battered by a monotonous and empty ocean; for Jenny's mind was indeed sea-water with the flotsam of wrecked information, with wonderful hues evanescent, with the sparkle and ripple of momentary joys, with the perpetual booming of discontent, sterile and unharvested.

One breezy June day, much the same sort of day as that when Jenny danced under the plane tree, Madame Aldavini told her she could give her a place as one of the quartette of dancers in a Glasgow pantomime.

'But, listen,' said Madame, 'what they want is acrobatic dancing. If you join this quartette, it does not mean you give up dancing – ballet-dancing, you understand: you will come back to me when the pantomime is over until you are able to join the Ballet at Covent Garden. You will not degrade your talent by sprawling over shoulders, by handsprings and splits and the tricks which an English audience likes. You understand?'

Jenny did not really understand anything beyond the glorious fact that in December she would be away from Hagworth Street and free at last to do just as she liked.

Mrs. Raeburn, when she heard of the proposal, declined to entertain its possibility. It was useless for Jenny to sulk and slam doors, and demand furiously why she had been allowed to learn dancing if she was not to be allowed ever to make a public appearance.

'Time enough for that in the future,' said her mother. 'There'll always be plenty of theatres.'

Jenny became desperate. Her dreams of a glorious freedom were fading. That night she took to bed with her a knife.

'What are you doing with that knife?' said May.

'I'm going to kill myself,' said Jenny.

Pale as a witch, she sat on the edge of the bed. White was her face as a countenance seen in a looking-glass at dawn. Her lips were closed; her eyes burned.

May shrieked.

'Mother – dad – come quick: Jenny's going to kill herself with the carving-knife.'

Mrs. Raeburn rushed into the room and saw the child with the blade against her throat. She snatched away the knife.

'Whatever was you going to do?'

'I want to go to Glasgow,' said Jenny; 'and I'll kill myself if I don't.'

'I'll give you "kill yourself",' cried Mrs. Raeburn, slapping her daughter's cheek so that a crimson mark burned on its dead paleness.

'Well, I will,' said Jenny.

'We'll see about it,' said Mrs. Raeburn. Jenny knew she had won; and deserved victory, for she had meant what she said. Her mother was greatly perplexed. Who would look after Jenny?

Madame Aldavini explained that there would be three other girls, that they would all live together, that she herself would see them all established, as she had to go north to give the final touches to a ballet which she was producing; that no harm would come to Jenny; that she would really be more strictly looked after than she was at home.

'That's quite impossible,' said Mrs. Raeburn.

Madame smiled sardonically.

'However,' Mrs. Raeburn went on, 'I suppose she's got to make a start some time. So let her go.'

Now followed an interlude from toe-dancing – an interlude which Jenny enjoyed, although once she nearly strained herself doing the 'strides.' But acrobatic dancing came very easily to her, and progress was much more easily discernible than in the long and tiresome education for the ballet.

Of the other three girls who were to make up the Aldavini Quartette, only one was still at the school. She was a plump girl called Eileen Vaughan, three years older than Jenny: prim and, in the latter's opinion, 'very stuck up.' Jenny hoped that the other two would be more fun than Eileen. Eileen was a pig, although she liked her name.

Great problems arose in Hagworth Street out of Jenny's embarkation upon the ship of life. So long as she had been merely a pupil of Madame Aldavini's, family opposition to her choice of a profession had slumbered; but with the prospect of her speedy debut it broke out again very fiercely.

Old Miss Horner had died soon after her letter of protest against the dancing notion, and Miss Mary was left alone in Carminia House – in isolated survival, a pathetic more than a severe figure. However, she ventured to pay a visit to her niece in order to present a final remonstrance, but she lacked the power of her two elder sisters. What they commanded she besought. What they declared she hinted. Mrs. Raeburn felt quite sorry for the poor old thing, as she nodded on about Salvation and Temptation and the Wages of Sin. Old Miss Horner used to be able to wing her platitudes with the flame of God's wrath, but Miss Mary let them appear as the leaden things they really were. She made no impression but that of her own loneliness, went back to Carminia House after declining a slice of cherry cake, and died shortly afterwards, to the great comfort of the Primitive Methodists of Sion Chapel, who gained velvet cushions for the pews in consequence and became less primitive than ever.

Mrs. Raeburn could not help speculating for an hour or two upon the course of Jenny's life if she had accepted her aunt's offer, but finally went to sleep thinking, anyway, it would be all the same a hundred years hence.

Mrs. Purkiss came and registered a vow never to come again if Jenny really went; but she had registered so many vows in her sister's hearing that Mrs. Raeburn had come to regard them with something of that familiarity which must ultimately dull the surprise of a Commissioner for Oaths, and treated them as a matter of course.

Uncle James Threadgale, with face as pale and square as ever, but with hair slightly damper and thinner, suggested that Jenny should come down to Galton for a bit and think it over. This offer being pleasantly declined, he gave her a roll of blue serge and asked a blessing on the undertaking.

Charlie, having found that he was easily able to keep all knowledge of his daughter's lapse into publicity from his fellow-workmen at the shop in Kentish Town, decided to celebrate her imminent departure to the boreal pole (Glasgow soon achieved a glacial topography in Hagworth Street) by giving a grand supper-party.

'We'll have old Vergoe and Madame Neverseenher' – his witty periphrasis for Aldavini – 'and a brother of mine you've none of you never seen either, a rare comic, or he used to be, though where he is now, well, that wants knowing.'

'What's the good of saying he's to come to supper, then?' enquired Mrs. Raeburn.

'Only if he's about,' explained Charlie. 'If he's about, I'd like Jenny here to meet him, because he was always a big hand at club concerts twenty years ago, before he went to Africa. Arthur his name *was*.'

'Oh, for goodness sake, stop your talking,' said Mrs. Raeburn.

'And you can't ask Madame,' announced Jenny, who was horrified by the contemplation of a meeting between her father and the dancing-mistress.

'*And* why not? *And* why not? Will anybody here kindly tell me why not?'

'Because you can't,' said Jenny decidedly.

'Of course not. The child's quite right,' Mrs. Raeburn corroborated.

'Well, of course, you all know better than the old man. But I daresay she'd like a talk about Paris with your poor old dad.'

However, notwithstanding the elision of all Mr. Raeburn's proposed guests from the list of invitations, the supper did happen, and the master of the house derived some consolation from being allowed to preside at the head of his own table, if not sufficiently far removed from his wife to enjoy himself absolutely. Mr. Vergoe, getting a very old man now, came with Miss Lilli Vergoe, still a second-line girl at the Orient Palace of Varieties; and Edie arrived from Brixton, where she was learning to make dresses. Eileen Vaughan came, at Mrs. Raeburn's instigation and much to Jenny's disgust; and Mr. Smithers, the new lodger, a curly-headed young draper's assistant, tripped down from his room upstairs. May, of course, was present; and Alfie sent a picture post-card from Northampton, showing the after-effects of a party. This was put up on the mantelpiece and greatly diverted the company. Mrs. Purkiss was invited, and pasty-faced Percy and Claude and Mr. Purkiss were also invited, but Mrs. Purkiss signalized her disapproval by taking no notice of the invitation, thereby throwing Mrs. Raeburn into a regular flutter of uncertainty. Nevertheless she turned up ten minutes late with both her offspring to everybody's great disappointment and Mrs. Raeburn's great anxiety, when she saw with what a will her nephews settled down to the tinned tongue.

The supper passed off splendidly, and nearly everything was eaten and praised. Mrs. Purkiss talked graciously to Mr. Smithers about the prospects of haberdashery and the principles of window-dressing and, somewhat tact-lessly, about the advantage of cash registers. Charlie gave a wonderfully humorous description of his first crossing of the English Channel. Percy and Claude ate enormously, and Percy was sick, to his uncle's immense entertainment and profound satisfaction, as it gave him an excuse to tell the whole story of the Channel crossing over again, ending up with: 'It's all right, Perce. Cheer up, sonny; Dover's in sight.'

Eileen ate self-consciously and gazed with considerable respectfulness at Miss Lilli Vergoe, who related pleasantly her many triumphs over the snares and duplicity of the new stage manager at the Orient. Mr. Vergoe chatted amiably with everybody in turn and made a great feature of helping the stewed tripe. May went into fits of laughter at everything and everybody, and Jenny discussed with Edie what style of dress should be made from the roll of blue serge presented to her by Uncle James.

After supper everybody settled down to making the evening a complete success.

Mr. Vergoe sang 'Champagne Charlie' and 'In her hair

she wore a white camellia,' and Mr. Raeburn joined in the chorus of the former with a note of personal satisfaction, while Mrs. Raeburn always said:

> 'Champagne Charlie *is* his name,
> Half a pint of porter *is* his game.'

Neither Miss Vergoe nor Miss Vaughan would oblige with a dance, to the great disappointment of Mr. Smithers who had hoped for a solution of many sartorial puzzles from such close proximity to two actresses. Jenny, however, was set on the table when the plates had been cleared away, and danced a breakdown to the great embarrassment of Mrs. Purkiss who feared for pasty-faced Percy and Claude's sense of the shocking.

Percy recited Casabianca, and Claude, though he did not recite himself, prompted his brother in so many of the lines that it became to all purposes a duet. Edie giggled in a corner with Mr. Smithers, and told the latter once or twice that he was a sauce-box and no mistake. Mr. Smithers himself sang 'Queen of my heart' in a mildly pleasant tenor voice, and, being encored, sang 'Maid of Athens,' telling Miss Vergoe, in confidence, that several persons had passed the remark that he was very like Lord Byron. To which Miss Vergoe, with some lack of appreciation, replied, 'What of it?' and sent Mr. Smithers headlong back to the readier admiration of Edie.

It was a very delightful evening indeed, the most delightful moment of which, perhaps, was Mrs. Purkiss's retirement with Percy and Claude, leaving the rest of the party to settle themselves round the kitchen fire, roast chestnuts, eat oranges and apples, smoke, and drink the various drinks that became their ages and tastes.

'And what's Jenny going to call herself on the stage?' asked Mr. Vergoe.

'What *does* the man mean?' said Mrs. Raeburn.

'Well, she must have a stage name. Raeburn is too long.'

'It's no longer than Vergoe,' argued Mrs. Raeburn, looking at Lilli.

'Oh, but she already had a stage name – so to speak,' explained the old man proudly. 'What's Jenny's second name?'

'Pearl,' said Mrs. Raeburn.

'Oh, mother, you needn't go telling everybody.'

'There you are,' said Charlie, who had waited for this moment fourteen years. 'There you are; I told you she wouldn't thank you for it when you would give it her. Pearl! Whoever heard? Tut-tut!'

'Why shouldn't she call herself Jenny Pearl – Miss Jenny Pearl?' said Mr. Vergoe. 'If it isn't a good Christian name, it's a very showy stage name, as it were – or wait a bit – what about Jenny Vere? There was a queen or something called Jennivere – no, now I come to think of it, that was Guineavere.'

'I can't think whatever on earth she wants to call herself anything different from what she is,' persisted the mother.

'Well, I don't know either, but it's done. Even Lilli here, she spells her first name differently – L-i-double-l-i, and Miss Vaughan here, I'll bet Vaughan ain't her own name – in a manner of speaking.'

'Yes it is,' said Miss Vaughan, pursing up her mouth so that it looked like a red flannel button.

Mr. Vergoe was right – Miss Eileen Vaughan in Camberwell was Nellie Jaggs. Jenny soon found that out when they lived together and wrote a post-card to Mr. Vergoe to tell him so.

'But why must she be Jenny Pearl?' asked Mrs. Raeburn. 'Although, mind, I don't say it isn't a very good name,' she added, remembering it was her own conjunction.

'It's done,' Mr. Vergoe insisted. 'More flowery – I suppose – so to speak.'

So Jenny Raeburn became Jenny Pearl, and her health was drunk and her success wished.

A few weeks afterwards she stood on Euston platform, with a queer feeling half-way between sickness and breath-lessness, and was met by Madame Aldavini with Eileen and two older girls, and bundled into a reserved compart-ment. Very soon she was waving a handkerchief to her mother and May, already scarcely visible in the murk of a London fog. Life had begun.

IX

Life, Art and Love

Eileen Vaughan was, of course, perfectly familiar to Jenny, but the two other girls who were to be her companions for several weeks had to be much observed during the first half-hour of the journey North.

Madame Aldavini was in a first-class compartment, as she wanted to be alone in order to work out on innumerable sheets of paper the arrangement of the new ballet. So the Aldavini Quartette shared between them the four corners of a third-class compartment. Jenny felt important to the world, when she read on the slip pasted to the window: 'Reserved for Aldavini Quartette, Euston to Glasgow.' It was written in looking-glass writing, to be sure, but that only made the slow deciphering of it the more delightful.

However, it was read clearly at last, and Jenny turned round once more to look at her companions. Immediately opposite was Valérie Duval – a French girl with black fountains of hair, with full red lips and a complexion that darkened from ivory to warm Southern roses when the blood coursed to her cheeks. Her eyes glowed under heavy brown lids as she talked sweetly in a contralto French accent. Soon she took Jenny on her knees and said:

'You will tell me all your secrets – yes?'

To which Jenny scoffingly answered:

'Secrets? I'm not one for secrets.'

'But you will confide to me all your loves – yes?'

'Love?' said Jenny, looking round over her shoulder at Valérie. 'Love's silly.'

Valérie smiled.

The other new friend was Winnie Ambrose – raspberries and cream and flaxen hair and dimpled chin and upper lip curling and a snub nose. She was one of those girls who never suggest the presence of stays, who always wear white blouses of crêpe de chine cut low round a plump neck. They have bangles strung on their arms, and each one possesses a locket containing the inadequate portrait of an inadequate young man. But Winnie was *very* nice, always ready for a joke.

The train swept them on northwards. Once, as it slowed to make a sharp curve, Jenny looked out of the window and saw the great express like a line of dominoes with its black and white carriages. There was not much to look at, however, as they cleft the grey December airs, as they roared through echoing stations into tunnels and out again into the dreary light. They ate lunch, and Jenny drank Bass out of a bottle and spluttered and made queer faces and wrinkled up her gay deep eyes in laughter unquenchable. They swept on through Lancashire with its chimneys and furnaces and barren heaps of refuse. They swung clear of these huddled populations and through the gathering twilight cut a way across the rolling dales of Cumberland. Jenny thought what horrible places they were, these sweeping moorland wastes with grey cottages no bigger than sheep, with switchback stone walls whence the crows flew as the train surged by. She was glad to be in the powdered, scented, untidy compartment in warmth and light. The child grew tired and, leaning her head on Valérie's breast, went to sleep; she was drowsily glad when Valérie kissed her, murmuring in a whisper melodious as the splash of the Saône against the warm piers of her native Lyons:

'Comme elle est gentille, la gosse.'

Pillowed thus, Jenny spent the last hours of the journey with the dark crossing of the border, waking in the raw station air, waking to bundles being pulled down and papers gathered together and porters peering in through the door. Madame Aldavini said before she left them:

'To-morrow, girls, eleven o'clock at the theatre.'

And all the girls said, 'Yes, Madame,' and packed themselves into a cab with velvet cushions of faded peacock-blue and a smell of damp straps. There they sat with bundles heaped on their knees, and were jolted through the cold Glasgow streets. It was Saturday night and all the kerbstones were occupied by rocking drunkards, except in one wide street golden and beautiful from which the cab turned off to climb laboriously the cobbles of a steep hill and pull up at last before a tall house in a tall, dark, quiet road.

They walked up the steps and rang the bell. The big door swung open, to Jenny's great surprise, apparently without human agency. They stood in the well of a great winding stone staircase, while a husky voice called from somewhere high above them to come up.

They had a large sitting-room too full of hangings and overburdened with photographs of rigid groups; but the fire was blazing up the chimney and the lamp was throwing a warm and comfortable halo on the ceiling. Jenny peeped out of the window and could see the black roofs of Glasgow in the starlight. They had tea when they arrived, with porridge which Jenny disliked extremely, and oatcakes which made her cough; and after tea they unpacked. It was settled that Jenny should sleep with Valérie. The bedroom was cosy with slanting bits of ceiling flung anywhere, like a box of toy bricks put carelessly away. The bed, to Jenny's enormous diversion, was buried in a deep alcove.

'Whoever heard?' she asked.

'We'll be all to ourselves,' said Valérie in her deep voice; and Jenny felt a thrill at the idea of lying snug in the alcove with Valérie's warm arm about her.

The sitting-room looked a different place when the four girls had scattered over it their various belongings, when they had flung all the antimacassars into the corner in a cold white heap, when they had stuck a fan-shaped line of photographs round the mirror over the mantelpiece – photographs of fluffy-haired girls in gay dancing attitudes, usually inscribed 'Yours sincerely Lottie, or Amy, or Madge, or Violet.'

When she had pulled off most of the blobs on the valance of the mantelpiece and examined all the photographs, Jenny sat down on the white rabbit-skin rug with her back to the high iron fender and looked at her companions – at Winnie sprawling over a shining leather arm-chair, twisting one of the buttons that starred its round back, while she read *Will He Remember?*; at Eileen writing home to Camberwell; at Valérie as deep in a horse-hair sofa as the shape of it allowed, smoking a cigarette. She thought, while she sat there in the warmth and quiet, how jolly it was to be quit of the eternal sameness of Hagworth Street. She almost felt that Islington no longer existed, as if up here in this Glasgow flat she were in a new world.

'This is nice,' she said. 'Give us a cigarette, Val, there's a duck.'

Bedtime came not at any fixed boring moment, but suddenly, with all the rapture of an inspiration. Bedtime came with Valérie taking, it seemed, hours to undress, as she wandered round the room in a maze of white lace and pink ribbons. Jenny lay buried in the deep feather bed, watching her shadow on the crooked ceiling, following with drowsy glances the shadowy combing of what, in reflection, seemed an absolute waterfall of hair.

Then suddenly Valérie blew out the candlelight.

'Oo-er!' cried Jenny. 'We aren't going to sleep in the dark?'

'Of course we are, kiddie,' said Valérie; and somehow darkness did not matter when Jenny could sail off into sleep clasping Valérie's soft hot hand.

Grey morning came with the stillness of Sunday in Glasgow, with raindrops pattering against the window in gusts of wind, with Mrs. McMeikan and breakfast on a tray.

'This is grand, isn't it?' said Jenny, and 'Oo-er!' she cried, as she upset the teapot all over the bed.

Then the bell had to be rung.

'Whoever heard of a bell-rope in such a place?' said Jenny, pulling it so hard that it broke. Then, of course, there was loud laughter, and when Mrs. McMeikan came in again Jenny buried herself in the bedclothes and Valérie had to explain what had happened.

'Eh, the wild wee lassie,' said the landlady, and the high spirits of the child, hidden by the patchwork quilt in the deep alcove, won the old Scotswoman's heart, so that whatever mischief Jenny conceived and executed under her roof was forgiven because she was a 'bonnie wean, and awfu' sma', she was thenkin', to be sent awa' oot tae airn her ain living.'

There was a rehearsal on Sunday because Madame Aldavini had to go back on Sunday night to London. The four girls walked along the grey Glasgow streets in the sound of the many footsteps of pious Presbyterian worshippers, until they arrived at the stage door of the Court Theatre. Jenny asked, 'Any letters for me?' in imitation of Valérie and Winnie.

'Any letters for Raeburn – for Pearl, I should say?'

Of course there was not so much as a post-card, but Jenny felt the prouder for asking.

The rehearsal of Jack and the Beanstalk went off with the usual air of incompleteness that characterizes the rehearsal of a pantomime. Jenny found that the Aldavini Quartette were to be Jumping Beans; and Winnie and Jenny and Valérie and Eileen jumped with a will and danced until they shook the boards of the Court Theatre's stage. Madame Aldavini went back to London, having left many strict injunctions with the three older girls never to let Jenny out of their keeping. But Jenny was not ambitious to avoid their vigilance. It was necessary, indeed, occasionally, to slap Eileen's face and teach her, but Winnie and Valérie were darlings. Jenny had no desire to talk to men, and if lanky youths with large tie-pins saluted her by the stage door, she passed on with her nose as high as a church tower. And when, lured on by Jenny's long brown legs and high brown boots and trim blue sailor dress, they ventured to remove the paper from their cuffs and follow in long-nosed, fishy-eyed pursuit, Jenny would catch hold of Valérie's hand and swing along in front of them as serenely cold as the Huntress Moon sailing over the heads of Bœotian swineherds.

Those were jolly days in Glasgow, sweet secluded days of virginal pastimes and young enjoyment. They danced at night in their green dresses and scarlet bean-blossom caps. They were encored by the shrewd Glasgow audience, who recognized the beauty and freshness and spirit of the four Jumping Beans. They walked through the grey Glasgow weather down Sauchiehall Street and stared at the gay shop-windows. They walked through wind-swept Kelvin Grove. They laughed at nothing, and gossiped about nothing, and ate large teas and smoked cigarettes and lolled in armchairs and read absurd stories and listened to Mrs. McMeikan's anecdotes with hardly concealed mirth. Nor did Mrs. McMeikan care a jot how much they laughed at her, 'sae bonny was their laughter.'

Everybody in the pantomime was very kind and very pleasant to Jenny. Everybody gave her chocolates and ribbons and photographs signed 'Yours sincerely Lottie, or Amy, or Madge, or Violet.' Everybody wanted her to be as happy and jolly as possible. She was a great favourite with the gallery boys, who whistled loudly whenever she came on. She was contented and merry. She did not feel that Winnie or Valérie or even Eileen was trying to keep her down. She knew they were loyal and was fond of them, but not so fond of them as they of her, although Eileen thought she should be snubbed now and then.

Jenny was at a critical age when she went to Glasgow. It was the time of fluttering virgin dreams, of quickening pulses and heartbeats unaccountable. If Jenny had been at a high school, it would have been the age of girlish adorations for mistresses. She might have depended on the sanctifying touch of some older woman with sympathy. She might have adopted the cloistral view of human intercourse, that light-hearted world of little intimate jokes and sentimental readings and petty jealousies for the small advantage of sitting next some reverend mother or calm and gentle sister.

However, it is not to be supposed that the transition from childhood to womanhood was altogether unmarked. There were bound to be moments of indestructible languor when she was content to be adored herself. Had she met Abelard, Abelard could have made her an Heloise. They existed truly enough, the passionate fevers and deep ardours of adolescence. They flowed up in momentary caresses and died as soon in profound shynesses. Now was the time to feed the sensuous imagination with poetry and lull the frightened soul with music. She should have been taken to enchanted lands.

There was nothing.

Here was a child worthy of a Naiad's maternity, if grace of limb counted immortally, and when for the first time she was given the world to look at, her finite vision and infinite aspirations were never set in relation to each other. She was given a telescope, and nobody had taken off the shutter. Her soul was a singing bird in a cage. Freedom was the only ideal. She might have been moved by Catholicism, but nobody gave it to her. It may be idle to speculate on the effect of incense-haunted chapels, of blazing windows and the dim accoutrements of Mass. Perhaps, after all, they would merely have struck her comically. Perhaps she was a true product of London generations, yet maybe her Cockney wit would have glittered more wonderfully in a richer setting – haply in Lacedæmon, with sea-green tunic blown to the outline of slim beauty by each wind coming southward from Thessaly.

Anyway, it was impossible to think of her enticed by the ready-made gallantries of raw-boned sawnies by the stage door of the Court Theatre. Her temperament found greater satisfaction in Valérie's more beautifully expressed adoration. The latter may not have roused her to encounter life, may not have supplied a purpose, a hope or a determination, but at least it kept her contented in the shy season of maidenhood. It helped to steer her course between incidental viciousness and eventful passion. She went back to Hagworth Street with no red thorns of impure associations to fester and gather. The days went by very quickly without any great adventures except the dance on the occasion of the pantomime's last night. Jenny was not invited to this entertainment. She was supposed to be too young, and her mouth went dry with disappointment and a lump of unshed tears came into her throat, and it almost seemed as if her heart must stop.

'I ought to go; oh, it is a shame! I ought to go.'

Jenny went up of her own accord to the stage manager himself and said:

'Please, Mr. Courtenay-Champion, why aren't I asked to the dance?'

'Good lord!' said Mr. Courtenay-Champion. 'A kid like you? No, my dear, you're too young. It goes on too late. After the show, some hours.'

But Jenny sobbed and cried, and was so clearly heartbroken by the idea of being left out that Mr. Courtenay-Champion changed his mind and told her she could come. She was instantly transfigured as by dazzling sunlight after days of mist. It was to be a splendid dance, with jellies and claret-cup; and Jenny went with Valérie to buy the widest pink sash that ever was known, and tied it in the largest pink bow that ever was seen. She danced every single dance and even waltzed twice with the great comedian Jimmy James, and what is more, told him he couldn't dance, to his great delight, for he had a sense of humour in addition to being a great comedian.

It really was a splendid evening, and perhaps the most splendid part of it was lying in bed with Valérie and talking over with her all the partners and taking them off with such excited demonstration of their methods that the bed became all untucked and had to be made over again before they could finally settle themselves down to sleep.

In February Jenny was back again in Hagworth Street, with memories of Jack and the Beanstalk fading slowly like the colours of a sunset. She had enjoyed her personal success in Glasgow, but already success was beginning to prove itself an empty prize – a rainbow bubble easily burst. The reason is obvious. Jenny had never been taught to concentrate her mind. She had no power of retrospective analysis. The applause endured a little while in her meditations, but gradually died away in the occupations of the present. She could not secure it as the basis of a wider success on the next occasion. She began to ask: 'What's the good of anything?' Within a few weeks of the resumption of ordinary life, the Glasgow theatre had become like a piece of cake that one eats unconsciously, then turns to find and discovers not. She was no farther forward on the road to independence. She became oppressed by the dead-weight of futurity.

At home, too, there was a real repression which she grew to hate more and more deeply on each occasion of its exercise. A breath of maternal interference and she would fly into a temper – a scowling, chair-tilting, door-slamming rage. She would fling herself out of the house with threats never to return. One day when she was reproached with staying out longer than was allowed, she rushed out again and disappeared. Her mother, in despair, went off to invoke the aid of Madame Aldavini, who wisely guessed that Jenny would be found with Valérie Duval. There she was, indeed, in Valérie's rooms in Soho, not at all penitent for her misbehaviour, but sufficiently frightened by Madame's threat of expulsion to come back home without argument.

Freedom was still Jenny's religion. She was much about with boys, but still merely for the life and entertainment of their company, for no sentimental adventures. It would have been wiser to let her alone, but nobody with whom she was brought into contact could realize the sexlessness of the child, or that the truest safeguard of a girl's virtue is familiarity with the aggregated follies of masculine adolescence.

Jenny fought her way desperately into her seventeenth year, winning freedom in jots. She liked most of anything to go to Collins' Music-hall with a noisy gang of attendant boys, not one of whom was as much a separate realized entity to her as even an individual sheep is to a shepherd. Alfie came home in the summer before her seventeenth birthday and abetted cordially her declarations of independence. May, too, was implicated in every plot for the subversion of parental authority.

Mrs. Raeburn worried terribly about her daughter's future. She ascribed her hoyden behaviour to the influence of the stage.

'We don't want your theatrical manners here,' she would say.

'Well, who put me on the stage?' Jenny would retort.

In the Christmastide after Alfie came home Jenny went to Dublin in a second Aldavini Quartette, and enjoyed herself more than ever. She had now none of the desire for seclusion that marked her Glasgow period, no contempt of man in the abstract, and was soon good friends with a certain number of young officers whom she regarded much as she regarded the boys of Islington.

One of them, Terence O'Meagh, of the Royal Leinster Fusiliers, made her his own special property; he was a charming, good-looking, conceited young Irishman, as susceptible to women as most of his nation, and endowing the practice of love with as little humour as most Kelts. He used to wait at the stage-door and drive her back to her lodgings in his own jaunting car. He used to give her small trinkets so innocently devoid of beauty as almost to attract by their artlessness. He was a young officer who had borne the blushing honours of a scarlet tunic for a very short while, so that, in addition to the Irishman's naïve assumption of universal popularity, he suffered from the sentiment that a soldier's red coat appeals to every woman.

Jenny, with her splendid Cockney irreverence, thought little of Mr. O'Meagh, less of his red coat, but a very great deal of the balmy February drives past the vivid green meadows of Liffey.

'You know,' Terence would say, leaning gracefully over the division of the car, 'you know, Jenny, our regiment – the 127th of the Line, as we call ours – was absolutely cut to pieces at Drieufontein; and at Riviersdorp they held the position against two thousand Boers.'

'Who cares?' said Jenny.

'You might take a little interest in it.'

'Well,' said Jenny, 'how can I?'

'But you might be interested because, after all, it is my regiment, and I'm awfully fond of you, little girl.'

'Don't be soppy,' Jenny advised him.

'You're so cursedly matter of fact.'

'Eh?'

'So – oh, well, damn it, Jenny, you don't seem to care whether I'm with you or not.'

'Why should I?'

'Any other girl would be fond of me.'

'Ah – any other girl would.'

'Then why aren't you?'

'Oh, you'll pass in a crowd.'

'Dash it, I'm frightfully in love with you,' vowed Terence.

'You date! What's the good of spoiling a fine day by being silly?'

'Damn it, nobody else but me would stick your rudeness.'

And Terence would sulk, and Jenny would hum, and the jaunting car would go jaunting on.

On the last night of the pantomime Mr. O'Meagh called for her as usual, and, as they drove off, said:

'Look here, Miss Jenny, you're coming back to my rooms with me to-night.'

'Am I?' said Jenny; 'that's news.'

'By Jove, you are!'

'No fear.'

'You shall.'

Terence caught hold of her hand.

'Let me go,' Jenny said.

'I'm damned if I will. Look here, you know, you can't make a fool of an Irishman.'

'That's quite right,' Jenny agreed.

'When an Irishman says he'll have a thing, he'll have it.'

'Well, you won't have Jenny Pearl.'

'Look here, I've been jolly good to you. I gave you—'

'What?' interrupted Jenny in dangerous tones. 'Look!'

She unbuckled a wrist-watch and flung it into the road.

'There's your watch, anyway. Going to get down and pick it up?'

Terence whipped up the horse.

'You little devil, you shall come with me.'

Jenny caught hold of the reins.

'Shut up!' said O'Meagh. 'Shut up! Don't you know better than that?'

'Well, stop,' said Jenny.

The subaltern, in order to avoid a scene, stopped.

'Look here,' Jenny told him. 'You think yourself a lad, I know, and you think girls can't say "no" to you; but I can, see? You and your little cottages for two! Not much! Try something softer next time. Ching-a-ling!' and Jenny slipped down from the car and vanished.

'Men,' she said to Winnie Ambrose, the only one left of the Glasgow Quartette. 'Men! I think men are awful. I do, really. Conceited? Oh no; it's only a rumour.'

It had been arranged by Madame Aldavini that Jenny, on her return from Dublin, should join the ballet of the opera at Covent Garden. Unfortunately her first appearance in London had to be postponed for a year owing to the fact of there being no vacancy. Jenny was disheartened. It was useless for Madame Aldavini to assure her that the extra year's practice would greatly benefit her dancing. Jenny felt she had been practising since the world was made. She continued to practise because there was nothing else to do, but time had quenched the fire of inspiration. She was tired of hearing that one day she might, with diligence and application, become a Prima Ballerina. She knew she was a natural dancer, but Terpsichore having endowed her with grace and lightness and twinkling feet, left the spirit that could ripen these gifts to some other divinity. She had, it is true, escaped the doom of an infant prodigy, but it might have been better to blossom as a prodigy than to lie fallow when the warmth and glory of the footlights were burning without her.

Meanwhile, Hagworth Street had not changed much in seventeen years. The tall plane tree at the end was taller. The London County Council, not considering it possessed any capacity for decoration, had neglected to lop off its head, and as there was no other tree in sight, did not think it worth the trouble of clipping to an urban pattern. Year by year it shed its bark and, purged of London vileness, broke in May fresh and green and beautiful. In October more leaves pattered down, more leaves raced along the gutters than on the night of Jenny's birth. The gas-jets burned more steadily in a mantle of incandescent light. This method of illumination prevailed indoors as well as outside, shedding acrid and sickly gleams over the front-parlour of Number Seventeen, shining, livid and garish, in the narrow hall. The knob was still missing from the bedstead, and for seventeen years Charlie had promised to get a new one. Charlie himself had changed very slightly. He still worked for the same firm in Kentish Town. He still frequented the Masonic Arms. He cared less for red neckties and seemed smaller than of old. Yet he could drink more. Although his hair was thinner, his eyebrows were more bushy, because he blew off his old ones in the course of an illustrated lecture on the management of gas-stoves. For the constant fingering of his ragged moustache he substituted a pensive manipulation of his exceptional eyebrows.

Mr. Vergoe was dead, and most of his property adorned his granddaughter's room in Cranbourne Street. She was still a second-line girl in the Corps de Ballet of the Orient Palace of Varieties. Jenny, however, possessed the picture of the famous dead Columbine. It hung beside a memorial card of the donor set in a shining black Oxford frame above the bed she shared with May. The room itself grew smaller every year. Jenny could not imagine that once to Edie and herself it had been illimitable. Nowadays it seemed to be all mahogany wardrobe and semi-circular marble-topped washstand and toilet-table and iron bedstead. On the door were many skirts and petticoats. On the walls were shrivelled fans with pockets that held curl-papers mostly. There was also a clouded photograph of Alfie, Edie, Jenny and May, of which the most conspicuous feature was the starched frills of Jenny, those historic frills that once, free of petticoats, had seemed a talisman to masculinity. The toilet-table was inhabited by a collection of articles that presented the most sudden and amazing contrasts. Next to a comb that might easily have been rescued from a dustbin was a brush backed with silver repoussé. Beside two or three pairs of nail-scissors was a scent-bottle with golden stopper. Jenny's nightgown was daintily ribboned and laced, and looked queerly out of place on the pock-marked quilt.

Mrs. Purkiss still visited her sister; but Jenny was not allowed to associate with Percy or Claude, both more pasty-faced than ever, because Percy was going to be a missionary and Claude was suspected of premature dissipation, having been discovered kissing the servant in the bathroom.

Mrs. Raeburn, in the jubilee of her age, was still a handsome woman, and was admired even by Jenny for her smartness. She still worried about the future of her children. She was more than ever conscious of her husband's inferiority and laughed over most of the facts of her life. May's back, however, and Jenny's perpetual riotousness caused her many misgivings. But Alfie was doing well and Edie seemed happy, making dresses over at Brixton. There had been no recurrence of Mr. Timpany, and she now viewed that episode much as she would have regarded a trifling piece of domestic negligence. As for the Misses Horner, their visit had long faded absolutely from her mind. It would have taken a very great emotional crisis to inspire such another speech as she made to them seventeen years ago. Charlie still snored beside her, as he had snored in sequel to seven or eight thousand nightly undressings. She still saw to the washing, added up the accounts, but always bought several new dresses and bonnets in spring and autumn. She still meant to read the papers this week, but never had time; and every night she hoped that all would go smooth. This habit of hope was to her what the candle-lit chapter of a Bible with flower-stained pages or counterpane prayers or dreams of greatness are to minds differently constituted. Her life was by no means drab, for she went often to the theatre and occasionally to the saloon bar of a discreet public-house where, in an atmosphere of whisky and Morocco leather, she would sometimes listen to Mrs. Purkiss's doubts of Jenny's behaviour, but more often tell diverting tales of Charlie.

Such was Hagworth Street when on a cold Sunday in the front of May Edie came over from Brixton. She looked pale and anxious as she sat for a while in the kitchen twisting black kid gloves round her fingers.

'How's Brixton, Edie?' asked her mother.

'Grand.'

'You've not been up to see us for a long time.'

'No-o-o,' agreed the eldest daughter.

'Busy?'

'Not so very. Only you never know when you will be. I'll go upstairs and take my things off. Come with us, Jenny,' she said, turning to her sister.

'There's a cheek. Whatever next?'

'Oh, you are hateful. Come on up.'

Jenny, with every appearance of unwillingness, followed Edie upstairs, and flung herself down on the bed they had once shared.

'Don't be all night,' she protested, as she watched Edie staring aimlessly at herself in the glass.

'Jenny,' said the latter suddenly, 'I done it.'

'Done what, you date?'

'Myself, I suppose.'

'What d'ye mean?'

'You know,' said Edie.

'Oh yes, I know, that's why I'm asking.'

'You remember that fellow I was going about with?'

'Bert Harding?'

'Yes, Bert.'

'You're never going to marry him, Edie?'

'I got to – if I can.'

Jenny sat up on the bed.

'You don't mean he's sprung it on you?'

'That's right,' said Edie.

'Whatever made you let – go on, Ede, you're swanking.'

'I wish I was.'

'You're not. Cri! how awful!'

'I am a fool,' said Edie helplessly.

'But can't you—'

'I tried. It wasn't no good.'

'Whatever will Alfie say?' Jenny wondered.

'What's it got to do with Alfie?'

'I don't know, only he's very particular. But this Bert of yours, I suppose he will marry you?'

'He says so. He says nothing wouldn't stop him.'

'Men!' cried Jenny. 'I think men are the dirtiest rotters on earth.'

'Bert isn't so bad,' said Edie in defence of her folly.

'Are you struck on him? You know, potty?'

'I like him very well.'

'Are you mad to marry him?'

'I must.'

'But you don't want to?'

'I wouldn't – not if I hadn't got to. I wouldn't marry anybody for a bit.'

'I wouldn't anyhow,' said Jenny decidedly.

'Don't talk silly. I've got to.'

'Oh, I do think it's a shame. A pretty girl like you, Ede. Men! Can he keep you? – comfortable and all that?'

'He's got enough, and he expects to make a bit more soon, and then there's my dressmaking.'

'Men!' declared Jenny. 'No men for me. I wouldn't trust any man.'

'Don't say anything to mother about it.'

'As if I should.'

The two sisters went downstairs.

'I'll bring him over soon,' said Edie.

'And I'll properly tell him off,' said Jenny.

'I hope you won't.'

'Crushed!' said Jenny half mocking, half kind.

A month went by, and Mr. Albert Harding had many important engagements. Another month went by and Edie began to fret.

Jenny went over to Brixton to see her sister.

'Looks as if this marriage was only a rumour,' she said.

'He hasn't got the time, not for a week or two.'

'What?' exclaimed Jenny.

'He's going to take me to the Canterbury to-morrow. He's all right, Jenny. Only he's busy. He is, really.'

Jenny, jolting homewards in the omnibus that night, wondered what ought to be done. Although she felt to the full the pity of a nice girl like Edie being driven into a hasty marriage, no alternative presented itself clearly. She thought with quickening heart, so terrible was the fancy, how she would act in Edie's place. She would run away out of the world's eyes, out of London.

Yet Edie did not seem to mind so much.

The malignity of men enraged her. The selfishness and grossness sickened her. Boys were different; but men, with their conceit and lies, were beasts. They should never make a fool of her. Never. Never. Then she wondered if her mother had been compelled to marry. On no other basis could her father be explained. Men were all alike. To sleep with a man, and lie awake watching his thick red neck, and be stroked by his hands rough as emery paper!

Whatever made Edie let Bert Harding spring it on her? Bert Harding. Greasy. Dark-eyed. Like a dirty foreigner. He was nice-looking after a fashion, yes; but even more conceited than most men. And Edie had *got* to marry him.

Alfie was on the doorstep when she reached home.

'You?' she said.

'Come over for the night. Got some business in Islington to-morrow morning.'

'Alfie, you know Bert Harding?'

'Yes.'

'You've got to make him marry Edie.'

'I'll smash his face in if he don't.'

'Yes, smash his face,' said Jenny. 'They'll be at the Canterbury to-morrow night.'

It was a poor fight in the opinion of the Westminster Bridge Road. Bert was overmatched. He was perfectly willing to marry Edie at once, as it happened, but Jenny enjoyed seeing one of his dark eyes closed up by her brother. Alfie, having done his duty, never spoke to Bert or Edie again.

'However could she have been so mad?' said Mrs.

Raeburn. 'Soft! soft! silly! That's you,' she went on, turning on her husband.

'Oh, of course it's me. Everything's me,' said Charlie.

'Yes, it is you. You can't say no to a glass of beer and Edie can't say no to a man.'

'What would you have done, mother,' asked Jenny, 'if Edie's Bert had gone away and left her?'

'She'd never have come inside my house again – not ever again.'

'You're funny.'

'Funny,' said Mrs. Raeburn. 'You try and be funny, and see what happens.'

'Who cares?' said Jenny. 'It wouldn't trouble me. I'm sick of this dog's island. But men. Whatever next? Don't you imagine I'll let any man spring it on *me*. Not much.'

'Don't you be too sure, Mrs. Clever,' said the mother.

'But I am. I'm positive. Love! There's nothing in it.'

'Hark at her,' jeered Charlie.

Jenny lay awake in a fury that night. One after another, man in his various types passed across the screen of her mind. She saw them all. The crimson-jointed, fishy-eyed Glasgow youths winked at her once more. The complacent subalterns of Dublin dangled their presents and waited to be given her thanks and kisses. Old men, from the recess of childish memories, rose up again and leered at her. Her own father, small and weak and contemptible, pottered across the line of her mental vision. Bert Harding was there, his black boot-button eyes glittering from a crowd of dirty rotters. And to that her sister had surrendered herself, to be pawed and mauled about and boasted of.

Ugh! Suddenly in the middle of her disgust Jenny thought she heard a sound under the bed.

'Oo-er, May!' she called out. 'May!'

'Whatever is it, you noisy thing?'

'Oo-er, there's a man under the bed! Oh, May, wake up, else we shall all be murdered!'

'Whatever next?' said May. 'Go to sleep.'

And just then the Raeburns' big cat, tired of his mouse-hole, came out from underneath the bed and walked slowly across the room.

X

Drury Lane and Covent Garden

To compensate Jenny for her disappointment over Covent Garden, Madame Aldavini secured a place for her in the Drury Lane pantomime. She was no longer to be the most attractive member of an attractive quartette, but one of innumerable girls who changed several times during the evening into amazingly complicated dresses, designed not to display individual figures, but to achieve broad effects of colour and ingenuity.

Straight lines were esteemed above dancing, straight lines of Frenchmen or Spaniards in the Procession of Nations, straight lines of Lowestoft or Dresden in the Procession of Porcelain, straight lines of Tortoise-shell Butterflies or Crimson-underwing Moths in the Procession of Insects. Jenny's gay deep eyes were obscured by tricolour flags or the spout of a teapot or the disproportionate antennæ of a butterfly. There was no individual grace of movement in swinging down the stage in the middle of a long line of undistinguished girls. If the audience applauded, they applauded a shaft of vivid colour, no more enthusiastically than they would have clapped an elaborate arrangement of limelight. Everything was sacrificed to the cleverness of a merely inventive mind. More than ever Jenny felt the waste of academic instruction in her art. She had been learning to dance for so many years, and there she was beside girls who could neither dance nor move, girls who had large features and showy legs and so much cubic space for spangles.

But if her personality did not carry over the footlights and reach the mighty audience of Drury Lane, behind the scenes it gradually detached itself from the huge crowd of girls. Great comedians with great salaries condescended to find out her name. Great principal boys with great expanses of chest nodded at her over furs. Dainty principal girls with dainty tiers of petticoats smiled and said good evening in their mincing, genteel, principal girl voices. Even the stage doorkeeper never asked her name more than once. Everybody knew Jenny Pearl, except the public. So many people told her she was sure to get on that she began to be ambitious again, and used to go, without being pressed, to Madame Aldavini's for practice. The latter was delighted and prophesied a career – a career that should date from her engagement (a real engagement this time) at Covent Garden in the spring.

Jenny's popularity at the theatre made her more impatient than ever of home. She bore less and less easily her mother's attempts to steer her course.

'You'll come to grief,' Mrs. Raeburn warned her.

'I don't think so.'

'A nice mess Edie made of things.'

'I'm not Edie. I'm not so soft.'

'You're not happy unless you're about with fellows.'

'Well, who else am I to go about with?'

'Why don't you stay at home and help your mother?'

'Yes, I daresay. I don't earn my keep without making my hands all ugly with work; oh no, it's only a rumour.'

'You can't cook a potato.'

'Who cares? You can't do the splits.'

'You're growing up a regular vulgar common girl. If I'd known what theatre manners were, you should never have gone on the stage.'

'My manners are all right, if they're let alone,' said Jenny. 'And, anyway, you put me on the stage.'

'Why you can't meet some nice young chap, and settle down comfortable with a home of your own, I can't think.'

'Like Edie, I suppose, and have a pack of kids. One after another. One after another. And a husband like Bert, so shocking jealous he can't see her look at another man without going on like a mad thing. Not this little girl.'

Jenny never told her mother that half the attraction of boys' society nowadays lay in the delight of making fools of them. If she had told her, Mrs. Raeburn might not have understood. Jenny was angry that her mother should suspect her of being fast. She was sure of her own remoteness from passionate temptation. She gloried in her security. She could not imagine herself in love, and laughed heartily at girls who did. She was engaged to sixteen boys in one year, to not one of whom was vouchsafed the light privilege of touching her cheeks. They presented her with cheap jewellery which she never returned on the decease of affection, and scarcely wore during its short existence.

It was put away in a cigar-box in a tangled heap of little petrified hearts.

Mrs. Raeburn, however, assuming in these despised youths a menace to her daughter's character, was never tired of dinning into her ears the tale of Edith's disaster. The more she scolded, the more she held a watch in her hand when Jenny came back from the theatre, the more annoying was Jenny, the longer did she delay her evening home-comings.

The fact that Bert and Edie had settled down into common-place married life did not make her regard more kindly the circumstance-impelled conjunction. She reproduced in her mental view of the result something of her mother's emotion immediately before her own birth. Long ago Mrs. Raeburn had settled down into an unsatisfied contentment; long ago she had renounced extravagance of hope or thought, merely keeping a hold on laughter; but Jenny felt vaguely the waste of life, the waste of love, the waste of happiness which such a marriage as Edie's suggested. She could not have formulated her impressions. She had never been taught to coordinate ideas. Her mind was a garden planted with rare shrubs whose labels had been destroyed by a careless gardener, whose individual existence was lost in a maze of rank weeds. Could the Fates have given her a rich revenge for the waste of her intelligence, Jenny should have broken the heart of some prominent member of the London School Board, should have broken his heart and wrecked his soul, herself meanwhile blown on by fortunate gales to Elysium.

May was often told of her sister's crusade, of the slain suitors too slow to race with Atalanta.

'Men *are* fools,' Jenny proclaimed. 'Soppy? oh no, it's only a rumour.'

'Did you see Fred to-night?'

'Yes; he saw me home.'

'What did he say?'

'Nothing much. I told him not to talk because he got on my nerves and I wanted to think about my new costume for the spring.'

'Didn't he mind?'

'I can't help his troubles. He asked if he might kiss me.'

'What did you say?'

'I told him after the next turning, and every time we came to the next turning I told him the next, till we got to our gate. I said good night and he said, "What about my kiss?" I said, "There's a cheek; you don't want much"; and he said, "I give you a brooch last week, Jenny"; and I said, "There's your brooch," and I threw it down.'

'What did he do?'

'He couldn't do much. I trod on it and ran in.'

'Somebody'll shoot you one day,' prophesied May.

'Who cares? Besides, they haven't got the pluck. Men are walking cigarettes, that's what men are.'

Drury Lane pantomime came to an end.

'And a good job,' said Jenny, 'for it isn't a pantomime at all; it's more of a Lord Mayor's show.'

Jenny now had to rehearse hard for the ballet at Covent Garden, but there was still plenty of time in the lengthening spring dusks with their silver stars and luminous horizons, to fool plenty of men. There was a quarrelsome interlude with Alfie on this account. The latter had rashly presented one of his own friends for Jenny's sport. The friend had spent most of his income on chocolates and pit-stalls, and at one swoop a whole week's salary on a garnet bracelet.

'Look here,' said Alfie. 'Don't you get playing your tricks on any of my friends, because I won't have it.'

'Hark at him. Hark at Alfred Proud. As if your friends were better than anyone else's.'

'Well, I'm not going to have fellows say my sister's hot stuff.'

'Who did?'

'Never mind who did. Somebody said it.'

'Arthur?'

Arthur was the melancholy Romeo introduced by Alfie.

'Somebody said you was to Arthur.'

'And what did he do?'

'He was quite disgusted. He walked away.'

'Didn't he have a fight over it?'

'No. He said he would have done, only you treated him so off-hand.'

'Well, he needn't come whistling outside for me no more.'

'You're not going to chuck him?'

'Chuck him? I never had him. He worried me to go out with him. I didn't want to go.'

'You'll get a bullet in your chest one of these days. You'll get shot.'

'Not by one of your massive friends.'

'Why not?'

'Why, there isn't hardly one of 'em as would have the pluck to hold a pistol, and not one as would have the money to buy one. I've properly rumbled your friends.'

'Well, don't say I never told you.'

'You and your friends' pistols!'

With the pride and insolence of maiden youth Jenny took the London streets. Through the transient April rains she came from Islington to Covent Garden every day. From King's Cross she rode on the green omnibus that jogged by the budding elms of Brunswick Square. Down Guilford Street she rode and watched its frail inhabitants coming home with their parcels of ribbons and laces. Through Great Queen Street into Long Acre she came, sitting alone on the front seat of the green omnibus more like a rosy lily now than a La France rose. Down Long Acre till she came to Bow Street, through which she would run to the theatre past the groups of porters who nodded and smiled at her, for they soon recognized the swift one running through the April rains.

Italian opera appealed to Jenny most. She did not care greatly for *Tannhäuser*, thinking the Venusberg ballet very poor and Venus herself a sight. Teutonic extravagance affected her with a slight sense of discomfort as of being placed too near trombones. Her training as a dancer had begotten a meticulous feeling for form which the expansive harmonies of Wagner disconcerted. Jenny did not enjoy suffering a sea-change. Novelty and strangeness were to her merely peculiar. Strauss would have bored her, not as Brahms might have bored her to somnolence, but as an irritating personality bores one to rudeness or sudden flight. To speculate how far it might have been advisable to hang her intelligence with Gothic tapestries is not worth while. Probably the imposition of decorated barbarism on her lucid and sensitive enjoyment of Verdi would have obscured the small windows of her soul with gloomy arras. Notwithstanding her education at the Board School, she had a view, and it was better she should preserve an instinct for a sanity that was sometimes bathos rather than that, in the acquirement of an epileptic appreciation, she should lose what was, after all, a classical feeling in her sensuous love of obvious beauty.

The sugar-plums of Italian opera melted innocently in her mouth, leaving behind them nothing but a memory of sweetness as one steps from a garden of shaded bird-song with a thought of music. Wagner was more intoxicating, but bequeathed no limpid exultation to the heart of the wearied listener. Moreover, she had a very real sense of being a square peg in a round hole when she and the other minions of Venus tripped round the frequent rocks of the Venusberg. It was as if a confectioner had stuck a shepherdess of pink icing on the top of a plum-pudding. Jenny felt, in her own words, that it was all unnatural. There was nothing of Walpurgis in their stereotyped allurement. It was Bobbing Joan in Canterbury Close. The violins might wail through the darkened opera-house, but an obese Tannhäuser caught by the wiles of an adipose Venus during the inexpressive seductions of an Italian ballet was silly; the poses to be sustained were fatiguing and ineffective. More fatiguing still was Jenny's almost unendurable waiting as a page while the competitors sang to Elizabeth. There were four pages in purple velvet tunics. Jenny looked her part, but the other three looked like Victoria plums. The one scene in German opera that she really enjoyed was the Valkyries' ride when she and a few selected girls were strapped high up to the enchanted horses and rocked exhaustingly through the terrific clamour.

But these excursions into Gothic steeps among the distraught populations of the North were not the main feature of the opera season. They were a tour de force of rocks in a dulcet enclosure. Over Covent Garden hung the magic of an easy and opulent decoration. It sparkled from the tiaras in the grand circle. It flashed from the tie-pins of the basses, from the rings of the tenors. It breathed on the oceanic bosoms of the contraltos. It trembled round the pleated hips of the sopranos. Everything was fat – a pasha's comfortable dream.

Jenny, being little and svelte, was distressed by the prevalent sumptuousness. A fine figure began to seem a fine ambition.

'My dear child, you are thin,' some gracious Prima Donna would murmur richly just before she tripped on to the stage to play consumptive Mimi.

Jenny could not see that she was advancing to fame at Covent Garden. Nor was she, indeed; but Madame Aldavini tried to console her by insisting upon the valuable experience and pointing out the products of success that surrounded her. Covent Garden was only a stepping-stone, Madame reminded her.

Here she was at seventeen without a chance to display

her accomplishments. It was more acting than dancing at Covent Garden. Jenny, too, was always chosen for such voiceless parts as were important. Some of these she did not like. In *Rigoletto*, for instance, Previtale, the great singer, expressed a wish that she should play the girl in the sack whom he has to fondle. Jenny did not like being fondled. Other girls would have loved the conspicuous attractions of Previtale, but Jenny thought his breath was awful, as indeed it was.

Her principal friend at Covent Garden was a girl called Irene, or rather spelt Irene, for she was always called Ireen. Irene Dale was a mixture of the odd and the ordinary in her appearance. At first glance she seemed the commonplace type produced in hundreds by English theatres. Perhaps the expression of her face in repose first suggested a possibility of distinction. The intensely blue eyes in that circumstance had a strange listless ardour as if she were dreaming of fiery moments fled long ago. The blue eyes were enhanced by hair, richly brown as drifted leaves in sunlight. Her straight mouth was prettiest when she was being pleasantly teased. Her nose came to an end, and then began again. Her chin was deeply cleft and her complexion full of real roses. In the company of Jenny Irene gave an impression of slowness; not that Jenny, except when late for rehearsal, ever seemed in a hurry, but with her there was always the suggestion of a tremulous agility. Irene had been at Madame Aldavini's school, where she and Jenny in their childhood had wasted a considerable amount of time in romping, but since they never happened to go on tour together, they never achieved a girlish friendship until at Covent Garden they found themselves dressing next to one another.

Jenny tried to inspire Irene with the hostility to men felt by herself. But Irene, although she enjoyed the lark, had a respect for men at the bottom of it all and would not always support Jenny in her freely expressed contempt. While she was at Covent Garden, Irene met a young man, unhealthily tall, who made much of her and gave her expensive rings and for an unpleasant fancy of his own took her to a fashionable milliner's and dressed her in short skirts. Jenny had heard something of Irene's Danby and was greatly annoyed by the latter's unsympathetic influence.

'Your Danby,' she would protest. 'Whatever can you see in him? Long idiot!'

'My Danby's a gentleman,' said Irene.

'Well, I think he looks terrible. Why, he wears his teeth outside.'

Then Jenny, meeting Irene and her Danby in Leicester Square, beheld her friend in the childish costume.

'Oh, sight!' she called out.

'You are rude,' said Irene.

'You're a very rude little girl,' said Danby; 'but will you come and have a drink with us?'

'No, thanks,' said Jenny, and passed on coldly. That evening she attacked Irene in the dressing-room.

'To let a man make such a shocking sight of you!'

'He likes to see me in short skirts.'

'Whatever for? And those boots! Ain't you afraid of getting the bird?'

'He wants me to marry him,' declared Irene.

'You soppy idiot, you ought to wear crape on your nose.'

'Why?'

'Your brains are dead.'

'Oh, you hateful thing!'

'Marry you? That's only a rumour, young Ireen. I've properly rumbled your Danby. Marry you! I don't think.'

'He is, when he comes back from Paris, and he said you were a very bad example for me.'

'Crushed!' said Jenny in mock humility. Then she went on: 'Yes, you and your Parises. Any old way, you can tell Tin Ribs from me I should be ashamed to make a girl I was fond of look such a terrible sight.'

'His brother said he'd like to be introduced to you.'

'Yes; I daresay. Tin Ribs the Second, I suppose. No, thanks, not this little girl.'

'You *are* mean.'

'Well, he'll only spring it on you, and then you'll wish you hadn't been so soft,' said Jenny.

London deepened into summer, and the golden people coming out of Covent Garden seemed scattered with star dust from the prodigal June stars, while the high moon made of Jenny a moonbeam as in white piqué she sat in the front of the green omnibus going home.

These were happy days at Covent Garden, and when the season ended Jenny was sorry. She did not enjoy Yarmouth with its swarming sands and goat-carriages and dust and fleas and switch-back flung down on the barren coast like a monstrous skeleton. She was glad to come back to London in the effulgence of a fine September; glad to rehearse again for the autumn Opera season, and pleased, when that was over, to return to Drury Lane for the Christmas pantomime.

After her second spring season of opera was over, she and Irene discussed the future. Danby had retired to Paris on his business: his rings sparkled unseen in the safe of a Camden Town pawnbroker, although the whisky and soda which they served to buy had long ceased to sparkle for Mrs. Dale. Irene said she was tired of being in three months and out three months.

'I think we ought to go to the Orient, Jenny.'

'I don't care where we go,' said Jenny.

'Well, let's.'

'All right. I'll meet you Camden Town station to-morrow. Don't you be late.'

'No fear.'

'Oh no, Mrs. Punctual, you're never late,' scoffed Jenny.

'Well, I won't be to-morrow.'

On the following morning Jenny dressed herself up to impress the ballet-master of the Orient, and arrived in good time at Camden Town station. Irene was nowhere in sight. Jenny waited half an hour. People began to stare at the sprays of lilac in her large round hat. Really they were looking at the blue facets of her eyes, and her delicate frowning eyebrows. But Jenny, feeling herself a-blush, thought it was the lilac, thought her placket was undone, thought there was a hole in her stocking, became thoroughly hot and self-conscious.

She waited another blushful quarter of an hour. Then,

thinking that Irene must surely have mistaken the meeting-place, she called at the shop in Kentish Town where her father worked and asked him if he'd seen Irene.

'Ireen Dale?' said Charlie.

'Yes. You know.'

'Haven't you seen her?'

'No.'

'Why, she was in here asking for you. She's been waiting outside Kentish Town station.'

'That's Mrs. Brains all over. Ta-ta!'

Jenny dashed off to Kentish Town, where she caught Irene on the verge of departure. Most of the way to the Orient they argued who was right.

When they reached the famous theatre of varieties Irene said she was afraid to go in.

'Who cares?' said Jenny. 'If they don't want us, they won't eat us, any old way.'

Monsieur Corontin, the Maître de Ballet, interviewed them in his little room that was hidden away at the end of one of the innumerable passages. He looked at Jenny curiously.

'Dance, please, miss.'

Jenny danced as well as she could in the diminutive room.

'Now, please, miss,' he said to Irene, who also danced.

'You are engaged,' said M. Corontin.

'Both?' asked Jenny.

'Both of you.'

They lost themselves several times in the course of their descent.

'What an unnatural place,' said Jenny. 'Gee! How many more stairs? I suppose we're ballet girls now.'

At home that evening Charlie remonstrated with his daughter for intruding upon him at Kentish Town.

'Don't come asking me for your flash friends,' he said. 'Why, the men wondered who you were.'

'Didn't they know I was your daughter?'

'I tried to pretend you wasn't, but one of 'em heard you calling me dad.'

'What did he say?'

'What did he say? He said, "Charlie, is your daughter a blinking princess?" '

'Well, you ought to have been very proud,' said Jenny.

'Proud, with all the men in the shop laughing at me? Why, they'll think I've no business to be working.'

'Oh, I've properly got the bird.'

'And don't you never recognize me in the street,' went on Charlie.

'Why ever not?'

'Well, look at you, look at your hat. People I know wonders whatever on earth you are.'

'Oh, my own father's ashamed of me now; and what about you? Beer and bed's all you think about.'

Jenny thought she would go and see Lilli Vergoe in Cranbourne Street, and tell her of the engagement.

Lilli sat with her feet on the mantelpiece smoking a cigarette.

'I've joined the ballet,' said Jenny.

'Where?'

'At the Orient.'

153

'You won't like it.'

'Who cares? I shan't stay if I don't.'

'Yes, you will. You'll stay. Everybody stays at the Orient. I've stayed there twelve years and I'm still a second-line girl. You'll stay twelve years and, if you don't get fat, you'll still be a second-line boy.'

'What about if I get married?'

'You'll still stay.'

'You'll give me a headache, you and your staying. I intend to enjoy myself. You're worse than a wet week, you are.'

Jenny was standing by the window looking down into Cranbourne Street baking in the July heat.

'Isn't it shocking hot?' said Lilli.

'I think summer's simply lovely,' Jenny answered.

XI

The Orient Palace of Varieties

The Orient Palace of Varieties rose like a cliff from the drapery shops of Piccadilly. On fine summer dusks, in a mist of golden light, it possessed a certain magic of gaiety; seemed to capture something of the torch-lit merriment of a country fair. As one loitered on the island, lonely and meditative, the Orient was alluring, blazed upon the vision like an enchanted cave, or offered to the London wanderer a fancy of the scents and glossy fruits and warblers of the garden where Camaralzaman lost Badoura; and in autumn, stained by rosy sunsets, the theatre expressed the delicate melancholy of the season. But when the rain dripped monotonously, when fogs transformed the town, when London was London vast and grey, the Orient became unreal like the bedraggled palaces of an exhibition built to endure for a little while. After all, it was an exotic piece of architecture, and evoked an atmosphere of falseness, the falseness of an Indian gong in a Streatham hall. Yet it had stood fifty years without being rebuilt. In addition to having seen two generations pass away, something in the character of its entertainment, in the lavishness of its decoration lent it the sacred permanence of a mausoleum, the mauso-leum of mid-Victorian amusement.

The Orient did not march with the times, rising from insignificance. It never owned a chairman who announced the willingness of each successive comedian to oblige with a song. Old men never said they remembered the Orient in the jolly old days, for they could not have forgotten it. In essentials it remained the same as ever. Dancers had gone; beauties had shrivelled; but their ghosts haunted the shadowy interior. The silver-footed coryphées now kept lodging-houses; the swan-like ballerinas wore elastic stockings; but their absence was filled by others: they were as little missed as the wave that has broken. The lean old vanities quizzed and ogled the frail ladies of the Promenade and sniffed the smoke-wreathed air with a thought of pleasures once worth enjoyment. They spent now an evening of merely sentimental dissipation, but because it was spent at the Orient, not entirely wasted; for the unchanged theatre testified to the reality of their youth. It may not have been able to rejuvenate them, but, as by a handkerchief that survives the departure of its owner, their senses were faintly stimulated.

The Orient was proud because it did not enter into competition with any other house of varieties; preened itself upon a cosmopolitan programme. With the snob-bishness of an old City firm, it declined to advertise its ware with eye-arresting posters, and congratulated itself on the inability to secure new clients. Foreigners made up a large proportion of the audience, and were apparently contented by equestrian mistresses of the *haute école,* by bewildering assemblages of jugglers, even by continental mediocrities for the sake of hearing their native tongue. They did not object to interminable wire-acts, and put up with divination feats of the most exhausting dullness. After all, these incidental turns must occur; but the ballets were the feature of the evening. For many who visited the Orient, the stream of prostitutes ebbing and flowing upon the Promenade was enough. Yet the women of the Orient Promenade would strike a cynic with uneasiness.

Under the stars, the Piccadilly courtesans affect the onlooker less atrociously. Night lends a magic of softness to their fretful beauty. The sequins lose their garishness; the painted faces preserve an illusion of reality. Moonlight falls gently on the hollow cheek; kindles a spark of youth in the leaden eye. The Piccadilly courtesans move like tigers in a tropic gloom with velvet blazonries and a stealthy splendour that masks the hunger driving them out to seek their prey. On the Orient Promenade the finer animalism has vanished; it was never more than superficially asthetic. The daughters of pleasure may still be tigers but they are naphtha-lit, pacing backwards and forwards in a cage. They all appear alike. Their hats are all too large; their figures are too brutal, their cheeks too lifeless. They are automatic machines of lust waiting to be stirred into action by pennies.

Under the stars they achieve a pictorial romance; but on the carpet of the Promenade, they are hard and heartless and vile. Their eyes are coins; their hands are purses. At their heels patter old men like unhealthy lapdogs; beefy provincials stare at them, their foreheads glistening.

Above all the Frangipani and Patchouli and Opoponax and Trèfle Incarnat steals the rank odour of goats. The orchestra thunders and crashes down below: the comfortable audience lean back in the stalls: the foreigners jabber in the gallery: the Orient claque interrupts its euchre with hired applause. The corks pop; the soda splashes; money chinks; lechery murmurs; drunkards laugh; and down on the stage Jenny Pearl dances.

The night wears on. The women come in continually from the wet streets. They surge in the cloak-room; quarrel over carrion game, blaspheme, fight and scratch. A door in the cloak-room (locked of course) leads into the passage outside the dressing-room, where Jenny changes five or six times each night. Every foul oath and every vile experience and every detestable adventure is plainly heard by twenty ladies of the ballet.

Dressing-room number forty-five was a long low room with walls of whitewashed brick. There was one window, seldom opened. There was no electric light and the gas-jets gave a very feeble illumination, so feeble that everybody always put on too much grease paint in their fear of losing an effect. The girls dressed on each side of the room at a wide deal board with forms to sit upon. There was a large wardrobe in one corner, and next to Jenny's place an open sink. The room was always dark and always hot. There were about eighty stone stairs leading up to it from the stage, and at least half a dozen ascents in the course of the evening. The dresser was a blowsy old Irishwoman more obviously dirty than the room, and there were two ventilators which gave a perpetual draught of unpleasant air.

The inspectors of the London County Council presumably never penetrated as far as Room 45, a fact which seemed to show that the extent of municipal interference had been much exaggerated.

The dressing-rooms were half on one side of the stage, half on the other. Those on the side nearer to the stage-door were less unpleasant. The architect evidently believed in the value of first impressions. Anybody venturing into either warren without previous acquaintanceship would have been bewildered by the innumerable rooms and passages tucked away in every corner and branching off in every direction. Some of the former seemed to have been uninhabited for years. One in particular contained an ancient piano, two daguerrotypes and a heap of mouldering stuffs. It might have been the cell where years ago a Ballerina was immured for a wrong step. It existed like a monument to the despair of ambition.

The Orient stifled young life. The Corps de Ballet had the engulfing character of conventual vows. When a girl joined it, she cut herself off from the world. She went there fresh, her face a mist of roses, hope burning in her heart, fame flickering before her eyes. In a few years she would inevitably be pale with the atmosphere, with grinding work and late hours. She would find it easy to buy spirits cheaply in the canteen underneath the stage. She would stop in one line, it seemed, for ever. She would not dance for joy again.

When Jenny went to the Orient first, she did not intend to stay long. She told the girls this, and they laughed at her. She did not know how soon the heavy theatre would become a habit; she did not realize what comfort exists in the knowledge of being permanently employed. Yet not even the Orient could throttle Jenny. She was not the daughter and granddaughter of a ballet girl. She inherited no traditions of obedience. She never became a marionette to be dressed and undressed and jigged, horribly and impersonally. She yielded up her ambition, but she never lost her personality. When soon after her arrival the Maître de Ballet took her in his dark little corner and pinched her arm, she struck him across the mouth, vowed she would tell the manager and burnt up his conceit with her spitfire eyes. He tried again later on, and Jenny told his wife, a yellow-faced fat Frenchwoman. Then he gave her up and, being an artist, bore her no malice, but kept her in the first line of boys.

It is not to be supposed that the eighty or ninety ladies of the ballet were unhappy. On the contrary, they were very happy and so far as it accorded with the selfishness of a limited company, they were well looked after. The managing director called them 'Children,' and was firmly convinced that he treated them as children. Actually, he treated them as dolls, and in the case of girls well into the thirties, with some of the sentimental indulgence lavished on old broken dolls. Perhaps it was the crowd of men who waited every night at the end of the long narrow court that led from Jermyn Street down to the Orient stage-door, which has helped to preserve the vulgar and baseless tradition of frailty still sedulously propagated. Every night, about half-past eleven, the strange mixture of men waited for the gradual exodus of the ladies of the ballet. A group of men, inherently the same, had stood thus on six nights of the week for more than fifty years.

They had stood there with Dundreary whiskers, in rakish full capes and strapped overalls. They had waited there with the muttonchop whiskers and ample trousers of the 'seventies. Down the court years ago had come the beauties, with their striped stockings and swaying crinolines and velvety chignons. Down the court they had tripped in close-fitting pleated skirts a little later, and later still with the protruding bustles and skin-tight sleeves of the 'eighties. They had taken the London star-light with the balloon sleeves of the mid-'nineties. They took the starlight now, as sweet and tender as the fairs of long ago. They came out in couples, in laughing compan-ies, and sometimes singly with eager searching glances. They came out throwing their wraps around them in the sudden coolness of the air. They lingered at the end of the court in groups delicate as porcelain, enjoying the freedom and reunion with life. Their talk was hushed and melodious as the conversation of people moving slowly across dusky lawns. They were dear to the imaginative observer. He watched them with pride and affection as he would have watched fishing-boats steal home to their haven about sunset. Every night they danced and smiled and decked themselves for the pleasure of the world. They rehearsed so hard that sometimes they would fall down after a dance, crying on the stage where they had fallen from sheer exhaustion. They were not rich. Most of them were married, with children and little houses in teeming suburbs. Many, of course, were free to accept the escort of loiterers by the stage-door. The latter often regarded the ladies of the ballet as easy prey, but the ladies were shy as antelopes aware of the hunter crawling through the grasses. They were independent of masculine patronage; laughed at the fools with their easy manners and genial condescension. They might desire applause over the footlights, but under the moon they were free from the necessity for favour. They had, with all its incidental humiliations, the self-respect which a great art confers. They were children of Apollo.

The difference between the gorgeousness of the ballet and the dim air of the court was unimaginable to the blockheads outside. They had seen the girls in crimson and gold, in purple and emerald, in white and silver; they had seen them spangled and glittering with armour; they had heard the tinkle of jewellery. They had watched their limbs; gloated over their poses. They had caught their burning glances; brooded on their lips and eyes and exquisite motion. Inflamed by the wanton atmosphere of the Orient, they had thought the ladies of the ballet slaves for the delight of fools; but round the stage-door, all their self esteem was blown away like a fragment of paper by a London night wind. Their complacent selves by most of the girls were brushed aside like boughs in a wood. Some, Jenny and Irene amongst them, would ponder awhile the silly group and gravely choose a partner for half an hour's conversation in a café. But somewhere close to twelve o'clock Jenny would fly, leaving not so much as a glass slipper to console her sanguine admirer. Home she would fly on the top of a tram and watch in winter the scudding moon whipped by bare blown branches, in summer see it slung like a golden bowl between the chimney stacks. The jolly adventures of youth were many, and the partnership of Jenny and Irene caused great laughter in the dressing-room when the former related each diverting enterprise.

The tale of their conquests would be a long one. Most of the victims were anonymous or veiled in the pseudonym of a personal idiosyncrasy. There was Tangerine Willy who first met them, carrying a bag of oranges. There was Bill Hair and Bill Shortcoat and Sop and Jack Spot and Willie Eyebrows and Bill Fur. They all of them served as episodes mirthful and fugitive. They were mulcted in chocolates and hansoms and cigarettes. They danced attendance, vainly dreaming all the time of conquest. Jenny held them in fee with her mocking eyes, bewitched them with musical derision, and fooled them as Hera fooled the passionate Titan.

In winter-time the balls at Covent Garden gave Jenny some of the happiest hours of her life. Every Tuesday fortnight, tickets were sent round to the stage-door of the Orient, and it was very seldom indeed that she did not manage to secure one. On the first occasion she went dressed as a little girl in muslin with a white baby hat and white shoes and socks and, wherever they might attract a glance, bows of pink silk. When the janitors saw her first, they nearly refused to admit such youthfulness; could not believe she was really grown up; consulted anxiously together while Jenny's slanting eyes glittered up to their majesties. They were convinced at last, and she enjoyed herself very much indeed. She was chased up the stairs and round the lobby. She was chased down the stairs, through the supper-room, in and out of half a dozen boxes, laughing and chattering and shrieking all the while. She danced nearly every dance. She won the second prize. Three old men tried to persuade her to live with them. Seven young men vowed they had never met so sweet a girl.

To the three former Jenny murmured demurely:

'But I'm a good little girl; I don't do those things.'

And of course they pointed out that she was much too young to come to so wicked a place as Covent Garden. And of course, with every good intention, they offered to escort her home at once.

With the seven young men's admiration Jenny agreed.

'I am sweet, aren't I? Oh, I'm a young dream, if you only knew.'

And as a dream was she elusive. She gloried in her freedom. She was glad she was not in love. She had no wish to do anything but enjoy herself to the top of her bent. And she succeeded. Then at half-past six o'clock of a raw November morning, she rumbled home to Hagworth Street in a four-wheel cab with five other girls – a heap of tangled lace. She went upstairs on tip-toe. She undressed herself somehow, and in the morning she woke up to find on each wrist, as testimony of the night's masquerade, a little pink bow, soiled and crumpled.

She went often after that first visit and had many adventures. On one occasion she fell in with the handsome wife of a Surrey publican, and drove back after breakfast beside her to whatever Surrey village Mrs. Argles astonished with her figure and finery. Irene came too, and the girls went to bed in a dimity-hung bedroom and were taken for a drive in the afternoon and sat so long in the cosy bar-parlour watching the dusk stealing through the misted trees that they decided to send a telegram to the theatre announcing their illness. Then they stayed another night and went for another drive, laughing and chatting down the deep Surrey lanes. After dinner Jenny went back to Hagworth Street, and had a flaming quarrel with her mother, who accused her of 'going gay'; demanded to know how she dared put in an appearance dressed in another woman's clothes; insisted that she was to come home always immediately after the theatre; forbade a hundred things, and had the door slammed in her face for the advice. There were mad days as well as spangled nights. There were days at the Zoo with Bill Fur, a schoolmaster always full of information until he found his hat in the middle of the giraffe's enclosure, or perceived his gloves viewed with dislike by a cassowary. Bill Fur, however, would gladly have lost more than gloves or hat to be free for a while from the Margate school where he taught delicate boys the elements of Latin. To himself he was Don Juan in bravery of black satin slashed with purple. To the world, he was a rather foolish middle-aged schoolmaster. To the girls he was, as Jenny put it, a scream.

Perhaps it was Colonel Walpole who first suggested to Jenny that all men were not merely ridiculous. From his seat in the front row stalls, he perceived her charm; sent round a note to the stage-door; took her out to supper and champagne. When he found she was a good girl, he seemed to like her more than ever, and gave her tea in the flat whose windows looked over the sunlit tree-tops of Green Park. He also gave her some pretty dresses and hats. The other girls whispered and giggled when Jenny's back was turned. Her mother was sharply inquisitive and extremely suspicious.

'Who cares?' said Jenny. 'There's nothing in it.'

Colonel Walpole took her for long motor drives, gave her salmon mayonnaise at Weybridge, chicken mayonnaise at Barnet, salmon mayonnaise at Henley, chicken mayonnaise at Cobham, and lobster au gratin at Brighton. Colonel Walpole was very paternal, and Jenny liked him. He had a cool, clean appearance and a pleasant voice. Whatever may have been his ultimate intentions, he behaved very well, and she was sorry when he went away on a Tibetan expedition.

'My Friend, the Prince, has gone away,' she told the girls; and 'Don't laugh,' she added, 'because I *don't* like it.'

Jenny was nineteen. The mark of the Orient was not yet visible. A few roses had withered, but eighteen months of the fusty old theatre had been balanced by laughter outside. There seemed to be no end to her enjoyment of life. In essentials she was younger than ever. Mrs. Raeburn worried ceaselessly; but her daughter was perfectly well able to look after herself. Indeed, what mistakes she made were due to wisdom rather than folly. She knew too much about men. She had 'properly rumbled' men. She was too much of a cynic to be taken in. Her only ambition was excitement; and love, in her opinion, did not provide it. She was always depressed by the sight of lovers. She hated the permanency of emotion implied by their perpetual association. She and Irene liked to choose a pair from the group of men who waited by the stage-door, as one picks out two horses for a race. The next evening the pair of last night would be contemptuously ignored and a fresh couple dangled at the end of a string, as long as their antics were novel enough to divert.

Jenny still vowed she had no intention of remaining at the Orient, and if people asked about her dancing she mocked.

'What's the good of working? You don't get nothing for it. I *could* have danced. Yes, once. But now. Well, I can now, only I don't want to. See? Besides, what's the good?'

If anyone had foretold a career, she would have mocked louder.

'You don't know the Orient, I reckon they don't *want* to see a girl get on at the Orient. If you make a success in one ballet, you're crushed in the next.'

One morning Jenny looked at herself in the glass.

'May,' she called out, 'I think if I was to get old, I'd drown myself. I would really. Thirty! What a shocking idea.'

'You date,' said May. 'Why, you're only nineteen.'

'Yes, I know, but I *shall* be thirty. Some fellow said so last night. I suppose I must have been twopence on the can, for I woke up thinking of it. Thirty! What an unnatural age! Who cares? Perhaps I shan't never be thirty.'

XII

Growing Old

In her twentieth year, when the Covent Garden season of balls was over, the dread of growing old sometimes affected Jenny: it came upon her in gusts of premonition and, like a phantom, intruded upon the emptiness of her mind. The nervous strain of perpetual pleasure had made her restless and insecure. Day by day she was forced into a still greater dependence on trivial amusement, notwithstanding that every gratified whim added the lean ghost of another dead hour to haunt her memory. Headaches overtook her more easily now, and fits of depression were more frequent. She was vaguely aware that something could cure her discontent, and once or twice in moments of extreme weakness caught herself envying the girls who seemed so happy with their mild lovers. She began to contemplate the prospect of mating with one of the swains who inhabited awkwardly enough the desolation of Sunday evenings. She even went so far as to award the most persistent an afternoon at the Hackney Furnishing Company; but when, blushful and stammering, he discussed with the shopman the comparative merits of brass and iron bedsteads, Jenny, suddenly realizing the futility of the idea, fled from the jungle of furniture.

These negotiations with domesticity drove her headlong into a more passionate pursuit of folly, so that, with the colourless shadow of mere matrimony filling her soul, her clutch upon the sweet present became more feverish. She watched the adventures of girlhood fall prettily about her; saw them like unsubstantial snowflakes that are effective only in accumulation. Yet the transitory lovers of the stage-door were beginning also to become intolerable. She could not brook, so slim and proud was she, their immediate assumption of proprietorship. She hated the cheapening of her kisses and their imperviousness to her womanhood.

Where among these eager-handed wooers was the prince of destiny? Not he with box-pleats underneath his eyes, nor he with the cold slick fingers, nor he peppered with blackheads. Love was a myth, a snare, a delusion of soppy women who sacrificed their freedom in marriage. She remembered how in old days Santa Claus had turned into her mother on tiptoe. Love was another legend. The emotion that begot the fancy of armed boyhood mischievous to man was as incredible to her as is the dimpled personification to a Hyde Park materialist.

Jenny asked Irene if the love of Danby had brought her satisfaction. When her friend said she rather liked him, she enquired what was the good of it all.

'You don't do nothing. You don't get married. You just walk round the houses when he's in London and when he's in Paris you swank all the time you're going over to

169

get married to him, and lark about with other fellows the same as I do. There's nothing in it.'

'Well, you needn't go giving me the bird.'

'I think he's making a proper fool of you. Why don't *I* fall in love? Because I'm not so soft. Besides, you're not in love. You're just walking round yourselves having a game with each other.'

'Oh well, what of it?' said Irene sulkily.

'Don't be silly. I never knew such a girl as you. You can't talk sensible for a minute. I want to know what this love is.'

'You'll find out one day.'

'Ah, one day. *One* day I shall go and drown myself. Ireen Dale, I think I'm funny. I do really. Sometimes I can dance all over the place and kick up a shocking row, laughing and that. And then I cry. Now what about? I ask you. What have I got to cry about? Nothing. I just sit and cry my eyes out over nothing.'

Jenny was beginning to take an interest in herself. Introspection was dawning on her mind. She did not practise the meditation of age, infirmity and death; when these spectres confronted her she dismissed them as too impalpable to count. Nor did she examine her conscience arduously like a Catholic neophyte. Unreasonable fits of weeping and long headaches were nevertheless disconcerting; and she was bound to search her mind for the cause.

The first explanation that presented itself was age; but she was unwilling to admit the probability of growing old at nineteen, and turned to health for the reason. She could not honestly assert that she was ill. Then she asked herself if disappointment was the cause, and wondered whether, if she were suddenly invited to head the Orient play-bill, she would be exhilarated out of tears for ever. Finally she decided, breathless in the solitude of a warm May dusk, that she wanted to fall in love. Desire, winged with the scent of lilac blossom, stole in through the sapphire window. Desire flooded her soul with ineffable aspirations. Desire wounded her heart as she whispered, timidly, faintly, 'darling, my darling.' From that moment she began to seek the unknown lover in the casual acquaintance. She began to imagine the electric light shining in the blue eyes of some newly met fellow was not electric light at all. She would meet him on the next day, and, beholding him starkly dull, would declare again that men were 'awful.' The readiness with which they all capitulated puzzled her. Why was she attractive? Irene told her she made eyes; but this was false, or if she did make eyes, they were made unconsciously. Men told her she led them on. There must be some lure in her personality fatal long before she attempted to exercise it; for, though latterly she had been deliberately charming to most men at first, she was so very ungracious the following day that anybody else but a man would have left her alone. The poor fools, however, seemed actually to rejoice in her hardness of heart. Moreover, why had this fascination never helped her to renown? She could dance better than many of the girls who were given Pas Seuls; but she had never escaped from the front line of boys. What was the good of working? Nothing came of it. She remained obscure and undefined to the public. It was not hers to trip from a rostrum into the affection of an audience. It was not hers to acknowledge the favour of applause by taking a call. There was no shower of carnations or rain of violets round her farewell curtseys. If she never danced again, it would not matter. Half bitterly she recalled the spangled dreams of childhood, and revived the splendour of a silver and pink ballet-skirt that now would seem such tawdry, trumpery apparel.

'Fancy,' she said to May; 'I used to want to be a Columbine and dance about Islington. Think of it. What an unnatural child.'

Columbine appeared fitfully in the Ballet-divertissements that opened the Orient's entertainment, but Jenny never portrayed that elusive personage. Certainly she played Harlequin once, when a girl was ill; and gay and sweet she looked in the trim suit chequered with black and gold.

Jenny wondered why she had longed to grow up.

'I used to think that it was glorious to be grown up. But there's nothing in it. There might be, but there isn't. I wish anyone could be what they thought they would be when they was kids.'

'Oh, Jenny, don't talk so much, and get dressed,' said Irene. 'Aren't you coming out to-night?'

'I suppose so,' Jenny answered. 'I wish I couldn't. I wish I'd *got* to meet somebody. There, now I've told you.'

'Hark at her. Hark at Jenny Pearl.'

'Oh, well, I'm sick of going out with *you*.'

'What a liberty! Why?'

'Oh, well, it's always the same.'

'You *are* mad. Whatever's wrong with you?'

'Don't talk so much, Mrs. Bigmouth. You get on my nerves.' Irene sulked awhile; then asked:

'Have you seen the peroxide they've sent up for our arms?'

'Oo-er! Why?'

'Mr. Walters said all the girls was to use it.'

'Oh, aren't they shocking, Ireen? I do think they're awful.'

'Somebody said the Hesperides didn't look nice from the front.'

Jenny examined the purple bottle which would idealize their forms to an Hellenic convention. After the first indignation had worn itself out, she began to be amused by the transformations of the drug. Lying in bed next morning, she began to play with the notion of dyeing her hair. The tradition of youthful fairness from the midst of which glowed her deep blue eyes was still vital in Hagworth Street. Other girls dyed their hair, and already once or twice Jenny had considered the step; but the exertion of buying the peroxide had hitherto stifled the impulse. Here, however, was the opportunity and surely the experiment was worth the trial. She jumped out of bed and examined herself critically in the toilet-glass; tried to picture the effect of fairness. It would be a change, anyhow: it would be something to vary the monotony of existence. It would be interesting to learn if her new appearance provoked admiration greater than ever. It would be interesting to see if the change impressed the authorities of the Orient. Best of all, perhaps, would be the exclamations of surprise when the dressing-room first beheld the alteration.

Having conceived the plan, she began to hate her present appearance, to ascribe to her present shade all the boredom that was clinging round her like a fog. Her own hair, paradoxically enough, came to be considered an unnatural colour. After all, she was really fair, and had been cheated of her natural hue merely by the freak of time. It was not as if she were truly dark. She could herself remember the glories of her complexion before they paled in the gloomy airs of the Orient. For a moment, however, the birth of artifice dismayed her. She wondered if, in addition to going fair, she would also go magenta like some of the girls who always made up. Again the phantom of age laughed over her shoulder; but the contemplation of futurity was fleeting, and she decided that if she were going fair, the sooner she went the better it would be: if she waited till thirty the world might laugh with reason. She would chance it. Jenny appropriated a bottle of the Management's peroxide that very night, and, excited by the prospect of entertainment, came home immediately after the performance, alarming Mrs. Raeburn so much by her arrival that the latter exclaimed:

'You *are* early. Is anything the matter?'

'Anything the matter? Whatever should be the matter?'

'Well, it's only a quarter to twelve.'

'Who cares?'

'Don't say that to me.'

'I shall say *what* I like, and I'm going to bed.'

May, however, was wide awake when Jenny reached their room; so the deed had to be postponed. May, elated by her sister's unaccustomed earliness, chattered profusely, and it was two o'clock in the morning before she fell asleep. Then Jenny crept out of bed and by the faint glimmer of gaslight achieved the transformation.

She woke up in the morning to May's cries of disgust.

'Oh, you sight! Whatever have you done?'

'*Don't* make such a shocking noise. I've gone fair.'

'Gone fair!' exclaimed her sister. 'Gone white, you mean. Get up and look at yourself. You look terrible.'

'What do you mean?' asked Jenny. 'Here, give me hold of the hand-glass.'

Her reflection upset her. She must have put on too much in the uncertain light.

'It's like milk,' cried May.

'Don't annoy me.'

'Oh, Jenny, it's awful. It's like that canary of Alfie's who died so sudden. It's shocking. What *will* all my friends say?'

'Who cares about your friends? *They're* nobody. Besides, it'll be quite all right soon. It's bound to sink in.'

'What will Alfie say?'

'Oh, damn Alfie.'

'There's a lady. Now swear.'

'Well, you annoy me. It's my own hair, isn't it?'

'Oh, it's your own hair right enough. Nobody else wouldn't own it.'

'I don't think I'll come down to breakfast this morning. Say I've got a most shocking headache, and fetch me up a cup of tea, there's a little love.'

'Mother'll only come up and see what's the matter, so *don't* be silly. You've got to go downstairs some time.'

'Oo-er, May, I wish I hadn't done it now. It's going whiter all the time. Look at it. Oh, what unnatural stuff. It can't go lighter than white, can it?'

Mrs. Raeburn, in the act of pouring out tea, held the pot suspended and, shaking with laughter, looked at her daughter. Charlie, too, happened to be at home.

'Good gracious alive!' cried the mother.

'I thought I'd see how it looked,' Jenny explained, with apologetic notes in her voice.

'You'll think your head right off next time,' said Charlie profoundly.

Jenny was seized with an idea.

'I had to do it for the theatre. At least, I thought – oh, well – *don't* all stare as if you'd never seen a girl with fair hair. You'll get used to it.'

'I shan't,' said Charlie hopelessly. 'I shouldn't never get used to that not if I lived till I was a hundred. Not if I never died at all.'

'Depend upon it,' said Mrs. Raeburn, 'her aunt Mabel will come and see us this very day and ask what I've been doing.'

'What about it?' said Jenny defiantly. 'Who's she? Surely I can do what I like with my own hair without asking *her*.'

'Now, what'ud you say if I went and dyed my hair?' asked Charlie. 'And come down with it the colour of an acid drop? That's what I'd like to know.'

A silence of pent-up laughter held the breakfast party while, under the mirthful glances of her mother and sister, Jenny began to regret the change. At last she volunteered:

'Oh, well, it's done now.'

'Done in, I should say,' corrected Charlie.

It was a gusty morning of clouds in early June, and the Hagworth Street kitchen was dark. The sun, however, streamed in for a moment in the wake of Charlie's correction, and Jenny's new hair was lighted up.

'Why, it's worse than I thought,' said Mrs. Raeburn. 'You look like a funny turn.'

'It looks like that ginger-beer we had on Whit-Monday,' said her father.

'Oh, who cares?' cried Jenny, flouncing upstairs out of the room. When she came down again, she was dressed to go out.

'You're never going out in broad daylight?' asked May.

'Let her go,' said Mrs. Raeburn. 'Her hat covers it up a *bit*. I only hope if we have company, she'll have the goodness to keep her hat on all the time.'

'Oh, yes, that would be a game of mine. I don't think,' protested Jenny.

The latter's belief in herself was restored by the attitude of the dressing-room. The girls all vowed the change improved her. There was an epidemic of peroxide, and Irene actually tarnished her own rich copper with the dye, so that for a while her hair seemed streaked with verdigris. Moreover, the unnatural fairness wore off as the weeks went by, and at last even the family was compelled to admit that she had not made a mistake. Only Alfie remained unconvinced, declaring she deserved a hiding for messing herself about. As for the suitors, they ran faster than before, but never swiftly enough to catch Jenny.

'I'm bound to get off with a nice young chap now,' she told the girls. 'I wish I could fall in love.'

'How would you like my Artie?' asked Elsie Crauford proudly.

'Your Artie? I don't think he's anything to tear oil-cloth over.'

'Didn't you think he looked nice in his evening dress?'

'Your Artie's never bought himself an evening dress? *What!* Girls, listen. The Great Millionaire's bought himself an evening dress.'

'You are rude, Jenny Pearl.'

'Well, I call it silly. Swanking round in evening dress with a bent halfpenny and his latchkey. And you needn't give me those perishing looks, young Elsie.'

'You are a hateful thing.'

'Your *Artie* in evening dress. Oh, no, it can't be done.'

'Shut up, Jenny Pearl,' cried Elsie, stamping her foot.

'Now get in a paddy. I suppose it was you edged him on to go without his dinner for a week to buy it.'

'I hope you'll fall in love, and I hope he'll spring it on you and go away to New Zealand the same as Nelly Marlowe's Jack did.'

'Oh! there's an unnatural girl! *Don't* you worry yourself. Not this little girl. Not Jenny Pearl. I wouldn't let any *man* make a fool of me.'

That night a thunderstorm ruined Jenny's hat.

Next day she bought another, pale green with rosy cherries bobbing at each side. 'I think this hat's going to bring me luck,' she announced.

'The cherries is all right, but green isn't lucky,' said Irene.

'Oh, well,' said Jenny, 'I'll chance it, any old way.'

XIII

The Ballet of Cupid

The thunderstorm which ruined Jenny's hat destroyed summer. Blowy August twilights began to harass the leaves: darkness came earlier, and people, going home, hurried through the streets where lately they had lingered. Jenny's new green hat with bobbing cherries seemed to have strayed from the heart of a fresher season, and passers-by often turned to regard her as she strolled down Coventry Street towards the Orient. September brought louder winds and skies swollen with rain; but Jenny, rehearsing hard for a new ballet on the verge of production, had no leisure to grumble at chilly dusks and moonless journeys home to Hagworth Street.

The Orient was in a condition of excitement, for the new ballet, like a hundred before it, was expected to eclipse entirely the reputation of its predecessors. Two Ballerinas had arrived from Rome, winter migrants who in their lightness and warmth would bring to London a thought of Italy. A Premier Danseur, more agile than a Picador, had travelled over from Madrid, and a fiery Maître de Ballet had been persuaded to forsake Milan. Yet the first night of Cupid was hard upon the heels of a theatre apparently utterly unprepared for any such date. The master carpenter was wrangling with the electrician. The electrician was insulting the wardrobe-mistress. The wig-maker was talking very rapidly in French to the costumier's draughtsman, who was replying in equally rapid Italian. From time to time the managing director shouted from the back of the promenade to know the reason for some delay. The new Maître de Ballet, having reduced most of the girls to hysteria by his alarming rages, abused his interpreter for misrepresenting his meaning. The Ballerinas from Rome were quarrelling over precedence, and the Spanish Danseur was weeping because the letters of his name were by four inches smaller than those which announced on the play-bills the advent of his feminine rivals. The call-boy was losing his youth. Everybody was talking at once and the musical director was always severely punctual.

When the dress rehearsal lasted eleven hours, everybody connected with the Orient prophesied the doom of Cupid; and yet on the twenty-first of September the ballet was produced with truly conspicuous success. The theme was Love triumphant through the ages, from the saffron veils and hymeneal torches and flickering airs of Psyche's chamber, through Arthur's rose-wreathed court and the mimic passions of Versailles, down to modern London transformed by the boy god to a hanging garden of Babylon.

The third scene was a Fête Champêtre after Watteau at sunset. Parterres of lavender and carnations bloomed at the base of statues that gradually disappeared in shadow as the sunset yielded to crimson lanterns. The scene was a harmony of grey and rose and tarnished silver. Love himself wore a vizard and the dances were very slow and stately. The leisured progress of the scene gave Jenny her first opportunity to scan the audience. She saw a clear-cut face dead white in the blue haze that hung over the stalls. She was conscious of an interest suddenly aroused, of an interest more profound than anything within her experience. For the first time the width of the orchestra seemed no barrier to intercourse. She felt she had only to lean gently forward from her place in the line to touch that unknown personality. She checked the impulse of greeting, but danced the rest of the movement as she had not danced for many months, with a joyful grace. When the tempo di minuetto had quickened to the pas seul of a Ballerina and the stage was still, Jenny stood far down in the corner nearest to the audience. Here, very close to the blaze of the footlights, the auditorium loomed almost impenetrable to eyes on the stage, but the man in the stalls, as if aware that she had lost him, struck a match. She saw his face flickering and, guided by the orange point of a cigar, whispered to Elsie Crauford, who was standing next to her:

'See that fellow in evening dress in the stalls?'

'Which one?'

'The one with the cigar — now — next to the fat man fanning himself. See? I bet you I get off with him to-night.'

'You think everybody's gazing at you,' murmured Elsie.

'No, I don't. But he is.'

'Only because he can see you're making eyes at him.'

'Oh, I'm not.'

'Besides, how do you know? He isn't waving his programme nor nothing.'

'No; but he'll be waiting by the stage door.'

'I thought you didn't care for fellows in evening dress,' said Elsie.

'Well, can't you see any difference between that fellow and your Artie?'

'No, I can't.'

'Fancy,' said Jenny mockingly.

The Ballerina's final pose was being sustained amid loud applause. The ballet-master began to count the steps for the final movement. The stage manager's warning had sounded. The curtain fell and eighty girls hurried helter-skelter to their rooms in order to change for the last scene.

'All down, ladies,' cried the call-boy, and downstairs they all trooped.

The curtain rose on Piccadilly Circus, grey and dripping. Sombre figures danced in a saraband of shadows to a yearning melody of Tschaikovsky. The oboe gave its plaintive summons; like sea-birds calling, the rest of the wood wind took up the appeal until it died away in a solitary flute, which sounded a joyful signal sweet and low. A cymbal crashed: a golden ray of light came slanting on to the stone figure of Cupid, infusing him with life until warm and radiant he sprang from his pedestal to bewitch the sad scene. Roses tumbled from the clouds; lilies sprang up, quivering in the wind of dancing motion. A fountain gushed from the abandoned pedestal: the scene was a furnace of colour. The Ballerinas led the Corps de Ballet in a Bacchic procession round and round the twirling form of Cupid. With noise of bell and cymbal, they ran leaping through an enchanted Piccadilly seen in amber or cornelian. They might have stepped from a canvas of Titian dyed by the sun of a spent Venetian afternoon. Individual members of the audience began to applaud and the isolated hand-claps sounded like castanets, until, as the dance became wilder, cheers floated on to the stage like the noise of waves heard suddenly over the brow of a hill.

Jenny, in a tunic of ivory silk sprayed with tawny roses, her hair bound with a fillet of gold, turned from the intoxication of the dance to search the stalls. Across the arpeggios of the misted violins, his eyes burned a path. Yet, although she knew that he asked for a signal to show her consciousness of him, she could not give one. Had his glances seemed less important, she would have smiled; but since for the first time in her life a man stirred her, bashfulness caught her icily and while her heart flamed her eyes were cold. The curtain fell, rising again at once to let the bouquets fall softly round the silver shoes of the Ballerinas. The odour of stephanotis, mingled with the sharper perfume of carnations, seemed almost visible. The emotion of the audience struck the emotion of the dancers and kindled a triumph. The man in the stalls leaned forward, and the intensity of his gaze was to Jenny as real an offering as a bouquet. The curtain fell for the last time and as it touched the stage, instead of hurrying to her dressing-room, she stood a moment staring at what, for the first time, seemed an agent of deprivation not relief. Suddenly, too, she realized that she was very lightly clothed, and as she walked slowly up the stone stairs to the dressing-room, was not sure whether she were sorry or glad.

In the crowd of chatting girls, Jenny began to call herself a fool, to rail at her weakness and to ascribe the whole experience to the extra Guinness of a first night. Yet all the time she wondered if he would be waiting at the end of the court; there had been no wave of hand or flutter of a programme to confirm the hopes of imagination. Moreover, what was he really like? Outside he would be 'awful,' like the rest of them. Outside he would smirk and betray his sense of ownership. Outside he would destroy the magic that had waked her at last from the dull sleep of ordinary life. She began to hurry feverishly her undressing, and the more she hurried, the more she dreamed. At last, having, as it seemed, exhausted herself with speed, she sat down on the bench and looking round perceived that the other girls were well in front of her. She lost confidence and wished for support in the adventure.

'Coming out to-night?' she asked Irene.

'If you like,' said the latter.

'I thought you'd got off,' said Elsie Crauford.

'Shut up, you.'

'Well, you told me you had.'

'What of it?'

'Just because my Artie's got an evening dress you're bound to swank you've got a young chap in evening dress.'

'Are you going to shut your mouth?' enquired Jenny, glinting. 'Because if you don't, Elsie Crauford, I shall hit you. Oh, yes, you can be very deedy over there in the corner, but if I punch into you there won't be quite so much of you and your evening dresses, you great silly fool.'

Elsie was silent and Jenny went on with her toilet.

'Is that right?' murmured Irene.

'Is what right?'

'About getting off with a fellow in the stalls?'

'You're not nosy, are you? Oh, no, it's only a rumour. But if you want to know, it's nothing to do with you.'

'You are a stuck-up thing. And do hurry up. Why, you haven't even begun to take off your make-up.'

Jenny, although she longed to be out of the theatre, could not be quick that night. As she watched the other girls leave the dressing-room, she asked herself why she had wanted Irene to wait for her. If he were outside, Irene would spoil it all; for, together, they would giggle and he would think what a shocking couple of girls he had fallen in with. She wished now that Irene would become impatient and go; but the latter seemed perfectly willing to dawdle, though by now they were the only two inhabitants of the dressing-room.

'Oh, do move yourself!'

'Oh, I can't, Ireen, so shut your noise. Whoever made these unnatural stays?'

'We shall get locked in,' said Irene.

But Jenny was dressed at last, and together they passed out into the cool September night. He was there. Instinctively Jenny recognized the careless figure in opera hat and full black cloak. She drew back and clutched her friend's wrist, aware of hot blushes that surely must flame visibly in the darkness.

'Who's he?' whispered Irene.

'Who's who?'

'The fellow by himself at the end of the court?'

'How ever on earth should I know? Do you think I'm a walking *Answers*?'

The two girls passed him by. He hesitated; then, as if by an effort, raised his hat.

Irene giggled foolishly.

'How dy'e do, Tootoose?' said Jenny, self-possessed through his embarrassment.

'I liked your dancing,' he said simply.

'Did you? Who ca—?' She stopped. Somehow the formula was inadequate.

'Can't we go and have supper somewhere?' he asked.

'Just as *you* like.'

'Where shall we go?'

'It doesn't matter to me,' said Jenny.

'Gatti's?'

'Um.'

'But do you like Gatti's?' persisted the stranger.

'It's all right.'

'We can all squash into a hansom, can't we?'

'Rather,' said Jenny.

They rattled off to Gatti's and were soon sitting on red velvet, rulers of gaiety.

'What's your name, Claude?' enquired Jenny.

'Raymond,' he said.

'Oo-er! What a soppy name!'

The young man hesitated. He looked for a moment deep into Jenny's eyes: perceived, it may be, her honesty, and said:

'Well, as a matter of fact, my real name is Maurice – Maurice Avery.'

'Oh, and he wasn't going to tell us,' cried Jenny, clapping her hands. 'We shall have to call him Careful Willie.'

'What do you think we are?' demanded Irene, huffed by his cautiousness.

'That's all right. He takes us for a couple of old tares. You, I, Us and Co are properly crushed.'

'No, I say, really, do forgive me for being a silly ass.'

'Now he's being rude to himself.'

Here a fat waiter interposed with a dish, and Avery had time to recover himself. Meanwhile, Jenny regarded him. She liked his fresh complexion and deep blue eyes. She liked better still his weak girlish mouth and white teeth. She liked best of all his manner, which was not too easy, although it carried some of the confidence of popularity.

'Whatever made you come on the first night? I think the ballet's rotten on the first night,' said Jenny.

'I'm awfully glad I did. But as a matter of fact I had to. I'm a critic. I'm going to write a notice of the ballet for the *Point of View*.'

Something in the intonation of this announcement would have warned anybody of the world that Avery's judgment had not long ago been demanded for the first time.

'A reporter?' asked Jenny.

'Well, a sort of reporter.'

'You don't look much like a reporter. I knew a reporter once who was going to photograph me in a bathing-dress for *Fluffy Bits*. But his flat was too high up for this little girl.'

187

Maurice Avery wished that Jenny were alone. He would in that case have attempted to explain the difference between a reporter and a dramatic critic. Under the circumstances, however, he felt that the subject should be dropped and turned politely to Irene.

'You're not talking much.'

'Ah, but I think the more.'

The conversation became difficult, almost as difficult as the macaroni au gratin which the three of them were eating. Maurice wished more than ever that Irene were out of the way. He possessed a great sense of justice which compelled him to be particularly polite to her, although his eyes were all for Jenny. The unsatisfactory meal evaporated in coffee, and presently they stood on the pavement.

'I say, I ought to drive you girls home,' said Maurice. 'But to-night I absolutely must get back and finish this notice in time to catch the three o'clock post. Couldn't we all three meet to-morrow?'

Inwardly he lamented the politeness which led him to include Irene in the suggested reunion.

'All right, Willie Brains,' said Jenny.

'Where?'

'Oh, I don't know. 3.30, outside the Palace. Good night.'

They shook hands discreetly, and though Maurice held Jenny's hand longer than was necessary, he held Irene's hand just as long in case she might have noticed and felt hurt by the greater attention paid to her friend.

Jenny and Irene turned in the direction of the Tube station by Leicester Square.

'He might have stood us a cab home,' complained the latter.

'Why should he?' said Jenny.

Irene looked at her in perplexity.

'You're usually the one to get all you can out of a fellow. And it was your turn to ask to-night.'

'I like Maurice,' Jenny replied. 'And what's more, I think I shall like him again to-morrow.'

The afternoon arrived. Jenny and Irene walking down Shaftesbury Avenue perceived Maurice gazing at the photographs outside the Palace.

'There he is,' cried Jenny.

Avery turned round.

'You *are* punctual,' he exclaimed.

Tea, at whatever tea-shop they drank it, was dull. The acquaintance did not seem to advance. They talked about such very dull subjects all the time that Jenny began to wonder if, after all, he were soppy.

When it was time for the girls to go into the theatre, Maurice said desperately:

'Could I drive you – both home to-night?'

At the last moment he was afraid to exclude Irene. 'I'll wait outside,' he went on, 'till you come out.'

Rain fell that night, and Maurice was glad when, along the court, he could see them strolling towards him.

'A hansom, eh?' he said. 'Or let's have a drink first.'

In the Monico, they sat round a table and nothing mattered to Maurice and Jenny, except eyes. The room seemed full of eyes, not the eyes of its chattering population, but their own. Never before had a London night seemed so gay. Never before had crème de menthe been dyed so richly green. They began to discuss love and jealousy. As Romeo hesitated before he joined the fatal masquerade, Maurice was seized with an impulse to make himself as poor a thing as possible.

'I couldn't be jealous,' he vowed. 'I think everybody can be in love with two or three people at once.'

'I don't,' said Jenny.

'Oh, yes, it's absurd to be jealous. Quite absurd. Different people suit different moods. The only trouble is when they meet.'

He had caught hold of Jenny's hand while they were speaking, and now she drew it away.

'I think I know what he means,' said Irene.

'You think so,' scoffed Jenny. 'You! You're potty, then.'

Maurice felt sorry for Irene and weakly took her hand. She let it recline in his, listless. It was cold and damp after Jenny's vitality.

'If I loved a man,' said Jenny, 'I should be most shocking jealous.'

'What would you do if you met him with another girl?' asked Maurice.

'I should never speak to him again.'

'Wouldn't that be rather foolish?'

'Foolish or not, that's what I should do.'

'Well, I'm not jealous,' vowed Maurice. 'I never have been.'

'Then you're silly,' asserted Jenny. 'Jealous? I'm terribly jealous.'

'It's a mistake,' said Maurice. 'It spoils everything and turns a pleasure into a nuisance.'

'I don't think I'm jealous of you know who,' put in Irene.

'Oh, him and you, you're both mad!' exclaimed Jenny. 'But if ever I love a man—'

'Yes,' said Maurice eagerly.

Two Frenchmen at the next table were shuffling the dominoes. For Maurice the noise had a strange significance, while he waited for the apodosis.

Jenny stared away up to the chandeliers.

'Well?' he said. Somebody knocked over a glass. Jenny shivered.

'It's getting late,' she said.

'What about driving home?' asked Maurice.

Outside it was pouring. They squeezed into a hansom cab. Again his politeness seemed bound to mar the evening.

'Let's see. Irene lives at Camden Town. We'd better drive to Islington first and leave Jenny, eh?'

Then Jenny said quite unaccountably to herself and Irene:

'No, thanks. We'll drive Ireen home first.'

Maurice looked at her quickly, but she gave no sign of any plan, nor did she betray a hint of the emotion he would have been glad to see.

With the glass let down against the rain, they were forced very near to one another as the horse trotted along Tottenham Court Road shining with puddles in the lamplight.

'This is jolly,' said Maurice, bravely putting an arm round each waist and holding Irene a little closer for fear she should feel that she was the undesired third person.

Having done this, he felt entitled to kiss Jenny first and turned towards her lips. She drew back whispering:

'Ah, so near and yet so far.'

Then, since he had offered to kiss Jenny, he felt bound to kiss Irene. The latter allowed the compliment as she would have let him pick up a handkerchief. Arrangements were made to meet again on the morrow at the same place, and at last the cab was pulled up some two hundred yards from Irene's house. Maurice jumped out and shook hands very politely and waved to her as she ran up a side-street. Then he sat back beside Jenny in the cab. The driver turned his horse and for a minute or two they travelled silently through the rain and lamplight.

'Jenny,' he whispered. 'Jenny, won't you kiss me now?'

She yielded herself to his arms, and while the wind rattled the glass shield, while the raindrops danced in the road before them, while lights faltered and went out in passing window-panes, Jenny nestled closer, ardent and soft and passionate.

'Are you glad we're alone?' he whispered.

'Rather.'

'I suppose you knew I've been burning all the time to sit with you like this?'

'No.'

'Oh, I have, Jenny. Jenny, I saw you when you first came on the stage, and afterwards I never saw anyone else. I wish you lived a thousand miles away.'

'Why?'

'Because then we should travel together for a thousand hours.'

'You date!'

'You're so delightful.'

'Am I?'

'I wish Irene weren't coming to-morrow. We shall have such a lot to talk about,' he vowed.

'Shall we?'

'What on earth made you ask her?'

'It's done now.'

Maurice sighed. Then he caught her close again and breathless they sat till Jenny suddenly cried:

'Gee! Here's Hagworth Street. Good night!'

At the end of the road, under the tall plane tree where once Jenny had danced, they sat in the old hansom cab, while the steam rose in clouds from the horse and the puddles sang with rain and the driver smoked meditatively. The world was fading away in sounds of traffic very remote. The wetness of the night severed them from humanity. They needed no blue Pacific haven to enrich their love. They perceived no omen in the desolation of the London night.

'What times we shall have together,' said Maurice.

'Shall we?' the girl replied.

'It's all happened so exactly right.'

'It does sometimes,' said Jenny.

The horse pawed the road impatient of the loitering. The driver knocked out the ashes of his pipe on the roof.

'I *must* go now,' she said.

'Must you?'

'Yes.'

'One more kiss.'

To Maurice each kiss of Jenny's seemed a first kiss.

'Isn't it glorious?' he exclaimed.

'What?'

'Oh, everything – life and London and you and I.'

He stood in the road and lifted her on to the pavement.

'Good night, my Jenny.'

'Good night.'

'To-morrow?'

'Rather.'

'Good night. Bless you.'

'Bless *you*,' she murmured. Then, surprised by herself, she ran through the rain as swift as the shadow of a cloud, while the horse trotted southward with a dreaming passenger.

XIV

Rain on the Roof

Upstairs in the room she shared with May Jenny sat before the glass combing her hair, while outside the rain poured down with volume increasing every moment. The wash of water through the black, soundless night lent the little room with its winking candle a comfortable security. The gentle breathing of May and the swish of the hairbrush joined the stream of rain without in a monotone of whisperings that sighed endlessly round Jenny's vivid thoughts. Suddenly she sprang from her reverie and, pulling up the blind with a rattle, flung open the window to dip her hands into the wet darkness. May sat up wild-eyed from sleep. The candle gasped and fluttered.

'Whatever is it?' cried May.

'Oh, Maisie, Maisie,' said her sister; 'it's raining real kisses to-night. It is, really.'

'Have you gone mad?'

'Oh, let me get into bed quick and dream. Oh, May, I'd go mad to dream to-night.'

And soon the rain washed down unheard, where Jenny, dreaming elusive ardours, ghostly ecstasies, lay still as coral.

XV

Cras Amet

The next morning sunlight shone in upon Jenny's rose-dyed awakening. Flushed with dreams she blinked, murmuring in sleepy surprise:

'Oo-er! if it isn't a fine day.'

'It's glorious,' corroborated May emphatically.

'Oh, it's lovely; let's all wave flags.'

'You were a mad thing last night,' said May.

'Don't take any notice, dee-ar. I was feeling funnified.'

'Opening the window like that and shouting out in your sleep and cuddling me all night long.'

'Did I?' enquired Jenny curiously.

'Did you? I should think you did. Not half.'

'Well, if you're a little love and make me a cup of tea, I'll tell you all about it.'

'About what?'

'About him. Oh, May, he's lovely. Oh, he's It.'

'Who is?'

'A fellow I met this week.'

'What, another?'

'Ah, but this one's the One and Only.'

'Go on, you soppy thing. I know your One and Onlies.'

196

'Oh, but May, he's a young dream, is My Friend the Prince. I'm going to meet him this afternoon with young Ireen.'

'And have a proper game with him, I suppose, and do the poor boy in and say goodbye.'

'I hope I shan't never say goodbye to him. Never, I do.'

'You have got it bad.'

'I know. Listen, May. He's rather tall and he's got a nice complexion, only his mother says he's rather pale, and he's got very white teeth and a mouth that's always moving, and simply glorious eyes.'

'What colour?'

'Blue. And he talks very nice and his name's Maurice. But whatever you do, don't say nothing to mother about it.'

'As if I should.'

Mrs. Raeburn came into the room at that moment.

'Are you lazy girls going to get up?'

'Oh, ma, *don't* be silly. Get up? Oh, what a liberty!'

'Lying in bed on this lovely morning,' protested Mrs. Raeburn.

'That's it. Now you carry on about the lovely morning. Young May's already woke me up once to look at the sun. All I know is it makes the room look most shocking dusty.'

The day deepened from a morning of pale gold to an amber afternoon, whose melting splendour suffused with a glittering haze the thin blue autumn air. Jenny stood pensive awhile upon the doorstep.

'Hark, what a noise the birds are all making. Whatever's the matter?'

'They're pleased it's fine,' said May.

'Oh, they're pleased too, are they?' Jenny exclaimed, as, with a long shadow leading her slim form, she went through a world of russet leaves and cheeping sparrows to meet her lover.

At the club there was a message from Irene to say she was ill and unable to keep the appointment.

'That's funny,' Jenny thought. 'Seems as if it's bound to be.'

Through Leicester Square she went with eyes that twisted a hundred necks in retrospect. Down Charing Cross Road she hurried, past the old men peering into the windows of bookshops, past the Delicatessen shops full of gold and silver paper, past a tall, gloomy church haunted by beggars, hurrying faster and faster until she swung into the sunlight of Shaftesbury Avenue. There was Maurice studying very earnestly the photographs outside the Palace Theatre.

'Here I am, Claude,' she laughed over his shoulder.

'Oh, I am glad you've come,' he said.

'Ireen couldn't come. She's ill. Shame, isn't it?'

'Really?' said Maurice, trying to seem concerned. 'Let's go and have tea.'

'Oh, you unnatural man. Aren't you sorry she's ill?'

'I can't be sorry you're alone. Where shall we have tea?'

'Where *you* like.'

'I know a funny little shop off Soho Square where there aren't many people.'

'Don't you like people, then?'

'Not always.'

Soho Square held the heart of autumn that afternoon.

London had surrendered this quiet corner to pastoral meditation. Here, among the noise of many sparrows and sibilance of dead leaves on the unfrequented pavement, one realized in the perishable hour's flight the immortality of experience.

'More birds,' said Jenny.

'Don't they make a row and don't the leaves look ripping in this light?'

'There's another one getting excited over the day.'

'Well, it is superb,' said Maurice. 'Only I wish there weren't such a smell of pickles. I say, would you mind going on ahead and then turning back and meeting me?'

'Oo-er, whatever for?'

'I want to see how jolly you'd look coming round the corner under the trees.'

'You are funny.'

'I suppose you think I'm absurd. But really, you know, you do look like a Dresden shepherdess with your heart-shaped face and slanting eyes.'

'Thanks for those few nuts.'

'No, really, do go on, won't you?'

'I certainly shan't. People would think we was mad.'

'What do people matter?'

'Hark at him. Now he's crushed the world.'

'One has to be fanciful on such an afternoon.'

'You're right.'

'I suppose I couldn't kiss you here?'

'Oh, of course. Wouldn't you like to sit down on the kerb and put your arm round my waist?'

'As a matter of fact, I should.'

'Well, I shouldn't. See? Where's this unnatural tea-shop?'

'Just here.'

'It looks like the Exhibition.'

It was a dim coffee-shop hung with rugs and gongs. The smoke of many cigarettes and joss-sticks had steeped the gloom with Arabian airs.

'It is in a way a caravanserai,' said Maurice.

'A what?' said Jenny.

'A caravanserai – a Turkish pub, if you like it better.'

'You and I *are* seeing life to-day.'

'I like my coffee freshly ground,' Maurice explained.

'Well, I like tea.'

'The tea's very good here. It's China.'

'But I think China tea's terrible. More like burnt water than tea.'

'I'm afraid you don't appreciate the East,' he said.

'No, I don't if it means China tea.'

'I wish I could take you away with me to Japan. We'd sit under a magnolia and you should have a kiss for every petal that fell.'

'That sounds rather nice.'

'You know you yourself are a bit Japanesy.'

'Don't say that. I hate to be told that.'

'It's the slant in your eyes.'

'I don't like my eyes,' said Jenny emphatically.

'I do.'

'One pleased, any old way.'

'I love your eyes,' said Maurice earnestly. 'But I made a mistake when I said you were Japanese. You're Slav – Russian, you know.'

'I must be a procession of all nations according to you.'

'But you are frightfully subtle.'

'Anything else? You're sure I'm not a bighead?'

'A what?' said Maurice.

'A pantomime bighead?'

Maurice laughed.

'Men always talk about my eyes,' Jenny went on. 'They often call me the girl with the saucy eyes, or the squinny eyes, *which* I don't like. And yet, for all my strange appearance, if I want a man to be struck on me, he always is.'

'Did you want me to be struck on you?'

'I suppose I must have.'

'Is that why you made us see Irene home first – so that you could be alone with me?'

'I suppose so. Any more questions? You're worse than my sister, and she'd ask the tail off a cat.'

'Hum!'

'Cheer up, Puzzled Willy.'

'Have you ever – er – well, insisted on having the person you wanted before?'

'No, I've not. Not like that. I can't make myself out sometimes. I don't understand myself. I do a thing all of a sudden and the next minute I couldn't tell anybody why I done it.'

'I might have thought you were running after me,' said Maurice.

'Who cares? If you did, it wouldn't matter to me. If I wanted you to make a fool of yourself, you'd make a fool of yourself.'

'But supposing I made a fool of you?' asked Maurice, slightly nettled.

'I don't think you could.'

'But I might. After all, I may be as attractive to women as you are to men. Perhaps we've both met our match. I admit you fascinate me. From the first moment I saw you, I wanted you. I told you that. And you?'

'I wanted you,' said Jenny simply.

'It is love at first sight. And yet, you know, I had an instinct to make you not like me.'

'You couldn't.'

'Couldn't I?' said Maurice, breathless. The heavy air of the coffee-shop vibrated with unheard passionate melodies.

'No,' said Jenny, gazing full at the young lover opposite, while Eros shook his torch, and the gay deep eyes, catching the warm light, shone as they had never shone for any man before. 'But why did you try to make me not like you?'

'I felt afraid,' said Maurice. 'I'm not very old, but I've made two girls unhappy and I had a presentiment that you would be the revenge for them.'

'I've made boys unhappy. Soppy boys,' said Jenny. 'And I thought you were sent to pay me out.'

'But I shall always love you,' said Maurice, putting his hand across the little table and clasping her fingers close.

'So shall I you.'

'We're lucky, aren't we?'

'Rather.'

'I feel sorry for people who aren't in love with you.'

'You date.'

'But don't let's talk here any more. Let's go back to my rooms,' he suggested.

'I've got to be in the theatre by half-past seven.'

'I know, but we've plenty of time. It's only just half-past five.'

'Where do you live?'

'Westminster. Looking over the river. I've got a largish studio. Quite a jolly room, I share the floor below with a friend.'

'What's he like?'

'Castleton? Funny chap. I don't expect you'd care for him much. Women don't usually. But don't let's talk about Castleton. Let's talk about Jenny and Maurice.'

Outside the fumes of the coffee-shop were blown away by soft autumnal breezes.

'We'll dash it in a taxi. Look, there's a salmon-coloured one. What luck! We must have that. They're rather rare. Taxi! Taxi!'

The driver of the favoured hue pulled up beside the pavement.

'Four-twenty-two Grosvenor Road, Westminster.'

'I wonder,' said Maurice, glancing round at Jenny and taking her slim gloved hand in his. 'I wonder whether taxis will ever be as romantic as hansoms. They aren't yet somehow. All the same, there's a tremendous thrill in tearing through this glorious September weather. Oh, London,' he shouted, bouncing in excitement up and down on the springy cushions, 'London, you're wonderful.'

Jenny shook his hand as a nurse reproves a child.

'Keep still,' she commanded. 'The man'll think you're potty.'

'But I am potty. You're potty. The world's potty, and

we're in love. My sweet and lovely Jenny, I'm in love with you.'

'There was a young lady called Jenny,
Whose eyes, some men said, were quite squinny.'

'Oh, Maurice, you *are* awful,' she protested.
But, Apollo urging him, Maurice would finish:

'When they said: "You're our fate,"
She replied, "It's too late."
So they went away sad and grew skinny.'

'Lunatic!' she said. 'And don't talk about getting thin.
Look at me. Nothing but skin and grief.'
'Nonsense,' said Maurice, and went on rhyming:

'There was a young lady said: "What!
My figure is going to pot."'

'And then two more lines that will have to be filled in like your figure, and then:

'They all of them said: "No it's not." '

'Well, you're not much more than a rasher of wind yourself,' commented Jenny.
'Ha! ha!' shouted Maurice. 'That's good. Hullo, here's Trafalgar Square. Aren't we going a pace down Whitehall? Jenny, there aren't any words for what I feel.'

He hugged her close.

'Oh, mind!' she protested, withdrawing from the embrace. 'People can see us.'

'My dear, they don't matter. They don't matter a damn. Not one of them matters the tiniest dash.'

Nor did they indeed to lovers in the warm apricot of a fine September sunset. What to them were dusty clerks with green shining elbows, and Government officials and policemen, and old women with baskets of tawny chrysanthemums? Fairies only were fit to be their companions. The taxi hummed on over the road shadowed by the stilted Gothic of the Houses of Parliament, hummed out of the shadow and into Grosvenor Road, where the sun was splashing the river with pools of coppery light. The stream was losing its burnished ripples and a grey mist was veiling the fire-crowned chimneys of Nine Elms when the taxi drew up by 422, Grosvenor Road.

'Right to the very top,' called Maurice. 'I do hope you don't mind.'

As he spoke he caught her round the waist and gathered her to his side to climb the stairs.

'It's an old house. I've got an attic for my studio. Castleton's out. An old woman buried somewhere near the centre of the earth cooks for me. When you see her, you'll think she's arrived via Etna. Jenny, I'm frightfully excited at showing you my studio.'

At last they reached the topmost landing, which was lit by a skylight opaque with spiders' webs and dust. The landing itself was full of rubbish, old clothes and tattered volumes and, as if Maurice sought to emulate Phaethon, a bicycle.

'Not in these!' said Jenny. 'You *don't* carry that up and down all these stairs every day?'

'Never,' said Maurice gaily. 'Not once since I carried it up for the first time a year ago.'

'You silly old thing.'

'I am. I am. But isn't it splendid to be able to be silly?'

He opened the door of the studio and Jenny walked into what seemed an astonishingly large room. There were windows at either end and a long skylight overhead. The ceiling was raftered and on the transverse beams were heaped all sorts of things that young men bring to London but never use, such as cricket-bats and tennis-racquets and skates.

The windows on one side looked out over the river, over barges going up on the full flood, and chimneys flying streamers of pearl-grey smoke. The windows on the other side opened on to a sea of roofs that rolled away down to a low line of purple cloud above whose bronzed and jagged edge the Byzantine tower of Westminster Cathedral stood in silhouette against a sky of primrose very lucent and serene.

There was a wide fire-place with a scarred rug before it and on either side a deal seat with high straight back. There were divans put up by Castleton along the white-washed walls, and shelves of tumbled books. Here and there were broken statues and isolated lead-bound panes of coloured glass, with an easel and a model's throne and the trunk of a lay figure. There was a large table littered with papers and tins of pineapple and a broken bag of oranges richly hued in the sunset. The floor was covered with matting, over which were scattered Persian rugs whose arabesques of mauve and puce were merged in a depth of warm colour by the fleeting daylight. On the walls were autotypes of Mona Lisa and Botticelli's Venus, of the Prince of Orange and little Don Baltazar on his great horse. There was also an alleged Rubens, the purchase of Maurice's first year at Oxford, from the responsibility of whose possessions he had never recovered. There were drawings on the wall itself of arms and legs and breasts and necks, and a row of casts in plaster of Paris. Here and there on shelves were blue ginger-jars, Burmese masks and rolls of Florentine end-papers. There was a grandfather-clock, lacquered and silent, which leaned slightly forward to ponder its appearance in a Venetian mirror whose frame was blown in a design of pink and blue roses and shepherds. The window-curtains were chintz in a pattern of faded crimson birds and brown vine-leaves stained with mildew. In one corner was a pile of brocaded green satin that was intended to cover the undulating horsehair sofa before the fire.

Maurice's room was a new experience to Jenny.

'What a shocking untidy place!' she exclaimed. 'What! It's like Madge Wilson's mother's second-hand shop in the New Kent Road. You don't *live* here?'

'Yes, I do,' said Maurice.

'Sleep here?'

'No; I sleep underneath. I've a bedroom with Castleton.'

'Untidy, like this is?'

'No, rather tidy. Bath-tub, Sandow Exerciser, and

photographs of my sisters by Ellis and Walery. Quite English and respectable.'

Jenny went on:

'Doesn't all this mess ever get on your nerves? Don't you ever go mad to clear it up?'

'You shall be mistress here and clear up when you like.'

'All right, Artist Bill. I suppose you are an artist?'

'I don't know what I am. I'd like best to be a sculptor. You must sit for me.'

'The only artist I ever sat for I took off my belt to in the finish.'

'Why?'

'He annoyed me. Go on. What else are you?'

'I'd like to be a musician.'

'You've got a jolly fine piano, any old way,' said Jenny, sitting down to a Bechstein grand to pick out some of Miss Victoria Monk's songs with the right hand while she held a cigarette in the left.

'Then I write a bit,' said Maurice. 'Criticisms, you know. I told you I wrote a notice of your ballet. I'm twenty-four and I shall come into a certain amount of money, and my people live in a large house in Surrey and oh, I – well – I'm a dilettante. Now you know my history.'

'Whatever on earth's a dilly— you do use the most unnatural words. I shall call you Dictionary Dick.'

'Look here, let's chuck explanations,' said Maurice. 'I simply must kiss you. Let's go and look out at the river.'

He pulled her towards the window and flung it wide open. Together they leaned out, smoking. The sparrows were silent now. They could hear the splash and gurgle

208

of the water against the piers, and the wind shaking the plane trees bare along the Embankment. They watched the lamplighter go past on his twinkling pilgrimage. They listened to the thunder of London streets a long way off. Their cigarettes were finished. Together they dropped to extinction in a shower of orange sparks below.

Maurice drew Jenny back into the darkening room.

'Look! The windows are like big sapphires,' he said, and caught her to his arms. They stood enraptured in the dusk and shadows of the old house. Round them Attic shapes glimmered: the gods of Greece regarded them: Aphrodite laughed.

'Don't all these statues frighten you?' said Jenny.

'No, they're too beautiful.'

'Oh!' screamed Jenny. 'Oh! She moved. She moved.'

'Don't be foolish, child. You're excited.'

'I must go to the theatre. It's late. I do feel silly.'

'I'll drive you down.'

'But I'll come again,' she said. 'Only next time we'll light the gas when it gets dark. I hate these statues. They're like skelingtons.'

'I'm going to make a statue of you. May I? Dancing?'

'If you like.'

'I adore you.'

'So do I you,' said Jenny.

'Not so much as I do.'

'Just as much, Mr. Knowall,' she said, shaking her head. They kissed once more.

'Jenny, Jenny!' It was almost a poignant cry. 'Jenny, I

wish this moment were a thousand years. But never mind, we shall always be lovers.'

'I hope we shall.'

'Why only hope? We shall. We must.'

'You never know,' she whispered. 'Men are funny; you never know.'

'Don't you trust me?'

'I trust nobody. Yes, I do. I trust you.'

'My darling, darling!'

Then downstairs they went, closer locked on every step, close together with hearts beating, the world before them and the stars winking overhead.

XVI

Love's Halcyon

The next fortnight passed quickly enough in the rapture
of daily meetings and kisses still fresh and surprising as
those first primroses of spring which few can keep from
plucking. There was nobody to interrupt the intimacy; for
Irene remained ill, and the rest of the world was as yet
unconscious of the affair. Nevertheless, with all these
opportunities for a complete understanding, the relation
of Maurice and Jenny to one another was still essentially
undefined. Their manner of life in that first fortnight of
mutual adoration had the exquisite and ephemeral beauty
of a daylong flower. It possessed the elusive joy that
mayflies have in dancing for a few sunny days above a glittering stream. It had the character of a pleasant dream,
where thought is instantly translated into action. It was
the opening of a poem by Herrick or Horace before the
prescience of transitoriness has marred the exultation
with melancholy.

Everything favoured a halcyon love. October had
come in windless and golden. Such universal serenity was
bound to preserve for lovers the illusion of permanence
that exists so poignantly in fine autumn weather, when

the leaves, falling one by one at rare intervals, scarcely express the year's decay. The sly hours stole onward in furtive disguises. Milk-white dawns evaporated in skies of thinnest azure and noons of beaten gold, while in pearl-grey dusks each day met its night delicately. For Maurice and Jenny even the night conjured no wintry thoughts, and when the moon came up round and tawny, floating unsubstantial above the black house-tops, an aged moon lacquered with rust, full of calamities, these lovers were not dismayed; although they were not influenced to quick and fervid enterprises.

No doubt, if they had wandered, treading violets under foot, beneath the silver moons of Spring, there would have been a more rapid encounter of emotions. But the tranquillity of nature affected Maurice particularly. He was like a man who, having endured the grief of long separation, meets his love in joyful security. It was as if with a sigh he folded her to his arms, conscious only of acquiring her presence. He had from the fret of London gained the quiet of high green cliffs and was no longer ambitious of anything save meditation on the beauty spread before his eyes. He had bought the much-desired book, and now was idly turning its leaves, safe in the triumph of possession.

Jenny, too, after her long experience of casual attraction, was glad to surrender herself to the luxury of absent effort; but in her case the feverishness of a child, who dreads any discussion that may rob the perfect hour of a single honeyed moment, made her fling white arms around his neck and hold him for her own against invisible thieves.

There exists in the heart of a London dawn a few minutes when the street lamps have just been extinguished, but before the sun has risen, when the city cannot fail to be beautiful even in its meanest aspects. At such an hour the Bayswater Road has the mystery of a dew-steeped glade; the Strand wears the frail hues of a sea-shell; Regent Street is crystalline. Even Piccadilly Circus stands on the very summit of the world, wind-washed and noble.

To Maurice and Jenny London was always a city seen at dawn, so many dull streets had been enchanted by their meetings, so many corners had been invested with the delight of the loved one's new appearance. But, though they were still imparadised, a certain wistfulness in looks and handclasps showed that they both instinctively felt they would never again tread the pavement so lightly, never again make time a lyric, life a measure.

On the afternoon before Jenny's birthday, she and Maurice had gone to Hampstead, there to discuss the details of a wonderful party that was to celebrate in the studio the lucky occasion. They had wandered arm in arm through the green alleys and orderly byways of the mellow suburb, dreaming away all senses of time and space. It was the culmination of St. Luke's little Summer, and nowhere had the glories been more richly displayed. Robins sang in Well Walk, and Michaelmas daisies splashed every garden with constellations of vivid mauve. After tea they walked up Heath Street and on a wooden seat stayed to watch the sunset. Below them the Heath rolled away in grassland to houses whose smoke was heavy on the dull crimson of a stormy dusk. The sun sank with an absence of effect which chilled them both. Night, with a cold wind that heralded rain, came hard on the heels of twilight. The mist rose thickly from the lower parts of the Heath, and the night's jewellery was blurred.

Maurice spoke suddenly as if to a signal.

'Jenny, we seem to have spent a very long time together now in finding out nothing.'

'What *do* you mean?' she asked.

'I mean – we've been together a frightful lot, but I don't know anything about you and you don't know anything about me.'

'I know you're a darling.'

'Yes, I know that, but—'

'What?' she broke in, 'well, if you don't properly go out with yourself.'

'No, I mean – bother about me being a darling – what I mean is – what are we going to do?'

'What do you want us to do?'

'You don't help me out,' he complained. 'Look here, are you really in love with me?'

'Of course I am,' she said softly.

'Yes, but really, violently, madly in love to the exclusion of everything else in the world?'

'Kiss me,' said Jenny, answering him from her heart.

'Kissing's too easy,' said Maurice. 'Kissing proves nothing. You've probably kissed dozens of men.'

'Well, why not?'

'Why not; good heavens, if I give up my whole being to you, do you mean to say you're not going to think anything of kissing dozens of men?'

'Don't be silly. To begin with, they did all the kissing.'

'That makes no difference.'

'I think it makes all the difference.'

'I don't,' he maintained.

'I do.'

'Look here, don't let's quarrel,' he said.

'I'm not quarrelling. You began.'

'All right. I know I did. Only do think things out.'

'What's the matter with your brain to-night?' Jenny asked.

'Why?'

'You've taken a sudden craze for thinking.'

'Oh, do be serious,' he said petulantly. 'Here are we. We meet. We fall in love at once. We roam about London in a sort of mist of love and we haven't settled anything.'

'Why can't we go on roaming about, as you call it?'

'We can – up to a point. Only—' he hesitated.

'Only what?'

'Look here. Are you sure I'm the right person, not a possible, but the person you've dreamed of, thought of?'

'I'm sure you're a darling.'

Jenny had no use for subtleties, no anxiety to establish the derivation of an affection which existed as a simple fact. She was not a girl to whose lips endearing epithets came easily. She had many words ready to describe everything except her deepest emotions. In love she became shy of herself. Maurice had a stock of sweet vocatives which she would have been too proud to imitate. 'Darling' said what she wished to say, and it was difficult even to say that.

'Well, do you want anybody else?' he asked.

215

'No.'

'You won't get tired of me in another month?'

'Don't be silly.'

'You said the other day you didn't trust anybody. Do you mean to say seriously that you don't trust me?'

'I suppose I do. You're different.'

'Only suppose?' asked Maurice.

'Well, I do.'

'You're not certain. Great heavens, child, can't you see what a terrible thing that is to say?'

'I don't see that it's so very terrible.'

'But it kills me dead. I feel all the time you think I'm masquerading. I feel like a figure with a mask in a carnival. I meet you in another mask. I say, "Take it off," and you won't. You shrivel up.'

'I don't know who you're getting angry with,' said Jenny. 'I haven't said nothing.'

'Nothing?' cried Maurice. 'It's nothing to tell somebody who adores you – good heavens, it's raining now! Of course, it *would* rain in the middle of grappling with a situation. What a damnable climate this is!'

'I'm glad you're going to quarrel with the weather a bit for a change,' said Jenny. 'I think you're in a very nasty mood.'

'You don't understand me,' said Maurice.

'I don't want to.' She spoke coldly.

'Jenny, I'm sorry I said that. Darling girl, do forgive me.'

The wind had risen to half a gale. Heath Street was full of people hurrying to shelter, and the entrance to the Tube station was crowded.

'Don't be angry with me,' Maurice whispered as the lift stopped. 'I was tired and foolish. Jenny, I'm sorry.'

'If any other man had spoken like you spoke,' said Jenny, 'I'd have got up and gone away and never seen him again, not ever, not however much I might want to, I wouldn't let myself. I couldn't. But now – now it's soppy me, I suppose.'

Further discussion was killed by the noise of the train, and Jenny and Maurice could only sit speechless gazing at a long line of damp people, most of them carrying rain-dabbled bunches of Michaelmas daisies. By the time Piccadilly was reached Maurice was himself again, full of plans for to-morrow's birthday party.

'Seeing those people in the Tube with those bluish flowers, what d'ye call them, made me think of a party I had for my birthday when I lived with an aunt in the country,' said Jenny.

As it was not yet time for her to go into the theatre, they turned aside into the Monico and drank Quinquina Dubonnet while the final arrangements were being made for the party.

'Now who exactly is coming?' asked Maurice.

'Ireen, if she's well enough, and Elsie Crauford, who isn't bad, but who's got to be told off sometimes, and Madge Wilson, who you haven't met, but she's a pretty girl, and Maudie Chapman and perhaps Gladys West. Oh, and can't I bring Lilli Vergoe? She's a bit old – you know – but she's a nice girl and I used to know her when I was little.'

'Right,' said Maurice. 'That makes seven. Then there'll

be me and Castleton and Cunningham and Ronnie Walker and probably one or two odd ones 'll drop in. You'll turn up about four – eh? It's lucky your birthday comes on a Sunday. Must you go now? All right, my sweet. Till to-morrow. By Jove, we'll have a great time, won't we?'

'Rather,' said Jenny.

Then just as she prepared to cross to the other side of Piccadilly, from the island on which they were standing, Maurice called her back.

'Jenny darling, I am forgiven, aren't I?'

'Of course.'

She looked back before she turned the corner into Regent Street and waved to him. He sighed and went off very happy to meet Castleton for dinner.

It was characteristic of Jenny that she issued her invitations very coldly. Most girls grew enthusiastic over such events, but Jenny did not believe in 'showing herself up' by demonstrations of delight.

'Coming to tea with that friend of mine to-morrow?' she asked Madge Wilson.

'Of course I am, duck, I'd love it,' said Madge, a round-faced, fluffy-haired girl, pretty, but always apt to be mistaken for somebody else.

'It's nothing to rave over,' said Jenny. 'It's in a studio something like your mother's shop. But there's a jolly fine piano and I dare say it won't be bad.'

'I shall love it,' said Madge.

'Well, don't wave too many flags.'

To the other girls Jenny offered the entertainment casually like a chocolate-cream.

Then she went to look for Lilli Vergoe in the dressing-room of the second line of girls. Lilli seemed much surprised by the invitation.

'You don't want me,' she said.

'Don't be silly. Why ever not?'

'Look at me.'

'I can't see nothing the matter.'

'I ask you, do I look like a birthday party? Never mind, kiddie, I'll come.'

'Don't make a favour of it, old girl. Only I thought you'd like it.'

'Why don't you ever come up to Cranbourne Street and see me?' asked Lilli.

'You're always miserable. It gets on my nerves.'

'I wish you would come sometimes. You've never been since that day you told me you'd joined the ballet.'

'Well, you was Melancholy Sarah that day, wasn't you, Lilli?'

The call-boy's summons closed the conversation, and Jenny ran off to her own dressing-room for the last touch of powder.

When she came out of the theatre that night, it was blowing a full October gale. There was nobody by the stage door in whom she felt the slightest interest; so without loitering and with pleasant anticipation of to-morrow's fun, she went straight home.

Mrs. Raeburn was sitting by the kitchen fire when Jenny got back.

'You're early,' she said.

'I know. There wasn't anything to stay out for. It's a

terrible night, pelting in rain. Shame after the glorious weather we've been having. It's my birthday to-morrow, too.'

'Good gracious!' exclaimed Mrs. Raeburn. 'And I'd forgotten all about it.'

'You always do,' said Jenny.

'I ought to have remembered this time. It was weather just like we've been having before you were born, and it come on to blow and rain just like this the very night. Twenty years! Tut-tut!'

'I don't feel a day older than fourteen,' asserted Jenny.

'Tell me, do you enjoy being alive?' asked Mrs. Raeburn.

'Oh, what a question, of course I do.'

'You don't ever feel it was a pity you ever come into the world?'

'Of course I don't. Why should I? I think I'm a very lucky girl.'

'You don't ever tell me anything about yourself,' said Mrs. Raeburn. 'So I don't know.'

'There's nothing to tell.'

'I wish you'd get married.'

'Whatever for?'

'Aren't you a bit gay?'

'Oh, I'm a regular old kerbstone fairy if you only knew. Shut up!' Jenny scoffed.

'Just lately haven't you been a bit gay?'

'Gay! Then you put your hand out to feel where you was. Gay! Of course not.'

'I wish you'd settle down,' urged the mother. 'There's a lot of nice young chaps as would be glad to marry you.'

'But I don't want to be married. I shan't ever get married. Ugh! Besides, what's "going on as I am" done? I'm enjoying myself.'

'Too much, I'm afraid,' said her mother.

'I don't want to get married,' Jenny repeated. 'I don't see that you did much good to yourself by getting married. I think you threw yourself away. Everybody must have liked you when you was a girl, and you go and marry Dad. I think you were potty. And yet you want me to do the same. I can't understand people.'

'Why couldn't you have been nicer to that young baker chap?'

'Young baker chap! Yes, then I woke up. Him! Why, he used to hang his shoulders up when he took off his coat. Besides, he's common.'

'You're getting very dainty.'

'Well, look at the men you want me to marry. Why, they're awful – like navvies half of them. Oh, don't carry on, mother. I know what I want.'

'Jenny,' said her mother sharply, 'you haven't done anything wrong, have you?'

'Of course not.'

'Don't do anything wrong, there's a good girl. I was very upset about Edie, but nothing to what I should be about you.'

'This little girl's all right. What's the matter with going to bed?'

'You go on up. I'll wait for your father.'

'You're in a funny mood to-night, Mrs. Raeburn,' said her daughter. 'Good night.'

When she reached the bedroom Jenny woke up her sister.

'Look here, young May, you haven't said anything to mother, have you, about My Friend the Prince?'

'Of course not, you great stupid. And don't wake me up to ask soppy questions.'

'Well, don't you, that's all, because I'll go straight off and live with one of the girls if you ever dare say a word about him. Mother wouldn't understand there's nothing in it.'

'You know your own business best,' said May sleepily.

'That's quite right,' Jenny agreed, and began to undress herself to a sentimental tune and the faint tinkle of hairpins falling on the toilet-table.

In bed, she thought affectionately of Maurice, of his gaiety and pleasant manner of speech, of his being a gentleman. He must be a gentleman because he never said so. Other girls had love affairs with gentlemen, but, with one or two exceptions, she believed they were all swankers. At any rate Maurice and Colonel Walpole were different from Irene's Danby (long idiot!) and Madge Wilson's Berthold (dirty little Hungrarian!) and Elsie Crauford's Artie (him!), all examples of swank. Still in some ways it was a pity that Maurice was a gentleman. It would never mean a wedding. Those photographs of his mother and sisters had crushed that idea. Even if he asked her to marry him, she wouldn't. Other girls might brag about their education, their schools in Paris, their better days and dead gentlemen fathers, but they were all ballet girls, not one of the Mrs. Bigmouths could get away from that fact. Ballet girls! They got a laugh in comic songs. Ballet girls and mothers-in-law! They might gabble in a corner to each other and simper and giggle and pretend, but they were ballet-hoppers. And what of it? Why not? Wasn't a ballet girl as good as anybody else! Surely as good as a stuck-up chorus girl, who couldn't dance and couldn't act and couldn't even sing sometimes. They might be fine women with massive figures or they might have sweetly pretty Chevy Chases and not mind what they did after supper, but they weren't any better than ballet girls.

After all, Maurice did not look down on her. He did not patronize her. He loved her. She loved him. With that thought flooding her imagination, Jenny fell asleep and lay buried in her deep white pillow like a rosebud in a snowdrift.

XVII

Columbine Asleep

Columbine lay sleeping on her heart. The long white hands were clasped beneath those cheeks round which tumbled the golden curls. The coverlet, thrown back in a restless dream, revealed her bent arms bare to the elbow. The nightgown allowed a dim outline of her shoulder to appear faintly, and where a pale blue bow had come untied, the dimple in her throat was visible. The gay deep eyes were closed beneath azure lids, but the pencilled eyebrows still slanted mockingly, and round her red lips was the curve of laughter. Awake, her complexion had the fragility of rosy porcelain: in sleep the colour fled, leaving it dead white as new ivory.

Columbine lay sleeping, a miniature stolen from the world's collection. The night wore on. The wind shook the old house. Dawn broke tempestuously.

Now should Harlequin have hurried down the unreal street and, creeping in magically, have kissed her a welcome to the sweet and careless 'twenties' that would contain the best of his Columbine's life.

XVIII

Sweet and Twenty

The studio, looking very cheerful for Jenny's birthday, had achieved a Sabbath tidiness. It was, to be sure, a tidiness more apparent than real, inasmuch at it consisted of pushing every disorderly object into a corner and covering the accumulation with an old Spanish cope. Beneath this semicircle of faded velvet lay onions and sealing-wax, palette, brushes, bits of cardboard, a mixture of knives and forks, a tin of pineapple still undefeated, many unanswered letters, a tweed overcoat, and other things that gave more to utility than beauty.

The fire blazed in the big fireplace and rippled in reflection about the sloping ceiling. Chairs were set in a comfortable crescent round the tea-table, and looked as invitingly empty as the Venetian mirror. The teacups, where each one held the fire's image, showed an opal in the smooth porcelain. Anticipation brooded upon the apartment, accentuated by the bell of a neighbouring church that rang in a quick monotone. In the high deal ingle sat three young men smoking long clay pipes; and by the window facing the river Maurice stood breathing upon the glass in order to record his love's name in evanescent charactery upon the misted surface.

At last the monotonous bell ceased its jangling. Big Ben thundered the hour of four, and the host, throwing up the window, leaned out to a grey, foggy afternoon.

'Here's Jenny,' he cried, drawing back so quickly into the studio that he banged his head against the frame of the window. The three young men in the ingle rose and, knocking out their pipes, stood with their backs to the fire in an attitude of easy expectation. Maurice by this time was dashing out into the street to welcome Jenny, who was accompanied by Irene.

'Hurrah,' he said. 'I was afraid you might get lost. How are you now?' he went on, turning to Irene.

'I'm quite all right now,' replied the latter.

'She's in the best of pink,' said Jenny.

'Pink enough to climb all these stairs?' asked Maurice, laughing.

'I expect so,' said Irene.

'Any of the others come yet?' Jenny enquired on the way up.

'Only Castleton and Cunningham and Ronnie Walker.'

'I mean any of the girls?'

'No, you're the first – and fairest.'

Irene, for all her optimism, was beginning to feel exhausted.

'I say, young Jenny, does your friend here – Maurice – I suppose I can call him Maurice?'

'Idiot! Of course.'

'Does Maurice live much higher?'

226

'Yes, you may well ask,' said Jenny. 'What! He's Sky-scraping Bill, if you only knew.'

'We're nearly there,' said Maurice apologetically. Outside the door of the studio they paused.

'What are their unnatural names?' asked Jenny, digging Maurice as she spoke.

'Cunningham, Castleton and Walker.'

'They sound like the American Comedy Trio that got the bird. You remember, Ireen. Who cares? I shall call them Swan and Edgar for short.'

'That's only two.'

'Oh, well, I can remember Walker.'

Maurice opened the door, and Cunningham, Castleton and Walker advanced to make their bows.

'This is Miss Pearl, and this is Miss Dale.'·

'Pleased to meet you,' said Irene.

Jenny said nothing, but shook hands silently, taking the measure of the trio with shrewd and vivid glances.

'Sit down, won't you?' said Cunningham.

'Have a chair?' Walker suggested.

Castleton looked at Jenny.

'Isn't he tall?' she commented. 'Doesn't he remind you of somebody?'

'No,' said Irene vaguely.

'He does me. That Russian juggler – you know – who was struck on Queenie Danvers. *You* know – the one we used to call Fuzzy Bill.'

'Oh, him?' said Irene.

'Call me Fuzzy Bill, won't you?' put in Castleton. 'It's a pleasantly descriptive name. I shall answer to that.'

Indeed, he did; for from that moment he became 'Fuz,' and never heeded a summons expressed differently.

Just then there was a ring at the front door, and down-stairs Maurice rushed to admit the visitors. Presently he came up again.

'Damned kids,' he grumbled.

'You don't mean to say they fetched you all that way for nothing?' exclaimed Jenny.

'It's good for him,' Ronnie Walker asserted.

'Yes, but what a dreadful thing,' said Jenny. 'Fancy tearing all that way for nothing. I should go mad, I should go bar-mee.'

Another ring punctuated Jenny's indignation. Everybody to be forewarned ran to the window.

'It is them this time. Gladys! Elsie!' she called. Then in critical commentary:

'What a dreadful hat Elsie's got on.'

'She bought it yesterday.'

'I don't think,' said Jenny. 'Or if she did, it must have lain in the window and got forgotten since the year before last. Besides, what a shocking colour. It's like anchovy paste.'

Madge Wilson and Maudie Chapman now appeared from round a corner, and, since Maurice was already on his way downstairs, Jenny ran after him to prevent a double journey.

'Wait, wait,' she called after him. 'Madge and Maudie are coming too.'

He stopped and waved to her.

'Jenny – quick, one kiss – over the banisters. Do.'

'Do, do, do, I want you to,' she mocked in quotation. But all the same she kissed him.

'I absolutely adore you,' he whispered. 'Do you love me as much to-day as you did yesterday?'

'Oh, I couldn't answer all that in my head. I should have to put it down on paper.'

'No, don't tease. Do you? Do you?'

'Of course, baby,' she assured him.

'Angel!' he shouted, and rushed downstairs two steps at a time to admit the bunch of guests on his doorstep.

In a minute or two the studio was full of introductions, in the middle of which Maudie Chapman, a jolly girl with a big nose and a loud voice, explained the adventures of Madge and herself in arriving at 422, Grosvenor Road.

'Where we got to, my dear, well, that wants knowing. I was saying, when we got off the tram at Vauxhall Bridge, "Whatever is this man's house?" and Madge she was giggling, and then I asked the time, and it was only half past three, and I said, "Whatever shall we do, we're most shockingly early." So we got inside a big building near here – full of pictures and a pond with gold-fish. I thought at first it was an aquarium, and then we saw some statues and I thought it was a Catholic church.'

'Isn't she a lad?' said Jenny, admiring the spirited piece of narrative.

'Well, we had a good look at the pictures, *which* we didn't think much of, and I slipped on the floor and burnt my hand on a sort of grating, and then we couldn't find the way out. We *couldn't* find the way out. We got upstairs somewhere, and I called out, "Management," and a fellow with his hair

229

nailed down and spectacles said: "Are you looking for the Watts?" and I said, "No, we're looking for the What Ho's!" and he said, "You've made a mistake, miss; they're in the National Gallery," and Madge, you know what a shocking giggler she is, she burst out laughing and I didn't know where to look. So I said, "Can you tell me where Grosvenor Road is?" and he looked very annoyed and walked off.'

'Oh, but it really was difficult to find the way out,' Madge corroborated.

'And what did you think of the pictures?' asked Ronnie Walker, who was a painter himself and still young enough to be interested in a question's answer.

'Oh, don't ask *me*,' said Maudie.

'Nor me,' said Madge.

'They never looked at no pictures,' said Jenny. 'I bet you they was all the time trying to get off with the keeper. I know Madge and Maudie.'

Castleton suddenly laughed very loudly.

'What's Fuz laughing at?' asked Jenny.

'I was thinking of Madge and Maudie getting off with the Curator of the Tate Gallery. It struck me as funny. I apologize.'

Jenny looked at him suspiciously. Castleton, however, large, wide-faced and honest, could not be malicious.

'Well, they do. They did at the Zoo once. Only he got annoyed when they asked him if he slept in a cage.'

At this point the bell interrupted reminiscence.

'That must be Lilli Vergoe,' said Jenny. 'I'll go down and let her in. She'll feel uncomfortable walking into a crowd by herself.'

'I'll come as well,' Maurice volunteered.

The two of them took almost longer to descend than to come up, so much discussion was there of the immortality of affection, so much weighing up of comparative emotion. When they reached the studio with Lilli, the party had settled down into various groups of conversation.

'What about tea?' said the host. 'Jenny shall pour out.'

'But what a terrible teapot,' cried the latter when she had accepted the task. 'It's like my sister's watering-can. What's the matter with it?'

'Age,' said Castleton solemnly. 'It's old Lowestoft. If you look inside, you'll see "A Present from Lowestoft."'

'Shut up,' said Maurice, 'and pass the Chelsea buns.'

'A bit of old Chelsea,' murmured Castleton.

'Shut up making rotten jokes,' said Cunningham.

'You must excuse him,' said Maurice. 'He isn't funny, but he's very nice. Good lord!' he went on. 'I've never wished Jenny "many happy returns of the day."'

'Yes, it's a pity you waited till after she'd seen those buns,' said Castleton. 'However!'

'And the cake,' said Maurice, diving into the cupboard.

'Don't look so sad,' Castleton whispered to the guest of honour. 'It isn't really a tombstone.'

'Isn't he awful?' said Jenny, laughing.

'I say,' cried Maurice. 'Look here!'

Across the white cake was written in pink icing: 'Sacred to the Memory of a Good Appetite.'

'Rotten!' said Cunningham. 'Castleton, of course?'

'Of course,' said Maurice. 'And now we haven't got any candles.'

'Let's light the gas instead,' Castleton suggested.

'You are mad,' said Jenny.

Tea went on with wild laughter, with clinking of saucers and spoons, with desperate carving of the birthday cake, with solemn jokes from Castleton, with lightning caricatures from Ronnie Walker.

Once Jenny whispered to Maurice:

'Why did you say I shouldn't like Fuz? I think he's nice. You know, funny; but very nice.'

'I'm glad,' Maurice whispered back. 'I like you to like my friends.'

After tea they all wandered round the studio in commentary of its contents.

'Maurice,' said Castleton, stopping before the wax model of an Aphrodite. 'You don't feed your pets regularly enough. This lady's outrageously thin.'

'Isn't he shocking?' said Maudie. 'What would you do with him?'

'He's a nut,' said Madge.

'Isn't he?' said Elsie and Gladys in chorus. These two very seldom penetrated beyond the exclamatory interrogative.

'A nut, you think?' said Castleton. 'A Brasilero of the old breed with waxed pistachios and cocoanut-matted locks? Or a nib? Fancy—'

'Oh, dry up,' said Maurice. 'I want the girls to look at this dancing girl.'

'No one couldn't stand in that posish,' said Jenny. 'Could they, Lilli?'

'Not very easily,' the latter agreed.

'Really?' asked Maurice, somewhat piqued.

'Of course they could,' Maudie contradicted.

'Certainly,' said Irene, highly contemptuous.

'I say they couldn't then,' Jenny persisted.

'She'd be a rotten dancer if she couldn't.'

'I don't think so,' Jenny said frigidly.

The girls unanimously attempted to get into the position conceived by Maurice; but in the end they all had to agree that Jenny and Lilli were right. The pose was impossible.

'Is that your mother?' asked Madge, pointing to Mona Lisa.

'Don't be silly, Madge Wilson,' Jenny corrected. 'It's a picture, and I *don't* think much of her,' she continued. 'What a terrible mouth. Her hands is nice, though – very nice. And what's all those rocks at the back – low tide at Clacton, I should think.'

'But don't you like her marvellous smile?' asked Maurice.

'I don't call that a smile.'

'I knew those flute-players annoyed her,' said Castleton. 'Down with creative criticism. She's nothing but a lady with a bad temper.'

'Of course she is,' said Jenny.

'Would you smile, Jenny, if Ronnie here painted you with a gramophone behind a curtain?'

'No, I shouldn't.'

'Catch the fleeting petulance, and you become as famous as Leonardo, my Ronnie.'

Don Baltazar was voted a little love with rather too big

a head, and the Prince of Orange was a dear. Botticelli's Venus was not alluded to. The acquaintanceship was not considered ripe enough to justify any comment in that direction; although later on Jenny, her eyelids feathered with mirth and flashing wickedly, sang, pointing to the embarrassed goddess: 'She sells seashells on the seashore.' Primavera concluded the tour of inspection, and by some Primavera herself was thought to be not unlike Jenny.

'She's more like one of those angels with candles at Berlin,' said Ronnie Walker.

'Anyway,' said Maurice, with a note of satisfaction, 'she's a Botticelli.'

'Well, now you've all settled my position in life,' said Jenny, 'what's Ireen?'

But somehow it was not so interesting to discover Irene's prototype, and her similarity to the ideal of any single old master was left undecided.

Now came the singing of coon songs with ridiculous words and haunting refrains, while dusk descended upon London. Maudie was at the piano, where a candle flickered on each side of the music and lit up the size of her nose. When all the favourites of the moment had been sung, older and now almost forgotten successes were rescued from the dust of obscurity.

'We *are* among the "has beens," ' said Jenny. 'Why, I remember that at the Islington panto when I went to see you, Lilli, and that's donkey's years ago. We've properly gone back to the year dot.'

Gradually, however, the jolly dead tunes produced a sentimental effect upon the party, commemorating as they did many bygone enjoyments. The sense of fleeting time, evoked by the revival of discarded melodies, began to temper their spirits. They sang the choruses more softly, as if the undated tunes had become fragile with age and demanded a gentler treatment. Perhaps in the gathering gloom each girl saw herself once more in short frocks. Perhaps Lilli Vergoe distinguished the smiling ghost of old ambition. Certainly Jenny thought of Mr. Vergoe and Madame Aldavini and the Four Jumping Beans.

Maudie Chapman suddenly jumped up:

'Somebody else's turn.'

Maurice looked at Cunningham.

'Won't you play some Chopin, old chap?'

'All right,' said Cunningham, a dark, very thin young man with a high, narrow face, seating himself at the piano. The girls composed themselves to listen idly. Maurice drew Jenny over to an arm-chair by the window. The studio grew darker. The notes of the piano with the rapid execution of the player seemed phosphorescent in the candlelight. The fire glowed crimson and dull. The atmosphere was wreathed with the smoke of many cigarettes. The emotions of the audience were swayed by dreams that, sustained by music, floated about the heavy air in a pervading melancholy, inexpressibly sensuous. It was such an hour as only music can attempt to portray. Here was youth in meditation untrammelled by the energy of action. Age, wrought upon by music, may know regret, but only youth can see aspiration almost incarnate. Jenny, buried in the arm-chair, with Maurice's caressing hand upon her cheeks, thought it was all glorious, thought that Cunningham played gloriously, that the river with a blurred light was glorious, that love was glorious. She had a novel wish to bring May to such a party, and wondered if May would enjoy the experience. Time as an abstraction did not mean much to Jenny; but as the plangent harmonies wrung the heart of the very night with unattainable desires, she felt again the vague fear of age that used to distress her before she met her lover. She caught his hand, clasping it tightly, twisting his fingers in a passionate clutch as if he were fading from her life into the shadows all around. She began to feel, so sharply the music rent her imagination, a pleasure in the idea of instant death, not because she disliked the living world, but because she feared something that might spoil the perfection of love: they were too happy. She knew the primitive emotion of joy in absolute quiescence, the relief of Daphne avoiding responsibility. Why could not she and Maurice stop still in an ecstasy and live like the statues opposite glimmering faintly? Then, with a sudden ardour, life overpowered the enchantment of repose; and she, leaping to meet the impulse of action, conscious only of darkness and melody, spurred, perhaps, by one loud and solitary chord, pulled Maurice down to her arms and kissed him wildly, almost despairingly. The music went on from ballade to waltz, from waltz to polonaise. Sometimes matches were lit for cigarettes, matches that were typical of all the life in that room, a little flame in the sound of music.

At last, on the delicate tinkle of a dying mazurka, Cunningham stopped quite suddenly, and silence succeeded for a while. Outside in the street was the sound of people walking with Sabbath footsteps. Out over the river there was a hail from some distant loud-voiced waterman. The church bell resumed its hurried monotone. Castleton got up and lit the gas. The windows now looked grey and very dreary; it was pleasant to veil them with crimson birds and vine-leaves. The fire was roused to a roaring blaze; the girls began to arrange their hair: it was time to think of supper. Such was Jenny's birthday — intolerably fugitive.

XIX

The Gift of Opals

Jenny did not see Maurice after the party until the following night, when he waited in the court to take her out.

'Come quick,' he said. 'Quick. I've got something to show you.'

'Well, don't run,' she commanded, moderating the pace by tugging at his coat. 'You're like a young racehorse.'

'First of all,' asked Maurice eagerly, 'do you like opals?'

'They're all right.'

'Only all right?'

'Well, I think they're a bit like soapsuds.'

'I'm sorry,' said Maurice, 'I've bought you opals for a birthday present.'

'I do like them,' she explained. 'Only they're unlucky.'

'Not if you're an October girl. They're very lucky then.'

They were walking through jostling crowds down Coventry Street towards the Café de l'Afrique, where Castleton would meet them to discuss a project of gaiety. Jenny's soft hand on his arm was not successful in banishing the aggrieved notes from Maurice's petulant defence of opals.

'Oh, you miserable old thing,' she said. 'Don't look so cross.'

'It's a little disappointing to choose a present and then be told by the person it's intended for that she dislikes it.'

'Oh, don't be silly. I never said I didn't like it. How could I? I haven't seen it yet.'

'It's hardly worth while showing it to you. You won't like it. I'd throw it in the gutter, if it wasn't for this beastly crowd of fools that will bump into us all the time.'

'You are stupid. Give it to me. Please, Maurice.'

'No, I'll get you something else,' he retorted, determined to be injured. 'I'm sorry I can't afford diamonds. I took a good deal of trouble to find you something old and charming. I ransacked every curiosity shop in London. That's why I couldn't meet you till to-night. Damned lot of use it's been. I'd much better have bought you a turquoise beetle with pink topaz eyes or a lizard in garnets or a dragon-fly that gave you quite a turn, it was so like a real one, or a—'

'Oh, shut up,' said Jenny, withdrawing her arm.

'It's so frightfully disheartening.'

'But what are you making yourself miserable over? I haven't said I don't want your present. I haven't seen it.'

'No, and you never will. Rotten thing!'

'You are unkind.'

'So are you.'

'Oh, good job.'

'You're absolutely heartless. I don't believe you care a bit about me. I almost wish I'd never met you. I can't think about anything but you. I can't work. What's the good of being in love? It's a fool's game. It's unsettling. It's hopeless. I think I won't see you any more after to-night. I can't stand it.'

239

Jenny had listened to his tirade without interruption; but now as they were passing the Empire, she stopped suddenly, and said in a voice cold and remote:

'Good night. I'm off.'

'But we're going to meet Castleton.'

'You may be. I'm not.'

'What excuse shall I make to him?'

'I don't care what you tell him. He's nothing to me. Nor you either.'

'You don't mean that?' he gasped.

'Don't I?'

'But Jenny! Oh, I say, do come into the Afrique. We can't argue here. People will begin to stare.'

'People! I thought you didn't mind about people.'

'Look here, I'm sorry. I am really. Do stay.'

'No, I don't want to.'

Jenny's lips were set; her eyes dull with anger.

'I know I'm a bad-tempered ass,' Maurice admitted. 'But do stay. I meant it to be such a jolly evening. Only I was hurt about the opals. Do stay, Jenny. I really am frightfully sorry. Won't you have the brooch? I'm absolutely to blame. I deserve anything you say or do. Only won't you stay? Just this once. Do.'

Jenny was not proof against such pleading. There was in Maurice's effect upon her character something so indescribably disarming that, although in this case she felt in the right, she, it seemed, must always give way; and for her to give way, right or wrong, was out of order.

'Soppy me again,' was all she said.

'No, darling you,' Maurice whispered. 'Such a darling,

too. I hope Castleton hasn't arrived yet. I want to tell you all over again how frightfully sorry I am.'

But when they had walked past the Buddha-like manager who, massive and enigmatical, brooded over the entrance to the café, they could see Castleton in the corner. It was a pity; for the constraint of a lovers' quarrel, not absolutely adjusted, hung over them still in the presence of a third person before whom they had to simulate ease. Maurice, indeed, was so boisterously cordial that Jenny resented his dramatic ability and, being herself incapable of simulation, showed plainly all was not perfectly smooth.

'What is the matter with our Jenny to-night?' Castleton enquired.

'Nothing,' she answered moodily.

'She feels rather seedy,' Maurice explained.

'No, I don't.'

'Do you like the opal brooch?' Castleton asked.

'I haven't seen it,' Jenny replied.

'I was waiting to give it to her in here,' Maurice suggested.

Jenny, who was examining herself in a pocket mirror, looked over at him from narrowing eyes. He turned to her, defending himself against the imputation of a lie.

'Castleton helped me to choose it. Look,' he said, 'it's an old brooch.'

He produced from his pocket a worn leather case on the faded mauve velvet of whose lining lay the brooch. It was an opal of some size set unusually in silver filigree with seed pearls and brilliants.

'It's rather pretty,' Jenny commented without enthusiasm.

In her heart she loved the old-fashioned trinket, and wanted to show her delight to Maurice; but the presence of Castleton was a barrier, and she was strangely afraid of tears that seemed not far away. Maurice, who was by now thoroughly miserable, offered to pin the brooch where it would look most charming; but Jenny said she would put it in her bag, and he sat back in the chair biting his lips and hating Castleton for not immediately getting up and going home. The latter, realizing something was the matter, tried to change the subject.

'What about this Second Empire masquerade at Covent Garden?'

'I don't think we shall be able to bring it off. Ronnie Walker would be ridiculous as Balzac.'

'There are others.'

'Besides, I don't think I want to be Théophile Gautier.'

'Don't be, then,' advised Castleton.

'Anyway, it's a rotten idea,' declared Maurice.

'What extraordinary tacks your opinions do take!' retorted his friend. 'Only this afternoon you were full of the most glittering plans and had found a prototype in 1850 for half your friends.'

'I've been thinking it over,' said Maurice. 'And I'm sure we can't work it.'

'Goodbye, Gustave Flaubert,' said Castleton. 'I confess I regret Flaubert; especially if I could have persuaded Mrs. Wadman to be George Sand and smoke a cigar. However, perhaps it's just as well.'

'Who's Mrs. Wadman?' asked Jenny.

'The aged female iniquity who "does" for Maurice and

me at Grosvenor Road. I'm sure on second thoughts it would be unwise to let her acquire the cigar habit. I might be rich next year, and I should hate to see her dusting, with a Corona Corona stuck jauntily between toothless gums.'

'Oh, don't be funny,' said Maurice. 'You've no idea how annoying you are sometimes. Confound you, waiter,' he cried, turning to vent his temper in another direction. 'I ordered Munich and you've brought Pilsener.'

'Very sorry, sir,' apologized the waiter.

'It was I who demanded the blond beer,' Castleton explained. Then, as the waiter retired, he said:

'Why not get him to come as Balzac?'

'Who?'

'The waiter.'

'Don't be funny any more,' Maurice begged wearily.

'Poor Fuz,' said Jenny. 'You're crushed.'

'I now know the meaning of Blake's worm that flies in the heart of the storm.'

Even Castleton was ultimately affected by the general depression; and Jenny at last broke the silence by saying she must go home.

'I'll drive you back,' said Maurice.

'Hearse or hansom, sir?' Castleton asked.

'Good night, Fuz,' said Jenny on the pavement. 'I'll bring Madge and Maudie to see you sometime soon.'

'Do,' he answered. 'They would invigorate even a sleepy pear. Good night, dear Jenny, and pray send Maurice back in a pleasanter mood.'

For a few minutes the lovers drove along in silence.

It was Maurice who spoke first:

'Jenny, I've been an idiot and spoilt the evening. Do forgive me, Jenny,' he cried, burying his face in her shoulder. 'My vile temper wouldn't have lasted a moment if I could just have been kissed once; but Castleton got on my nerves and the waiter would hover about all the time and everybody enraged me. Forgive me, sweet thing, will you?'

Jenny, abandoning at once every tradition of obstinacy, caught him to her.

'You silly old thing.'

'I know I am, and you're a little darling.'

'And he wasn't ever going to see me again. What a liberty! Not ever.'

'I am an insufferable ass.'

'And he wished he'd never met me. Oh, Maurice, you do say unkind things.'

'Were you nearly crying once?' he asked. 'When I gave you the brooch?'

'Perhaps.'

'Jenny, precious one, are you nearly crying now?' he whispered.

'No, of course not.'

Yet when he kissed her eyelids they were wet.

'Shall I pin the brooch now?'

She nodded.

'Jenny, you don't know how I hate myself for being unkind to you. I hate myself. I shall fret about this all night.'

'Not still a miserable old thing?' she asked, fingering

the smooth face of the opal that had caused such a waste of emotion.

'Happy now. So happy.' He sighed on her breast.

'So am I.'

'You're more to me every moment.'

'Am I?'

'You're so sweet and patient. Such a pearl, such a treasure.'

'You think so.'

'My little Queen of Hearts, you've a genius for love.'

'What's that?'

'I mean, you're just right. You never make a mistake. You're patient with my wretched artistic temperament. Like a perfect work of art, you're a perfect work of love.'

'Maurice, you *are* a darling,' she sighed on the authentic note of passionate youth in love.

'When you whisper like that, it takes my breath away . . . Jenny, are you ever going to be more to me even than you are now?'

'What do you mean, more?' she asked.

'Well, everything that a woman can be to a man. You see I'm an artist, and an artist longs for the completion of a great work. My love for you is the biggest thing in my life so far, and I long to complete it. Don't you understand what I mean?'

'I suppose I do,' she said very quietly.

'Are you going to let me?'

'Some day I suppose I shall.'

'Not at once?'

'No.'

'Why not? Don't you trust me?'

'Yes.'

'Well?'

'Kiss me,' she said. 'I can't explain. Don't let's talk about it any more.'

'I can't understand women,' Maurice declared.

'Ah!'

She smiled; but in the smile there was more of sadness than mirth.

'Why waste time?' he demanded passionately. 'Heaven knows we have little enough time. Jenny, I warn you, I beg you not to waste time. You're making a mistake. Like all girls, you're keeping one foot in a sort of washy respectability.'

'Don't go on,' Jenny said. 'I've told you I will one day.'

'Why not come abroad with me if you're afraid of what your people will say?'

'I couldn't. Not while my mother was alive.'

'Well, don't do that; but still it's easy enough not – to waste time. Your mother need never find out. I'm not a fool.'

'Ah, but I should feel a sneak.'

Maurice sighed at such scruples.

'Besides,' she added, 'I don't want to – not yet. Can't we be happy like we have been? I will one day.'

'You can't play with love,' Maurice warned her.

'I'm not. I'm more in earnest than what you are.'

'I don't think you are.'

'But I am. Supposing if you got tired of me?'

'I couldn't.'

'Ah, but that's where men are funny. All of a sudden you might take a sudden fancy to another girl. And then what about me? What should I do?'

'It comes to this,' he argued. 'You don't trust me yet. You don't believe in me. Good heavens, what can I do to show you I'm sincere?'

'Can't you wait a little while?' she gently asked.

'I must.'

'And you won't ask me again?'

'I won't promise that.'

'Well, not for a long time?' Jenny pleaded.

'I won't even promise that. You see I honestly think you're making a mistake – a mistake for which you'll be very sorry one day. I wish you understood my character better.'

'All men are the same.' She sighed out the generalization.

'That's absurd, my dear girl. I might as well say all women are the same.'

'Well, they are. They're all soppy.'

'Isn't it rather soppy to go as far as you have with me, and not go farther?' Maurice spoke tentatively.

'Oh, *I've* properly joined the soppy brigade. I did think I was different, but I'm not. I'm well in the first line.'

'Don't you think,' Maurice suggested, '– of course, I'm not saying you haven't had plenty of experience – but don't you think there's a difference between a gentleman and a man who isn't a gentleman?'

'I think gentlemen are the biggest rotters of all.'

'I don't agree with you.'

'I do. Listen. You asked me just now to come away with you. You didn't ask me to marry you.'

Maurice bubbled over with undelivered explanations.

'Wait. I wouldn't marry you, not if you asked me. I don't want you to ask me. Only—'

'Only what?' Maurice enquired gloomily.

'Only if I did all you wanted, I'd be giving everything – more than you'd give, even if you married a ballet girl.'

'Do let me explain,' Maurice begged. 'You absolutely misunderstand me . . . Oh lord, we're nearly at Hagworth Street . . . I've only time to say quite baldly what I mean. Look here, if you married me you wouldn't like it. You wouldn't like meeting all my people and having to be conventional and pay calls and adapt yourself to a life that you hadn't been brought up to. I'd marry you like a shot. I don't believe in class distinction or any of that humbug. But you'd be happier not married. Can't you see that? You'd be happier the other way . . . There's your turning. There's no time for more . . . Only do think over what I've said and don't misjudge me . . . darling girl, good night.'

'Good night.'

'A long kiss.'

Reasons, policies, plans and all the paraphernalia of expediency vanished when she from the steps of her home listened to the bells of the hansom dying away in the distance, and when he, huddled in a corner of the cab, was conscious but of the perfume of one who was lately beside him.

In her bedroom Jenny examined the brooch. Perhaps what showed more clearly than anything the reality of her love was the affection she felt for Maurice when he was away from her. She was never inclined to criticize faults so easily forgotten in the charms which she remembered more vividly. Now, with the brooch before her, as she sat dangling her legs from the end of the bed, she recalled lovingly his eagerness to display the unfortunate opal. She remembered the brightness of his blue eyes and the vibrant attraction of his voice. He was a darling, and she had been unkind about opals. He was always a darling to her. He never jarred her nerves or probed roughly a tender mood.

Jenny scarcely sifted so finely her attitude towards Maurice. She summed him up to herself in a generalization. In her mind's eye he appeared in contrast to everybody else. All that the rest of mankind lacked he possessed. Whatever mild approval she had vouchsafed to any other man his existence obliterated. She had never created for herself an ideal whose tenuity would one day envelop a human being. Therefore, since there had never floated through her day-dreams a nebula with perfect profile, immense wealth and euphonious titles, Maurice had not to be fitted in with a preconception. Nor would it be reasonable to identify her with one of the world's Psyches in love with the abstraction of a state of mind and destined to rue its incarnation. She had, it may be granted, been inclined to fall in love in response to the demand of her being; but it would be wrong to suppose her desire was gratified by the first person who came along. On the contrary, Maurice had risen suddenly to overthrow all that had gone before, and, as it seemed now, he was likely to overthrow anything that might come after.

Sitting on the edge of the bed, she was hypnotized into

a meditative coma by the steady twin flames of the candle and its reflection in the toilet-glass. She was invested with the accessories favourable to crystal-gazing, and the brooch served to concentrate faculties that would under ordinary circumstances have lacked an object. Contrast as an absolute idea is often visualized during slightly abnormal mental phases. Fever often fatigues the brain with a reiteration of images in tremendous contrast, generally of mere size, when the mind is forced to contemplate again and again with increasing resentment the horrible disparity between a pin's point and a pyramid. In Jenny's mind Maurice was contrasted with the rest of the universe. He was so overpowering and tremendous that everything else became a mere speck. In fact, during this semi-trance, Jenny lost all sense of proportion, and Maurice became an obsession.

Then suddenly the flame of the candle began to jig and flicker; the spell was broken, and Jenny realized it would be advisable to undress.

Action set her brain working normally, and the vast absorbing generalization faded. She began to think again in detail. How she longed for to-morrow, when she would be much nicer to Maurice than she had ever been before. She thought with a glow of the delightful time in front of them. She pictured wet afternoons spent cosily in the studio. She imagined herself, tired and bored, coming down the court from the stage-door, with Maurice suddenly appearing round the corner to drive weariness out of London. It was glorious to think of someone who could make the worst headache insignificant and turn the most unsatisfactory morning to a perfect afternoon. Quickened by such thoughts she got into bed without waking May, so that in a flutter of soft kisses she could sink deliciously to sleep, enclosed in the arms of her lover as an orchard by sunlight.

About two o'clock Jenny woke up to another psychic experience not unusual with hypersensitive temperaments. The ardour of the farewell embrace had consumed all the difficulties of the situation discussed on the journey home. This ardour of merely sensuous love had lasted long enough to carry her off to sleep drowsed by a passionate content. Meanwhile her brain, working on what was originally the more vital emotion, brought her back to consciousness in the middle of the problem's statement. Lying there in the darkness, Jenny blushed hotly, so instant was the mental attitude produced by Maurice's demand. In previous encounters over this subject, her suitors had all been so manifestly contemptible their expectations so evident from the beginning that their impudence had been extinguished by the fire of merely social indignation. Jenny had defeated them as the representative of her sex rather than as herself. She had never comprehended as a feasible proposition the application of their desires to herself. They were a fact merely objectively unpleasant like monkeys in a cage, physically dangerous, however, with certain opportunities that Jenny's worldly wisdom would never afford. In the case of Maurice the encounter was actual, involving a clash of personalities: the course of her behaviour would have to be settled. No longer fortified by the hostility of massed opinion, she would be compelled to entrust her decision to personal resolution and individual judgment. For the first time she was confronted with the great paradox that simultaneously restricts and extends a woman's life. She remembered the effect of Edie's announcement of surrender. It had sickened her with virginal wrath and impressed her with a sense of man's malignity, and now here was she at the cross-roads of experience with signposts unmistakable to dominate her mental vision.

It was not astonishing that Jenny should blush with the consciousness of herself as a vital entity; for the situation was merely an elaboration of the commonplace self-consciousness incident to so small an action as entering alone a crowded room. Years ago, as a little girl, she had once woken up with an idea she no longer existed, an idea dispelled by the sight of her clothes lying as usual across the chair. Now she was frightened by the overwhelming realization of herself: she existed too actually. This analysis of her mental attitude shows that Jenny did not possess the comfortable mind which owes volition to external forces. Her brain registered sensations too finely; her sense of contact was too fastidious. Acquiescence was never possible without the agony of experience. Her ambition to dance was in childhood a force which was killed by unimaginative treatment. Once killed, nothing could revive it. So it would be with her love. In the first place, she was aware of the importance of surrender to a man. She did not regard the step as an incident of opportunity. All her impulses urged her to give way. Every passionate fire and fever of love was burning her soul with reckless intentions. On the other hand, she felt that if she yielded herself and tasted the bitterness of disillusionment, she would be for ever more liable to acquiesce. She would demand of her lover attributes which he might not possess, and out of his failure by the completeness of her personality she would create for herself a tragedy.

Finally a third aspect presented itself in the finality of the proposed surrender. She was now for the first time enjoying life with a fullness of appreciation which formerly she had never imagined. She was happy in a sense of joy. When Cunningham was playing in the studio, she had felt how insecure such happiness was, how impatient of any design to imprison it in the walls of time. Indeed, perhaps she had seen it escaping on the echoes of a melody. Then suddenly over all this confusion of prudence, debate, hesitation, breathless abandonment and scorching blushes, sleep resumed its sway, subduing the unnatural activity of a normally indolent mind.

She lay there asleep in the darkness without a star to aid or cross her destiny. She and her brooch of opals were swept out into the surge of evolution; and she must be dependent on a fallible man to achieve her place in the infallible scheme of the universe.

XX

Fête Galante

For some weeks after the incident of the opal, there was no development of the problem of behaviour. Maurice did not refer to the subject, and Jenny was very glad to put it out of her mind. As if by tacit agreement, they both took refuge from any solution in a gaiety that might have been assumed, so sedulously was it cultivated. Everything else was set aside for a good time, and though there were interludes when in the seclusion of an afternoon spent together they would recapture the spirit of that golden and benign October, these lovers generally seemed anxious to share with their friends the responsibilities of enjoyment.

Thus it came about that a polity of pleasure was established whose citizens were linked together by ties of laughter. This city state of Bohemia, fortified against intrusion by experiences which the casual visitor was not privileged to share, stood for Jenny as the solidest influence upon her life so far. It gave her a background for Maurice, which made him somehow more real. Without this little society, acknowledging herself and him as supreme and accepting their love as the pivot on which its own existence revolved, she would have seen her lover as an actuality only when they were making love. Out of her sight, he would have faded into the uncertain mists of another social grade, floated incorporeal among photographs of Ellis and Walery in a legend of wealth and dignity beyond her conception. To Fuz and Ronnie and Cunningham she could talk of Maurice, thereby gleaning external impressions which confirmed her own attitude. In this atmosphere her love assumed a sanity and normality that might otherwise easily have been lost.

It must not be supposed that this little republic was content with the territory of 422 Grosvenor Road. On the contrary, throughout October, November and December there were frequent sallies against convention and raids upon Philistia. There were noisy tea-parties in hostile strongholds like the Corner House, where ladies were not permitted to smoke and customers were kindly requested to pay at the desk. Perhaps their most successful foray was upon a fashionable tea-shop in St. James's Street, where a florin was the minimum charge for tea to include everything; on this occasion, prepared for by rigorous fasting, it included a very great deal. There were attempts by Ronnie Walker to make the girls enjoy picture-galleries, by Cunningham to convert them to Symphony Concerts. And once they all went to see a play by Mr. Bernard Shaw. But Painting, Music and the Drama could not compete with skating rinks, where several elegant and accomplished instructors complained of their rowdiness. But, as Jenny said, 'What of it? *We're* enjoying ourselves, any old way.'

The pinnacle of their gay ambition was a Covent Garden Ball. This entertainment had continually to be postponed for lack of funds; for, though a Covent Garden Ball has usually a sobering, even a chilling effect upon the company, it has dare-devil pretensions which Maurice and his retinue would not exploit without being assured of a conspicuous success.

So the Second Empire Masquerade was planned and debated a long time before it actually happened. That it happened at all was due to the death of Maurice's great-aunt, who left him one hundred pounds. This legacy, being unexpected, was obviously bound to be spent at once. As the legatee pointed out to Jenny one dripping afternoon in early January, as they sat together in the studio:

'It's practically like finding money in the road. I know that one day my stockbroker uncle will leave me two thousand pounds. He's told me so often to raise my spirits on wet week-ends at his house. I've planned what to do with that. Every farthing is booked. But this hundred I never thought of. I was beginning to despair of ever raising the cash for Covent Garden, and here it is all of a sudden.'

'You're not going to spend a hundred pounds in one evening?' Jenny exclaimed.

'Not all of it, because you've got to buy yourself some furs and three hats and those silk stockings with peach-coloured clocks – oh yes, and I've got to buy you that necklace of fire opals which we saw in Wardour Street and also that marquise ring, and I've got to buy myself a safety razor and a box of pastels, and I simply must get Thackeray's *Lectures on the English Humorists* for Fuz.'

'There won't be much left of your hundred pounds,' said Jenny.

'Well, let's draw up an estimate. I'll write down the possibles and then we'll delete nearly all of them.'

Maurice got up from his chair and wandered round the room in search of note-paper. Not being able to find any, he pinned a large sheet of drawing-paper to a board and produced a pencil.

'Look at him,' laughed Jenny. 'Look at the Great Millionaire. Just because he's come into money, he can't write on anything smaller than a blanket.'

'It's not ostentation,' Maurice declared. 'It's laziness – a privilege of the very poor, as you ought to know by this time. I can't find any note-paper.'

'I should think you couldn't. I wonder you can find yourself in this room.'

'Come along,' urged the owner of it. 'We must begin. Maurice and Jenny. Then Fuz and Maudie, Ronnie and Irene, Cunningham and Madge. Any more you can think of?'

'You don't mean to say you've taken that unnatural piece of paper just to write those few names which we could have thought of in our heads. What would you do with him?'

'We want another eight,' Maurice declared.

'Oh no, eight's plenty.'

'Perhaps it is,' he agreed. 'Well now, Maurice will be Théophile Gautier – no, he won't – the red waistcoat knocks him out – Edmond de Goncourt? No, he had a moustache. Chopin? Long hair. Look here, I don't think we'll be anybody in particular. We'll just be ladies and gentlemen of the period. You know you girls have got to wear crinolines and fichus and corkscrew curls?'

'Like we used to wear in Bohême in the Opera?'

'That's it. You must see about your dresses at once. Good ones will cost about ten pounds to hire, and that ought to include some decent paste.'

'We shan't have to pay for our tickets.'

'Good. Four guineas saved. Dresses? Say twenty pounds for the eight of us. Supper with fizz another ten quid. Four salmon-coloured taxis with tips, ten pounds.'

'How much?' Jenny exclaimed. 'Ten pounds just to take us to Covent Garden Ball and back?'

'Ah, but I've a plan. These salmon-coloured taxis are going to be the *chef d'œuvre* as well as the *hors d'œuvre* of the entertainment. Hush, it's a secret. Let me see our tickets – four guineas – forty-four pounds four shillings. Well, say fifty quid to include all tips and breakfast.'

'Well, I think it's too much,' Jenny declared.

'Not too much for an evening that shall be famous over all evenings – an evening that you, my Jenny, will remember when you're an ancient old woman – an evening that we'll talk over for the rest of our lives.'

While Maurice was speaking, the shadow of a gigantic doubt passed over Jenny's mind. She endured one of those moments when only the profound uselessness of everything has any power to impress the reason. She suffered a complete loss of faith and hope. The moment was one of those black abysses before which the mind is aghast at effort and conceives annihilation. In the Middle Ages such an experience would have been ascribed to the direct and personal influence of Satan.

'What's the matter?' Maurice asked. 'You look as if you didn't believe me.'

But, while the question was still on his lips, the shadow passed, and Jenny laughed.

The famous evening was finally assigned to the twenty-seventh of January. The four girls took their places in the ballet as usual and, meeting from time to time in evolutions, would murmur as they danced by, 'To-night, what, what?' or 'Don't you wish it was eleven?' They would look at each other, too, from opposite sides of the stage, smiling in the sympathy of anticipated pleasure. When the curtain fell they hurried to their dressing-rooms to exchange tights and spangles for mid-Victorian frocks, whose dainty lace made all the other girls very envious indeed. Some were so envious as to suggest to Jenny that another colour would have suited her better than pink or that her hair would be more becoming *en chignon* than curled. But Jenny was not deceived by such professions of amiable advice.

'Yes, some of you would like to see me with my hair done different. Some of you wouldn't be half pleased if I went out looking a sight. Oh no, it's only a rumour. Thanks, I'm not taking any. I know what suits me better than *anyone*, *which* pink does.'

'Don't take any notice of them,' Maudie whispered to her friend.

'Take notice of them. What? Why, I should be all the time looking. My eyes would get as big as moons. They've been opened wide enough since I came to the Orient, as it is.'

At last, having survived every criticism, the four girls

were ready. The hall-porter's boy carried their luggage out to the salmon-coloured taxis, whose drivers looked embarrassed by the salmon-coloured carnations which Maurice insisted they should wear. The latter with Fuz, Ronnie and Cunningham stood in the entrance of the court, wrapped in full cloaks and wearing tall hats of a bygone fashion. They were leaning gracefully on their tasselled canes as the girls came along the court towards them. It was romantic to think that other girls in similar frocks had trod the same path and met men dressed like them fifty years ago. This sweet fancy was vividly brought home to them when an old cleaner, grimed with half a century of Orient dust, passed by the laughing, chattering group and, as she shuffled off towards Seven Dials, looked back over her shoulder with an expression of fear.

'Marie thinks we're ghosts,' laughed Madge.

'Isn't it dreadful to think she was once in the ballet?' said Jenny. 'Poor old crow, I do think it's dreadful.'

The eight of them shivered at the thought.

'Really?' said Maurice. 'How horrible.'

'Yes, some man sprung it on her,' said Jenny. 'And she went away to have a baby and when she come back her place was filled. So they said she could come back as a dresser, *which* she did, and then she began to drink and became a cleaner. That's your men.'

The episode was a gaunt intrusion upon gaiety; but it was soon forgotten in the noise and sheen of Piccadilly. The taxis with much hooting hummed through the dazzling thoroughfares into the gloom and comparative stillness of Long Acre. As usual they tried to cut through Floral Street, only to be turned back by a policeman; but without much delay they swept at last under the great portico of the Opera House. Here many girls, blown into Covent Garden by the raw January winds, gave the effect of thistledown, so filmy were their dresses; and the rigid young men, stopping behind to pay their fares, looked stiff and awkward as groups of Pre-Raphaelite courtiers. Commissionaires decorated the steps without utility. In the vestibule merry people were greeting each other and nodding as they passed up and down the wide staircase. Here and there an isolated individual, buttoning and unbuttoning his gloves with unconscionable industry, gazed anxiously at every swing of the door. Presently Jenny and Madge and Maudie and Irene were ready and, as on the arms of their escort they took the floor of the ballroom, might have stepped from a note-book of Gavarni.

Covent Garden balls are distinguished by the atmosphere of a spectacle which pervades them. The floor itself has the character of an arena encircled by tiers of red boxes, many of which display marionettes, an unobtrusive audience, given over to fans and the tinkle of distant laughter; while the curtained glooms of others are haunted by invisible eyes. Here are no chaperons struggling with palms and hair-nets through a wearisome evening, creaking in wicker chairs and discussing draughts with neighbours. The old men, searching for bridge-players, are absent. There is neither host nor hostess; and not one anæmic young débutante is distressed by the bleakness of her unembarrassed programme.

Maurice announced that he had taken a box for the

evening, so that his guests would be able, when tired of dancing, to cheat fatigue. Then he caught Jenny round the waist and, regardless of their companions, the two of them were lost in the tide of dancers. They were only vaguely conscious of the swirl of petticoats and lisp of feet around their course. In the irresistible sweep of melodious violins all that really existed for Maurice and Jenny was nearness to each other, and eyes ablaze with rapture; and for him there was the silken coolness of her curls, for her the fever of his hand upon her waist.

During the interval between the sixth and seventh waltzes, Maurice, breathless at the memory of their perfect accord, said:

'I wonder if Paolo and Francesca enjoy swooning together on the winds of hell. Great Scott! as if one wouldn't prefer the seventh circle to bathing in pools of light with a blessed damozel. I'm surprised at Rossetti.'

'Who's she?'

'The blessed damozel?'

'No – Rose Etty.'

'Oh, Jenny, don't make me laugh.'

'Well, I don't know what you're talking about.'

'I was speculating. Hark! They're playing the Eton Boating Song. Come along. We mustn't miss a bar of it.'

In the scent of Frangipani and Jicky and Phulnana the familiar tune became queerly exotic. The melody, charged with regret for summer elms and the sounds of playing-fields, full of the vanished laughter of boyhood, held now the heart of romantic passion. It spoke of regret for the present rather than the past and, as it revelled in the lapse of moments, gave expression to the dazzling swiftness of such a night in a complaint for flying glances, sighs and happy words lost in their very utterance.

'Heart of hearts,' whispered Maurice in the swirl of the dance.

'Oh, Maurice, I do love you,' she sighed.

Now the moments fled faster as the beat quickened for the climax of the dance. Maurice held Jenny closer than before, sweeping her on through a mist of blurred lights in which her eyes stood out clear as jewels from the pallor of her face. Round the room they went, round and round, faster and faster. Jenny was now dead white. Her lips were parted slightly, her fingers strained at Maurice's sleeve. He, with flushed cheeks, wore elation all about him. No dream could have held the multitude of imaginations that thronged their minds; and when it seemed that life must end in the sharpness of an ecstasy that could never be recorded in mortality, the music stopped. There was a sound of many footsteps leaving the ballroom. Jenny leaned on Maurice's arm.

'You're tired,' he said. 'Jolly good dance that.'

'Wasn't it glorious? Oh, Maurice, it was lovely.'

'Come and sit in the box when you've had some champagne, and I'll dance with the girls while you're resting. Shall I?'

She nodded.

Presently Maurice was tearing round the room with Maudie, both of them laughing very loudly; while Jenny sat back in a faded arm-chair thinking of the old Covent Garden days and nights, and wondering how before she met Maurice she could ever have fancied she was happy. In a few minutes Fuz came into the box to ask if she wanted to dance.

'No, I'm tired,' she told him.

'It's just as well, perhaps,' he said gravely. 'For I am what you would describe as a very unnatural dancer.'

'Oh, Fuz,' she laughed, 'are you? Oh, you must dance once round the room with me before it's over. Oh, you must. It tickles my fancy, the idea of Fuz dancing.'

'At last I've earned a genuine laugh.'

'Oh, Fuz, doesn't anyone else ever laugh at you, only me?'

'Very rarely.'

'Shame!'

'So it is.'

'Aren't Maurice and Maudie making a terrible noise?'

'They're certainly laughing loud enough,' Fuz agreed. 'But Maurice is always in spirits. I don't think he knows the meaning of depression.'

'Doesn't he then!' Jenny exclaimed. 'I think he gets *very* depressed sometimes.'

'Not deeply. It's never more than a passing mood.'

'That's quite right. It is a mood. But he works himself up into a state over his moods.'

'Tell me, dear Jane—' said Castleton suddenly. 'No, on second thoughts, I won't ask.'

'Oh, do tell me.'

'No, it's not my business. Besides, you'd be annoyed, and I've no wish to make our Jenny angry.'

'I won't be angry. Do tell me, Fuz, what you was going to ask.'

'Well, I will,' he said after a pause. 'Jenny, are you very fond of Maurice?'

'Oh, I love him.'

'Really love him?'

'Of course.'

'But you'd soon get over it if——'

'If what?'

'If Maurice was – was a disappointment – for instance, if he married somebody else quite suddenly? Don't look so frightened; he's not going to, as far as I know; or likely to, but if . . . would it upset your life?'

Jenny burst into tears.

'My dearest Jane,' Castleton cried. 'I was only chaffing. Please don't cry Jenny, Jenny, I'm only an inquisitive, speculative jackanapes. Maurice isn't going to do anything of the kind. Really. Besides, I thought – oh, Jane – I'm terribly ashamed of myself.'

'Maurice said I shouldn't like you,' Jenny sobbed. 'And I don't. I hate you. Don't stay with me. Go out of the box. I'm going home. Where's Maurice? I want Maurice to come to me.'

'He's dancing,' said Castleton helplessly. 'Jane, I'm an absolute beast. Jane, will you marry me and show your forgiving nature?'

'Don't go on teasing me,' sobbed Jenny, louder than ever. 'You're hateful. I hate you.'

'No, but I mean it. Will you, Jenny? Really, I'm not joking. I'd marry you to-morrow.'

Jenny's tears gradually turned to laughter, and at last she had to say:

'Oh, Fuz, you're hateful, but you are funny.'

'It's a most extraordinary thing,' he replied, 'that the only person I don't want to laugh at me must do it. Jane!' He held out his hand. 'Jane, are we pals again?'

'I suppose we've got to be,' Jenny pouted.

'Good pals and jolly companions?'

'Oh, whoever was it said that to me once?' cried Jenny. 'Years and years ago. Oh, whoever was it?'

'Years and years?' echoed Castleton, quizzing. 'Who are you, ancient woman?'

'Don't be silly. It was. Someone said it when I was a little girl. Oh, Fuz, I'd go raving mad to remember who it was.'

'Well, anyway, I've said it now. And is it a bargain?'

'What?'

'You and I being pals?'

'Of course.'

'Which means that when I'm in trouble, I go to Jane for advice, and when Jane's in trouble, she comes to Fuz. Shake hands on that.'

Jenny, feeling very shy of him for the first time during their acquaintanceship, let him take her hand.

'And the tears are a secret?' he asked.

'Not if Maurice asks me. I'd have to tell him.'

'Would you? All right, if he asks, tell him.'

Maurice, however, did not ask, being full of arrangements for supper and in a quandary of taste between Pol Roger and Perrier Jouet.

'What about Perrier without Jouet?' Castleton suggested. 'It would save money.'

266

Supper (and in the end Maurice chose Pommery) was very jolly; but nothing for the lovers during the rest of the evening reached the height of those first waltzes together. After supper Fuz and Jenny danced a cake-walk, and Ronnie tried to hum a favourite tune to Cunningham in order that he could explain to the conductor what Ronnie wanted. Nothing came of it, however, as the latter never succeeded in disentangling it from two other tunes. So, with laughter and dancing, they kept the night merry to the last echo of music, and when at about half-past six they all stood in the vestibule waiting for the salmon-coloured taxis to drive them home, all agreed that Maurice had done well.

'And I've not done yet,' he said. 'I suppose you all think you're going home to tumble sleepily into bed. Oh no, we're going to have breakfast first at the old Sloop, Greenwich.'

'Greenwich?' they repeated in chorus.

'I've ordered a thumping breakfast. The drive will do us good. We can see the dawn break over the river.'

'And put our watches right,' added Castleton.

'Then you girls can be driven home (your bags are all inside the taxis) and sleep all the rest of the morning and afternoon.'

Maurice was so eager to carry this addendum that none of them had the heart to vote firmly for bed.

'I don't mind where we go,' said Ronnie. 'But why Greenwich in particular? We can see the dawn break over the river just as well at Westminster.'

'Greenwich is in the manner,' Maurice answered.

267

'What manner?'

'The crinoline manner. The Sloop is absolutely typic-
ally mid-Victorian and already twice as romantic as your
crumbling Gothic or overworked Georgian.'

So the taxis hummed off to Greenwich through the
murk of a wet and windy January morning. Waggons were
being unloaded in Covent Garden as they started; and
along the Strand workers were already hurrying through
the rain. It was still too dark to see the river as they spun
over Waterloo Bridge, but the air blew in through the open
windows very freshly. In the New Kent Road factory girls,
shuffling to work, turned to shout after the four taxis; and
Madge Wilson leaned out to wave to the shutters of her
mother's shop as they passed.

All the way Jenny slept in Maurice's arms, and he from
time to time would bend over and kiss very lightly the
sculptured mouth. In Deptford High Street the grey dawn
was beginning to define the houses, and in a rift of the
heavy clouds stars were paling.

Jenny woke up with a start.

'Where am I? Where am I?' Then, aware of Maurice,
she nestled closer.

'You've been asleep, dearest. We're almost at Greenwich.
It's practically morning now.'

'I'm cold.'

'Are you, my sweet? I thought this fur coat would keep
you warm. It's yours, you know. I bought it for you to-day
– yesterday, I mean.'

'It's lovely and warm,' she said, 'but I'm so sleepy.'

'You are so perfect when you're lying asleep,' he said; 'I

must make a statue of you. I shall call it The Tired Dancer. I'll begin as soon as possible and finish it this Spring.'

'I wish Spring would come quick,' she murmured. 'I'm sick of Winter.'

'So am I,' he agreed. 'And we shall have the most exquisite adventures in the spring. We'll go out often into the country. Long country walks will do you good.'

'Rather.'

'Hullo!' cried Maurice. 'Here we are at the Sloop. I hope breakfast is ready.'

There was, however, no sign of life in the hotel by the water's side. It stared at them without any welcome.

'What an extraordinary thing,' said Maurice. 'I'll ring the bell. Great Scott! I never posted the letter telling them about breakfast.'

'What would you do with him?' said Madge.

'Never mind. It's absurd to keep us waiting like this. We can surely get breakfast.' He pealed the bell loudly as he spoke.

'Can't you get in, sir?' asked one of the drivers.

'And it's coming on to rain,' said Jenny.

Maurice pealed the bell louder than ever; and finally a sad-eyed porter in shirt-sleeves opened the door and surveyed the party over a broom.

'We want breakfast,' said Maurice, 'breakfast for eight.'

'Breakfast always is at eight,' the man informed them.

'Breakfast for eight people and as quickly as possible.'

The man looked doubtful.

'Good heavens!' Maurice cried irritably. 'Surely in any decent hotel you can get breakfast for eight.'

269

'What are you?' the man asked. 'Theatricals?'

'No, no, no, we've been to a fancy dress ball – and we want breakfast.'

In the end they were admitted and, a chamber-maid having been discovered on a remote landing, the girls were shown into a bedroom.

'I thought this hotel professed to cater for excursions of pleasure,' said Maurice frigidly.

'We don't get many of 'em here in winter.'

'I'm not surprised. Good lord, isn't the fire lighted in the coffee-room?'

'We don't use the coffee-room much – except for political meetings. Greenwich has gone out from what it used to be.'

The girls came in pale and tired, and the party forgathered round the coffee-room grate, from which a wisp of smoke ascended in steady promise.

'Well, Maurice,' said Castleton, 'I think very little of this ravished conservatory into which your historic sense has led us. How do you like Greenwich, girls?'

The girls all sighed.

'They don't.'

'Hullo, here's a waiter,' said Cunningham, turning round. 'Good morning, waiter.'

'Good morning, sir.'

'Is breakfast going to be long?'

'It's on order, sir. Eggs and bacon, I think you said.'

'I should think somebody probably did. In fact I'd almost bet on it,' said Castleton. 'What's the time, waiter?'

'I don't know, sir, but I'll find out for you.'

'I always thought Greenwich was famous for its time.'

'Whitebait, sir, more than anything.'

Castleton sighed; and Maurice, who had gone downstairs to reassure the household, came back trying to look as if waiting for breakfast on a January morning after dancing all night was one of the jolliest experiences attainable by humanity.

'Maurice,' said Ronnie Walker, 'we think your night was splendid. But we think your morning is rotten.'

'Oh, Maurice, why didn't you let us go to bed?' Jenny grumbled.

'You can't really blame the hotel people,' Maurice began.

'We don't,' interrupted Cunningham severely. 'We blame you.'

'I also blame myself,' said Ronnie, 'for giving way to your mad schemes.'

'You're right,' Jenny put in. 'I think we were all mad. What must they have thought of us – a party of loonies, I should say.'

'I meant it to be very charming,' Maurice urged in apology.

'Oh, well, it'll all come out in the wash, but I wish they'd bring in this unnatural breakfast.'

The company sighed in unison, and, as if encouraged by such an utterance of breath, the wisp of smoke broke into a thin blue flame.

'Come, that's better,' said Maurice, unduly encouraged. 'The fire's burning up quite cheerfully.'

This and the entrance of breakfast revived everybody,

and when a genuine blaze crackled in the grate they thought Greenwich was not so bad after all; though Maurice could not persuade anybody to stand by the bleak windows flecked with raindrops and watch the big ships going out on the ebb.

'But what shall we do?' Jenny demanded. 'I can't go home after the milk. I shall get into a most shocking row.'

'You can explain matters,' Cunningham suggested.

'Yes, I should say. Who'd believe we should be so mad as to rush off to Greenwich on a pouring morning for breakfast? No, I must say I slept with Ireen.'

'Well, why don't you come back and go to bed at my place?' Irene suggested. 'You can go home tea-time.'

'All right. I will.'

Maudie and Madge decided to copy the example of the other two, by going back together to Mrs. Wilson's house near the Elephant and Castle.

'Only we ought to change our clothes first,' Jenny said. 'What of it though? We've got cloaks.'

'I shouldn't mind changing,' said Castleton. 'These claret-coloured overalls of mine will inevitably attract the public vision.'

'Rot!' said Maurice. 'We can all drive down to the Elephant – although, by the way, we ought to stop at the Marquis of Granby and look at the Museum.'

'To the deuce with all museums,' cried Ronnie. 'I want my bed.'

'You are an unsporting lot,' Maurice protested. 'Then we'll stop at the Elephant, and the girls can go home in two taxis and we'll go back in the others.'

So it was arranged; and, having paid the bill and politely assented to the waiter's suggestion that they should come over in the summertime to a whitebait dinner, they left behind them the Sloop Hotel, Greenwich.

On the way back to London, Maurice attempted to point out to Jenny the foolishness of her present style of living.

'All this fuss about whether you go home before or after the milk. I can't understand why you let yourself be a slave to a family. I really can't.'

'But I'm not,' said Jenny indignantly. 'Only that doesn't say I'm going to live with you, if that's what you mean.'

Somehow the wet and dreary morning gave a certain crudity of outline to the situation, destroying romantic enchantments and accentuating the plain and ugly facts.

'You'd be ever so much happier if you did.'

'Oh, well, who cares?'

'I wish you wouldn't say that.'

'Well, what an unnatural time to talk about where I'm going to live and what I'm going to do.'

'It's extraordinary,' said Maurice, 'how much you're influenced by the unimportant little things of life. I'm as much in love with you now as I was last night when we were waltzing. You're not.'

'I don't love anything now except bed.'

'Yet I'm just as tired as you are.'

'Who cares?'

'Damn it, don't go on saying that. I can't think where you got hold of that infernal expression.'

'You *are* in a nasty mood,' said Jenny sullenly.

'So are you.'

'Well, why did you drag me out all this way in the early morning?'

'I wanted you to enjoy yourself. I wanted to round off a glorious evening.'

'I think a jolly good sleep rounds off a glorious evening, or anything else, best of all.'

'I think you sleep too much,' argued Maurice, who was so tired himself that he felt bound to contest futilely every point of the discussion.

'Well, I don't. That's where you and me don't agree.'

'You're always sleeping.'

'Well, if I like it, it needn't trouble you.'

'Nothing troubles me,' Maurice answered with much austerity. 'Only I wish to goodness you'd behave reasonably. Look here, you're an artistic person. You earn your living by dancing. You don't want to take up with a lot of old women's notions of morality. If you reject an experience, you'll suffer for it. Chance only offers you Life – I mean Life only offers you Chance—' But it did not matter much what he meant, for by now Jenny was fast asleep.

XXI

Epilogue

Jenny went to bed at Irene's house in Camden Town and slept soundly till four o'clock in the afternoon. Then she got up, dressed herself and prepared to face the storms of 17 Hagworth Street.

When she walked into the kitchen, the family was assembled in conclave round the tea-table. The addition of her brother to the usual party of three made her exclaim in surprise from the doorway:

'Oo-er, there's Alfie.'

'So you've come back?' said Mrs. Raeburn.

'Yes, I went to Covent Garden Ball.'

'I wonder you dare show your face.'

'Why not?' asked Jenny, advancing towards the table.

'Oh, leave her alone, mother,' said May. 'She's tired.'

'You dare tell me what I'm to do,' Mrs. Raeburn threatened, turning sharply to her youngest daughter.

Jenny began to unbutton her gloves, loftily unconscious of her mother's gaze which was again directed upon her.

'How's yourself, young Alf?' she lightly enquired.

'Better than you, I hope,' came the morose reply muffled by a teacup.

'Perhaps you'd like us to help you off with your things?' Mrs. Raeburn suggested sarcastically.

'Eh?' Jenny retorted, pointing a cold insolence of manner with arched contemptuous eyebrows.

'Don't you try and defy me, miss,' Mrs. Raeburn warned her. 'Because you know I won't have it.'

'Who cares? I haven't done nothing.'

Alfie guffawed ironically.

'I wonder you aren't afraid to make a noise like that with such long ears as you've got,' said Jenny. 'I should be.'

Alfie muttered something about sauce under his breath, but ventured no audible retort.

'Well, what's the matter?' Jenny asked. 'Get it over and done with.'

'Where were you last night?'

'I told you. At Covent Garden Ball.'

'And afterwards?'

'I went home with Ireen.'

'And that's a bloody lie,' shouted Alfie. 'Because I saw you go off with a fellah.'

'What of it, Mr. Nosy Parker? And don't use your navvy's language to me, because I don't like it.'

'That's quite right,' May agreed. 'He ought to be ashamed of himself.'

'You shut up, silly kid,' Alfie commanded.

Here Charlie entered the dispute.

'There's no call to swear, Alf. I can argue without swearing and so can you.'

'It was you that learned him to swear. He's heard you

often enough,' Mrs. Raeburn pointed out. 'But that's no reason why Alfie should.'

Jenny, more insolently contemptuous than ever, interrupted the side-issue:

'When you've finished arguing which is the biggest lady and gentleman in this room, perhaps you'll let me finish what I was going to say.'

'I'd hold my tongue if I was you,' her brother advised. 'You're as bad as Edie, with more swank.'

'Don't talk to me. You!' said Jenny, stamping with rage. 'You, all hair-oil, a walking Woodbine.' Then, with head thrown back and defiant underlip, she continued:

'That's quite right about my driving off with a gentleman.' In the tail of the 'g' was whipcord for Alfie's self-esteem.

'Gentleman,' he sneered.

'*Which* is more than *you* could ever be, any old way.'

'Or want to,' Alfie growled. 'Thanks, I'm quite content with what I am.'

'You can't have many looking-glasses down at your workshop then. Look at Mr. Quite Content. How much do they pay you a week to be all the time spying after your sister?'

'Well, anyway, I caught you out, my girl.'

'No, you didn't. I say I *did* drive off with a gentleman, but there was a crowd of us. We went to have breakfast at Greenwich.'

'Now that's a place I've often meant to go to and never did,' said Charlie. 'What's it like?'

'You keep quiet, you silly old man,' his wife commanded. 'As if she went near Greenwich. What a tale!'

'It isn't a tale,' Jenny declared. 'I did. Ask Maudie Chapman and Madge Wilson and Ireen. They were all there.'

'Oh, I don't doubt they're just as quick with their tongues as what you are,' said Mrs. Raeburn. 'A nice lot you meet at that theatre.'

'Jest leave the theatre alone,' her daughter answered. 'It's better than this dog's island where no one can't let you alone for a minute because they're so ignorant that they don't know nothing. I say I did go to Greenwich.'

'I don't see why the girl shouldn't have gone to Greenwich,' Charlie interposed. 'I keep telling you I've often thought of going there myself.'

'Jenny never speaks only what's the truth,' May asserted.

'Yes, and a lot of good it does me,' said Jenny indignantly. 'I'd better by half tell a pack of lies, the same as other girls do.'

'What she wants,' said Alfie sententiously, 'is a jolly good hiding. Look at her. There's a fine sister for a chap to have – nothing but paint and powder and hair-dye, looking like a tart.'

Jenny stood silent under this; but the upper lip was no longer visible. Her cheeks were pale: her eyes mere points of light. May was the first to speak in defence of the silent one.

'Brothers!' she scoffed. 'Some girls would be a sight better without brothers. Hateful things!'

Jenny's feelings had been so overwrought by the fatigue of the dance followed by this domestic scene that May's gallant sally should have turned contempt to tears. But

Alfie had enraged her too profoundly for weeping, and though tear-drops stood in her eyes, they were hard as diamonds.

'You oughtn't to talk to her like that, my boy,' Charlie protested. 'You're talking like a clergymen I once did some work for. He said, "I'm not satisfied with this here box, Mr. Raeburn" – well, he said more than that – and I said, "I'm not satisfied with your tone of voice," and—'

'For goodness' sake, Charlie, keep your tongue quiet,' his wife begged. 'Look here, Jenny,' she went on, 'I won't have these hours kept, and that's all about it. Wherever you were last night, you weren't at home where you ought to be, and where you shall be as long as you live with me. Now that's all about it, and don't give me any back-answers, because I know what's right and I'm your mother.'

'I think you're a bit hard on the girl, Florrie, I do really,' said the father. 'She takes after her dad. I was always one for seeing a bit of life. What I says is, "Let the young enjoy themselves."'

'What you say is neither here nor there,' replied Mrs. Raeburn. 'You never did have any sense, you haven't got any sense now, and you never will have any sense.'

'When you've done nagging at one another, all of *you*, I'm off,' said Jenny deliberately.

'Off?' Mrs. Raeburn echoed.

'I'm going to live at Ireen Dale's for the future. This!' She looked round the kitchen. 'Pooh!'

'You're not going to leave home?' Mrs. Raeburn asked.

'Aren't I? Who says so? I'm going now. You!' she said

279

bitterly to her brother. 'You've done a lot, Mr. Interfering Idiot. It's time you looked about for some girl to marry you, so as you can poke your nose into her business. Goodbye, all. I'll come over to tea soon, that is if you aren't all ashamed to have tea with a tart.'

As she turned abruptly to go, Alfie asked his mother why she didn't lock her in a bedroom.

'It wouldn't be any good,' said the latter.

'No, it wouldn't,' Jenny vowed. 'I'd kill myself sooner than sleep here another night.'

'You're a dreadful worry to me,' said Mrs. Raeburn slowly and earnestly.

'Send on my things to 43 Stacpole Terrace, Camden Town,' replied the daughter. 'You needn't think you'll get me back by keeping them, because you won't.'

'You'll come and see us?' asked Mrs. Raeburn, who seemed now to accept defeat meekly.

'Yes, as long as you keep Mr. Nosy Parker Puppydog outside. Brother! Why if you only knew, he wears that jam-pot round his neck to hide where his head's come off.'

Presently the front door slammed.

XXII

The Unfinished Statue

Maurice, on being informed of the decisive step which Jenny had taken, asked her why she had not taken the more decisive step of avowing his protection.

'Because I don't want to. Not yet. I can't explain why. But I don't. Oh, Maurice, don't go on asking me any more.'

'It's nothing to do with your people. Because you evidently don't mind hurting their feelings in another way.'

'Going to live at Ireen's isn't the same as living with you.'

'You needn't live with me openly. Nobody wants you to do that. Only—'

'It's not a bit of good your going on,' she interrupted. 'I've told you I will one day.'

'One day,' he sighed.

It was a fine February that year, coming in with a stir of Spring. Maurice felt in accord with the season's impulse, and became possessed with the ambition to create a work of art. He suggested that Jenny should come daily to the studio and sit for his statue of The Tired Dancer.

'I'm sure my real vocation is plastic,' he declared. 'I can write and I can play, but neither better than a lot of other people. With sculpture it's different. To begin with, there isn't such competition. It's the least general of the arts, although in another sense it's the most universal. Again, it's an art that we seem to have lost. Yet by every rule of social history, it is the art with which the present stage of evolution should be most occupied. In this era of noise and tear the splendid quiescence of great sculpture should provoke every creative mind. I have the plastic impulse, but so far I've been content to fritter it away in bits and pieces of heads and arms and hands. I must finish something; make something.'

Jenny was content to sit watching him through blue wreaths of cigarette smoke. She found a sensuous delight in seeing him happy and hearing the flow of his excited talk.

'Now I must mould you, Jenny,' he went on, pacing up and down in the midst of the retinue of resolutions and intentions. 'By gad! I'm thrilled by the thought of it. To possess you in virgin wax, to mould your delicious shape with my own hands, to see you taking form at my compelling touch. By gad! I'm thrilled by it. What's a lyric after that? I could pour my heart out in every metre imaginable, but I should never give anything more than myself to the world. But if I make a glorious statue of you, I give you – you for ever and ever for men to gaze at and love and desire. By gad! I'm thrilled by the thought of it. There's objective art. Ha! Poor old poets with their words. Where are they? You can't dig your nails into a word. By Jove, the Nereids in the British Museum. You remember those Nereids, darling?'

Jenny looked blank.

'Yes, you do. You said how much you liked them. You must remember them, so light and airy that they seem more like clouds or blowballs than solid marble.'

'I think *all* the statues we saw were very light and airy, if it comes to that,' said Jenny.

Maurice gave up pacing round the room and flung himself into a chair to discuss details of the conception.

'Of course, I'd like you to be dressed as a Columbine: and yet, I don't know, it's rather obvious.'

'I could wear my practice dress.'

'What's that like?'

'I've got two or three. Only the nicest is my grey tarlington.'

'Eh?'

'You know, very frilly musling. Just like a ballet skirt, only you needn't wear tights.'

'I didn't hear what you said. I know, tarlatan. Nice frizzy stuff. That sounds good. And it won't matter crumpling it?'

'Of course not.'

'Because, you see, I want you to be lying on a pile of rugs and cushions just as if you'd been dancing hard and had fallen asleep where you sank down.'

So, in the time of celandines and snowdrops, Jenny would come to the studio every day; and when they had lunched together intimately and delightfully, she would go downstairs to change her frock, while Maurice arranged her resting-place.

The dove-grey tarlatan skirt, resilient like the hair-spring of a watch, suited the poise of Jenny's figure. She wore grey silk stockings clocked with vivid pink, a crêpe de Chine blouse the colour of mist, and round her head a fillet of rosy velvet. Altogether, she looked an Ariel woven magically from the smoke of London. Once or twice she actually fell fast asleep among the rugs; but generally she lay in a dream, just conscious of the flow of Maurice's comments and rhapsodies.

'It's an extraordinary thing,' he began on one occasion, 'but as I sit here fashioning your body out of wax, you yourself become every moment more and more of a spirit. I've a queer fancy working in my brain all the time that this is really you, here under my hands. I suppose it's the perpetual concentration on one object that puts everything else out of proportion. One thing, however, I do realize: you're making yourself every day more necessary to my life. Honestly, when you're not here, this studio is infernal. You seem to endow it with your presence, to infuse it with your personality. It's so romantic, you and I all alone on the tops of the houses, more alone than if we were on a beach in winter. I wish I could tell you the glorious satisfaction I feel all the time.'

'Darling,' she murmured drowsily.

'Sleepy girl are you?'

'A bit.'

Just then a knock came at the door, and Ronnie Walker looked in.

'Hullo, Ronnie,' said Maurice, with a hint of ungraciousness in his tone.

'I say, old chap, would you think me an intrusive scoundrel if I made some drawings of Jenny?'

Maurice's annoyance at interruption was mollified by the pride of ownership.

'Rather not. Any time. Why not now?'

So Ronnie sat there, making little *croquis* of Jenny with soft outlines elusive as herself. After a while, with his sketch-book under his arm, he stole quietly from the room. The next day he came back with two water-colours of which the first showed a room shadowy with dawn and Jenny fast asleep before a silver mirror, wrapped in a cloak of clouded blue satin. The second represented a bedroom darkened by jalousies faintly luminous with the morning light, while through one chink, glittering with motes, a narrow sunbeam made vivid her crimson lips.

The painter showed his pictures to Maurice.

'Oh, Ronnie,' said the latter. 'You put me out of temper with my own work.'

'My dear chap, I'm awfully sorry,' apologized Ronnie, and, without waiting, hurried from the studio.

'Whatever's the matter?' asked Jenny, woke up by this brief interview.

'I wish people wouldn't come in and interrupt me when I'm at work,' Maurice grumbled. 'It's frightfully inconsiderate. You don't want to look at damned paintings when you're working in another medium.'

'Who were they of?'

'You, of course.'

'Why didn't he show them to me?'

'Because I jumped down his throat, I suppose.'

'Whatever for?'

'Can't you understand how annoying it must be to have to look at another person's treatment of your subject?'

'I think it was very nasty of you not to let him show me the pictures.'

'You seem more interested in Ronnie's work than in mine.'

'Well, you never let me look at what you've done.'

'It isn't finished yet.'

'You *can* be horrid.'

'Look here, Jenny, for goodness' sake don't start criticizing me. I can't stand it. I never could. I've noticed lately you've taken to it.'

'Oh, I've not.'

'Well, you give me that impression.'

Jenny rose from the cushions and, running her hands down the tarlatan till it regained its buoyancy, she moved slowly across to Maurice's side.

'Kiss me, you silly old thing, and don't say any more unkind things, because they make me unhappy.'

Maurice could not be disdainful of her as, leaning over him, she clasped cool hands beneath his chin and with tender kisses up-rooted from his forehead a maze of petulant lines.

'You little enchanting thing,' he murmured. 'You disarm me with your witcheries.'

'And he's not going to be cross any more.'

'He can't be. Alas, my sweet one is too sweet.'

'If you only knew what it meant for Jenny Pearl to be the soppy one.'

'That's love,' Maurice explained.

'Is it? I suppose it is.'

The sunshine of February was extinguished by a drench of rain. March came in with storms of sleet followed by a long stretch of dry easterly gales, when the studio, full of firelight and daffodils, was a pleasant refuge from the grey winds. After Ronnie's visit the statue had been put aside for a while; the lovers spent most of their time in hearthrug conversations, when Jenny would prattle inconsequently of youthful days and Maurice would build up a wonderful future. Vexatious riddles of conduct were ignored like the acrostics of old newspapers, and Jenny was happier than she had ever been. Her nature had always demanded a great deal from the present. Occurrences the most trivial impressed themselves deeply upon her mind, and it was this zest for the ephemeral which made her recollections of the past so lively. As a natural corollary to this habit of mind, she was profoundly deficient in speculation or foresight. The future exhausted her imagination at once: her intellect gasped long before she reached the prospect of eternity. A month made her brain reel.

Having succeeded in postponing all discussion of their mutual attitude, Jenny set out to enjoy the present which endowed her with Maurice's company, with fragrant intimacies and long, contented hours. He himself was most charming when responsibilities whether of art or life were laid aside. Jenny, a butterfly herself, wanted nothing better than to play in the air with another butterfly.

Then Maurice suddenly woke up to the fact that, Summer being imminent, no more time must be wasted. Work on the statue was resumed in a fever of industry.

April came in more like a beldame than a maid. In the studio, now full of rose-pink tulips, the statue rapidly progressed. One morning April threw off her disguises and danced like a fairy.

'I shall finish the model to-day,' Maurice announced.

The sun went in and out all the afternoon. Now the windows were a-wash with showers; in a moment they were sparkling in a radiancy.

'Finished,' the artist cried, and dragged Jenny to look and admire.

'Jolly fine,' she declared. 'Only it isn't very like me. Never mind, position in life's everything,' she added, as she contemplated her sleeping form.

'Not like you,' said Maurice slowly. 'You're right. It's not! Not a bit! Damn art!' he cried, and, picking up the wax model, flung it with a crash into the fire-place.

Jenny looked at Maurice, perplexity and compassion striving with disapproval in her countenance; then she knelt to rescue a curved arm, letting it fall back listlessly among the other fragments when she realized the ruin.

'You *are* mad. Whatever did you want to do that for?'

'You're right. It's not you. Oh, why did I ever try? Ronnie could do it with a box of damned paints. Why couldn't I? I know you better than Ronnie does. I love you. I adore every muscle and vein in your body. I dream day and night of the line of your nose. Why couldn't I have given that in stone, when Ronnie could show the world your mouth with two dabs of carmine? What a box of trickery life is. Here am I burning with ambition to create a masterpiece. I fall in love with a masterpiece. I have every opportunity,

288

a flaming inspiration and nothing comes of it. Nothing. Absolutely nothing. But, by Jove, something must. Do you hear, Jenny? I won't be put off any longer. If I can't possess your counterpart, I must possess you.'

During this speech a storm of hail was drumming on the windows; but while Maurice strained her to his heart in a long silence, the storm passed and the sun streamed into the warm, quiet room. On the window-sill a solitary sparrow cheeped at regular intervals, and down in the street children were bowling iron hoops that fell very often.

'Jenny, Jenny,' pleaded Maurice, relaxing the closeness of his embrace. 'Don't play at love any more. Think what a mistake, what a wicked mistake it is to let so much of our time go by. Don't drive me mad with impatience. You foolish little girl, can't you understand what a muddle you're making of life?'

'I want to wait till I'm twenty-one,' she said.

It meant nothing to her, this date; but Maurice, accepting it as an actual pledge of surrender, could only rail against her unreasonableness.

'Good heavens! What for? You are without exception the most amazing creature? Twenty-one! Why twenty-one? Why not fifty-one? Most of all, why not now?'

'I can't. Not now. Not when I've just left home. I should feel a sneak. Don't ask me to, Maurice. If you love me, as you say you do, you'll wait a little while quite happy.'

'But don't you want to give yourself to me?'

'I do, and then again I don't. Sometimes I think I will, and then sometimes I think I don't want to give myself to any man.'

'You don't love me.'

'Yes, I do. I do. Only I hate men. I always have. I can't explain more than what I've told you. If you can't understand, you can't. It's because you don't know girls.'

'Don't know girls,' he repeated, staggered by the assertion. 'Of course I understand your point of view, but I think it's stupid and irrational and dangerous – yes – dangerous . . . Don't know girls? I wish I didn't.'

'You don't,' Jenny persisted.

'My dear child, I know girls too well. I know their wretched stammering temperaments, their inability to face facts, their lust for sentiment, their fondness for going half-way and turning back.'

'I wish you wouldn't keep on walking up and down. It makes me want to giggle. And when I laugh, you get angry.'

'Laugh! It is a laughing matter to you. To me it's something so serious, so sacred, that laughter no longer exists.'

Jenny thought for a moment.

'I believe,' she began, 'I should laugh whatever happened. I don't believe anything would stop me laughing.'

Just then, away downstairs, the double knock of a telegraph boy was heard, too far away to shake the nerves of Jenny and Maurice, but still sufficiently a reminder of another life outside their own to interrupt the argument.

'I wonder if that's for me,' said Maurice.

'You'd better go down and see, if you think it is.'

'Wait a minute. Old Mother Wadman may answer the door.'

Again, far below, they heard the summons of humanity.

'Damn Mrs. Wadman. I wish she wouldn't go fooling out in the afternoon.'

'Why don't you go down, Maurice? He'll go away in a minute.'

Once more, very sharply, the herald demanded an entrance for events and emotions independent of their love, and Maurice unwillingly departed to admit them.

Left alone in a tumult of desires and repressions, Jenny felt she would like to fling herself down upon the rugs and cry. Sentiment, for an instant, helped the cause of tears, when she thought of the many hours spent on that pile, drowsily happy. Then backwards and forwards went the image of her lover in ludicrous movement, and the whole situation seemed such a fuss about nothing. There was a merciless clarity about Jenny's comprehension when, urged by scenes of passion, she called upon her mind for a judgment. Perhaps it was the fatalism of an untrained reason which taught her to grasp the futility of emotional strife. Or it may have been what is called a sense of humour, which always from one point of view must imply a lack of imagination.

Maurice came back and handed her the telegram:

Uncle Stephen died suddenly in Seville come home at once you must go out and look after aunt Ella please dear Mother

'She's fond of you, isn't she?'

Maurice looked puzzled.

'Your mother, I mean.'

'Why?'

'I don't know. I think she's written very nice, that's all. I wish you hadn't got to go away though.'

'Yes, and to Spain of all places. This is the uncle I was telling you about. I come into two thousand pounds. I must go.'

'I wish you hadn't got to go away,' she repeated sorrowfully. 'Just when the weather's getting fine too. But you must go, of course,' she added.

Jenny wrung this bidding out of herself very hardly, but Maurice accepted it casually enough. Suddenly he was seized with an idea:

'Jenny, this two thousand pounds is the key to the situation.'

'What?'

'Of course I can,' he assured the air. 'I can settle this on you. I can provide for you, whatever happens to me. Now there's absolutely no reason why you shouldn't give way.'

'I don't see that two thousand pounds makes *any* difference. What do you think I am?'

'I'm not buying you, my dear girl. I'm not such a fool as to suppose I could do that.'

'No, you couldn't. No man could buy me.'

'I'm very glad of it,' he said. 'What I mean is that now I've no scruples of my own to get over. This is certain. I know that if anything happens to me, you would be all right. Jenny, you must say "yes." '

'I've told you I will one day. Don't keep on asking. Besides, you're going away. You'll have other things to think about besides your little Jenny. Only come back soon, Maurice, because I do love you so.'

'Love me!' he scoffed. 'Love me! Rot! A woman without the pluck to trust herself to the lover talks of love. It means nothing, this love of yours. It's just a silly fancy. Love hasn't widened your horizon. Love hasn't given your life any great impetus. Look at me – absolutely possessed by my love for you. That's passion.'

'I don't think it's much else, I don't,' said Jenny.

'How like a girl. How exactly like every other girl. Good lord, and I thought you were different. I thought you wouldn't be so blind as to separate love from passion.'

'I don't. I do love you. I do want you,' she whispered. 'Just as much as you want me, but not now. Oh, Maurice, I wish you could understand.'

'Well, I can't,' he said coldly. 'Look here, you've quarrelled with your mother. That's one obstacle out of the way.'

'But it isn't. She's still alive.'

'You've known me long enough to be sure I'm not likely to turn out a rotter. You needn't worry about money, and – you love me or pretend to. Now why in the name of fortune can't you be sensible?'

'But there'll come a moment, Maurice darling, and I think it will come soon, when I shall say "yes" of my own accord. And whatever you said or done before that moment couldn't make me say "yes" now.'

'And meanwhile I'm to go on wearing myself out with asking?'

'No,' she murmured, afire with blushes at such revelation of himself. 'No, I'll say "Maurice" and then you'll know.'

'And I'm to go off to Spain with nothing to hope for but "one day, one day"?'

'You'll have other things to think about there?'

'You're rather amusing with your proposed diversions for my imagination. But, seriously, will it be "yes" when I come back, say, in a fortnight?'

'No, not yet. Not for a little while. Oh, don't ask me any more; you are unkind.'

Maurice seemed to give up the pursuit suddenly.

'I shan't see you for some time,' he said.

'Never mind,' Jenny consoled him. 'Think how lovely it will be when we do see each other.'

'Goodbye,' said Maurice bluntly.

'Oh, what an unnatural way to say goodbye.'

'Well, I've got to pack up and catch the 6.30 down to Claybridge. I'll write to you.'

'You needn't trouble,' she told him, chilled by his manner.

'Don't be foolish, I must write. Goodbye, Jenny.'

He seemed to offer his embrace more from habit than desire.

'I've got to change first,' she said, making no movement towards the enclosure of his arms. It struck them both that they had passed through a thousand emotions, he in the sculptor's blouse of his affectation, she in her tarlatan skirt.

'It's like a short story by de Maupassant,' said Maurice.

'Is it? You and your likes! I'm like a soppy girl.'

'You are,' said Maurice with intention. To Jenny, for the first time, he seemed to be criticizing her.

'Thanks,' she said, as with a shrug of the shoulder and curl of the lip, she walked out of the studio, coldly hostile.

The rage was too deep to prevent her from arranging her hair with deliberation. Nor did she fumble over a single hook in securing the skirt of ordinary life. Soon Maurice was tapping at the door, but she could not answer him.

'Jenny,' he called, 'I've come to say I'm a pig.'

Still she did not answer; but when she was perfectly ready, flung open the door and said tonelessly:

'Please let me pass.'

Her eyes, resentful, their lustre fled, were dull as lapis lazuli. Her lips were no longer visible.

'You mustn't go away like this. Jenny, we shan't see one another for a fortnight or more. Don't let's part bad friends.'

'Please let me pass.'

He stood aside, outfaced by such determination, and Jenny, with downcast eyes intent upon the buttoning of her glove, passed him carelessly.

'Jenny!' he called desperately over the banisters. 'Jenny! Don't go like that. Darling, don't; I can't bear it.' Then he ran to catch her by the arm.

'Kiss me goodbye and be friends. Do, Jenny. Jenny! Do! Please! I can't bear to see your practice dress lying there on the floor.'

Sentiment had its way this time, and Jenny began to cry.

'Oh, Maurice,' she wept. 'Why are you so unkind to me? I hate myself for spoiling you so, but I must. I don't care about anything excepting you. I do love you, Maurice.'

In the dusty passage they were friends again.

'And now my eyes is all red,' she lamented.

'Never mind, darling girl. Come back while I get some things together, and see me off at Waterloo, will you?'

She assented, and enlaced they went up again to the studio.

'It's all the fault of that rotten statue,' he explained. 'I was furious with myself and vented it on you. Never mind. I'll begin again when I come back. Look, we'll put the tarlatan away in the drawer I take my things out of. Shall we?'

Soon they were driving in a hansom cab towards the railway station.

'We always seem to wind up our quarrels in cabs,' Maurice observed.

'I don't know why we quarrel. I hate quarrelling.'

'We won't any more.'

As the horse strained up through the echoing cavern of Waterloo, they kissed each other goodbye, a long, long kiss.

There were still ten minutes before the train left, and among the sweep of hurrying passengers and noise of shouting porters to an accompaniment of whistling, rumbling trains, Maurice tried to voice the immortality of his love.

'Great Scott, I've only a minute,' he said suddenly. 'Look, meet me on Monday week, the twenty-third, here, at three-thirty. Three-thirty from Claybridge. Don't forget.'

'Take your seats, please,' a ticket inspector shouted in their ears. Maurice jumped into his compartment and wrote quickly on an envelope: '3.30. Waterloo. Ap. 23. Claybridge.'

'Goodbye, darling, darling girl. I'll bring you back some castanets and a Spanish frock.'

'Goodbye. See you soon.'

'Very, very soon. Think of me.'

'Rather.'

The train went curling out of the station.

'I shall be early in the theatre to-night,' Jenny thought.

XXIII

Two Letters

Hôtel de Paris, Sevilla, Spain.
April 17.

My dear and lovely one,

I've not had time to write before. I meant to send you a letter from the train, but I left all my notepaper and pencils in the station restaurant at a place called Miranda, and went to sleep instead.

I find that my uncle has left me more than I expected – five thousand pounds, in fact. So I want to buy you a delightful little house somewhere quite close to London. You could have a maid and you could go on dancing if you liked. Only I do want you to say Yes at once. I want you to write by return and tell me you're going to give up all doubts and worries and scruples. Will you, my precious?

I've got another splendid plan. I want you to come and join me in Spain in about a week. I shall be able to meet you in Paris, because I am going to escort my aunt so far on the way home. Fuz will look out your trains. You must *come. He can arrange to give you any money you want. We need not stay away very long – about a month. Sevilla is perfect. The weather is divine. Get yourself some cool frocks. We'll sit in*

the Alcazar garden all day. It's full of lemon trees and foun-
tains. In the evening we'll sit on a balcony and smoke and
listen to guitars.

My darling, I do so adore you. Please, please, come out to
Spain and give up not knowing your own mind. I miss you
tremendously. I feel this beautiful city is wasted without you.
I'm sure if you determined not to bother about anything but
love, you'd never regret it. You wouldn't really. Dearest,
sweetest Jenny, do come. I'm longing for my treasure. It's
wonderfully romantic sitting here in the patio of the hotel – a
sort of indoor garden – and thinking so hard of my gay and
sweet one away in London. Darling, I'm sending you kisses
thick as stars, all the way from Spain. All my heart.

Your lover,

Maurice.

Jenny was lying in bed when she received this letter. The
unfamiliar stamp and crackling paper suited somehow
the bedroom at Stacpole Terrace to which she was not yet
accustomed. Such a letter containing such a request would
have seemed very much out of place in the little room she
shared at home with May. Here, so dismal was the prospect of life, she felt inclined to abandon everything and
join her lover.

The Dales were a slovenly family. Mr. Dale himself was
a nebulous creature whom rumour had endowed with
a pension. It never specified for what services nor even
stated the amount in plain figures; and a more widely
extended belief that the household was maintained by
the Orient management through Winnie and Irene Dale's

dancing, supplanted the more dignified tradition. Mr. Dale was generally comatose on a flock-exuding chair-bed in what was known as 'dad's room.' There in the dust, surrounded by a fortification of dented hatboxes, he perused old Sunday newspapers whose mildewed leaves were destroyed biennially like Canterbury Bells. Mrs. Dale was a beady-eyed, round woman with a passion for bonnets, capes, soliloquies and gin. Her appearance and her manners were equally unpleasant. She possessed a batch of grievances of which the one most often aired was her missing of the Clacton Belle one Sunday morning four years ago. Jenny disliked her more completely than anybody in the world, regarding her merely as something too large and too approximately human to extirpate. Winnie Dale, the smoothed-out replica of her mother, was equally obnoxious. She had long lost all the comeliness which still distinguished Irene, and possessed an irritating habit of apostrophizing her affection for a fishmonger – some prosperous libertine who occasionally cast an eye, glazed like one of his own cod's, at Jenny herself. Ethel, the third sister, was still in short frocks because her intelligence had not kept pace with her age.

'The poor little thing talks like a child,' Mrs. Dale would explain. 'So I dresses her like a child. It's less noticeable.'

'*Which* is silly,' Jenny used to comment. 'Because she's as tall as a house and *everybody* turns round to look after her.'

Jenny would scarcely have tolerated this family for a week, if she had been brought at all closely or frequently into contact with them; but so much of the day was spent

with Maurice and all the evening at the theatre that
Stacpole Terrace implied little beyond breakfast in bed
and bed itself. Sometimes, indeed, when she went home to
tea at Hagworth Street and saw the brightness of the glass
and shimmer of clean crockery, she was on the verge of
sinking her pride in a practical reconciliation. Nine weeks
passed, however, making it more difficult every day to
admit herself in the wrong; although, during the absence
of Maurice, it became a great temptation. Therefore when
this letter arrived from Spain, inviting her to widen the
breach with her family, she was half inclined to play with
the idea of absolute severance. Flight, swift and sudden,
appealed to her until the difficulty of making arrangements
began to obscure other considerations. The thought of
packing, of catching trains and steamers, of not knowing
exactly what frocks to buy, oppressed her; then a fear took
hold of her fancy lest, something happening to Maurice,
she might find herself alone in a foreign city; and at the
end of it all there was her childhood in a vista of time, her
childhood with the presence of her mother brooding over
it, her mother dearly loved whatever old-fashioned notions
she preserved of obedience and strictness of behaviour. It
would be mean to outrage, as she knew she would, her
mother's pride, and to hand her over to the criticisms of
a mob of relatives. It would be mean to desert May, who
even now might be crying on a solitary pillow. But when
she went downstairs dressed and saw the Dale family in
morning deshabille, uncorseted, flabby and heavy-eyed,
crouching over the parlour fire, and when she thought
of Maurice and the empty studio, Jenny's resolution was

shaken and she was inclined to renounce every duty, face every difficulty and leave her world behind.

'You do look a sulky thing,' said Irene. 'Coming to sit round the fire?'

'No, thanks,' said Jenny, 'I haven't got the time.'

'Your young chap's away, isn't he?' asked Winnie.

'What's it got to do with you where he is?'

Jenny was in a turmoil of nervous indecision, and felt that whatever else she did, she must be quit of Stacpole Terrace for that day at least. She debated the notion of going home, of telling her mother everything; but the imagination of such an exposure of her most intimate thoughts dried her up. It would be like taking off her clothes in front of a crowd of people. Then she thought of going home without reference to the past; but she was prevented by the expectation of her mother's readiness to believe the worst, and the inevitably stricter supervision to which her submission would render her liable. In the end, she compromised with her inclination by deciding to visit Edie and find out what sort of sturdy rogue her nephew was by now.

Edie lived at Camberwell in a small house covered with Virginia creeper not yet in leaf, still a brownish red mat which depressed Jenny as she rattled the flap of the letter-box and called her sister's name through the aperture. Presently Edie opened the door.

'Why if it isn't Jenny. Well I never, you are a stranger.'

Edie was shorter than Jenny and more round. Yet for all her plumpness she looked worn, and her slanting eyes, never so bright as Jenny's, were ringed with purple cavities.

'How are you, Edie, all this long time?'

'Oh, I'm grand; how's yourself?'

'I'm all right.'

The two sisters were sitting in the parlour, which smelt unused, although it was covered with lengths of material and brown-paper patterns. By the window was a dress-maker's bust, mournfully buxom. Jenny compared it with the lay figure in the studio and smiled, thinking how funny they would look together.

'I wish Bert was in,' said Edie. 'But he's away on business.'

Just then a sound of tears was audible, and the mother had to run out of the room.

'The children gets a nuisance,' she said, as she came back comforting Eunice, a little girl of two.

'Isn't she growing up a little love?' said Jenny. 'Oh, I do think she's pretty. What glorious eyes she's got.'

'They're like her father's, people say; but young Norman, he's the walking life-like of you, Jenny.'

'Where is the rogue?' his aunt enquired.

'Where's Norman, Eunice?'

'Out in the garding digging gwaves,' said Eunice in a fat voice.

Jenny had a sudden longing to have a child of her own and live in a little house quite close to London.

'Why, I don't believe you've ever seen Baby,' said Edie.

'Of course I have, but not for some months.'

They went upstairs to look at Baby, who was lying asleep in his cot. Jenny felt oppressed by the smallness of the bedroom and the many enlargements of Bert's likeness in youth which dwarfed every other ornament. They recurred everywhere in extravagantly gilt frames; and the original photograph was on the chest of drawers opposite one of Edie wearing a fringe and balloon sleeves.

'There's another coming in five months,' said Edie.

'Go on. How many more?'

'I don't know – plenty yet, I expect.'

The magic home that for a few moments had enchanted the little house was dispelled. Moreover, at tea Norman smeared his face with jam, and snatched, and kicked his mother because she slapped his wrist.

'Why do you let him behave so bad?' asked Jenny, unconscious that she was already emulating her own hated Aunt Mabel.

'I don't, only he's such a handful; and his dad spoils him. Besides, anything for a bit of peace and quiet. Bert never thinks what a worry children is, and as if I hadn't got enough to look after, he brought back a dog last week.'

'Why didn't you tell him off?'

'Oh, it's easier to humour him. You'll find that out quick enough when you're married yourself.'

'Me married? I don't think.'

On the way to the theatre that evening Jenny almost made up her mind to join Maurice, and would probably have been constant to her resolve, had it not been for one of those trivial incidents which more often than great events change the whole course of a life.

Because she did not like the idea of sitting in meditation opposite a row of inquisitive faces, she took a seat outside the tramcar that came swaying and clanging down the Camberwell New Road. It was twilight by now and, as the tramcar swung round into Kennington Gate, there was a wide view of the sky full of purple cloudbanks, islands in a pale blue luminous sea where the lights of ships could easily be conjured from the uncertain stars contending with the afterglow of an April sunset. Jenny sat on the back seat and watched along the Kennington Road the incandescent gas suffuse room after room with a sickly phosphorescence in which the inhabitants seemed to swim like fish in an aquarium. All the rooms thus illuminated looked alike. All the windows had a fretwork of lace curtains; all the tables were covered with black and red chequered cloths on which was superimposed half a white cloth covered with the remains of tea; all the flower vases wore crimped paper petticoats; all the people inside the cheerless rooms looked tired.

Jenny pulled out the foreign letter and read of sunlight and love. She began to visualize herself with a red rosebud in her mouth, to hear the melodious clap of castanets and toreadors singing. She began to dream of kisses amid surroundings something like the principal scene of an Orient ballet, and, as London became more and more intolerably dreary, over her senses stole the odour of a cigar that carried her mind racing back to the past. Somewhere long ago her mother, wanting to go away with someone, had stayed behind; and for the first time Jenny comprehended mistily that now forgotten renunciation. She fell to thinking of her mother tenderly, began to be oblivious of interference, to remember only her merry tales and laughter and kindness. The strength which long ago enabled Mrs. Raeburn to refuse the nice little house and the Ralli car seemed to find a renewed power of expression in her daughter. At present, Jenny thought, kisses in Spain must still be dreams. That night, in the cheerless parlour of the Dales, she wrote in watery ink to Maurice that she could not meet him in Paris.

43 STACPOLE TERRACE, CAMDEN TOWN
Friday.

My darling Maurice,

I cant come to Spain – I cant leave my mother like that – I should feel a sneak – hurry up and come home because I miss you very much all the time – It's no use to wish I could come – But I will tell you about it when you come home – I wish you was here now. With heap's of love from your darling Jenny.

Ireen sends her love and hopes your having a good time.

XXIV

Journey's End

Jenny received a post-card from Maurice in answer to her letter. She was glad he made no attempt to argue a point of view which his absence had already modified more persuasively than any pleading. During the summer, perhaps on one of those expeditions long talked of, she would make him her own with one word; having sacrificed much on account of her mother, she was not prepared to sacrifice all; and when Maurice came back, when she saw his blue eyes quick with love's fires, and knew again the sorcery of hands and breathless enfolding of arms, it would be easy upon his heart to swoon out of everything except compliance. Aglow with tenderness, she wrote a second letter hinting that no chain was wanting but the sight of him to bind her finally and completely. Yet with whatever periphrasis she wrapped it round, the resolve was not to be expressed with a pen. Recorded so, it seemed to lose something vital to its beauty of purpose. However thoughtfully she wrote and obliterated and wrote again, at the end it always gave the impression of a bargain. She tore the letter up. No sentence she knew how to write would be heavy with the velvet glooms of summer nights, prophetic of the supreme moment now at hand when girl-hood should go in a rapture.

A week went by, and Jenny received another post-card postponing the date of his return to May the first. She was much disappointed, but took the envelope he had given her at Waterloo, and altered, half in fun, half seriously, April 23 to May 1.

The night before she was to meet Maurice, there was a heavy fall of rain, reminding her of the night they first drove home together. She lay awake listening to the pervading sound of the water and thinking how happy she was. There was no little sister to cuddle now; but with the thought of Maurice on his way home to her kisses, her imagination was full of company. It was a morning of gold and silver when she was first conscious of the spent night. The room was steeped in rich illuminations. Sparrows twittered noisily, and their shadows would sometimes slip across the dingy walls and ceiling. 'To-day,' thought Jenny, as, turning over in a radiancy of dreams and blushes and murmurous awakenings, she fell asleep for two more slow hours of a lover's absence. The later morning was passed in unpicking and re-shaping the lucky green hat which had lain hidden since the autumn. There was no time, however, to perfect the restoration; and Jenny had to be content with a new Saxe blue dress in which she looked very trim and eager under a black mushroom hat a-blow with rosebuds.

It was about two o'clock when she went down the steps of 43 Stacpole Terrace in weather fit for a lovers' meeting. Great swan-white clouds breasted the deepening azure of May skies. The streets were dazzlingly wet with the night's rain, and every puddle was as blue as a river. In front gardens the tulips burned with fiery jets of colour, and the lime-tree buds were breaking into vivid green fans through every paling; while in the baskets of flower-women cowslips fresh from chalky pastures lay close as woven wool. Every blade of grass in the dingy squares of Camden Town was of emerald, and gardeners were strewing the paths with bright orange gravel. Children were running against the wind, pink balloons floating in their wake. Children solemnly holding paper windmills to catch the breeze were wheeled along in mail-carts and perambulators. Surely of all the lovers that went to keep a May-day tryst, none ever went more sweet and gay than Jenny.

She left the Tube at Charing Cross and, being early, walked along the Embankment to Westminster Bridge. As she crossed the river, she looked over the splash and glitter of the stream towards Grosvenor Road and up at Big Ben, thinking, with a sigh of content, how she and Maurice would be sitting in the studio by four o'clock. At Waterloo there was half an hour to wait for the train; but it was not worth while to buy a stupid paper when she could actually count the minutes that were ticking on with Maurice behind them. It was 3.25. Her heart began to beat as the enormous clock hand jerked its way to the time of reunion. Not because she wanted to know, but because she felt she must do something during that last five minutes, Jenny asked a porter whether this was the right platform for the 3.30 from Claybridge.

'Just signalled, miss,' he said.

Would Maurice be looking out of the window? Would he be brown with three weeks of Spanish weather? Would he be waving, or would he be . . .

The train was curling into the station. How much happier it looked than the one which curled out of it three weeks ago. Almost before she was aware of the noise, it had pulled up, blackening the platform with passengers that tumbled like chessmen from a box. Maurice was not immediately apparent, and Jenny in search of him worked her way against the stream of people to the farther end of the train. She felt an increasing chill upon her as the contrary movement grew weaker and the knots of people became more sparse; so that when beyond the farthest coach she stood desolate under the station roof and looked back upon the now almost empty line of platform, she was frozen by disappointment.

'Luggage, miss?' a porter asked.

Jenny shook her head and retraced her steps regretfully, watching the satisfied hansoms drive off one by one. It was impossible that Maurice could have failed her: she must have made a mistake over the time. She took the envelope from her bag and read the directions again. Could he have come on the 23rd after all? No, the post-card was plain enough. The platform was absolutely empty now, and already the train was backing out of the station.

With an effort she turned from the prospect and walked slowly towards the exit. Then she had an idea. Maurice must have missed the 3.30 and was coming by the next. There was another in half an hour, she found out from a porter, but it came in to a platform on the opposite side of the station. So she walked across and sat down to wait less happily than before, but, as the great hand climbed up towards the hour, with increasing hopefulness.

Again the platform was blackened by emerging crowds. This time she took up a position by the engine. A cold wave of unfamiliar faces swept past her. Maurice had not arrived. It was useless to wait any longer. Reluctantly she began to walk away, stopping sometimes to look back. Maurice had not arrived. With throbbing nerves and sick heart Jenny reached York Road and stood in a grey dream by the edge of the pavement. A taxi drew up alongside, and she got in, telling the man to drive to 422 Grosvenor Road.

The river still sparkled and Big Ben had struck four o'clock, but they were not sitting together in the studio. The taxi had a narrow escape from a bad accident. Ordinarily Jenny would have been terrified; but now, bitterly and profoundly careless, she accepted the jar of the brakes, the volley of recriminations and the gaping of foot passengers with remote equanimity. Notwithstanding her presentiment of the worst, as the taxi reached the familiar line of houses by which she had so often driven passionate, sleepy, mirthful, sometimes one of a crammed jolly party, sometimes alone with Maurice in ecstasies unparagoned, Jenny began to tell herself that nothing was the matter, that when she arrived at the studio he would be there. Perhaps, after all, he thought he had mentioned another train: his post-card in alteration of the date had not confirmed the time. Already she was beginning to rail at herself for being upset so easily, when the taxi stopped and Jenny alighted. She let the man drive off before she rang. When he was out of sight she pressed the studio bell three times so that Maurice should not think it was 'kids'; and ran down the steps and across the road looking up to the top floor for the heartening wave. The windows were closed: they seemed steely and ominous. She rang again, knowing it was useless; yet the bell was often out of order. She peered over at the basement for a glimpse of Mrs. Wadman. Hysterical by now, she rang the bells of other floors. Nobody answered: not even Fuz was in. Wings of fire, alternating with icy fans, beat against her brain. The damnable stolidity of the door enraged her and, when she knocked, its impassiveness made her numb and sick. Her heart was wilting in a frost and, as the last cold ache died away in oblivion, arrows of flame would horribly restore it to life and agony. She rang the bells again one after another: she rang them slowly in studied permutations: quickly and savagely she pressed them all together with the length of her forearm. The cherubs on the carved porch turned to demons, and from demons vanished into nothing. The palings on either side of the steps became invalid, unsubstantial, deliquescent like material objects in a nightmare. A catastrophe of all emotion collapsed about her mind and, when gladly she seemed to be fainting, Jenny heard the voice of Castleton a long way off.

'Oh, Fuz, where is he? Where's Maurice?'

'Why, I thought you were meeting him. I've been out all day.'

Then Jenny realized the door was still shut.

'He wasn't there. Not at Waterloo.'

She was walking slowly upstairs now beside Castleton. The fever of disappointment had left her and, outwardly tranquil, she was able to explain her reeling agitation. The studio looked cavernously empty; already on the well-remembered objects lay a web of dust. The jars still held faded pink tulips. The fragments of The Tired Dancer still littered the grate.

'Wait a minute,' Castleton said; 'I'll see if there's a letter for me downstairs.'

Presently he came back with a sheet of crackling paper.

'Shall I read you what he says?'

Jenny nodded, and, while he read, wrote with her finger, '3.30 Claybridge,' many times in the dust that lay thick on the closed lid of the piano.

This was the letter:

Dear Castleton,

I've settled not to come back to England for a while. One makes plans and the plans don't come off. I can't work in England and am better out of it. Let me hear that Jenny is all right. I think she will be. I didn't write to her. I just sent a postcard saying I should not be at Waterloo on the first of May. I expect you'll think I'm heartless, but something has gone snap inside me and I don't honestly care what you think. I'm going to Morocco in two or three days. I want adventure. I'll send you a cheque for my share of the rent in June. If you write, write to me at the English Post Office, Tangiers.

                              Yours,
                                 Maurice Avery

'Is that what he says?' Jenny asked.

'That's all.'

'And he wants to hear I'm all right?'

'He says so.'

'Tell him from me this little girl's all right,' said Jenny. 'There's plenty more mothers got sons. Plenty. Tell him that when you write.'

Her sentences rattled like musketry. Castleton stared vaguely in the direction of the river as if a friendship were going out on the tide.

'But I don't want to write,' he said. 'I couldn't. Still, there's one thing. I don't believe it's another woman.'

'Who cares if it is?' There was a wistfulness about her brave indifference. 'Men are funny. It might be.'

'I don't somehow think it is. I'd rather not. I was very fond of him.'

'So was I,' said Jenny simply. 'Only he's a rotter like all men.'

It was strange how neither of them seemed able to mention his name. Already he had lost his individuality and was merged in a type.

'What will you do?' Castleton asked.

'There's a question. How should I know?'

Before her mind life like a prairie rolled away into distance infinitely dull.

'It was a foolish question. I'm sorry. I wish you'd marry me.'

Jenny looked at him with sad eyes screwed up in perplexity.

'I believe you would, Fuz.'

'I would. I would.'

'But I couldn't. I don't want to see any of you ever again.'

Castleton seemed to shrink.

'I'm not being rude, Fuz, really. Only I don't want to.'

'I perfectly understand.'

'You mustn't be cross with me.'

'Cross! Oh, Jane, do I sound cross?'

'Because,' Jenny went on, 'if I saw you or any of his friends, I should only hate you. Goodbye, I must run.'

'You're all right for money?' Castleton stammered awkwardly. 'I mean – there's – oh, damn it, Jenny.'

He pounded over to the window, huge and disconsolate.

'Why ever on earth should I want money? What's the matter with next Friday's Treasury?'

'Perhaps, Jenny, you would come out with me once, if I waited for you one night?'

'Please don't. I should only stare you out, I *wouldn't* know you. I don't ever ever want to see any of you again.'

She ran from the studio, vanishing like a flame into smoke.

That night when Jenny went back alone to Stacpole Terrace, she saw on the table in the cheerless parlour the post-card from Maurice, and close beside it the green hat bought in September still waiting to be re-shaped for the spring. She threw it into a corner of the room.

XXV

Monotone

Jenny's first thought was an impulse of revenge upon the opposite sex comparable with, but more drastic than, the resolution she had made on hearing of Edie's disaster. She would devote her youth to 'doing men down.' It was as if from the desert of the soul seared by Maurice, the powers of the body were to sweep like a wild tribe maiming the creators of her solitude. Maurice had stood for her as the epitome of man, and it was to be expected that when he fell, he would involve all men in the ruin. This hostility extended so widely that even her father was included, and Jenny found herself brooding upon the humiliation of his share in her origin.

This violent enmity finding its expression in physical repulsion defeated itself, and Jenny could no longer attract victims. Moreover, the primal instincts of sex perished in the drought of emotion; and soon she wished for oblivion, dreading any activity of disturbance. The desert was made, and was vast enough to circumscribe the range of her vision with its expanse of monotony. Educated in Catholic ideals, she would have fled to a nunnery, there coldly to languish until the fires of divine adorations should burst from the ashes of earthly love. Nunneries, however, were outside Jenny's set of conceptions. Death alone would endow her with painless indifference in a perpetual serenity; but the fear of death in one who lacked ability to regard herself from outside was not mitigated by pictorial consolations. She could never separate herself into audience and actor. Extinction appalled one profoundly conscious of herself as an entity. By such a stroke she would obliterate not merely herself, but her world as well. Suicides generally possess the power of mental dichotomy. They kill themselves, paradoxically, to see the effect. They are sorry for themselves, or angry, or contemptuous: madness disintegrates their sense of personality so that the various components run together. In a madman's huggermugger of motives, impulses and reasons, one predominant butchers the rest for its own gratification. Whatever abnormal conditions the shock of sorrow had produced in Jenny's mental life, through them all she remained fully conscious of her completeness and preserved unbroken the importance of her personality. She could not kill herself.

The days were very long now, nor would she try to quicken them by returning to the old life before she met Maurice. She would not with two or three girls pass in review the shops of Oxford Street or gossip by the open windows of her club. In the dressing-room she would sit silent, impatient of intrusion upon the waste with which she had surrounded herself. The ballets used to drag intolerably. She found no refuge from her heart in dancing, no consolation in the music and colour. She danced listlessly, glad when the task was over, glad when she came out of the theatre and equally glad to leave Stacpole Terrace on the next day. In bed she would lie awake meditating upon nothing; and when she slept, her sleep was parched.

'Buck up, old girl, whatever's the matter?' Irene would ask, and Jenny, resentful, would scowl at the gaucherie. She longed to be with her mother again, and would visit Hagworth Street more often, hoping some word might be uttered that would make it easy for her to subdue that pride which, however deeply wounded by Maurice, still battled invincibly, frightening every other instinct and emotion. But when the words of welcome came, Jenny, shy of softness, would carry off existence with an air, tears and reconciliation set aside. It was not long before the rumour of her love's disaster was carried in whispers round the many dressing-rooms of the Orient. Soon enough Jenny found the girls staring at her when they thought her attention was occupied. She had always seemed to them so invulnerable that her jilting excited a more than usually diffused curiosity; but for a long time, though many rejoiced, no girl was brave enough to ask malicious questions, intruding upon her solitude.

June came in with the best that June can give of cloudless weather, weather that is born in skies of peach-blossom, whose richness is never lost in wine-dark nights pressed from the day's sweetness. What weather it would have been for the country! Jenny used to sit for hours together in St. James's Park, scratching aimlessly upon the gravel with the ferrule of her parasol. Men would stop and sit beside her, looking round the corners of their eyes like actors taking a call. But she was scarcely aware of their presence and, when they spoke, would look up vaguely perplexed so that they muttered apologies and moved along. Her thoughts were always travelling through the desert of her soul. Unblessed by mirage, they travelled steadily through a monotony towards an horizon of brass. Her heart beat dryly and regularly like the tick of a clock, and her memory merely recorded time. No relic of the past could bring a tear; even the opal brooch was worn every day because it happened to be useful. Once a letter from Maurice fell from her bag into the lake, and she cared no more for it than the swan's feather beside which it floated.

July came in hot and metallic. Every sunset was a foundry, and the nights were like smoke. One day towards the end of the month Jenny, walking down Cranbourne Street, thought she would pay a visit to Lilli Vergoe. The room had not changed much since the day Jenny joined the ballet. Lilli, in a soiled muslin dress, was smoking the same brand of cigarettes in the same wicker-chair. The same photographs clung to the mirror, or were stacked on the mantelshelf in palisades. The walls were covered with Mr. Vergoe's relics.

'Hullo, Jenny! So you've found your way here at last. What's been wrong with you lately? You're looking thin.'

'It's this shocking hot weather.'

'Why, when you came here before and I said it was hot, you said it was lovely.'

'Did I?' asked Jenny indifferently. 'I must have been potty.'

'How's your mother? And dad? And young May?'

'All right. I'm living along with Ireen Dale now.'

'I know. Whatever made you do that?'

'Why shouldn't I?'

'I shouldn't call them your style,' said Lilli positively.

'Ireen's nice.'

'Yes, she's all right. But Winnie Dale's dreadful. And look at her mother. She's like an old charwoman. And that youngest sister.'

'Oh, them, I never see *them*.'

'You've heard about me, I suppose?'

'No, what?' asked Jenny, politely inquisitive.

'I've turned suffragette.'

'You never haven't? Oh, Lil, what a dreadful thing!'

'It's not. It's great. I used to think so myself, but I've changed my mind.'

'Oh, Lilli, I think it's terrible. A suffragette? But what an unnatural lot of women you must go around with.'

'They're not,' said Lilli, loud in defence of her associates.

'A lot of Plain Janes and No Nonsense with the hair all screwed back. I know. And all walking on one another's petticoats. Suffragette Sallies! What are they for? Tell me that.'

'Hasn't it never struck you there's a whole heap of girls in this world that's got nothing to do?'

Lilli spoke sadly. There was a life's disillusionment in the question.

'Yes; but that doesn't say they should go making sights of themselves, shouting and hollering. Get out! Besides, what's the Salvation Army done?'

'You don't understand.'

'No, and I don't want to understand.'

'Why don't you come round to our club? I'll introduce you to Miss Bailey.'

'Who's she?'

'She's the President.'

Jenny considered the offer a moment. Soon she decided that, dreary as the world was, it would not be brightened by an introduction to Miss Bailey. In the dressing-room that night, during the wait between the two ballets, Elsie Crauford, who had long been waiting for an opportunity to avenge Jenny's slighting references to Artie's evening dress, thought she would risk an encounter.

'I didn't know your Maurice had gone quite sudden,' she said. 'Aren't you going to do anything about it?'

'You've blacked your nose, Elsie Crauford.'

'Have I? Where?' Elsie had seized a hand-glass.

'Yes, you have, poking it into other people's business. You curious thing! What am I going to do about it? Punch into you, if you're not sharp.'

'He seemed so fond of you, too.'

'You never saw him but once, when you blew in with the draught in that flash hat of yours.'

'No, but Madge Wilson told me you were absolutely mad about one another. It seems so funny he should leave you. But Madge said it wouldn't last. She said you weren't getting a jolly fine time for nothing. Funny thing, you always knew such a lot before you got stuck on a fellow yourself. What you weren't going to do! You aren't so much cleverer than us after all.'

'*Who* told you?' demanded Jenny.

321

'Madge Wilson did.'

'Don't take any notice of *her*,' Maudie Chapman advised at this point. 'You jest shut up, Elsie Crauford. Always making mischief.'

'I'm tired of Jenny Pearl's always knowing better than anyone without being told off.'

'Told off? Who by? *You?*' gasped Jenny. 'Why, you dirty little Wurzit, there's nothing of you to tell off. You ought to go to Brighton and show yourself for a penny like eels in vinegar or mites in cheese. No wonder your Artie's took to wearing glasses. He's worn his eyes out looking for you, *I* should say. Tell *you* off!'

Then Madge Wilson herself came into the dressing-room.

'Hullo, duck,' she said, surprised by Jenny's apparent re-entry into society.

'Are you speaking to me, Madge Wilson? Because I don't want to talk to you. A nice friend. Hark at your fine friends, girls. They're the rotters that take you off behind your back.'

'Whatever's the matter?' Madge asked.

'Yes, you don't know, do you? But I wouldn't be a sneak like you, you soppy, two-faced thing! I'd say out what I thought and not care for anyone. I wasn't getting a jolly fine time for nothing? And what about you, Mrs. Straightcut? But that's the way. Girls you think are your friends, girls *you* take out and give a good time, they're the first to turn round on you. I wonder you haven't all gone hoarse with the way you've talked me to pieces these last weeks. A lot of mares! That's all you are in this theatre. Mrs. Bigmouths, every one of you. Worse than a lot of case-keepers. I know you. I can hear you mumbling and whispering in corners. "Have you heard about Jenny Pearl? Isn't it shocking? Oh, I do think it's a dreadful thing. What a terrible girl." Coo! and look at *you*. Married women! Yes, and what have you married? Why, there isn't a girl in this dressing-room whose husband can afford to keep her. Husbands! Why, they're no better than—'

'She's been going out with Lilli Vergoe,' interrupted Elsie sneeringly. 'Jenny Pearl's turned into a suffragette.'

'What of it? That's better than turning into an old pastry which is what you'll do. You and your six pairs of gloves that your Artie bought you. Well, if he did, *which* I don't think, he must have broke open the till to do it.'

Madge Wilson's disloyalty effected for Jenny what nothing else had done. It made the blood course fast, the heart beat: it kindled her eyes again. That night in bed, she thought of falseness and treachery and cried herself to sleep.

XXVI

In Scyros

The outburst against feminine treachery had an effect upon Jenny's state of mind beyond the mere evoking of tears. These were followed by a general agitation of her point of view, necessitating an outlet for her revived susceptibleness to emotion. A less sincere heart would have been caught on the rebound; but she and men were still mutually unattractive. The consequence of this renewed activity of spirit, in the aspect of its immediate cause, was paradoxical enough; for when Jenny thought she would try the pretensions of Suffragism, no clear process of reasoning helped her to such a resolve, no formulated hostility to man. Whatever logic existed in the decision was fortuitous; nor did she at all perceive any absence of logic in throwing in her lot with treacherous woman.

Lilli Vergoe was proud of such a catechumen, and made haste to introduce her to the tall house in Mecklenburg Square, whose elm-shadowed rooms displayed the sober glories of the Women's Political, Social and Economic League. Something about the house reminded Jenny of her first visit to Madame Aldavini's School; but she found

Miss Bailey less alarming than the dancing mistress as, rising from masses of letters and scarlet gladioli, she welcomed the candidate. Miss Bailey, the President of the League, was a tall handsome woman very unlike Jenny's conception of a suffragette. She had a regular profile, a thin high-bridged nose, and clearly cut determined lips. Her complexion was pale, her hair brown and rich. Best of all Jenny liked her slim hands and the voice which, though marred by a slight huskiness due to public speaking, was full of quality and resonance. She was one of those women who, carrying in their presence a fine tranquillity at once kindly and ascetic, imbue the onlooker with their long and perceptive experience of humanity. She was in no sense homely or motherly; indeed, she wore about her the remoteness of the great. Yet whatever in her general appearance seemed of marble was vivified by clear hazel eyes into a reality of womanhood.

'And so you're going to join our club?' enquired Miss Bailey.

Jenny, although she had intended this first visit to be merely empirical, felt bound to commit herself to the affirmative.

'You'll soon know all about our objects.'

'Oh, I've told her a lot already, Miss Bailey,' declared Lilli with the eagerness of the trusted school-girl.

'That's right,' said Miss Bailey, smiling. 'Come along then, and I will enroll you, Miss—'

'Pearl,' murmured Jenny, feeling as if her name had somehow slipped down and escaped sideways through her neck. Then with an effort clearing her throat, she added, 'Jenny Pearl,' blushing furiously at the confession of identity.

'Your address?'

'Better say 17 Hagworth Street, Islington. Only I'm not living there just now. Now I'm living 43 Stacpole Terrace, Camden Town.'

'Have you a profession?'

'I'm on the stage.'

'What a splendid profession, too – for a woman. Don't you think so?'

Jenny stared at this commendation of a state of life she had always imagined was distasteful to people like Miss Bailey.

'I don't know much about splendid, but I suppose it's all right,' she agreed at last.

'Indeed it is. Are you at the Orient also?'

'Yes. You know. In the ballet,' said Jenny quickly, so that the President might not think she was trying to push herself unduly.

'I don't believe there's anything that gives more pleasure than good dancing. Dancing ought to be the expression of life's joy,' said the older woman, gazing at the pigeon-holes full of docketed files, at the bookshelves stuffed with dry volumes of Ethics and Politics and Economics, as if half regretting she, too, was not in the Orient Ballet. 'Dancing is the oldest art,' she continued. 'I like to think they danced the spring in long before calendars were made. Your subscription is half a crown a year.'

Jenny produced the coin from her bag; and it said much for Miss Bailey's personality that the new member to adorn the action did not wink over her shoulder at Lilli.

'Thank you. Here's the badge. It's copied from an old Athenian medal. This is Pallas Athene, the Goddess of Wisdom.'

'She isn't much to look at, is she?' commented Jenny.

'My dear child, that's the owl.'

Jenny turned the medal over and contemplated the armed head. Then she put it carefully away in her purse, wondering if the badge would bring her luck.

'Now, I shall let Lilli show you round the club rooms, for I'm very busy this afternoon,' said Miss Bailey in gentle dismissal.

The two girls left the study and set out to explore the rest of the house. Over the mantelpiece of the principal room Jenny saw Mona Lisa and drew back so quickly that she trod on Lilli's foot.

'I'm not going in there,' she said.

'Why not? It's a nice room.'

'I'm not going in. I don't want to,' she repeated, without any explanation of her whim.

'All right. Let's go downstairs. We can have tea.'

It was a fine afternoon towards the end of July, so the tea-room was empty. Jenny looked cautiously at all the pictures, but none of them conjured up the past. There was a large photograph of the beautiful sad head of Jeanne d'Arc, but Jenny did not bother to read that it came originally from the church of St. Maurice in Orleans. There were a number of somewhat dreary engravings of famous pioneers of feminism like Mary Wollstonecraft, whose faces, she thought, would look better turned round to the wall. Below these hung several statistical maps showing the density of population in various London slums with black splodges for criminal districts. Most of the furniture was of green fumed oak fretted with hearts, and the crockery that lived dustily on a shelf following the line of the frieze came from Hanley disguised in Flemish or Breton patterns, whose studied irregularity of design and roughness of workmanship were symbolic of much. In order, apparently, to accentuate the flimsiness of the green fumed oak, there were several mid-Victorian settees that, having faded in back rooms of Wimpole Street and Portman Square, were now exposed round the sides of their new abode in a succession of hillocks. On the wall by the door hung a framed tariff, on which poached eggs in every permutation of number and combination of additional delicacies figured most prominently. Here and there on tables not occupied with green teacups were scattered pamphlets, journals, and the literary propaganda of the feminine movement. The general atmosphere of the room was permeated by an odour of damp toast and the stale fumes of asthma cigarettes.

'What an unnatural smell,' murmured Jenny.

'It's those asthma cigerettes,' Lilli explained. 'One of the members has got it very bad.'

Jenny was glad to escape very soon after tea, and told her friend a second visit to Mecklenburg Square was not to be done.

'I used to think they was nice houses when I passed by the other side in that green 'bus going to Covent Garden, but I think they're *very* stuffy, and what wall-paper! More like blotting-paper.'

However, one Saturday evening in August, as Jenny was leaving the theatre, Lilli begged her to come and hear Miss Ragstead speak on the general aims of the movement, with particular attention to a proposed demonstration on the occasion of the re-opening of Parliament.

'When's the old crow going to speak?' Jenny enquired.

'To-morrow evening.'

'On a Sunday?'

'Yes.'

So because there was nothing else to do and because nowadays Sunday was a long grim moping, a procession of pretty hours irrevocable, Jenny promised to accompany her friend.

It was a wet evening, and Bloomsbury seemed the wettest place in London as the two girls turned into the sparse lamplight of Mecklenburg Square and hurried along under the dank fast-fading planes and elms. Inside the house, however, there was an air of energetic jollity owing to the arrival of several girl students from Oxford and Cambridge, who stumped in and out of the rooms, greeting each other with tales of Swiss mountains and comparisons of industry. In their strong low-heeled boots they stumped about consumed by holiday sunshine and the acquisition of facts. With friendly smiles and fresh complexions, they talked enthusiastically to several young men whose Adam's apples raced up and down their long necks, giving them the appearance of chickens swallowing maize very quickly.

'Talk about funny turns,' whispered Jenny.

'They're all very clever,' Miss Vergoe apologized, as she steered her intolerant friend past the group.

'Yes, I should say they ought to be clever, too. They *look* as though they were pecking each other's brains out.'

Miss Bailey encountered them here.

'Why, this is capital,' she said. 'Miss Ragstead won't be long now. Let me introduce a dear young friend of mine, Miss Worrill.'

'How are you?' Miss Worrill asked heartily.

She was a pleasant girl dressed in Harris tweed strongly odorous from the rain. Her hair might have been arranged to set off her features to greater advantage, and it was a pity her complexion was spoilt by a network of tiny purple veins which always attracted the concentration of those who talked to her. Jenny began to count them at once.

'Come to hear Connie Ragstead?' asked Miss Worrill. 'Jolly good crowd for August,' she went on, throwing a satisfied glance round the room. 'Have you ever heard her?'

'No,' Jenny replied, wondering why something in this girl's way of speaking reminded her of Maurice.

'You'll like her most awfully. I met her once at the Lady Maggie "Gaudy." '

'At the what?'

'Our Gaude at Lady Margaret's. Festive occasion and all that. I say, do you play hockey? I'm getting up a team to play at Wembley this winter.'

'My friend and I are too busy,' Miss Vergoe explained, looking nervously round at Jenny to see how she took the suggestion.

'But one can always find time for "ecker." '

'I *could* find time to fly kites. Only I don't want to,' said Jenny dangerously. 'You see I'm on the stage.'

'I'm frightfully keen on the stage,' Miss Worrill volunteered. 'I believe it could be such a force. I thought of acting myself once – you know, in real plays, not musical comedy, of course – only I took up "stinks" instead. A friend of mine was in the *Ecclesiasuzæ* at the Afternoon Theatre. She wore a *rather* jolly vermilion tunic and had bare legs. Absolutely realistic.'

Jenny now began to giggle, and whispered 'Cocoanut knees' to Lilli, who, notwithstanding the importance of the occasion, also began to giggle. So Miss Worrill, presumably shy of their want of sensibility, retired.

Soon, when the rumour of the speaker's arrival ran round the assemblage, a general move was made in the direction of the large room on the first floor. Jenny, as she entered with the stream, saw Leonardo's sinister portrait and tried to retreat; but there were too many eager listeners in the way, and she had to sit down and prepare to endure the damnable smile of La Gioconda that seemed directed to the very corner where she was sitting.

During the earlier part of Miss Ragstead's address, Jenny's attention was chiefly occupied by her neighbours. She thought that never before was such a collection of freaks gathered together. Close beside her, dressed in a green djibbeh embroidered with daisies of terra-cotta silk, was a tallowy woman who from time to time let several books slide from her lap on to the floor – a piece of carelessness which always provoked the audience to a lullaby of protest. In front of this lady were two Hindu students with flowing orange ties; and just beyond her, in black velvet, was a tall woman with a flat, pallid face, who gnawed alternately her nails and the extinguished end of a cigarette. Then came a group of girl students, all very much alike, all full of cocoa and the binomial theorem; while the rest of the audience was made up of typists, clerks, civil servants, copper-workers, palmists, nurses, Americans and poets, all lending their ears to the speaker's words as in the Zoological Gardens elephants, swaying gently, offer their trunks for buns. Gradually, however, from this hotch-potch of types, the personality of the speaker detached itself and was able to impress Jenny's attention. Gradually, as she grew tired of watching the audience, she began to watch Miss Ragstead and, after a critical appreciation of her countenance, to make an attempt to comprehend the intention of the discourse.

Miss Constance Ragstead was a woman of about forty, possessing much of the remote and chastened beauty that was evident in Miss Bailey. She, too, was pale, not unhealthily, but with the impression of having lived long in a rarefied atmosphere. Virginity has its fires, and Miss Ragstead was an inheritor of the spirit which animated Saint Theresa and Mary Magdalene of Pazzi. Her social schemes were crowned with aureoles, her plans were lapped by tenuous gold flames. She was a mystic of humanity, one who from the contemplation of mortality in its individual aspirations, had arrived at the acknowledgement of man as a perfect idea and was able from his virtues to create her theogony. This woman's presence implied the purifica-tion of ceaseless effort. Activity as expressed by her was a sacrament. It conveyed the isolated solemnity of a force that does not depend for its reality on human conceptions or practical altruism. Her activity was a moral radium never consumed by the expenditure of its energy; it was dynamic whether it effected little or much. When she recalled the factory in which for a year she had worked as a hand, the enterprise was hallowed with the romance of a saint's pilgrimage. When she spoke of her green garden, where June had healed the hearts of many young women, she seemed like an eremite in whose consolation was absolute peace. Her voice was modulated with those sweet half-tones that thrushes ring upon the evening air; and since they were produced suddenly with no hint of premeditation, the feeblest listener was at some time inevitably waylaid.

It was not astonishing Jenny should find herself caught in the melodious twilight of the oration, should find that the craning audience was less important than the speaker. She came to believe that Mona Lisa's smile was kindlier. She began to take in some of the rhetoric of the peroration:

'I wish I could persuade you that if our cause is a worthy cause, it must exist and endure through the sanity of its adherents. It must never depend upon the trivial eccentricities of a few. I want to see the average woman fired with zeal to make the best of herself. I do not want us to be contemptuously put aside as exceptions. Nor am I anxious to recruit our strength from the discontented, the disappointed and the disillusioned. Let us do away with the reproach that we voice a minority's opinion. Let us preserve the grace and magic of womanhood, so that with the spiritual power of virginity, the physical grandeur of

333

motherhood, in a devoted phalanx huge as the army of Darius, we may achieve our purpose.'

Here the speaker paused and, as if afraid she might be deemed to offer counsels of pusillanimity, broke forth more passionately:

'But because I wish to see our ambition succeed through the aggregate of dignified opinion, I do not want to discredit or seek to dishearten the advance-guard. Let us who represent the van of an army so mighty as to be mute and inexpensive, let us, not thinking ourselves martyrs nor displaying like Amazons our severed breasts, let us resolve to endure ignominy and contempt, slander, disgrace and imprisonment. Some day men will speak well of us, some day the shrieking sisterhood will be forgotten, and those leaders of women whom to-day we alone venerate, will be venerated by all. Pay no heed to that subtle propaganda of passivity. Reject the lily-white counsels of moderation. Remember that without visible audible agitation this phlegmatic people cannot be roused. Therefore I call on you who murmur your agreement to join the great march on Westminster. I implore you to be brave, to despise calumny, to be careless of abuse and, because you believe you are in the right, to alarm once more this blind and stolid mass of public opinion with the contingency of your ultimate triumph.'

The speaker sat down lost in the haze which shrouds a room full of people deeply wrought by eloquence and emotion. There was a moment's silence and then, after prolonged applause, the audience began to babble.

Jenny sat still. She had not listened to the reasoned

arguments and statistical illustrations of the main portion of the speech, nor had she properly comprehended the peroration. Yet she was charged with resolves, primed with determination and surgingly impelled to some sort of action. She was the microcosm of a mob's awakening to the clarion of an orator. A cataract of formless actions was thundering through her mind; the dam of indifference had been burst by mere weight of rhetoric, that powerful dam proof against the tampering of logic. Perhaps she was passing through the physical crisis of conversion. Perhaps, in her dead emotional state, anything that aroused her slightly would have aroused her violently. No doubt a deep-voiced bishop could have secured a similar result, had she been leaning against the cold stone of a cathedral rather than the grey flock wall-paper of Mecklenburg Square.

'I'd like to talk to her,' she told Lilli.

'She doesn't half stir you up, eh?'

'I don't know so much about stirring up, Mrs Pudding,' said Jenny, unwilling to admit any renascence of sensibility. 'But I think she's nice. I'd like to see what sort she'd be to talk to quiet.'

No opportunity for a conversation with Miss Ragstead presented itself that evening; but Lilli, somewhat elated by the capture of Jenny, told Miss Bailey of her admiration, and the President, who had been attracted to the neophyte, promised to arrange a meeting. Lilli knew better than to breathe a word to Jenny of any plan, and merely threw out a casual suggestion to take tea at the club.

So without any premonitory shyness Jenny found herself talking quite easily in a corner of the tea-room to Miss

Ragstead, who was not merely persuasive with assemblages, but also acutely sympathetic with individuals.

'But I don't want a vote,' Jenny was saying, 'I shouldn't know what to do with it. I don't see any use in it. My father's got one and it's a regular nuisance. It keeps him out late every night.'

'My dear, you may not want a vote,' said Miss Ragstead. 'But I do, and I want the help of girls like you to get it. I want to represent you. As things are now, you have no say in the government of yourself. Tell me, now, Jenny – I'm going to call you Jenny straight away – you wouldn't like to be at the mercy of one man, would you?'

'But I wouldn't. Not me,' said Jenny. Yet somehow she spoke not quite so bravely as once, and even as the assertion was made, her heart throbbed to a memory of Maurice. After all she had been at the mercy of one man.

'Of course you wouldn't,' Miss Ragstead went on. 'Well, we women who want the vote have the same feeling. We don't like to be at the mercy of men. I suppose you'd be horrified if I asked you to join our demonstration in October?'

'What, walk in procession?' Jenny gasped.

'Yes, it's not so very dreadful. Who would object? Your mother?'

'She'd make fun of it, but that wouldn't matter. She'd make everyone laugh to hear her telling about me in a procession.'

Jenny remembered how her mother had teased her father when she saw him supporting a banner of the Order of Foresters on the occasion of a beanfeast at Clacton.

'Well, your lover?'

Jenny looked sharply at Miss Ragstead to ascertain if she were laughing. The word sent such a pang through her. It was a favourite word of Maurice.

'I haven't got one,' she coldly answered.

'No?' said Miss Ragstead, gently sceptical. 'I can hardly believe that, you know, for you surely must be a most attractive girl.'

'I did have one,' said Jenny, surprised out of her reserve. 'Only we just ended it all of a sudden.'

'My dear,' said Miss Ragstead softly, 'I don't think you're a very happy girl. I'm sure you're not. Won't you tell me about it?'

'There's nothing to tell. Men are rotters, that's all. If I thought I could pay them out by being a suffragette, I'd *be* a suffragette, and chance getting the bird all round.'

Jenny spoke with decision, pointing the avowal by flinging her cigarette into the grate.

'Yes, I know that's a reason with some. But I don't think that revenge is the best of reasons, somehow. I would rather you were convinced that the movement is right.'

'If it annoys men, it must be right,' Jenny argued. 'Only I don't think it does. I think they just laugh.'

'I see you're in a turbulent state of mind,' Miss Ragstead observed. 'And I'm glad in a way, because it proves that you have temperament and character. You ought to resent a wrong. Of course, I know you'll disagree with me when I tell you that you're too young to be permanently injured by any man – and, I think I might add, too proud.'

'Yes, I am most shocking proud,' Jenny admitted,

looking down on the floor and, as it were, regarding her character incarnate before her.

'But it's just these problems of behaviour under difficulties that our club wants to solve. I'd like to put you on the road to express yourself and your ambitions without the necessity of – say marriage for convenience. You're a dancer, aren't you?'

'Um, a ballet girl,' said Jenny as usual, careful not to presume the false grandeur of an isolated stellar existence.

'Are you keen on your dancing?'

'I was once. When I began. Only they crush you at the Orient. Girls there hate to see you get on. I'm sick of it.'

'I wonder,' said Miss Ragstead half to herself, 'I wonder if active work for the cause would give you a new zest for life. It might: you feel all upside down just now, don't you?'

'I feel as if nothing didn't matter. Not *any*thing,' replied Jenny decidedly.

'That's terrible for a girl of your age. You can't be more than eighteen or nineteen.'

'Twenty-one in October.'

'So much as that? Yes' – the older woman continued after a reflective pause – 'yes, I believe you want some spur, some excitement quite outside your ordinary experience. You know I am a doctor, so without impertinence I can fairly prescribe for you.'

'Well, what have I got to do?' Jenny asked. She was almost fascinated by this lady with her cool hands and deep-set, passionate eyes.

'I wish I could invite you to spend some time with me in Somerset, but I'm too busy now for a holiday. I feel rather uncertain whether, after all, to advise you to plunge into the excitement of this demonstration. And yet I'm sure it would be good for you. Dear child, I hope I'm not giving bad advice,' said Miss Ragstead earnestly as she leaned forward and took hold of Jenny's hand.

So it came about that Jenny was enrolled in the ranks of the great demonstration that was to impress the autumnal sessions of Parliament. She kept very quiet about her intention and no one, except Lilli, knew anything about it. The worst preliminary was the purple, green and white sash which contained her unlucky colour. Indeed, at first she could hardly be persuaded to put it across her shoulders. But when the booming of the big drum marked the beat, she felt aflame with nervous expectation and never bothered about the sash or the chance of casual recognition.

The rhythm of the march, the crashing of the band, the lilting motion, the unreality of the crowds gaping on the pavements intoxicated her, and she went swinging on to the tune in a dream of excitement. In the narrower streets the music blazed with sound and fury of determination, urging them on, inspiring them with indomitable energy, inexorable progress. The tops of the houses here seemed to converge, blotting out the sky; and Jenny felt that she was stationary, while they moved on like the landscape of a cinematograph. As the procession swept into Trafalgar Square with its great open space of London sky, the music unconfined achieved a more poignant appeal and infected the mass of arduous women with sentiment, making their temper the more dangerous. The procession became a pilgrimage to some abstract nobility, to no set place.

339

Jenny was now bewitched by the steady motion into an almost complete unconsciousness of the gaping sight-seers, thought of them, if she thought of them at all, as figures in a fair-booth to be knocked carelessly backwards as she passed, more vital than they were with their painted grins.

In Whitehall the air was again charged with anger. The tall banners far ahead floated on airs of victory. The mounted women rode like conquerors. Then for an instant as Jenny heard from one of the pavement-watchers a coarse and mocking comment on the demonstrations, she thought the whole business mere matter for ridicule and recalled the circus processions that flaunted through towns on sunny seaside holiday mornings long ago. Soon, however, the tune re-established itself in her brain, and once more she swept on to the noble achievement. The houses grew taller than ever; faded into remote mists; quaked and shimmered as if to a fall. Far down the line above the brass and drums was a sound of screaming, a dull mutter of revolution, a wave of execration and encouragement. The procession stopped dead: the music ceased in discords. Two or three of the women fainted. The crowd on either side suddenly came to life and pressed forward with hot inquisitive breath. Somewhere, a long way off, a leader shrieked, 'Forward.' Policemen were conjured from the quivering throng. Somebody tore off Jenny's sash. Somebody trod on her foot. The confusion increased. Nothing was left of any procession: everyone was pushing, yelling, groaning, scratching, struggling in a wreck of passions. Jenny was cut off from the disorganized

340

main body, was helpless in a mob of men. The police were behaving with that magnificent want of discrimination which sometimes characterizes their behaviour in a crisis of disorder. Their tactics were justified by success, and as they would rely on mutual support in the official account of the riot, individual idiocy would escape censure.

In so far as Jenny was pushing her way out of the mob, was seeking desperately to gain the sanctuary of a side street and for ever escape from feminine demonstrations, she was acting in a way likely to cause a breach of the peace. So it was not surprising that a young plough-boy lately invested with uniform should feel impelled to arrest her.

'Now then, you come along of me,' commanded the yokel, as a blush ebbed and flowed upon his cheeks glistening with down and perspiration.

'Who are you pushing, you?' cried Jenny, enraged to find her arm in the tight grasp of a podgy, freckled hand.

'You ought to be ashamed of yourself,' he declared.

'Don't speak to me, you. Why, what *are* you? Invisible blue when you're *wanted*. Let go of me. I won't be held. I wasn't doing anything. I was going home. Let go.'

The young policeman, disinclined to risk the adventure single-handed, looked round for a fellow-constable to assist at the conveyance of Jenny to the station. All his companions, however, seemed busily engaged tugging at recalcitrant women; and instead of being congratulated on his first arrest, a well-groomed man, white with rage, shouted: 'Look here, you blackguard, I've got your number and I'll have your coat off for this. This lady was doing absolutely nothing but trying to escape from the crowd.'

The young policeman looked about him once more with watery, unintelligent eyes. He was hoping that someone would arrest the well-groomed man; but as nobody did, and as the latter was not unlike the Captain of the Volunteer Company from whose ranks he had climbed into the force, the novice released his grip of Jenny and said:

'Now, you be off. You won't get another chance.'

'No, you turnip-headed bumpkin,' shouted the well-groomed man, 'and nor will you, when I've had five minutes at Scotland Yard. I'm going to watch you, my friend. You're not fit for a position of responsibility.'

Jenny, free of the crowd, walked through the peace of Whitehall Court and promised herself that never again would she have anything to do with suffragettes.

'Soppy fools,' she thought, 'they can't do nothing. They can only jabber, jabber.' She reproached herself for imagining it was possible to consummate a revenge on man by such means. She had effected nothing but the exposure of her person to the freckled paws of a policeman.

'Not again,' said Jenny to herself, 'not ever again will I be such a silly, soppy idiot.'

In the distance she could still hear the shouting of the riot; but as she drew nearer to Charing Cross railway station, the noise of trains took its place.

XXVII

Quartette

Suffragism viewed in retrospect was shoddy embroidery for the *vie intérieure* of Jenny. There was no physical exhilaration for her in wrestling with policemen, and the intellectual excitement of controversy would never be likely to appeal to a mind naturally unfitted for argument. There was, too, about her view of the whole business something of Myrrhine's contempt. She may have been in an abnormal condition of acute hostility to the opposite sex; but as soon as she found herself in a society whose antipathy towards men seemed to be founded on inability to attract the hated male, all her common sense cried out against committing herself to such a devil-driven attitude. She felt that something must be wrong with so obviously an ineffective aggregation of Plain Janes. She was not concerned with that unprovided-for surplus of feminine population. She had no acquaintance with that asceticism produced by devotion to the intellect. She perceived, though not consciously, the inherent weakness of the whole movement in its failure to supply an emotional substitute for more elemental passions.

Jenny was shrewd enough to understand that leaders

like Miss Bailey and Miss Ragstead were logically justified in demanding a vote. She could understand that they would be able to use it to some purpose; but at the same time she realized that to the majority of women a vote would be merely an encumbrance. Jenny also saw through the folly of agitation that must depend for success on equality of physique, and half divined that the prime cause of such extravagance lay in the needs of feminine self-expression. Nuns are wedded to Christ; suffragists, with the notable exceptions of those capable of sustaining an intellectual predominance, must remain spiritual old maids. As Jenny asked, 'What do they all want?' Very soon the inhabitants of Mecklenburg Square became as unreal as unicorns, and the whole episode acquired the reputation of an interlude of unaccountable madness from the memory of which the figure of Miss Ragstead stood out cool and tranquil and profoundly sane. Jenny would in a way have been glad to meet her again; but she was too shy to suggest meeting outside the domain of the Women's Political, Social and Economic League, and their auspices were now unimaginable. In order to avoid the whole subject, Jenny began to avoid Lilli Vergoe; and very soon, partly owing to the opportunities of propinquity, partly owing to a renewed desire for it, her friendship with Irene Dale was reconstituted on a firmer basis than before.

Six months had now elapsed since that desolate first of May. The ballet of Cupid was taken off about the same time, and the occupation of rehearsing for a new one had steered Jenny through the weeks immediately following Maurice's defection. She was now dancing in a third ballet in which she took so little interest that no account of it is necessary. The pangs of outraged love were drugged to painlessness by time. From a superficial standpoint the wounds were healed, that is, if a dull insensibility to the original cause of the evil be a cure. Jenny no longer missed Maurice on particular occasions and, having grown used to his absence, was not aware she missed him in a wider sense. Love so impassioned as theirs, love lived through in moments of individual ecstasy, was in the verdict of average comment a disease; but average comment failed to realize that, like the scarlet fever of her youth, its malignant influence would be extended in complications of abnormal emotional states. Average comment did not perceive that the worst tragedies of unhappy love are not those which end with death or separation. Nor did Jenny herself foresee the train of ill that in the wake of such a shock to her feelings would be liable to twist her whole life awry.

With Maurice she had embarked on the restless ocean of an existence lived at unusually high pressure. She had conjured for her soul dreams of adventure, fiery-hearted dreams which would not be satisfied by the awakenings of commonplace dawns. Time had certainly assuaged with his heavy anodyne the intimate desire for her lover; but time would rather aggravate than heal the universal need of her womanhood. These six months of seared emotions and withered hopes were a trance from which she would awake on the very flashing heels of the last mental and physical excitement.

It was said in the last chapter that a less sincere heart

would have been caught on the rebound. Such hearts are dragged but a little way down into the depths of misery; for they have not fallen from great heights. Jenny on the first of May fell straight and deep as a plummet to the bed of the ocean of despair, there to lie long submerged. But to one who had rejected death life would not hold out oblivion. Life with all its cold insistence called her once more to the surface; thence to make for whatever beach chance should offer. Jenny, scarcely conscious of any responsibleness for her first struggles, clutched at Suffragism – a support for which life never intended her. However, it served to help her ashore; and now, with some of the cynicism that creeps into the adventurer's life, she looked around for new adventures. Her desire to revenge herself on men was superseded by anxiety to rediscover the savour of living. Her instinct was now less to hurt others than to indulge herself. A year's abstention from the episodic existence spent by Irene and her before Maurice had created an illusion of permanence, had given that earlier time a romantic charm; and a revival of it seemed fraught with many possibilities of a more widely extended wonder. One evening late in October she asked Irene casually, as if there had been no interval of desuetude, whether she were coming out. To this enquiry her friend, without any manifestation of surprise, answered in the affirmative. It was characteristic of both girls, this manner of resuming a friendship.

Now began a period not worth a detailed chronicle, since it was merely a repetition of a period already discussed – a repetition, moreover, that like most anachronisms seemed after other events jejune and somewhat tawdry. The young men were just as young as those of earlier years; but Irene and Jenny were older and, if before they had found it hard to tolerate these ephemeral encounters, they found it harder still now. The result of this was that, where once a single whisky and soda was enough, now three or four scarcely availed to pass away the time. Neither of the girls drank too much in more than a general sense, but it was an omen of flying youth when whiskies were invoked to give an edge to existence.

One evening they sat in the Café de l'Afrique, laughing to each other over the physical and social oddities of two Norwegians who had constituted themselves their hosts on the strength of a daring stage-door introduction. As Jenny paused in her laughter to catch some phrase of melody in the orchestra, she saw Castleton drawing near their table. He stopped in doubt and looked at her from wide, grey eyes very eager under eyebrows arched in a question. She returned his gaze without a flicker of recognition and, bowing imperceptibly, he passed out into the night. The doors swung together behind him, and Jenny striking a match from the stand on the table, set the whole box alight to distract Irene's attention from what she feared in the blush of a memory.

'Come on; let's go,' she said to her friend.

So the girls left the two Norwegians desolate and volubly unintelligible.

One morning in November Irene came into Jenny's room at Stacpole Terrace.

'My Danby's coming home this week,' she announced. 'And his brother, too.'

347

Jenny often thought to herself that Danby was a riddle. It was four years now since he and Irene had been reputed in love; yet nothing seemed to have happened since the day when for a fancy he dressed his sweetheart in short frocks. Here he was coming back from France as he had come back time after time in company with his brother, at the notion of meeting whom Jenny had always scoffed.

'What of it?' she said.

'Now don't be nasty, young Jenny. I shall be glad to see him.'

'I suppose this means every minute you can get together for a fortnight, and then he'll be off again for six months. Why doesn't he marry you?'

'He's going to,' Irene asserted, twisting the knob on the corner of the bed round and round until it squeaked. 'But I don't want to get married, not yet.'

'Oh no, it's only a rumour. Whyever not? If I loved a fellow as you swank you love Danby, I'd get married quick enough.'

'Well, you didn't—'

'That's enough of you,' said Jenny, sitting up in bed. 'No, I know I didn't. But that was different.'

'Why was it different? My Danby's a gentleman.'

'Yes, when he's asleep. He *can't* be much or he wouldn't have dressed you up such a sight. I'd like to see a man make such a poppy-show of me,' cried Jenny, indignant at the recollection of the incident.

'Oh, well, he doesn't do it now,' said Irene pacifically. 'Aren't you coming out with us?'

'You're very free all of a sudden with your Danby,'

Jenny continued mockingly. 'I remember when you was afraid for your life some girl would carry him off under your nose. Yet you let him go all the time to France. I think you're silly.'

Jenny could not refrain from teasing Irene. The habit was firmly established and, although she had not now the sense of outraged independence which prompted her attitude in old days, she kept it up because such rallying was easier than sympathetic attention.

'His brother Jack says he'd like to meet you.'

Jenny laughed derisively.

'I thought you weren't giving your Danby away with a pound of nothing. Do you remember when I used to call Jack Danby Tin Ribs the Second and you used to get so ratty?'

'Well, what a liberty,' said Irene, laughing at the now almost forgotten insult.

Towards the dripping fog-stained close of November Arthur and Jack Danby arrived from Paris and, tall as lamp-posts, waited for the two girls at the top of the court in Jermyn Street. It did not strike Jenny at the time that the appointment seemed girt with intrigue, as if whispers had gone to the making of it, whispers that voiced a deceitful purpose in her friend. Jenny had often arraigned the methods of Mrs. Dale and denounced the encouragement of Winnie and Irene in any association whose profit transcended its morality. But she never really understood Irene, and her teasing was a sign of this. She accepted her place at Jack Danby's side without suspicion; and was only dimly aware of the atmosphere of satisfaction which clung to the two brothers and her friend.

In the bronzed glow of the Trocadero grill-room she had an opportunity of studying the two men, and because the result of this was a decided preference for Jack, she lost any suspicion of a plot and appeared almost to enjoy his company.

All Arthur Danby's features, even his teeth, seemed excessively pointed, while his thinness and length of limb accentuated this peaked effect of countenance. His complexion had preserved the clearness of youth, but had become waxy from dissipation, and in certain lights was feathered with fine lines that looked like scratches on a smooth surface. His eyelids were puffy and tinged slightly round the rims with a redness which was the more obvious from the vivid light blue eyes it surrounded. A certain diabolic strangeness redeemed the whole effect from mere unpleasantness. Jack Danby was not so tall as his brother, and his features were less sharply pointed, although they were as clearly defined. He had similar eyes of almost cobalt blue when contrasted with the dead whiteness of a skin that gave the impression of being powdered. The younger brother's eyes preserved more fire and seemed under the influence of suggestive conversation to be lighted up from behind in a way that sent a sudden breathlessness through many women. Jenny, when she looked at him full, was aware less of his eyes than of her own, which seemed to her to be kindling in the dry sparks that were radiated by his; and even as she felt scorched by the brain which was thus expressed, her own eyes would melt, as it were, to meet appropriately the liquid softness that succeeded. His lips were never remarkably red and, as the evening advanced, they adopted the exact shade of his complexion, which from paleness took on the lifeless monotone of colour that is seen in the rain-soaked petal of a pink rose. Danby's mouth curved upwards, and when he smiled, he only smiled on one side of his face. The immediate impression he conveyed was that of profound lassitude changed by any topic of sly licentiousness to a startling concentration.

A pictorial representation of the party might have some decorative value. The two brothers had ordered red mullet, which lay scattered about their plates in mingled hues of cornelian, rose and tarnished copper. Their wine was Lacrima Christi of the precise tint to carry on the scheme of colour. Jenny and Irene were drinking champagne whose pale amber sparkled against the prevailing lustre, contrasting and lightening the arrangement of metallic tints, just as Jenny's fair hair set off and was at the same time enhanced by Irene's copper-brown. As a group of revellers the four of them composed into a rich enough study in *genre*, and the fanciful observer would extract from the position of the two men a certain potentiality for romantic events as, somewhat hunched and looking up from down-turned heads, they both sat with legs outstretched to the extent of their length. The more imaginative observer would perceive in the group something unhealthy, something *faisandé*, an air of too deliberate enjoyment that seemed to imply a perfect knowledge of the limitations of human pleasure. These men and girls aimed no arrow of fleeting gaiety to pierce in a straight, sharp course the heart of the present. Sophistication clung to them, and weariness. That senescent October moon which a year ago marked the end of love's halcyon would have been a suitable light for such a party. Jenny herself had gone back to that condition of cynicism which before the days of Maurice was due to ignorance, but was now a profounder cynicism based on experience. Irene had always been sceptical of emotional heights, had always accepted life sensually without much enthusiasm either for the gratification or the denial of her ambitions. As for the two men, they had grown thin on self-indulgence.

'Fill up your glasses, girls,' said Arthur.

'Fill up,' echoed Jack. 'Is there time for another bottle?' he added anxiously.

'This cheese is very good,' commented Arthur.

'Delicious,' the other agreed.

'You two seem to think of nothing but eating and drinking,' said Jenny distastefully.

'Oh no, we think of other things, don't we, Jack?' contradicted the older brother, with a sort of frigid relish.

'Rather,' the younger one corroborated, looking sideways at Jenny.

'We must have a good time this winter,' Arthur announced. 'We needn't go back to Paris for a month or two. We must have a good time at our flat in Victoria.'

'London's a much wickeder city than Paris,' said Jack, addressing the air like some pontiff of vice. 'I like these November nights with shapes of women looming up through the fog. A friend of mine—' As Jack Danby descended to personal reminiscence, he lost his sinister power and became mean and common. 'When I say friend

– I should say business friend, eh, Arthur?' he asked, smiling on the side of his face nearer to his brother. 'Well, he's a lord as a matter of fact,' he continued in accents of studied indifference.

'Tell the girls about him,' urged his brother, and 'Fill up your glasses,' he murmured as, leaning back in his chair, he seemed to fade away into clouds of smoke blown from a very long, thin and black cigar.

'This lord – I won't tell you his name—' said Jack. 'He wanders about in fogs until he meets a shape that attracts him. Then he hands her a velvet mask and takes her home. What an imagination!' chuckled the narrator.

'Well, I call him a dirty rotter,' said Jenny.

'Do you?' asked Jack as if struck by the novelty of such a point of view.

The lights were being extinguished now. The quenching of the orange illumination, and the barren waste of empty tables, gave the grill-room a raffish look which consorted well with the personalities of the two brothers. The party broke up in the abrupt fashion of England, and within a few minutes of sitting comfortably round a richly lighted supper-table, the two girls were seated in a dark taxi on the way to Camden Town.

'How do you like Jack Danby?' Irene enquired.

'He's all right. Only I don't know – I think if I'd met him last year I'd have thought him a swine. I think I must be turning funny. What are they – these long friends of yours?' she added after a pause. 'What do they do in Paris?'

'They bring out books,' Irene informed her.

'Books?' echoed Jenny. 'What sort of books?'

'Ordinary books, I suppose,' said Irene, slightly huffed by Jenny's contemptuous incredulity.

'Well, what do they want to live in Paris for, if they're ordinary books?'

'That's where their business is.'

'Funny place to do a business in ordinary books?'

'I don't see why.'

'Oh, well, it doesn't matter. But *I* think it's funny, that's all. You *are* deep, Ireen.'

'Oh yes,' said Irene, looking out of the window at the waves of light that broke against the window with each passing street lamp. 'You always say that, but I'm not near so deep as what you are.'

'Yes, you are, because I'm always catching you out in a lie *which* you don't me.'

'No, because I'm not so nosy.'

'Now don't be silly and get in a paddy about nothing,' Jenny advised. 'You can't help having funny friends. Only what I can't understand is myself. I think they're both beasts, and yet I'd like to see them again. That's where I'm funny, I think.'

Irene assumed an attitude of lofty indifference.

'There's no need for you to see them again, if you don't like them. Only they give you a good time, and Arthur gave me some glorious rings.'

'*Which* your mother pawned,' interrupted Jenny.

'And he's going to marry me,' Irene persisted.

'Yes, if you get married after dinner when he's drunk.'

'Oh, well, what of it? You're not so clever as what you make out to be.'

354

'That's quite right,' said Jenny, lapsing into a gloom of introspection.

Lying awake that night in the bewilderment of a new experience, the image of Jack Danby recurred to her like the pale image of a sick dream at once repulsive and perilously attractive. Time after time she would drive him from her mind, but as fast as he was banished, his slim face would obtrude itself from another quarter. He would peep from behind the musty curtains, he would take form in the wavering grey shadow thrown upon the ceiling by the gas. He would slide round pictures and materialize from the heap of clothes on the wicker arm-chair by the bed.

One other image could have contended with him; but that image had been finally exorcized by six months of mental discipline. All that was left of Maurice was the fire he had kindled, the fire of passion that, lying dormant since his desertion, was now burning luridly in Jenny's heart.

XXVIII

St. Valentine's Eve

The supper at the Trocadero only marked the first of many such evenings spent in the company of Irene and the two brothers. However much one side of Jenny's character might despise Jack Danby, to another side he was strangely soothing. When she was beside Maurice, every moment used to be haunted by its own ghost, bitter-sweet with the dread of finality. Danby's effect was that of a sedative drug whose action, however grateful at the time, is loathed in retrospect, until deprivation renews desire. Jenny found herself longing to sit near him and was fretful in his absence because, not being in love with him, he did not occupy her meditations pleasantly. He was worth nothing to her without the sense of contact. He was a bad habit: under certain conditions of opportunity in association he might become a vice.

Evolution, in providence for the perpetuation of the species, has kept woman some thousands of years nearer to animals than man. Hence their inexplicableness to the majority of the opposite sex. Men have built up a convention of fastidious woman to flatter their own sexual rivalry. Woman is relinquished as a riddle when she fails to conform to masculine standards of behaviour. Man is accustomed to protest that certain debased – or rather highly specialized – types of his own sex are unreasonably attractive. He generally fails to perceive that, when a woman cannot find a man who is able to stimulate her imagination, she often looks for another who will gratify her senses.

Maurice was never the lover corresponding most nearly with an ideal of greensick maiden dreams. Jenny's sensibility had not been stultified by these emotional ills, so that when he crossed her horizon, she loved him sanely without prejudice. She made him sovereign of her destiny because he seemed to her fit for power. He completely satisfied her imagination; and, having made a woman of her, he left a libertine to reap what he had sown.

Jack Danby possessed the sly patience of an accomplished rake. He never alarmed Jenny with suggestions of escort, with importunity of embraces. His was the stealthy wooing of inactivity and smouldering eyes. He would let slip no occasion for interpreting life to the disadvantage of virtue; he was always sensually insistent. He and his brother, offspring of a lady's maid and an old demirep, owed to their inheritance of a scabrous library the foundations of material prosperity. They owed also their corrupt breed which, through some paradox of healing, might be valuable to women in the mood for oblivion whom the ordinary anæsthetics of memory had failed.

One Saturday night early in January, Arthur suggested that the two girls should come to tea the next day and spend the evening at the flat in Victoria. Irene looked at Jenny, and Jenny nodded her approval of the plan.

Greycoat Gardens lay between the Army and Navy Stores and Vincent Square. The windows at the back looked out over the playground of an old-fashioned charity school and the roof made a wave in that sea of roofs visible from the studio window in Grosvenor Road. But that was ten months ago.

When Jenny and Irene reached the Gardens, the mud-splashed January darkness had already fallen; but for some reason the entrance-hall of the block containing the Danbys' flat was not yet lighted up. It seemed cavernous and chill: the stone stairs were repellent and the whole air full of hollow warnings. Half-way up, a watery exhalation filtered through the frosted glass of a flat's front door in a cold effulgence which added eerily to the lifelessness of all the other doors. The Danbys lived at the very top, and it took all Irene's powers of persuasion to induce Jenny to complete the ascent. At last, however, they gained their destination and immediately on the shrilling of an electric bell walked through a narrow hall misty with the fumes of Egyptian cigarettes. The sitting-room looked cosy with its deep crimson paper and fireglow and big armchairs heaped with downy cushions. Yet the atmosphere had the sickly oppression of an opiate, and it did not take Jenny long to pull back the purple velvet curtains and throw open the window to the raw winter night.

'It's like being in a bottle of port in this room. Phew! I shall have a most shocking headache soon,' she prophesied.

'Won't you leave your coats and things in my room?' said Jack Danby.

'That's not such a dusty idea. Come on, young Ireen.'

The two girls followed their host to his room which was hung with rose du Barri draperies prodigally braided with gold.

'What a glorious room,' cried Jenny.

'You think so?' asked its owner.

'Rather.'

The evening passed away without any development of the situation. The girls looked at books and pictures according to the custom of first visits, and drank Green Chartreuse after the supper which they had helped to lay. They also smoked many fat Egyptian cigarettes during an evening of heavy silences, broken by the crunch of subsiding coal and occasional cries that floated in from neighbouring slums across the stillness of a wet Sunday night.

As Jenny paused on the step of the taxi that was to drive them home, Jack Danby held her hand very tightly.

'You'll come again?' he asked.

'Of course.'

After this first visit Jenny and Irene spent almost every afternoon at the flat in Greycoat Gardens. Jenny liked the sensation of Jack Danby brushing against her, of the sudden twitches he would give her hands, nor did she resent an unexpected kiss with which he once burnt her neck as she leaned over the table looking at a portfolio of Lancret's engravings.

Arthur Danby went back to Paris in advance of his brother, and Jenny fell into the habit of visiting the flat alone. Jack still never startled her with sudden importunities, never suggested the existence of another point of view beside her own. He seemed perfectly content to watch her enjoyment of his luxury and heavy comfort.

One Sunday afternoon in the middle of February – St. Valentine's Eve, to be precise – when the snowdrops drift in myriads across the London parks, Jenny went to pay her farewell visit. Jack Danby was leaving England on the next day to rejoin his brother in Paris. Before she came away from Stacpole Terrace, Jenny had arranged for Irene to pick her up in the course of the evening, so that they could go back together. For some reason she was very particular in exacting a strict promise from Irene not to fail her.

'What a fuss about nothing,' grumbled her friend.

'Oh, well, Ireen, I don't like coming back alone on a Sunday night. I hate Sunday, and you know it.'

Jenny, buried in a big armchair, dozed away the afternoon as usual and after tea sat staring into the fire, while Danby from the hearth-rug assiduously stroked the slim white hand that drooped listlessly over an arm of the chair. A steady drench of rain had set in with the dusk and, being close under the roof, they could hear the gurgle and hiss of the flooded gutters. Neither of them made a move to turn on the electric light or stir the lowering fire to flame. Danby even denied himself three or four cigarettes so that the magnetic current of sensuousness should not be interrupted. Inch by inch he drew closer to Jenny, sliding noiselessly over the thick fur of the rug. He was now near enough to kiss slowly her bare forearm and separately each supple finger. Jenny leaned back unconscious of him, though remotely pleased by his kisses, in her dull hell of memory where repressed inclinations smouldered like the fire on which her eyes were fixed. What a fool she had been for the sake of a silly powerlessness to take the plunge. It was bound to be taken in the end – with someone. But Maurice was a rotter, and would he after all have been worthy of the ultimate sacrifice? Would he not have tired and put her under an even more severe humiliation? Toys were good enough for Maurice. It was ridiculous to make life a burden for the sake of one man. Twenty-two next October. How quickly the years were flying. So, in a maze of speculation, regret and resolution, Jenny lay back in the deep armchair while Jack Danby drugged her with kisses. She drew her arm away at last, feeling hungry in a vague way.

'What's the time?' she asked, yawning.

'It must be after nine.'

'Good lord, and we haven't had supper yet.'

'Are we going to wait for Irene?' he enquired.

'Not for supper. She is late. I won't half tell her off.'

Danby had risen from the hearth-rug and turned on the light. Jenny was poking the fire vigorously.

'I've got *pâté de foie gras*,' he informed her.

'Ugh, what horrible-looking stuff,' she said.

'Don't you like it?'

'I never tried it.'

'Try now,' Danby urged.

'No, thanks; it looks like bad butter.'

The rain increased in volume as the evening wore on. Still Irene did not come. It struck eleven o'clock, and Jenny said she would wait no longer.

'I'll get a cab,' said Danby.

'No; don't leave me here all alone,' cried Jenny.

'Why should you go home at all to-night?' Danby breathed in a parched whisper.

Jenny pressed her face against the jet-black window-pane and suddenly away beyond Westminster there was a low bourdon of thunder.

'Stay with me,' pleaded Danby; 'it's such a night for love.'

'Who cares?' murmured Jenny. 'I've only myself to think about.'

'What did you say?' he asked.

'Nothing.'

'But you will stay?'

She nodded.

XXIX

Columbine at Dawn

Columbine, leaden-eyed, sat up in the strange room, where over an unfamiliar chair lay huddled all her clothes. Through the luminous white fog of dawn a silver sun, breasting the house-tops, gleamed very large. Wan with a thousand meditations, seeming frail as the mist of St. Valentine's morning, suddenly she flung herself deep into the pillow and, buried thus, lay motionless like a marionette whose wire has snapped.

XXX

Lugete, O Veneres

The silver dawn was softened to a mother-of-pearl morning that seemed less primal than autumnal. When Danby came into the sitting-room, he found Jenny, fully dressed for departure, crouched over the ashes of last night's fire. He had a pinched, unwholesome look so early in the day, and was peevish because Jenny's presence kept him from summoning the housekeeper to bring up breakfast.

'We must get something to eat,' he said.

'I don't want anything,' said Jenny.

'Why not?'

'I've got a headache.'

Danby tried to appear sympathetic; but his hands so early were cold as fish, and his touch made Jenny shrink.

'What a nuisance packing is. I've got a fearful lot to do to get to Charing Cross in time for the boat train.'

Like many other people he tried to demonstrate his sympathy by enlarging on his own trials.

'Well?' said Jenny, regarding him from eyes pin-pointed with revulsion in a critical survey that was not softened by the grey morning light, for whatever silkiness clung to the outside air was lost in the stale room.

'I wish I hadn't got to go away,' said Danby awkwardly.

'Why?' Jenny asked, screwing up her eyes as if she had perceived upon the wall an unpleasant insect.

'Well, it seems a pity now that we've – we've got to know each other better.'

'You don't think,' said Jenny, chiselling the words from the very bedrock of her contempt, 'you *don't* think that because I've been in your flat all a night, you know me? Why I don't know myself even. You don't think if I did, I'd have stayed with a long worm like *you*?'

'You're damned unromantic, my beauty.'

'Don't call me *your* beauty. Swear, yes – that suits you. But don't call me yours, because I'm not yours or *any* man's. What I done, I done because I wanted to: but I don't belong to *any*body.'

'You little spitfire,' said Danby, 'I believe you'd stick a knife into me, if you had one.'

'And that's just where you're quite wrong,' Jenny contradicted from some lofty plane unattainable by him. 'You're not worth killing. Get me a taxi, please. I want to go back.'

'Aren't you going to come and see me off?' he asked in a ludicrous attempt at sentiment.

'See you off? You must think I'm potty. See *you* off? Oh yes, that's a game of mine seeing off clothes-props. If you can't move,' she added, 'I can. Let me pass, please.'

Jenny walked towards the door of the contaminated flat followed by Danby in a state of weak bewilderment.

'You'll write to me, little girl?' he asked, making a motion to detain her hand.

'You seem to think I'm struck on you,' she rapped out. 'But I'm not.'

'Well, why did you—'

'Ah, Mr. Enquire Within,' she interrupted, 'you're right. Why?'

'Surely,' he persisted, 'the first person who—'

'The first! Hark at Mr. Early Bird. If you go out with your long soppy self like that, you'll miss your train. Ching-a-ling.'

So Jenny parted from Mr. Jack Danby as long ago she had parted from Mr. Terrence O'Meagh of the Royal Leinster Fusiliers. It was typical of her pride that in order to rob Danby of any satisfaction in his achievement, she should prefer to let him assume he was merely one of a crowd, a commonplace incident in her progress. Anything seemed more suitable to the fancy of such a despicable creature than the self-congratulation of the pioneer.

Yet, though she bore herself so bravely from the hated room which had witnessed the destruction of her inaccessibility, when she was seated alone in the taxi whirring back to Camden Town, Jenny was very near to an emotional collapse. This was averted by an instinct to review the several aspects of the experience. The actual event, happening in the normal course of a temperament's advance to completeness, scarcely distressed her. On the other hand, the circumstances and actors were abhorrent. The very existence of the Danbys was an outrage, and as for Irene, her behaviour was treachery incarnate. What added bitterness to her meditations was the reflection that however contemptuous she might show herself of the two brothers, they, with Irene to voice their absence, would have the laugh

366

on their side. From one point of view it had been a skilful seduction effected with the deliberation of use. Jenny was maddened by the thought that Irene would believe she had been unable to avoid it, that she had been bewitched by Jack Danby's dissolute accomplishments. She would never be able to impress Irene's stolidity with the fact that she had used Danby for her own purpose. Irene would be bound to consider the wretched business a justification of her own dependence on the elder brother. She would triumph with damaging retorts, pointing out the fallibility of other girls when brought beneath the Danby sway, citing Jenny in a manner that would infuriate her with the impotence of argument. All larger issues were obscured by this petty annoyance, and at first her regrets were confined to wishing she had played the inevitable drama of womanhood in some secret place with only her own soul for audience. Why had she stayed at Greycoat Gardens last night?

After the first vexation at her loss of prestige, deeper commentaries upon the act wrote themselves across her mind. She had intended, while her mother was still alive, to be rigidly unassailable. There was weakness in her failure to sustain this resolution, and Jenny loathed weakness. What had made her carry through this experience against the finest influence upon her life? Well, it was done; but the knowledge of it must be kept from her mother. Regrets were foolish; yet she would make some reparation. She would go and live at home again and, before anything, please her mother for a long time to come. She would be extra nice to May. She would be – in parental terminology – a really good girl.

Whatever agony Maurice's love had caused her to bear this sacrifice of her youth upon a tawdry altar had finally and effectually deadened. Now she could meet without a tremor the cause of all the miserable business. Things might have been different, were fidelity an imaginable virtue. But it was all over now; she had consummated the aspirations of youth. There should be an end of love henceforth. For what it was worth of bitter and sweet, she had known it. No longer was the viceroy of human destiny a riddle. He had lost his wings and lay like a foundling in the gutter. No more of such a sorry draggled god for her. Jenny's ambition now was in reconciliation with her mother to be re-established in the well-beloved house in Hagworth Street, and in affection for old familiar things to forget the wild adventures of passion.

The taxi swept on down the Hampstead Road until it turned off on the right to Camden Town, whose curious rococo squares, mildewed and queerly ornamented, seemed the abode of a fantastic depression. For all the sunlight of St. Valentine, the snowdrops looked like very foolish virgins as they shivered in the wind about the blackened grass, good sport for idle sparrows. The impression of faded wickedness made on Jenny's mind by Stacpole Terrace that morning suited her disgust. Every window in the row of houses was askew, cocking a sinister eye at her reappearance. Every house looked impure with a smear of green damp over the stucco. Stacpole Terrace wore an air of battered gaiety fit only for sly entrances at twilight and furtive escapes in the dawn; while in one of the front gardens a stone Cupid with broken nose smirked perpetually at whatever shady intrigue came under his patronage.

It was nearly eleven o'clock when Jenny, entering the sitting-room, found Irene bunched sloppily over the fire. Mrs. Dale and her youngest daughter were busy in the kitchen. Winnie was not yet out of bed and the head of the family was studying in the dust of his small apartment the bargains advertised in yesterday's paper.

'Why didn't you call for me last night?' Jenny demanded straight and swift.

'Oh, well, it was too wet,' grumbled Irene, covering as well as she could her shame with nonchalance.

'Ireen, I think you're a rotter. I think you're real mean and nothing won't ever make me believe you didn't do it for the purpose. Too wet!'

Irene declined to admit herself in the wrong.

'Well, it was too wet. You could easy have come home in a taxi, if you wanted to.'

Jenny stamped with rage.

'What I *could* have done hasn't got nothing to do with it at all, and you know it hasn't. You said you were coming for me and you didn't, and I say you're a sneak. Because you and your massive sister behave anyhow, you'd like to make everyone else as bad.'

Irene, contending even with unclasped stays, made an effort at dignity.

'You can just shut up, Jenny Pearl, because you know very well my mother wouldn't allow me to *do* anything. You know that.'

Jenny fumed with indignation.

369

'Your mother? Why, when she's got half a bottle of gin to cry with over her darling Ireen or darling Winnie, she's *very* glad to pawn what her darlings get given to them.'

'Well, don't stay here any more, if you don't like it,' said Irene surlily.

'Thanks, you don't suppose I'd go on living in what's no better than a common case-house, and which in fact all the houses round this part are.'

'Are they?' sneered Irene.

'Yes.'

'You've got very good,' said Irene, bitterly sarcastic, 'since this night out.'

'Which you meant for me to spend out from the moment you introduced me to him.'

'What do you take me for?' enquired Irene rashly.

'I take you for what you are – a rotter. Yes! and think what you will be one day – I know – a dirty old woman in a basement with a red petticoat and a halfpenny dip and a quartern of gin.'

Irene's imagination was not extensive enough to cap this prophecy, so she poked the fire instead of making the attempt.

'Nobody wants you to stay here,' she muttered, weakly reiterative.

'Don't you worry yourself. I'm going upstairs to pack my things up now.'

Jenny was not able to make a completely effective departure with cab at the door and heaped-up baggage, because her taxi back from Victoria and the payment of a week's board at Stacpole Terrace had exhausted her ready money. However, she had the satisfaction of seeing her portmanteau, her hatbox and a small bag stacked in tapering stories upon the bedroom floor, there to await the offices of Carter Paterson.

Mrs. Dale emerged from the kitchen at the rumour of change and, as morning did not evoke sentiment, indulged in a criticism of Jenny's personal appearance.

'I don't like that hat of yours and never did,' she announced. 'I can't get used to these new-fangled fashions and never shall.'

'What of it?' said Jenny with marked indifference.

'Oh, nothing at all, if it pleases you. You've got to wear it and I suppose there's nothing more to be said. But I think that hat is vulgar. Vulgar it would have been called when I was a girl. And I can't think what you want to go all of a sudden for like this. It isn't often I make a beefsteak pudding.'

Jenny was in a flutter to be away.

'Goodbye, Mrs. Dale,' she said firmly.

'Well, goodbye, Jenny. You mustn't mind shaking hands with me all covered in suet. As I say, it's very seldom I do make a beefsteak pudding. I won't disturb my old man. He's busy this morning. Come and tell us soon how you get on.'

It was a relief to be seated inside the tram and free of Stacpole Terrace. It was pleasant to change cars at the Nag's Head and behold again the well-known landscape of Highbury. A pageant of childish memories, roused by the sight of the broad pavements of Islington, was marshalled in Jenny's brain. Somehow on the visits she had paid her home during the last year these aspects were obscured by the consciousness of no longer owning any right to them.

371

Now, really going home, she turned into Hagworth Street with a glow of pride at seeing again its sobriety and dignity so evident after the extravagant stucco and Chinese balconies of Camden Town's terraces and squares. There was Seventeen, looking just the same, prophetic of refuge and solid comfort to the exile. She wondered what freak of folly had ever made her fancy home was dingy and unpleasant, home that held her bright-eyed mother's laugh, her absurd father always amusing, and her little sister May. Home was an enchanted palace with more romance in each dear room than was to be found elsewhere in the world. Home was alive with the past and preserved the links which bound together all the detached episodes of Jenny's life. As she turned into the garden that once had seemed a district, as she rattled the letter-box – in the days of her estrangement she always rang the bell – remorse came welling up in tears. She remembered what good times had been recurrent through the past, tea-parties and pantomimes and learning to ride a bicycle in the warm sunsets of June. And in the house opposite nothing was altered, not a fold of the lace curtains, not a leaf of the dusty aspidistra that took all the light in the ground-floor window.

What a long time they were opening the door. She rattled the letter-box again and called out to May. It was like coming home after summer holidays by the blue sparkling sea, coming home to dolls and toys and the long, thin garden at the back which from absence had acquired an exaggerated reputation for entertainment.

Suddenly May opened the door, peeping round over the latch, much scared apparently.

'How quick you've been,' she said.

'Quick?' repeated Jenny.

'Didn't you get my telegram?'

'No,' said Jenny, and perceiving that May's eyes were red with weeping, her delightful anticipation was clouded with dread. 'What did you want to telegraph for? Not – not about mother?'

May nodded.

'She isn't dead?' Jenny gasped.

'No, she isn't dead. But she's had to be took away. You know. To an asylum.'

'Go on,' said Jenny. 'Oh, what a dreadful thing.'

'Well, don't stand there,' May commanded. 'There's been crowd enough round here this morning as it is.'

In the kitchen she unfolded the story. It seemed that for the last fortnight their mother had been queer.

'Oh, she was funny,' said May. 'She used to sit moping over the fire – never doing nothing and saying all the time how her head hurt.'

'Didn't dad fetch in a doctor?' Jenny demanded.

'Not at first he wouldn't. You know what dad's like. I said she was really ill and he kept on saying: "Nonsense, why look at me. I'm as ill as I can be, but I don't want no doctor. I've got a sort of a paralytic stroke running up and down my arm fit to drive anybody barmy. And here am I going off to work so cheerful, the chaps down at the shop say they don't know how I does it." '

'He ought to be bumped,' Jenny asserted wrathfully. 'I only wish I'd been at home to tell him off. Go on about mother. And why wasn't I sent for directly?' she asked.

'Well, I did think about fetching you back. But I didn't really think myself it was anything much at first. She got worse all of a sudden like. She took a most shocking dislike to me and said I was keeping her indoors against her will, and then she carried on about you, said you was – well, I don't know what she didn't say. And when the doctor came, she said he was a detective and asked him to lock you and me both up, said she had the most wicked daughters. I was quite upset, but the doctor he said not to worry as it was often like that with mad people, hating the ones they liked best. And I said, "She's never gone mad? Not my mother? Oh, whatever shall I do?" And he said, "She has," and then she started off screaming enough to make anyone go potty to hear her, and a lot of boys come and hung about by the gate and people was looking out of windows and the greengrocer was ringing all the time to know if there was any orders this morning.'

'When was all this?' asked Jenny, frozen by the terrible narrative.

'This morning, I keep telling you.'

'Just now.'

'No, early. They come and took her away to an asylum somewhere in the country and we can go and see her once a fortnight. But she's very ill, the doctor says – some sort of abscess on her brain.'

'Where's dad?'

'He went round to the Arms. He said he felt quite shaky.'

Jenny sat mute and hopeless. Would her mother never recognize her? Would she die in the belief that she was neither loved nor appreciated?

XXXI

A Document in Madness

Ashgate Asylum was a grey accumulation of stone, standing at the head of a wide avenue of beech trees on a chalky ridge of the Chiltern Hills. Here in a long ward lay Mrs. Raeburn, fantasies riding day and night through the darkness of her mind.

Jenny and May used to go once a fortnight to visit her sad seclusion. In a way it was a fruitless errand of piety; for she never recognized her daughters, staring at them from viewless eyes. Nobody else in the family made the slow, dreary journey through the raw spring weather. To be sure every fortnight Charlie intended to go; but something always cropped up to prevent him, and as he was unable to realize the need for instancy, he finally made up his mind to postpone any visit to the early summer, when, as he optimistically announced, it would no doubt be time to fetch his wife home completely cured.

Jenny and May used to be met at the railway station by the asylum brougham, which would bear them at a jogging pace up the straight melancholy avenue and set them down by the main entrance beside which hung the huge bell-chain whose clangour seemed to wake a multitude of unclean spirits. Often, as they walked nervously over the parquet of the lobby ample as a cloister and past a succession of cheerful fire-places, Jenny would fancy she heard distant screams, horrid cries travelling down the echoing corridors that branched off at every few paces. The nurse who was directing them would talk away pleasantly without apparent concern, without seeming to notice those patients allowed a measure of liberty. Jenny and May, however, could hardly refrain from shrieking out in terror as they shivered by these furtive, crouching shapes whose gaze was concentrated on things not seen by them. In the long ward at whose extreme end their mother's bed was situated, these alternations of embarrassment and fear became even more acute. Nearly all the occupants of the beds had shaved heads which gave them, especially the grey-haired women, a ghastly appearance. Many of them would mutter audible comments on the two girls as they passed along, comparing them extravagantly to angels or to long-lost friends and relatives. Some would whimper in the terrible imagination that Jenny and May had arrived to hurt them. The girls were glad when the battery of mad eyes was passed and they could stand beside their mother's bed.

'Here are your daughters come all this long way to see you, Mrs. Raeburn,' the nurse would announce, and 'Well, mother,' or 'How are you now, mother?' they would shyly enquire.

Mrs. Raeburn could not recognize them, but used to regard them from wide-open eyes that betrayed neither friendliness nor dislike.

'Won't you say you're glad to see them?' the nurse would ask.

Then sometimes Mrs. Raeburn would bury herself in the bedclothes to lie motionless until they had gone, or sometimes she would count on her fingers mysterious sums and ghostly numerals comprehended in the dim mid-region where her soul sojourned. If Jenny or May looked up in embarrassment, they would see all around them reasonless heads, some smiling and bobbing and beckoning, some grimacing horribly, and every one, save the listless head they loved best, occupied with mad speculations upon the identity of the two girls. After every visit, as hopelessly they were leaving the ward, the nurse would say:

'I expect your mother will be better next time you come and able to talk a bit.'

They would be shown into a stuffy little parlour while the brougham was being brought round, a stuffy little room smelling of plum-cake and sherry. In the window hung a cage containing an old green paroquet that all the time swore softly to itself and seemed in the company of the mad to have lost its own clear bird's intelligence. Then back they would drive along the straight wet avenue in a sound of twilight gales, back to the rain-soaked dreary little station in whose silent waiting-room they would sit, crying softly to themselves, until the Marylebone train came in.

These visits continued for six weeks, and then, on the fourth visit, just as April had starred the Chilterns with primroses, the nurse whispered while they were walking through the ward's distraught glances:

377

'I think your mother will know you to-day.'

'Why?' Jenny whispered back.

'I think she will, somehow.'

Up the ward they went with hearts beating expectant, while the voices of the mad folk chattered on either side. 'Look at her golden hair,' 'That's St. Michael. Holy Michael, pray for us.' One young woman with pallid, tear-washed face was moaning: 'Why can't I be dead, oh, why can't I be dead?' An old woman, grey as an ash tree, was muttering very quickly to herself: 'Oh, God help me; Oh, dear Lord help me!' on and on without a pause in the gibbering re-iteration. Some of the patients waved and bobbed as usual, mopping and mowing and imparting wild secrets from the wild land in which they lived, and others scowled and shook their twisted fists. This time, indeed, their mother did look different, as if from the unknown haunted valleys in which her soul was imprisoned she had gained some mountain peak with a view of home.

'How are you, mother?' Jenny asked.

Mrs. Raeburn stared at her perplexed, but not indifferent. Nor did she try to hide herself as usual. Suddenly she spoke in a voice that to her daughters seemed like the voice of a ghost.

'Is that little May?'

May's ivory cheeks were flushed with nervous excitement as, by an effort of brave will, she drew near to the mad mother's couch.

'Yes, it is little May,' said Mrs. Raeburn, fondling her affectionately. 'Poor little back. Poor little thing. What a dreadful misfortune. My fault, all my fault. I shouldn't

378

have bothered about cleaning up so much, not being so far gone as I was. Poor little May. I'm very ill – my head is hurting dreadfully.'

Suddenly over the face of the tortured woman came a wonderful change, a relief not mortal by its radiance. She sank back on her pillow in a vision of consolation. Jenny leaned over her. 'Mother,' she whispered, 'don't you know me? It's Jenny! Jenny!' she cried in agony of longing to be recognized.

'Jenny,' repeated the mother as if trying to make the name fit in with some existing fact of knowledge. 'Jenny?' she murmured more faintly. 'No, not Jenny, Cupid.'

'What's she mean?' whispered May.

'She's thinking of the ballet. It was last time she saw me on the stage.'

'Cupid,' Mrs. Raeburn went on. 'Yes, it's Cupid. And Cupid means love. Love! God bless all good people. It's a fine day. Yes, it is a fine day. I'm very fond of this window, Carrie; I think it's such a cheerful view. Look at those lovely clouds. What a way you can see – right beyond the "Angel" to the country. Those aunts are coming again. Tut, tut. What do *they* want to come here for? They shan't have her, they shan't have my Jenny. Jenny!' cried Mrs. Raeburn, recognizing at last her best-loved daughter, 'I meant you to be so sweet and handsome, my Jenny! Oh, be good, my pretty one, my dainty one. I wish you'd see about that knob, Charlie. You *never* will remember to get a new one.'

Then, though her eyes were rapturous and gay again, her mind wandered farther afield in broken sentences.

'I think you'd better kiss her goodbye,' the nurse said.

Softly each daughter kissed that mother who would always remain the truest, dearest figure in their lives.

Downstairs in the stuffy little parlour, Dr. Weever interviewed them.

'Who ever allowed you two girls to come here?' he asked sharply. 'You've no business to visit such a place. You're too young.'

'Will our mother get better?' Jenny asked.

'Your poor mother is dying and you should be glad, because she suffers great pain all the time.' His voice was harsh, but nevertheless full of tenderness.

'Will she die soon?' Jenny whispered. May was sobbing to herself.

'Very soon.'

'Then I'd better tell my father to come at once?'

'Certainly, if he wants to see his wife alive.'

Jenny did not go to the Orient that night, and when her father came in, she told him how near it was to the end.

'What, dying?' said Charlie, staggered by a thought which had never entered his mind. 'Dying? Go on, don't make a game of serious things like death.'

'She is dying. And the doctor said if you wanted to see her alive, you must go at once.'

'I'll go to-night,' said Charlie, feeling helplessly for his best hat.

Just then came a double-knock at the door.

'That means she's dead already,' said Jenny in a dull monotone.

XXXII

Pageantry of Death

Mr. Raeburn determined that, if there had sometimes been a flaw in his behaviour towards his wife when alive, there should be no doubt about his treatment of her in death. Her funeral should be famous for its brass-adorned oaken coffin, splendidly new in the gigantic hearse. There should be long-tailed sable horses with nodding plumes, and a line of mourning coaches. Mutes should be everywhere and as many relatives as could be routed out within the time. Black silks and satins, jet and crape and sombre stuffs should oppress the air and Death with darkling wings should overshadow Islington. Many mourners were gathered together whose personalities had never played any part in Jenny's life; but others arrived who had in the past helped her development.

Mrs. Purkiss came, escorted by Claude Purkiss representing with pale face and yellow silky moustache the smugness of himself and Percy the missionary. Claude's majority would occur in May, when he would be admitted to a partnership in the business. Already a bravery of gold paint, symbolizing his gilt-edged existence, was at work adding 'And Son' to 'William Purkiss.' Uncle James

Threadgale made the journey from Galton, bringing with him Mrs. Threadgale the second – a cheerful country body who pressed an invitation upon Jenny and May to visit them. Uncle James did not seem to have altered much, and brought up with him a roll of fine black cloth for Jenny, but was so much upset on realizing he had omitted May from his thoughtfulness that immediately upon his arrival he slipped out to buy a similar roll for her. The two lodgers were present as a mark of respect to the dead woman who had been so admirable a landlady; and both of them with kindly tact announced they were going away for a few days. Alfie, of course, was there with his fiancée, whom Jenny somewhat grudgingly admitted to be very smart. Edie came with the children and her husband. His arrival caused a slight unpleasantness, because Alfie said he would rather not go at all to the funeral than ride with Edie and Bert. But in the end a compromise was effected by which he and his Amy occupied a coach alone. After these mourners came a cortège of friends and cousins, all conspicuously black, all intent to pay their homage of gloom.

Jenny, when she had made herself ready, sat on the end of the bed and laughed.

'I can't help it, May. I know it's wicked of me. But I can't keep from laughing, I can't really.'

'Well, don't let any of them downstairs hear you,' begged May, 'because *they* wouldn't understand.'

'It doesn't mean I'm not sorry about mother because I laugh. And I believe she'd be the first to understand. Oh, May, what a tale she'd have made of it, if she'd only been alive to see her own funeral. She'd have kept anyone in fits of laughter for a week.'

Even during the slow progress of the pomp, Jenny in the first coach with her father and May was continually on the verge of laughter because, just as by a great effort she had managed to bring her emotions under control, Aunt Mabel had tripped over her skirt and dived head foremost into the carriage that was to hold Claude, Uncle James and his wife, and herself. Moreover, to make matters worse, her father's black kid gloves kept splitting in different places until, by the time the cemetery was reached, his hands merely looked as if they were plentifully patched with court-plaster. It was blue and white April weather, fit for cowslips and young lambs, when the sombre people darkened the vivid wet grass round the grave. During the solemnity and mournfulness of the burial service Jenny stood rigid and pale, more conscious of the wind sighing through the yew trees than of finality and irremediable death. She was neither irritated nor moved by the sniffling of those around her. The fluttering of the priest's surplice and the tear-dabbled handkerchiefs occupied her attention less than the figure of a widow looking with sorrowful admiration at a tomb-stone two hundred yards away. She did not advance with the rest to stare uselessly down on the lowered coffin. The last words had been said: the ceremony was done. In the sudden silver wash of an April shower they all hurried to the shelter of the mourning coaches. Jenny looked back once, and under the arc of a rainbow saw men with gleaming spades: then she, too, lost in the dust and hangings of the heavy equipage, was jogged slowly back to Islington.

Funerals, like weddings, are commonly employed by families to weld broken links in the chain of association with comparisons of progress and the condolences or congratulations of a decade's chance and change. Jenny could not bear to see these relations cawing like rooks in a domestic parliament. She felt their presence outraged the humour of the dead woman and pictured to herself how, if her father had died, her mother would have sent them all flapping away. She did not want to hear her mother extolled by unappreciative people. She loathed the sight of her sleek cousin Claude, of Alfie glowering at Edie, of her future sister-in-law picking pieces of white cotton off her skirt, of Edie brushing currants from the side of Norman's mouth. Finally, when she was compelled to listen to her father's statement of his susceptibility to the knocks of a feather on receiving the news of his wife's death, she could bear it no longer, but went upstairs to her bedroom, whither Aunt Mabel presently followed in search.

'Ah, Jenny, this is a sad set out and no mistake,' Mrs. Purkiss began.

Jenny did not deign to pay any attention, but looked coldly out of the window.

'You must feel quite lost without her,' continued the aunt, 'though to be sure you didn't trouble her much with your company this last year. Poor Florrie, she used to fret about it a lot. And your father wasn't much use – such an undependable sort of man as he is. Let's all hope, now he's got two motherless girls to look after, he'll be a bit more strict.'

'I wish you wouldn't keep on at me, Auntie,' Jenny protested, 'because I shall be most shocking rude to you in a minute, which I shouldn't like to be at such a time.'

'Tut-tut, I wish you could control that temper of yours; but there, I make allowances, for I know you must be feeling it all very much, especially as you must blame yourself a bit.'

Jenny turned sharply round and faced her aunt.

'What for?' she demanded.

'Why, for everything. Nothing'll ever convince me it wasn't worry drove your poor mother into the grave. Your Uncle William said the same when he heard of it. He was *very* disappointed to think he couldn't come to the funeral; but, as he said, "what with Easter almost on us and one thing and another, I really haven't got the time." '

Mrs. Purkiss had seated herself in the armchair and was creaking away in comfortable loquacity.

'I think it's nothing more than wicked to talk like that,' Jenny declared indignantly. 'And, besides, it's silly, because the doctor said it was an abscess, nothing else.'

'Ah, well, doctors know best, I dare say; but we all have a right to our opinions.'

'And you think my leaving home for a year killed my mother?'

'I don't go so far as that. What I said was you were a worry to her. You were a worry when you were born, for I was there. You were a worry when you would go on the stage against whatever I said. You were a worry when you dyed your hair and when you kept such disgraceful late hours and when you went gallivanting about with that young fellow. However, I don't want to be the one to rub in uncomfortable facts at such a time. What I came up to ask was if you wouldn't like to come and stay with us for a little while, you and May. You'll have to get an extra servant to look after the lodgers if your father intends keeping things on as they were, and you'll be more at home with us.'

Mrs. Purkiss spoke in accents almost ghoulish, with a premonitory relish of macabre conversations.

'Stay with you?' repeated Jenny. 'Stay with *you*? What, and hear nothing but what I ought to have done? No, thanks; May and I'll stay on here.'

'You wouldn't disturb your Uncle William,' Mrs. Purkiss continued placidly, 'if that's what you're thinking of. You'd be gone to the theatre, when he reads his paper of an evening.'

'If I went to stay anywhere,' said Jenny emphatically, 'I should go and stay with Uncle James at Galton. But I'm not, so please don't keep on, because I don't want to talk to *any*body.'

Mrs. Purkiss sighed compassionately and vowed she would forgive her niece under the circumstances, would even spend the evening in an attempt to console the sad household of Hagworth Street.

'But I want to be alone, and so does May.'

'Well, I always used to say you was funny girls, and this proves my words true. Anyone would think you'd be glad to talk about your poor mother to her only sister. But no, girls nowadays seem to have no civilized feelings. Slap-dashing around. In and out. Nothing but amuse themselves, the uncultivated things, all the time. No wonder the papers carry on about it. But I'm not going to stay where I'm not wanted and don't need any innuendives to go.'

Here Mrs. Purkiss rose from the chair and, having in a majestic sweep of watered silk attained the door, paused to deliver one severe speculation.

'If you treated your poor mother as you behave to your aunt, I'm not surprised she got ill. If my Percy or my Claude behaved like you – well, there, but they don't, thank goodness.'

Jenny listened, quite unmoved, to the swishing descent of her aunt. She was merely glad to think her rudeness had been effectual in driving her away, and followed her downstairs very soon in order to guarantee her departure.

One by one the funereal visitors went their ways. One by one they faded into the sapphire dusk of April. Some went in sable parties like dilatory homing cattle, browsing as they went on anecdotes of the dead. On the tail of the last exit, their father, somewhat anxiously as if afraid of filial criticism, went also. He sat for a long time, as he told them afterwards, without drinking anything, the while he stared at his silk hat enmeshed in crape, and when he did drink he called for stout.

The two girls stayed alone in the parlour with little heart to light the gas, with little desire to talk after the mournful buzz which had filled the house all day. The lodgers being gone, no responsibility of general illumination rested with Jenny or May. Soon, however, they moved in accord to the kitchen, where on each side of the glowing fire they listened to the singing of a kettle and the tick of the American clock. An insistent loneliness penetrated their souls. In that hour of sorrow and twilight, they drew nearer to one another than ever before. Outside a cat was wailing, and far down the road a dog, true to superstition, howled at intervals. The kitchen was intolerably changed by Mrs. Raeburn's absence. Jenny suddenly realized how lonely May must have been during those weeks of illness and suspense. She herself had had the distractions of the theatre, but May must have moped away each heavy moment.

'I wonder where Ruby is now?' said Jenny suddenly.

'Fancy! I wonder.'

They sighed. The old house in Hagworth Street seemed, with the death of its laughing mistress, to have lost its history, to have become merely one of a dreary row.

'Oh, May, look,' said Jenny. 'There's her apron, never even gone to the wash.'

After that the sisters wept quietly; while Venus dogged the young moon down into the green West, and darkness shrouded the grey Islington street.

XXXIII

Loose Ends

For all that Jenny was so contemptuous of her aunt's opinion at the time of its expression, when she came to weigh its truth she found it somewhat disturbing. Was an abscess indeed the sole cause of her mother's madness and death? And could Aunt Mabel have any justification for so cruelly hinting at a less obvious cause? Jenny herself possessed a disconcerting clarity of intuition which she inherited from her mother, who might have divined the progress of the Danby incident and brooded over it too profoundly in the absence of her daughter. Indeed, she might have been actually goaded into sheer madness by a terrible consciousness of that rainy St. Valentine's eve; for it was strange that her sanity should fly for ever on the very next morning. It was horrid to think that all night long her mother, kept awake by pain, might have been conscious of her actions. Yet the doctor had so confidently blamed the abscess for everything. Moreover, in the asylum her mother had seemed just as much distressed by the thought of May's back as anything else. Sensitiveness to her mother's feelings had led Jenny into wrecking her own happiness with Maurice, but even Fortune could scarcely be so fierce as to drive her mother mad on account of the pitiful corollary to that ruined love. Yet it might be so, and if it were, what remorse would burden her mind everlastingly! And now it was too late for explanations. Jenny, having felt all through her mother's life an inability to confide in her completely, now when she was dead developed an intense desire to pour out her soul, to acquaint her with every detail of experience and even to ascertain if her own passionate adventures had been foreshadowed in her mother's life.

Meanwhile, with all these potential horrors of culpable actions, there was the practical side of the future to consider. In a week the lodgers would return, and a servant must be found at once to help May. She herself would do as much as possible, but most of her energy was sapped by the theatre. She wished her father had the smallest conception of management. The death of his wife, however, seemed to have destroyed what small equipment of resolution he possessed, and the Masonic Arms received him more openly, more frequently than ever.

Jenny debated the notion of leaving the Orient and applying all her mind to keeping house; but it was too late for her temperament to inure itself to domesticity without the spur of something sharper than mere pecuniary advantage. Perhaps it would be better to give up the house in Hagworth Street and take a smaller one, where, on the joint earnings of herself and her father, he and the two sisters could live in tolerable comfort. Perhaps she might even accept the risk of setting up house with May alone. But thirty shillings a week was not a large sum for two girls, one of whom must be well dressed and able to hold her own in company where dress counted for a good deal. The more she thought of it, the more impossible did it seem to give up the theatre. Those few days of absence proved how intimately her existence was wrapped up in the certainty of an evening's employment. As the time had drawn on for going down to the Orient, she had become restless in the quiet of home. However much she might scoff at it, there was wonderful comfort in the assurance of a cheerful evening of dressing-room gossip. Besides, there was always the chance of an interesting stranger in front or of suddenly being called upon to play a noticeable part, though that pleasure grew more and more insipid all the time. There was, however, still a certain agree-able reflection in the consciousness of looking pretty and knowing that a few eyes every night remarked her face and figure. And even if these consolations of theatrical existence failed, there was a great satisfaction in making up and leaving, as it were, one's own discontented body behind.

For a time everything went on as usual, and nobody put forward any definite proposal involving a change either of residence or mode of life. Jenny began to think she was doomed to settle down into perpetual dullness and never again to be launched desperately on a passionate adventure. She was beginning to be aware how easy it was for a woman to belie the temperament of her youth with a common-place maturity. By the end of the summer their father had already advanced so far on the road to moral and financial disintegration as to make it evident to Jenny and May that they must fend for themselves. One lodger, an old clerk in a Moorgate firm of solicitors, had already left; the other, a Cornishman working in a dairy, would soon be carrying the result of his commercial experience back to his native land. Neither of the girls liked the prospect of new lodgers and both were nervous of affording shelter to possible thieves or murderers. Nor did May in particular enjoy the supervision of the servant or wrestling with the slabs of unbaked dough which heralded her culinary essays. So at last she and Jenny decided the house was altogether too large and that they must give notice to quit.

'And aren't I to give no opinion on the subject of my own house?' asked their father indignantly.

'You?' cried Jenny. 'Why should you? You don't do nothing but drink everything away. Why should we slave ourselves to the death keeping you?'

'There's daughters!' Charlie apostrophized. 'Yes, daughters is all very nice when they're small, but when they grow up, they're worse than wives. It comes of being women, I suppose.' And Charlie, as if sympathizing with his earliest ancestor, sighed for Eden. 'Look here, I don't want to take my hook from this house.'

'All right, stay on then, stupid,' May advised; 'only Jenny and I are going to clear off.'

'Stay on by yourself,' Jenny continued in support of her sister, 'and a fine house it'll be in a year's time. No one able to get in for empty bottles and people all around thinking you've opened a shooting-gallery, I should say.'

'Now don't keep on,' said Charlie. 'Because I want to have a lay down, so you can just settle it as you like.'

It was Sunday afternoon and no problems of future arrangements were serious enough to interrupt a lifelong habit.

'It's no good talking to him,' said Jenny scornfully; 'what we've got to do is give notice sharp. I hate this house now,' she added, savagely appraising the walls.

So it was settled that after so many years the Raeburns should leave Hagworth Street. Charlie made no more attempts to contest the decision, and acquiesced almost cheerfully when he suddenly reflected that public-houses were always handy wherever anyone went, 'though, for all that,' he added, 'I shall miss the old Arms.'

'Fancy,' said Jenny, 'who'd have thought it?'

On the following Sunday afternoon Mr. Corin the remaining lodger came down to interview his hostesses.

'I hear you're leaving then, Miss Raeburn,' he said. 'How's that?'

'It's too hard work for my sister,' Jenny answered very politely. 'And besides, she don't care for it, and nor don't I.'

'Well, I'm going home-along myself in November month, I believe, or I should have been sorry to leave you. What I came down to ask about was whether you'd let a bedroom to a friend of mine who's coming up from Cornwall on some law business in connection with some evidence over a right of way or something. A proper old mix up, I believe it is. But I don't suppose they'll keep him more than a week, and he could use my sitting-room.'

Jenny looked at May.

'Yes, of course, let him come,' said the housewife. 'But when will it be?'

'October month, I believe,' said Mr. Corin. 'That's when the witnesses are called for.'

Everything seemed to happen in October, Jenny thought. In October she would be twenty-two. How time was flying, flying with age creeping on fast. In the dreariness of life's prospect even the arrival of Mr. Corin's friend acquired the importance of an expected event, and, though neither of the sisters broke through custom so far as to discuss him beforehand, the coming of Mr. Corin's friend served as a landmark in the calendar like Whitsuntide or Easter. Meanwhile, Mr. Raeburn, as if aware of the little time left in which the Masonic Arms could be enjoyed, drank more and more as the weeks jogged by.

Summer gales marked the approach of autumn, and in the gusty twilights that were perceptibly earlier every day, Jenny began to realize how everything of the past was falling to pieces. There was an epidemic of matrimony at the theatre, which included in the number of its victims Maudie Chapman and Elsie Crauford. Of her other companions Lilli Vergoe had left the ballet and taken up paid secretarial work for some misanthropic society, while the relations between Irene and herself had been grimly frigid ever since the quarrel. New girls seemed to occupy old places very conspicuously, and all the stability of existence was shaken by change. Only the Orient itself remained immutably vast and austere, voracious of young life, sternly intolerant of fading beauty, antique and unscrupulous.

Jenny was becoming conscious of the wire from which she was suspended for the world's gaze, jigged hither and thither and sometimes allowed to fall with a flop when fate desired a new toy. The ennui of life was overwhelming. A gigantic futility clouded her point of view, making effort, enjoyment, sorrow, disappointment, success equally unimportant. She was not induced by that single experience of St. Valentine's eve to prosecute her curiosity. This may have been because passion full-fed was a disillusionment, or it may have been that the shock of her mother's madness appeared to her as a tangible retribution. Everything was dead. Her dancing, like her life, had become automatic, and even her clothes lasted twice as long as in the old days.

'I can't make out what's happened to everybody,' she said to May. 'No fellows ever seem to come round to the stage door now. All the girls have either got married or booked up that way. Nobody ever wants to have larks like we used to have. You never hardly hear anybody laugh in the dressing-room now. I met someone the other day who knew me two years ago and they said I'd gone as thin as a threepenny-bit.'

Jenny meditated upon the achievement of her life up to date and wrote it down a failure. Where was that Prima Ballerina Assoluta who with pitter-pat of silver shoes had danced like a will-o'-the-wisp before her imagination long ago? Where was that Prima Ballerina with double-fronted house at Ealing or Wimbledon and meek, adoring husband? Where, indeed, were all elfin promises of fame and fairy hopes of youth? They had fled, those rainbow-winged deceivers, together with short frocks accordion-pleated and childhood's tumbled hair. Where was that love so violent and invincible that even time would flee in dismay before its progress? Where, too, was the laughter that once had seemed illimitable and immortal? Now there was nothing so gay as to keep even laughter constant to Jenny's world. For her there was no joy in lovely transience. She knew by heart no Horatian ode which, declaiming against time, could shatter the cruelty of impermanence. Without an edifice of love or religion or art or philosophy, there seemed no refuge from decay.

When the body finds existence a mock, the mind falls back upon its intellectual defences. But Jenny had neither equipment, commissariat nor strategic position. She was a dim figure on the arras of civilization, faintly mobile in the stressful winds of life. She was a complex decorative achievement and should have been cherished as such. Therefore at school she was told that William the Conqueror came to the throne in 1066, that a bay is a large gulf, a promontory a small cape. She had been a plaything for the turgid experiments of parrots in education by simple facts, facts so sublimely simple that her mind recorded them no more than would the Venus of Milo set down on a bench before a pupil teacher. When she was still a child, plastic and wonderful, she gave her dancing and beauty to a country whose inhabitants are just as content to watch two dogs fight or a horse die in the street. When ambition withered before indifference, she set out to express herself in love. Her early failures should not have been fatal, would not have been if she had possessed any power of mental recuperation. But even if William the Conqueror had won his battle at Clacton, the bare knowledge of it would not have been very useful to Jenny. Yet she might have been useful in her beauty, could some educationalist have perceived in her youth that God as well as Velazquez can create a thing of beauty. She lived, however, in a period of enthusiastic waste, and now brooded over the realization that nothing in life seemed to recompense one for living, however merrily, however splendidly the adventure began.

Such was Jenny's mood when, just after her twenty-second birthday, Mr. Corin announced that his friend Mr. Z. Trewhella would arrive in three days' time.

XXXIV

Mr. Z. Trewhella

Mr. Corin was anxious to make his friend's visit to London as pleasant as possible and, in zeal for the enjoyment of Zachary Trewhella, to impress him with the importance and knowingness of William John Corin. By way of extirpating at once any feeling of solitude, he was careful to invite Jenny and May to take tea with them on the afternoon following Trewhella's arrival. The first-floor sitting-room, once in the occupation of Mr. Vergoe, looked very different nowadays; and indeed no longer possessed much character. Corin's decorative extravagance had never gone beyond the purchase of those glassy photographs of City scenes in which from a confusion of traffic rise landmarks like St. Paul's or the Royal Exchange. These destined ultimately to adorn the best parlour of his Cornish home were now propped dismally against the overmantel, individually obscured according to the vagaries of the servant's dusting by a plush-bound photograph of Mr. Lloyd George. The walls of the room were handed over to wall-paper save where two prints, billowy with damp, showed Mr. Gladstone looking at the back of Mr. Spurgeon's neck over some tabulated observations on tuberculosis among cows.

Zachary Trewhella did more than share his friend's sitting-room: he occupied it, not so much actively, as by sheer inanimate force. To see him sitting in the armchair was to see a boulder flung down in a flimsy drawing-room. He was a much older man than Corin, probably about thirty-eight, though Jenny fancied he could not be less than fifty. His eyes, very deep brown and closely set, had a twinkle of money, and the ragged moustache probably concealed a cruel and avaricious mouth. His hands were rough and swollen with work and weather: his neck was lean and his pointed ears were set so far back as to give his high cheek-bones over which the skin was drawn very taut a prominence of feature they would not otherwise have possessed. He belonged to a certain type of Cornish farmer, a little more than fox, a little less than wolf, and judged by mere outward appearance, particularly on this occasion of ill-fitting broadcloth and celluloid collar, he would strike the casual glance as mean of form and feature. Yet he radiated force continually and though actually a small man produced an effect of size and power. It was impossible definitely to predicate the direction of this energy, to divine whether it would find concrete expression in agriculture or lust or avarice or religion. Yet so vitally did it exist that from the moment Trewhella entered Corin's insignificant apartment, the room was haunted by him, and not merely the room, but Hagworth Street itself and even Islington.

'Well, Zack,' said Mr. Corin, winking at the two girls, and for effect lapsing into broadest dialect. 'What du 'ee thenk o' Lonnon, buoy, grand auld plaäce 'tis, I b'liv?'

'I don't know as I've thought a brae lot about it,' said Zack.

'He's all the time brooding about this right of way,' Mr. Corin explained.

Jenny and May were frankly puzzled by Trewhella. He represented to them a new element. Jenny felt she had received an impression incommunicable by description, as if, having been flung suddenly into a room, one were to try to record the experience in terms of the underground railway.

The farmer himself did not pay any attention to either of the girls, so that Jenny was compelled to gain her impression of him as if he were an animal in a cage, funny or dull or interesting, but always remote. She was content to watch him eat with a detached curiosity that prevented her from being irritated by his deliberation or, after noisy drinking, by the colossal fist that smudged his lips dry.

'Ess,' Trewhella announced after swallowing a large mouthful of plum-cake. 'Ess, I shall be brim glad when I'm back to Trewinnard. 'Tis my belief the devil's the only one to show a Cornishman round London fitty.'

Mr. Corin laughed at this sardonic witticism, but said he was going to have a jolly good try at showing Zack the sights of the town that very night.

'You ought to take him to the Orient,' May advised.

'By gosh, and that's a proper notion,' said Corin, slapping his thigh. 'That's you and me to-night, Zack.'

'What's the Orrient?' enquired Trewhella.

'Haven't you never heard of the Orient?' Jenny gasped, her sense of fitness disturbed by such an abyss of ignorance.

'No, my dear, I never have,' replied Trewhella, and for the first time looked Jenny full in the face.

'I dance there,' she told him, 'in the ballet.'

The Cornishman looked round to his friend for an explanation.

'That's all right, boy,' said Corin jovially. 'You'll know soon enough what dancing is. You and me's going there to-night.'

Trewhella grunted, looked at Jenny again and said after a pause: 'Well, being in the city, I suppose we must follow city manners, but darn 'ee, I never thought to go gazing at dancing like maidens at Petertide.'

Corin chuckled at the easy defeat of the farmer's prejudice, and said he meant to open old Zack's eyes before he went back to Cornwall, and no mistake.

Soon after this the two girls left the tea-party and, while Jenny dressed herself to go down to the theatre, they discussed Mr. Z. Trewhella.

'Did you ever hear anyone talk so funny? Oh, May, I nearly split myself for laughing. Oh, he talks like a coon.'

'I thought he talked like a gramophone that wants winding up,' said May.

'But what a dreadful thing to talk like that. Poor man, it's a shame to laugh at him though, because he can't help it.' Jenny was twisting round to see that no dust lay on the back of her coat.

'I wonder what he'll think of you dancing,' May speculated. 'But I don't expect he'll recognize you.'

'I think he will, then,' contradicted Jenny as she dabbed her nose with the powder-puff. 'Perhaps you never noticed, but he looked at me very funny once or twice.'

'Did he?' said May. 'Well, I'm jolly glad it wasn't me or I should have had a fit of the giggles.'

Presently, under the scud of shifting clouds, Jenny hurried through the windy shadows of twilight down to the warm theatre. When she was back in the bedroom that night, May said:

'Mr. Trewhella's struck on you.'

'What do you mean?'

'He is – honest. He raved about you.'

'Shut up.'

'He went to see you dance and he's going again to-morrow night and all the time he's in London, and he wants you and me to go to tea again to-morrow.'

'I've properly got off,' laughed Jenny, as down tumbled her fair hair and as she with a single movement shook it free of a day's confinement.

'Do you like him?' May enquired.

'Yes, all right. Only his clothes smell funny. Lavingder or something. I suppose they've been put away for donkey's years. Well, get on with it, young May, and tell us some more about this young dream.'

'You date,' laughed her sister. 'But don't make fun of the poor man.'

'Oh, well, he is an early turn, now isn't he, Maisie? What did dad say to him?'

'Oh, dad. If beer came from cows, dad would have had plenty to say.'

'You're right,' agreed Jenny, standing rosy-footed in her night-gown. She gave one critical look at her image in the glass, as if in dreams she meant to meet a lover, then put out all lights and with one leap buried herself in the bedclothes.

On the following afternoon during tea Mr. Trewhella scarcely took his eyes off Jenny.

'Well, how did you enjoy the ballet?' she enquired.

'I don't know so much about the ballet. I was all the time looking for one maid in that great old magic lantern of a place, and when I found her I couldn't see her so well as I wanted. But, darn'ee, I will to-night. William John!'

'Zack?'

'William John, if it do cost a golden guinea to sit down-along to-night, we'm going to sit in they handsome chairs close up to the harmony.'

'That's all right, boy,' chuckled Corin. 'We'll sit in the front row.'

'That's better,' sighed Trewhella, much relieved by this announcement.

When Jenny said she must go and get ready for the theatre, the farmer asked if he might put her along a bit of the way.

'If you like,' she told him. 'Only I hope you walk quicker than what you eat, because I shall be most shocking late if you don't.'

Trewhella said he could walk just as quick as she'd a mind to; but Jenny insured herself against lateness by getting ready half an hour earlier than usual.

They presented a curious contrast, the two of them walking down Hagworth Street. There was a certain wildness in the autumnal evening that made Trewhella look less out of keeping with the city. All the chimneys were flying streamers of smoke. Heavy clouds, streaked with dull red veins, were moving down the sky, and the street corners looked very bare in the wind. Trewhella stalked on with his long, powerful body bent forward from crooked legs. His twisted stick struck the pavement at regular intervals: his Ascot tie of red satin gleamed in the last rays of the sunset. Beside him was Jenny, not so much shorter actually, but seeming close to him very tiny indeed.

'Look, you maid,' said Trewhella when after a silent hundred yards they were clear of the house, 'I never seed no such a thing as your dancing before. I believe the devil has gotten hold of me at last. I sat up there almost falling down atop of 'ee. Yet I'm the man who's sat thinking of heaven ever since I heard tell of it. Look, you maid, will you be marrying me this week and coming home-along back to Cornwall?'

'What?' cried Jenny. 'Marry you?'

'Now don't be in a frizz to say no all to once. But hark what I do tell 'ee. I've got a handsome lill farm set proper and lew – Bochyn we do call it. And I've got a pretty lill house all a-shining wi' brass and all a-nodding wi' roses and geraniums, where a maid could sit looking out of the window like a dove if she'd a mind to, smelling the stocks and lilies in the garden and harking to the sea calling from the sands.'

'Well, don't keep on so fast,' Jenny interrupted. 'You *don't* think I'd marry anyone I'd only just seen? And besides you don't hardly know me.'

'But I do know you're the only maid for me, and I can't go back without you. That's where it's to. When I've been preaching and sweating away down to the chapel, when I've been shouting and roaring about the glories of heaven, I've all the time been thinking of maids' lips and wondering how I didn't care to go courting. I'm going to have 'ee.'

'Thanks,' said Jenny loftily. 'I seem to come on with the crowd in this scene. I don't want to marry you.'

'I don't know how you can be so crool-hearted as to think of leaving me go back home-along and, whenever I see the corn in summertime, keep thinking of your hair.'

'But I'm not struck on you,' said Jenny. 'You're too old. Besides, it's soppy to talk like that about my hair when you've never hardly seen it at all.'

Trewhella seemed oblivious to everything but the prosecution of his suit.

'There's hundreds of maids have said a man was too old. And what is love? Why, 'tis nothing but a great fire burning and burning in a man's heart, and if 'tis hot enough, it will light a fire in the woman's heart.'

'Ah, but supposing, like me, she's got a fireproof curtain?' said Jenny flippantly.

Trewhella looked at her, puzzled by this counter. He perceived, however, it was hostile to his argument and went on more earnestly than before:

'Yes, but you wouldn't have me lusting after the flesh, I that found the Lord years ago and kept Him ever since. I that showed fruits of the Spirit before any of the chaps in the village. I that scat up two apple orchards so as they shouldn't go to make cider and drunkenness. You wouldn't have me live all my life in a whorage of thoughts?'

405

'Who cares what you do?' said Jenny, getting bored under this weight of verbiage. 'I don't want to marry.'

'I've been too quick,' said Trewhella. 'I've been led away by my preacher's tongue. But you'll see me there in front of 'ee to-night,' he almost shouted. 'You'll see me there gazing at 'ee, and I don't belong to be bested by nothing. Maid nor bullock. Good night, Miss Raeburn, I'll be looking after William John.'

'Good night,' said Jenny pleasantly, relieved by his departure. 'I'll see you in front, then.'

She thought as she said this how utterly inappropriate Trewhella and Corin would look in the stalls of the Orient. She fancied how the girls would laugh and ask in the wings what those strange figures could be. It was lucky none of them were aware they lodged in Hagworth Street. What a terrible thing it would be if it leaked out that such unnatural-looking men, with such a funny way of talking, lodged at Jenny Pearl's. The thought of the revelation made her blush. Yet Corin had not seemed extraordinary before the arrival of his friend. It was Trewhella who had infected them both with strangeness. He had an intensity, a dignity that made him difficult to subdue with flippancy. He never seemed to laugh at her retorts, and yet underneath that ragged moustache he seemed to be smiling to himself all the time. And what terrible hands he had. More like animals than hands. When Jenny caught his eye glinting down in the stalls, she wished she were playing anything but an Ephesian flute-girl, for Ephesian flute-girls, owning a happier climate, dressed very lightly.

'He sat there looking me through and through,' she told

406

May, 'till I nearly run off to the side. He stared at me just like our cat stares at the canary in the window next door.'

'It's not a canary,' May corrected. 'It's a goldfinch.'

'Now don't be silly, and shut up, you and your gold-finches. Who cares if it's a parrot? You know what I mean. Tell me what I'm to do about Borneo Bill.'

May began to laugh.

'Well, he is. He's like the song.'

On the next day Mr. Corin interviewed Jenny about the prospects of his friend's suit.

'You know, Miss Raeburn, he's very serious about it is Zack. He's accounted quite a rich man down West. 'Tis his own farm freehold – and he's asked Mr. Raeburn's permission.'

'Well, that wins it!' Jenny proclaimed. 'Asked my father's permission? What for? What's it got to do with him who I marry? Thanks, I marry who I please. What a liberty!'

Mr. Corin looked apologetic.

'I only told you that so as you shouldn't think there was anything funny about it. I never saw a man so dead in earnest, and he's a religious man, too.'

'Well, I'm not,' Jenny retorted. 'I don't see what reli-gion's got to do with marrying.'

'You come to think of it, Miss Raeburn, it's not such a bad offer. I don't believe you could meet with a safer man than Zack. I suppose if he's worth a dollar, he's worth three hundred pounds a year, and that's comfortable living in Cornwall.'

'But he's old enough to be my father,' Jenny contended.

'He looks older than what he is,' continued Mr. Corin plausibly. 'Actually he isn't much more than thirty-five.'

'Yes, then he woke up,' scoffed Jenny.

'No, really he isn't,' Corin persisted. 'But he's been a big worker all his life. Thunder and sleet never troubled him. And, looking at it this way, you know the saying, "'Tis better to be an old man's darling than a young man's slave."'

'But I don't like him – not in the way that I could marry him.' Jenny had a terrible feeling of battered down defences, of some inexorable force advancing against her.

'Yes; but you might grow to like him. It's happened before now with maids. And look, he's willing for'ee to have your sister to live with you, and that means providing for her. What 'ud become of her if anything happened to you or your father?'

'She could go and live with my sister Edie or my brother.'

'Yes, but we all know what that may mean, whereas if she comes to live with you, Zack will be so proud of her as if she were his very own sister.'

Jenny was staggered by the pertinacity of this wooing and made a slip.

'Yes; but when does he want to marry me?'

The pleader was not slow to take hold of this.

'Then you'll consider it, eh?'

'I never said so,' Jenny replied in a quick attempt to retrieve her blunder.

'Well, he wants to marry you now to once.'

'But I couldn't. For one thing I couldn't leave the theatre all in a hurry. It would look so funny. Besides—'

'Well, Zack said, "Don't worry the maid, William John, but leave her find out her own mind and I'll bide here-along till she do know it." '

Mr. Corin dwelt on the magnanimity of his friend and having, as he thought, made a skilful attack on Jenny's prejudice, retired to let his arguments sink in. He had effected even more than he imagined by his cool statement of the proposal. Put forward by him, devoid of all passion and eccentricity of language, it seemed a very businesslike affair. Jenny began to think how such a step would solve the problem of taking a new house, of moving the furniture, of providing for May, of getting rid of her father, now daily more irritating on account of his besotted manner of life. All the girls at the theatre were marrying. It was in the air. She was growing old. The time of romantic adventure was gone. The carnival was petering out in a gloomy banality. Change was imminent in every direction. Why not make a clean sweep of the old life and, escaping to some strange new existence, create a fresh illusion of pleasure? What would her mother have said to this offer? Jenny could not help feeling she would have regarded it with very friendly eyes, would have urged strongly its acceptance. Why, she had even been anxious for Jenny to make a match with a baker; and here was a prosperous man, a religious man, a steady man, inviting her to be mistress almost of a country estate. She wished that Mr. Z. Trewhella were not so willing to wait. It made him appear so sure, so inevitable. And the time for moving was getting very near. Change was in the air. Jenny thought she would sound May's views on the future in the case of sudden accident or any deliberate alteration of the present mode of life.

'Where would you live if I went away?' she asked.

'What do you mean?' said May, looking much alarmed by the prospect and turning sharply on her pillow.

'I mean who would you live with? Alfie or Edie?'

'Neither,' May affirmed emphatically.

'Why not?'

'Because I wouldn't.'

This reply, however unsatisfactory it might have been to a logician, was to Jenny the powerfullest imaginable.

'But supposing I got married?' she went on.

'Well, couldn't I live with you? No, I suppose I couldn't,' said May dejectedly. 'I'm a lot of good, aren't I? Yes, you grumble sometimes, but how about if you was like me?'

Jenny had always accepted May's cheerfulness under physical disability so much as a matter of fact that a complaint from her came with a shock. More than ever did the best course for May seem the right course for Jenny. She recalled how years ago her mother had entrusted May to her when a child. How much more sacred and binding was that trust now, when she who imposed it was dead.

'Don't get excited,' said Jenny, petting her little sister. 'Whatever I done or wherever I went, you should come along of me.'

May, not to display emotion, said:

'Well, you needn't go sticking your great knee in my back.' But Jenny knew by the quickness with which she fell asleep that May was happy and secure.

'I'm going to have a rare old rout-out this morning,'

Jenny announced when she woke up to the sight of an apparently infinitely wet day, a drench from dawn to nightfall in a grey monotony of sky.

About eleven o'clock the rout-out began, and gradually the accumulated minor rubbish of a quarter of a century was stacked in various heaps all over the house.

'What about mother's things?' May enquired.

'I'm going to put them all away in a box. I'm going through them this afternoon,' said Jenny.

'I've promised to go out and see some friends of mine this afternoon,' said May. 'So I'll leave them to you because they aren't tiring.'

'All right, dee-ar.'

After dinner, when her sister had gone out and Jenny, except for the servant, was alone in the old house, she began to sort her mother's relics. One after another they were put away in a big trunk still plentifully plastered with railway labels of Clacton G.E.R. and Liverpool Street, varied occasionally by records of Great Yarmouth. Steadily the contents of the box neared the top in ordered layers of silk dresses and mantles. Hidden carefully in their folds were old prayer books and thimbles, ostrich plumes and lace. Jenny debated for a moment whether to bury an old wax doll with colourless face and fragile baby-robes of lawn – a valuable old doll, the plaything in childhood of the wife of Frederick Horner the chemist.

'I suppose by rights Alfie or Edie ought to have that,' Jenny thought. 'But it's too old for kids to knock about. If they remember about it, they can have it.'

So the old doll was relegated to a lavendered tomb.

'After all,' thought Jenny, '*we* weren't even allowed to play with it. Only just hold it gently for a Sunday treat.'

Next a pile of old housekeeping books, figured all over in her mother's neat thin handwriting, were tied round with a bit of blue ribbon and put away. Then came the problem of certain pieces of china which Mrs. Raeburn when alive had cherished. Now when she was dead Jenny felt they should be put away with other treasures. These ornaments were vital with the pride of possession in which her mother had enshrined them and should not be liable to the humiliation of careless treatment.

At last only the contents of the desk remained, and Jenny thought it would be right to look carefully through these that nothing which her mother would have wished to be destroyed should be preserved for impertinent curiosity. The desk smelt strongly of the cedar-wood with which it was lined, and the perfume was powerfully evocative of the emotions of childish inquisitiveness and awe that once it had always provoked. Here were the crackling letters of the old Miss Horners, and for the first time Jenny read the full history of her proposed adoption. 'Good job that idea got crushed,' she thought, appalled by the profusion of religious sentiment and half annoyed by their austere prophecies and savage commentaries upon the baby Jenny. In addition to these letters there was a faded photograph of her parents in earliest matrimony and another photograph of someone she did not recognize – a man with a heavy moustache, and by the look of his clothes prosperous.

'Wonder who he was,' Jenny speculated. 'Perhaps that

man who was struck on her and who she wouldn't go away with.' This photograph she burned. Suddenly, at the bottom of the packet of letters, Jenny caught sight of a familiar handwriting which made her heart beat with the shock of unexpected discovery.

'However on earth did that come there?' she murmured as she read the following old letter from Maurice.

422 G.R.
Friday.

My little darling thing,

I've got to go away this week-end, but never mind, I shall see you on Tuesday, or anyway Wednesday for certain. I'll let you know at the theatre. Good night, my sweet one. You know I'm horribly disappointed after all our jolly plans. But never mind, my dearest, next week it will be just as delightful. 422 kisses from Maurice.

The passion which once had made such sentences seem written with fire had long been dead. So far as the author was concerned, this old letter had no power to move with elation or dejection. No vestige even of fondness or sentiment clung to this memorial of an expected joy. But why was it hidden so carefully in her mother's desk, and why was it crumpled by frequent reading? And how could it have arrived there in the beginning? It was written in February, after Jenny had left home. She must have dropped it on one of her visits, and her mother finding it must have thought there was something behind those few gay words. Jenny tried to remember if she had roused the suspicion of an intrigue by staying for a week-end with some girl friend. But, of course, she was away all the time, and often her mother must have thought she was staying with Maurice. All her scruples, all her care had gone for nothing. She had wrecked her love to no purpose, for her mother must have been weighed down by the imagination of her daughter's frailty. She must have brooded over it, fed her heart with the bitterness of disappointment and, ever since that final protest which made Jenny leave home, in gnawing silence. Jenny flung the letter into the fire and sat down to contemplate the dreadful fact that she had driven her mother slowly mad. These doctors with their abscess were all wrong. It was despair at her daughter's behaviour which had caused it all. She went into the kitchen and watched the servant wrestle inadequately with her work; then wandered back to the parlour and slammed the lid of the trunk down to shut out the reproach of her mother's possessions. It was growing late. Soon she must get ready to start for the theatre. What a failure she was. The front-door bell rang and Jenny, glad of relief from her thoughts, went to open it. Trewhella, wringing wet, stepped into the passage.

'Why, Miss Raeburn,' he said, 'here's a grand surprise.'

'Have you had your tea?' the hostess enquired.

'Ess, had tea an hour ago or more. Dirty weather, 'tis, sure enough.'

He had followed her into the parlour as he spoke, and in the grey gloom he seemed to her gigantic and like rock immovable.

'Finished your business?' she asked, oppressed by the silence which succeeded his entrance.

'Ess, this right of way is settled for good or bad, according to which one's happy. And now I've got nothing to do but bide for your answer.'

The lamplighter's click and dying footfall left the room in a ghostly radiance, and the pallid illumination, streaming through the lace curtains, threw their reflection upon the walls and table in a filigree of shadows.

'I'll light the gas,' said Jenny.

'No, don't; but hark to what I do say. I'm regular burnt up for love of 'ee. My heart is like lead, so heavy for the long waiting. Why won't 'ee marry me, my lovely? 'Tis a proper madness of love and no mistake. Maid Jenny, what's your answer?'

'All right. I will marry you,' she said coldly. 'And now let me turn on the gas.'

She struck a match, and in the wavering glow she saw his form loom over her.

'No,' she half screamed; 'don't kiss me. Not yet. Not yet. People can see through the windows.'

'Leave 'em stare so hard as they've a mind to. What do it matter to us?'

'Now don't be silly. I don't want to start kissing. Besides, I must run. I'm late for the theatre.'

'Darn the theatre. You don't want to go there no more.'

'I *must* give a fortnight's notice.'

Mr. Z. Trewhella, a little more than fox, perceived it would not take much to make her repudiate her promise and wisely did not press the point.

'Will I put 'ee down-along a little bit of the road?' he asked.

'No, no. I'm in a hurry. Not to-night.'

Presently, in the amber fog that on wet nights suffuses the inside of a tram, Jenny rode down towards the Tube station, picturing to herself her little sister in a garden of flowers.

XXXV

Marriage of Columbine

Trewhella spent in Cornwall the fortnight during which Jenny insisted on dancing out her contract with the Orient. The withdrawal, ostensibly to prepare his mother for the wife's arrival, was a wise move on his part; for Jenny was left merely with the contemplation of marriage as an abstract condition of existence, undismayed by the presence of a future husband whom she did not regard with any affection. She did not announce her decision to the girls in the theatre until the night before her departure. At once ensued a chorus of surprise, encouragement, speculation and good wishes.

'If I don't like Cornwall,' Jenny declared, 'I shall jolly soon come back to dear old London. Don't you worry yourselves.'

'Write to us, Jenny,' the girls begged.

'Rather.'

'And mind you come and see us first time you get to London.'

'Of course I shall,' she promised and, perhaps to avoid tears, ran quickly down the court, with her box of grease paints underneath her arm.

'Good luck,' cried all the girls, waving farewell in silhouette against the dull orange opening of the stage door.

'See you soon,' she called back over her shoulder. 'Goodbye, all.'

Another chorus of goodbyes travelled in pursuit along the darkness as, leaving behind her a legend of mirth, an echo of laughter, she vanished round the corner.

Jenny and Trewhella were married next morning in a shadowy old church from whose gloom the priest emerged like a spectre. She was seized with a desire to laugh when she found herself kneeling beside Trewhella. She fell to wondering how May was looking behind her, and wished, when the moment came for her father to give her away, that he would not clip his tongue between his teeth as if he were engaged on a delicate piece of joinery. Mr. Corin, too, kept up a continuous grunting and, when through the pervading silence of the dark edifice any noise echoed, she dreaded the rustle of Aunt Mabel's uninvited approach. It did not take so long to be married as to be buried, and the ceremony was concluded sooner than she expected. In the registry she blushed over the inscription of her name, and let fall a large blot like a halo above her spinsterhood. Luckily there was no time for jests and banqueting as, in order to arrive in Cornwall that night, it was necessary to catch the midday train from Paddington. Jenny looked very small beneath the station's great arch of dingy glass, and was impressed by the slow solemnity of Paddington, so different from the hysteria of Waterloo and frosty fog of Euston. Trewhella, leaning on his blackthorn, talked to their father and Mr. Corin, while the two girls ensconced themselves in the compartment.

'Take your seats,' an official cried, and when Trewhella had got in, Mr. Raeburn occupied the window with his last words.

'Well, I shan't go down to the shop to-day, not now. Let's have a line to say you've arrived all safe. You know my address after I clear out of Hagworth Street.'

'So long, dad,' said Jenny awkwardly. Neither she nor May had ever within memory kissed their father; but on this last opportunity for demonstrative piety they compromised with sentiment so far as each to blow him a kiss when the train began to move, and in token of good-will to let for a little while a handkerchief flutter from the window.

There was no one else in the carriage besides themselves, and in the stronger light that suddenly succeeds a train's freedom from stationary dimness, Jenny thought how lonely they must look. To be sure, May's company was a slight solace, but that could neither ease the constraint of her attitude towards Trewhella nor remove the sense of imprisonment created by his proximity. It was a new experience for her to be compelled to meet a man at a disadvantage, although as yet the nearness of freedom prevented the complete realization of oppression. Trewhella himself seemed content to sit watching her, proud in the consciousness of a legalized property.

So the green miles rolled by until the naked downs of Wiltshire first hinted of a strange country, and in a view of them through the window Trewhella seemed to gather from their rounded solitudes strength, tasting already, as it were, the tang of the Cornish air.

'Well, my lovely, what do 'ee think of it all?'

'It's nice, I like it,' replied Jenny.

Conversation faltered in the impossibility of discussing anything with Trewhella, or even in his presence. Jenny turned her mind to the moment of first addressing him as Zachary or Zack. She could not bring herself to mouth this absurd name without an inward blush. She began to worry over this problem of outward behaviour, while the unusual initial twisted itself into an arabesque at once laughable and alarming. And she was Mrs. Z. Trewhella. Jenny began to scrabble on the pane filmed with smoke the fantastic initial. As for Jenny Trewhella, madness would have to help the signature of such an inapposite conjunction. Then, in a pretence of reading, she began to study her husband's countenance, and with the progress of contemplation to persuade herself of his unreality. Sometimes he would make a movement or hazard a remark, and she, waking with a start to his existence, would ponder distastefully the rusted neck, the hands like lizard skin, and the lacklustre nails frayed by agriculture.

The train was rocking through the flooded meads of Somerset in a desolation of silver, and the length of the journey was already heavy on Jenny's mind. She had not travelled so far since she was swept on to the freedom of Glasgow and Dublin. Now, with every mile nearer to the West, her bondage became more imminent. Trewhella loomed large in the narrow compartment as Dawlish was left behind. They seemed to be travelling even beyond the sea itself, and Jenny was frightened when she saw it lapping the permanent way as they plunged in and out of the hot-coloured Devonshire cliffs. Exeter with its many small gardens and populated back windows had cheered her, and Plymouth, grey though it was, held a thought of London. Soon, however, they swung round the curve of the Albert Bridge over the Tamar and out of Devon. Sadly she watched the Hamoaze vanish.

'Cornwall at last,' said Trewhella, with a sigh of satisfaction. ''Tis a handsome place, Plymouth, but I do dearly love to leave it behind me.'

The heavy November twilight caught them as the train roared through the Bodmin valley past hillsides strained with dead bracken – like ironmould, Jenny thought. St. Austell shone white in the aquamarine dusk, and darkness wrapped the dreary country beyond Truro. Every station now seemed crowded with figures, whose unfamiliar speech had a melancholy effect upon the girls in inverse ratio to the exhilaration it produced in Trewhella. Jenny thought how little she knew of her destination: in fact without May's company she might as well be dead – into such an abyss of strange gloom was she being more deeply plunged with every mile. Trewhella, as if in reply to her thoughts, began to talk of Trewinnard.

'Next station's ours,' he said. 'And then there's a seven-mile drive; so we shan't get home-along much before half-past eight.'

'Fancy, seven miles,' said Jenny.

'Long seven mile 'tis, too,' he added. 'And a nasty old road on a dark night. Come, we'll set out our passels.'

It was like action in a dream to reach down from the rack various parcels and boxes, to fold up cloaks and collect umbrellas. Jenny watched from the window for the twinkle of town lights heralding their stopping-place; but without any preliminary illumination the train pulled up at Nantivet Road.

'Here we are,' shouted Trewhella, and as the girls stood with frightened eyes in the dull and tremulous light of the platform, he seemed fresh from a triumphant abduction. The luggage lay stacked in a grey pile with ghostly uncertain outlines. The train, wearing no longer any familiar look of London, puffed slowly on to some farther exile, its sombre bulk chequered with golden squares, the engine flying a pennant of sparks as it swung round into a cutting whence the sound of its emerging died away on the darkness in a hollow moan. The stillness of the deep November night was now profound, merely broken by the rasp of a trunk across the platform and the punctuated stamping of a horse's hoof on the wet road.

'That's Carver,' said Trewhella, as the three of them, their tickets delivered to a shadowy figure, walked in the direction of the sound.

'Carver?' repeated Jenny.

'My old mare.'

The lamps of the farm cart dazzled the vision as they stood watching the luggage piled up behind. To the girls the cart seemed enormous: the mare of mammoth size. The small boy who had driven to meet them looked like a gnome perched upon the towering vehicle, and by his smallness confirmed the impression of hugeness.

'Well, boy Thomas,' said his master in greeting.

'Mr. Trewhella!'

'Here's missus come down.'

'Mrs. Trewhella!' said the boy in shy welcome.

'And her sister, Miss Raeburn,' added the farmer.

Jenny looked wistfully at May as if she envied her the introduction with its commemoration of Islington.

'Now come,' said Zachary, 'leave me give 'ee a hand up.'

He lifted May and set her down on the seat. Then he turned to his wife.

'Come, my dear, leave me put 'ee up.'

'I'd rather get in by myself,' she answered.

But Trewhella caught her in his arms and with a kiss deposited her beside May. Thomas was stowed away among the luggage at the back; the farmer himself got in, shook up Carver and, with a good night to the porter, set out with his bride to Bochyn.

The darkness was immense: the loneliness supreme. At first the road lay through an open stretch of flat boggy grassland, where stagnant pools of water glimmered with the light of the cart lamps as the vehicle shambled by. After a mile or so they dipped down between high hedges and overarching trees that gave more response to their lights than the open country, whose incommensurable blackness swallowed up their jigging, feeble illumination.

'It smells like the inside of a flower-shop, doesn't it?' said May. 'You know, sort of bathroom smell. It must be glorious in the daytime.'

'Yes, 'tis grand in summertime, sure enough,' Trewhella agreed.

The declivity became more precipitous, and the farmer pulled up.

'Get down, you, boy Thomas, and lead Carver.'

Thomas scrambled out, and with a loud 'whoa' caught hold of the reins.

'It's like the first scene of a panto. You know, demons and all,' said Jenny.

Indeed, Thomas, with his orange-like head and disproportionately small body, had a scarcely human look, leading the great mare whose breath hung in fumes upon the murky air. At the walking pace May was able to distinguish ferns in the grass banks and pointed them out to Jenny, who, however, was feeling anxious as in the steep descent the horse from time to time slipped on a loose stone. Down they went, down and down through the moisture and lush fernery. Presently they came to level ground and the gurgle of running water. Trewhella pulled up for Thomas to clamber in again. Beyond the rays of their lamps, appeared the outline of a house.

'Is this a place?' Jenny asked.

''Tis Tiddleywits,' Trewhella answered. 'Or belonged to be rather, for there's nothing left of it now but a few mud walls. A wisht old place, 'tis.'

On restarting, they splashed through a stream that flowed across the road.

'Oo-er,' cried Jenny, 'take care, we're in the water.'

Trewhella laughed loudly, and a moorhen waking in sudden panic rose with a shrill cry from a belt of rushes.

'Oo-er, I'm getting frightened,' said Jenny. 'Put me down. Oh, May, I wish we hadn't come.'

Trewhella laughed louder than before. The wish appealed in its futility to his humour.

Now came a slow pull up an equally deep lane, followed at the summit by another stretch of open country very wild. Suddenly the mare swerved violently. Jenny screamed. A long shape leaned over them in menace.

'Ah, look! Oh, no! I want to go back,' she cried.

'Steady, you devil,' growled Trewhella to the horse. ''Tis nothing, my dear, nothing only an old stone cross.'

'It gave me a shocking turn,' said Jenny.

'It made *me* feel rather funny,' said May. 'You know, all over like.'

The girls shivered, and the cart jogged on across the waste. They passed a skewbald sign-post crowded with unfamiliar goblin names, and a dry tree from which once depended, Trewhella assured them, the bodies of three notorious smugglers. One of the carriage candles proved too short to sustain the double journey and presently flickered out gradually, so that the darkness on one side seemed actually to advance upon them. After a long interval of silence Trewhella pulled up with a jerk.

'Listen,' he commanded.

'Oh, what is it?' asked Jenny, with visions of a murderer's approach. On a remote road sounded the trot of horses' hoofs miles away.

'Somebody coming after us,' she gasped, clutching May's sleeve.

'No, that's a cart; but listen, can't you hear the sea?'

Ahead of them in the thick night like the singing of a kettle sounded the interminable ocean.

'Wind's getting up, I believe,' said Trewhella. 'There's an ugly smell in the air. Dirty weather, I suppose, dirty weather,' he half chanted to himself, whipping up the mare.

Soon, indeed, with a wide sigh that filled the waste of darkness, the wind began to blow, setting all the withered rushes and stunted gorse bushes hissing and lisping. The effort, however, was momentary; and presently the gust died away in a calm almost profounder than before. After another two miles of puddles and darkness, the heavy air was tempered with an unwonted freshness. The farmer again pulled up.

'Now you can hark to it clear enough,' he said.

Down below boomed a slow monotone of breakers on a long flat beach.

'That's Trewinnard Sands, and when the sea do call there so plain, it means dirty weather, sure enough. And here's Trewinnard Churchtown, and down-along a bit of the way is Bochyn.'

A splash of light from a dozen cottages showed a squat church surrounded by clumps of shorn pine trees. The road did not improve as they drew clear of the village, and it was a relief after the jolting in and out of ruts to turn aside through a white gate, and even to crunch along over a quarter of a mile of rough stones through two more gates until they reached the softness of farmyard mud. As they pulled up for the last time, between trimmed hedges of escallonia a low garden gate was visible; and against the golden stream suffused by a slanting door, the black silhouette of a woman's figure, with hand held up to shade her eyes.

'Here we are, mother,' Trewhella called out. Then he

lifted down the two girls, and together they walked up a flagged path towards the light. Jenny blinked in the dazzle of the room's interior. Old Mrs. Trewhella stared critically at the sisters.

'Yon's a wisht-looking maid,' she said sharply to her son, with a glance at May.

'Oh, they're both tired,' he answered gruffly.

'And what do 'ee think of Cornwall, my dear?' asked the old woman, turning to the bride.

'I think it's very dark,' said Jenny.

XXXVI

The Tragic Loading

The bridal feast was strewn about the table; the teapot was steaming; the cream melted to ivory richness and, among many more familiar eatables, the saffron cake looked gaudy and exotic. After the first bashful make-weights of conversation, Jenny and May put their cloaks down, took off wraps, and made the traveller's quick preparation for a meal which has expected their arrival for some time. Then down they all sat, and with the distraction of common hunger the painful air of embarrassment was temporarily driven off. Old Mrs. Trewhella was inclined with much assertion of humility to yield to Jenny her position at the head of the table; but she, overawed by the prodigal display of new dishes, of saffron cake and pasties and bowls of cream, prevailed upon the older woman to withhold her resignation.

The living-room of Bochyn was long, low, and raftered, extending apparently to the whole length of the farm-house, except where a parlour on the left of the front door usurped a corner. Very conspicuous was the hearth, with its large double range extravagantly embossed with brass ornaments and handles. On closer inspection the ironwork itself was hammered out into a florid landscape of pagodas, mandarins and dragons. Jenny could not take her eyes off this ostentatious piece of utility.

'Handsome slab, isn't it?' said Trewhella proudly.

'Slab?'

'Stove – we do call them slabs in Cornwall.'

'It's nice. Only what a dreadful thing to clean, I should say.'

'Maid Emily does that,' explained Mrs. Trewhella.

Jenny turned her glances to the rest of the room. By the side of the slab hung a copper warming-pan holding in ruddy miniature the room's reflection. Here were also brass ladles and straining spoons and a pair of bellows, whose perfectly circular box was painted with love-knots and quivers. On the high mantelpiece stood several large and astonished china dogs with groups of roughly cast, crudely tinted pottery including Lord Nelson and Elijah, all set in a thicket of brass candlesticks. Indeed, brass was the predominant note in the general decoration. The walls were shining with tobacco boxes, snuffers, sconces and trays. Very little space on the low walls could be found for pictures; but one or two chromo-lithographs, including Cherry Ripe and Bubbles, had succeeded in establishing a right to be hung. All down the middle of the room ran a long oak trestle-table, set with Chippendale chairs at the end which Jenny and the family occupied, but where the rest of the household sat, with benches. The five windows were veiled in curtains of some dim red stuff, and between the two on the farther side from the front door stood an exceptionally tall grandfather's clock, above whose face, in a marine upheaval that involved the sun, moon and stars' united rising, a ship rocked violently with every swing of the pendulum. A door at the back opened to an echoing vault of laundries, sculleries, larders and pantries, while in the corner beyond the outhouse door was a dark and boxed staircase straight and steep, a cavernous staircase gaping to unknown corridors and rooms far away.

Old Mrs. Trewhella suited somehow that sinister gangway; for, being so lame as to depend on a crutch, the measured thump of her progress was carried down the gloom with an eternal sameness of sound that produced in the listener a sensation of uneasiness. She had a hen-like face, the brightness of whose eyes was continually shuttered by rapid blinks. Her hair, very thin but scarcely grey, was smoothed down so close to give her head the appearance of a Dutch doll's. She had a slight moustache and several tufted moles. There was much of the witch about her and more of the old maid than the mother.

When the new arrivals had been seated at the table for some minutes, the rest of the household trooped in through the outhouse door. Thomas Hosken led the procession. His face under the glaze of soap looked more like an orange than ever, and he had in his walk the indeterminate roll of that fruit. Emily Day came next, a dark slip of a maid with long-lashed stag's eyes, too large for the rest of her. She was followed by Dicky Rosewarne, a full-blooded, handsome, awkward boy of about twenty-three, loose-jointed like a yearling colt and bringing in with him a smell of deep-turned earth, of bonfires and autumn leaves. Bessie Trevorrow the dairy-maid, ripe as a pippin, came in, turning down the sleeves of a bird's-eye print dress over forearms that made Jenny gasp. She could not reconcile the inconsistencies of feature in Bessie, could not match the burning almond eyes with the coarse lips, nor see how such weather-stained cheeks could belong to so white a neck. Last of all came Old Man Veal, whose duties and status no one rightly knew. The household individually slid into their separate places along the benches with side-long shy greetings to Jenny and May, who for their part would have sat down with more ease to supper with a flock of sheep. One chair still remained empty.

'Where's Granfa Champion?' asked Trewhella.

'Oh, my dear life, that old man is always last,' grumbled Mrs. Trewhella. 'What a thing 'tis to have ancient old relations as do never know to come in to a meal. Go find him, boy Thomas,' she added, with a sigh.

Thomas was much embarrassed by this order, and a subdued titter ran round the lower part of the table as Thomas made one of his fruit-like exits to find Granfa Champion.

'He's my uncle,' explained Mrs. Trewhella to Jenny. 'A decent old man as anyone could wish to meet, but most terrible unknowing of the time. I believe he's so old that time do mean nothing to him. I believe he's grown to despise it.'

'Is he very old?' asked Jenny for want of anything better to say.

'Well, nobody do know how old he is. There's a difference of twenty years in the opinions you'll hear put about. Poor old soul, he do give very little trouble at all. For when the sun do shine, he's all the time walking up and down the garden, and when 'tis dropping, he do sit in his room so quiet as a great old lamb.'

Here Thomas came back with positive news.

'Mr. Champion can't get his boot off and he's in some frizz about it.'

'How can't he get his boot off? How didn't 'ee help him?'

'So I did,' said Thomas. 'But he wouldn't hear nothing of what I do know about boots, and kept on all the time telling what a fool I was. I done my best with 'en.'

At this moment Granfa Champion himself appeared, his countenance flushed with conquest, his eyes shining in a limpid blue, his snow-white hair like spindrift round his face.

'Come in, you Granfa,' his nephew invited.

'Be the maids come?' he asked.

'Ess, ess, here they are sitting down waiting for 'ee.'

Mr. Champion advanced with a fine stateliness and nobility of welcome. Indeed, shy as she was, his entrance tempted Jenny to rise from her chair.

'Come, leave me look at 'ee,' said Granfa, placing his hands on her shoulders.

'Keep quiet, Uncle,' said Mrs. Trewhella. 'You'll make her fire up.'

'Ah, nonsense,' contradicted the old man. 'That's nothing. I do dearly love to see maids' cheeks in a blush. Wish you well, my lovely,' he added, clasping Jenny's hands. 'I'm terrible hurried I wasn't here to give 'ee a welcome by the door.'

Jenny liked this old man, who for the exile from a distant country by his age and dignity and sweetness conjured a few tears of home. The supper, a late meal for such a household, went its course at a fair speed; for they were all anxious to be off to bed with the prospect of work in the windy November dawn. Soon they all vanished through the outhouse door, and Granfa with lighted candle, a hot brick wrapped in flannel under his arm, twinkled slowly up to bed through the hollow staircase. The rest of them were left alone in silence. It was ten o'clock, and the fire was already paling behind the fluted bars of the slab.

'Well, I suppose you're thinking of bed?' suggested Mrs. Trewhella.

May looked anxiously at her sister.

'Yes, I suppose we are,' Jenny agreed.

Zachary began to whistle a Sankey hymn tune.

'You'll be wishing to unpack your things first,' continued Mrs. Trewhella.

'Yes, I ought to unpack,' Jenny said in a frozen voice.

'I've put May in the bedroom next to you. Come, I'll show 'ee.'

Zachary still sat whistling his hymn tune. A bird shielded from view by the window-curtain stirred in its cage. Mrs. Trewhella lighted three candles. Cloaks were picked up and flung over arms, and in single file the three figures, each with her winking guide, vanished up the staircase.

'What a long passage,' whispered Jenny when they stood in a bunch at the top.

Mrs. Trewhella led the way to the bride's chamber.

433

'You're here, where the wives of the Trewhellas have slept some long time.'

After the low room downstairs the bedroom seemed enormous. The ceiling in Gothic irregularities of outline slanted up and up to cobwebs and shadows. It was a great barn of a room. A tall four-post bed, hung with faded tapestries of Love and War, was set off by oak chests-of-drawers and Court cupboards. The floor was uneven, strangely out of keeping with the rose-infested Brussels carpet so vividly new. Most of the windows, latticed and small, were set flush with the floor; but high up in a dormer was a large window with diamonded panes, uncurtained, black and ominous. A couple of tall cheval-glasses added to the mystery of the room with their reduplication of shadowy corners.

'And May's in here,' Mrs. Trewhella informed them, leading the way. 'The loft begins again after your bedroom, so the ceiling isn't so tall.'

Certainly, May's room was ordinary enough, even dainty, with the dimity curtains and wall-paper of bows and forget-me-nots. Round the toilet-table crackled a pink chintz valance, draped in stiffest muslin.

Mrs. Trewhella looked closely at Jenny for a moment before she left them.

'You're thin, my dear,' she commented. 'Ah, well, so was I; and I can mind the time when they wondered what a man could see in such a maid. The men was all for plumpness then. Wish you good night.'

The old woman thumped off down the corridor, her candle a-bob with every limping step.

'What a dreadful place,' said Jenny.

434

'Don't let's stay,' said May eagerly. 'Don't let's stay. Let's go back – now – now.'

'*Don't* be silly. How can we? But we never oughtn't to have come. Oh, May, I only wish I could sleep in here with you.'

'Well, why don't you?' suggested May, who was shocked to see how the usually so indomitable sister was shaking with apprehension. 'There's plenty of room and I'd chance what *he* says.'

Jenny pulled herself together by a visible effort.

'No, I can't go on sleeping with you. I've *got* to be married, now I've done it.'

The two sisters, as if drawn by some horrid enchantment, went back to the bride's room.

'How big that candle looks, doesn't it, but small in one way. May, I'm frightened,' whispered the bride.

There was a rattle of falling plaster, a squeak, a dying scamper.

'Oo-er, what was that?' cried May.

'Rats, I suppose. Oh, this is a shocking place,' said Jenny, trembling. 'Never mind, it's got to be done. It's got to be finished some day. It'll be all the same in a hundred years, and anyway, perhaps it won't be so bad in the morning. May!' she added sharply.

'What?'

'Why, when you come to think of it, the second ballet's well on now and here am I starting off to undress in this dog's island. Let's go back to your room for a minute.'

Again the sisters sought May's kindlier room and Jenny had an idea.

'May, if we pushed your bed back close to the wall, you could tap sometimes, and if I was awake in the night I'd hear you. May, don't go to sleep. Promise you won't go to sleep.'

They pushed the bedstead back against the ribbons and forget-me-nots. Then Jenny, summoning every tradition of pride, every throb of determination, kissed May and ran to the lonely Gothic room, where the flame of the solitary candle burned so still and shapely in the breathless night. She undressed herself in a frenzy. It was like falling into a river to enter those cold linen sheets and, worse, to lie there with pulses thudding and breast heaving under a bravery of new pink bows and ribbons. It could not be long now. She sat up in bed thinking to tap on the wall; but the tapestried head-piece muffled the sound. May, however, heard and rapped her answer.

'To-morrow,' vowed Jenny, 'I'll slit those unnatural curtains with my scissors so as I can tap easily.'

Then down the passage she heard her husband's tread. He was still whistling that tune, more softly indeed, but with a continuous reiteration that was maddening. Round the door his shadow slipped before him. Jenny hid beneath the bedclothes, breathing faster than a trapped bird. She heard his movements slow and dull and heavy, accompanied by the whistling, the endless damnable whistling. Then the light went out and, as if he walked on black velvet, Trewhella stole nearer to the bed.

XXXVII

Columbine in the Dark

Jenny lay awake in a darkness so intense, so thick, so material that her effort to repulse it produced the illusion of a suffocating fabric desperately torn. What ivory cheeks were hidden by the monstrous gloom, what sparkling eyes were quenched in the dry mouth of night.

'Oh, morning, morning,' she moaned. 'Come quickly, oh, do come quick.'

Far away in the blackness a cock crowed. She from London did not understand its consolation. Trewhella, sleeping soundly as he was wont to sleep on market nights, did not stir to the appeal. Jenny lay sobbing.

'What's it all for?' she asked. Then sleep, tired of love's cruelty, sent rosy dreams to comfort her, and in the morning, when she woke, her husband was gone from her side. It was a morning of moist winds and rich November sunlight, of pattering leaves and topaz lights, full of seagulls' wings and the cawing of rooks.

A little sister stood by the end of the bed.

'Oh, get in beside me,' Jenny cried.

And whatever else was mad and bad, there would always be that little sister.

XXXVIII

The Alien Corn

Bochyn was built to escape as easily as possible the many storms of the desolate country that surrounded it. The windows in the front of the house looked out between two groves of straight Cornish elms over a moist valley to a range of low hills, whose chequered green and brown surface in the perpetual changes of light and atmosphere took on the variety and tralucence of water or precious stones; and not merely their peripheral tints, but even their very contours seemed during the courses of the sun and moon hourly to shift. Behind the house was the town-place, a squelchy courtyard hemmed in by the stables and full of casual domestic animals. From here a muddy lane led up to the fields on the slopes above, slopes considerably more lofty than those visible from the front windows and ending in a bleak plateau of heather and gorse that formed the immediate approach to the high black cliffs of many miles of coast. The house itself was a long two-storied building flanked by low grey stone hedges feathered with tamarisks and fuchsias. The garden, owing principally to the care of Granfa Champion, had an unusual number of flowers. Even now in November the dahlias were not over, and against the walls of the house pink ivy-leaved geraniums and China roses were in full bloom. The garden itself ended indeterminately, with no perceptible line of severance, in the moors or watery meads always vividly coloured, and in summer creaming with meadow-sweet. At the bottom of the garden was a rustic gazebo, from which it was possible to follow the course of the stream up the valley between cultivated slopes that gave way to stretches of gorse and bracken, until the valley swept round out of sight in thick coverts of dwarfed oaks. Westward in the other direction the stream, flowing straighter and straighter as it neared the sea, lost itself in a brown waste of sand, while the range whose undulations it had followed sank abruptly to a marsh. This flatness made the contrary slope, which jutted forward so as to hide the actual breaking of the waves, appear portentously high. Indeed, the cliffs on that side soon reached three hundred feet, and on account of their sudden elevation looked much higher. The stream spread out in wide shallows to its outlet, trickling somewhat ineffectively in watery furrows through the sand.

On the farther side of the brown waste, where not even rushes would grow, so complete and perpetual was the devastation of the gales, a line of towans followed the curve of the coast, a desolate tract, grey-green from the rushes planted to bind the shifting surface, and preserving in its endless peaks and ridges the last fantastic glissades and diversely elevated cones into which the wind had carved and gathered and swept the sand. Mostly, these towans presented to the beach a low line of serrated cliffs perhaps forty feet high; but from time to time they would break away to gullies full of fine drifted sand, whose small cavities hoarded snail-shells wind-dried to an ætherial lightness, and rabbit-bones bleached and honeycombed by weather. After a storm the gullies gave an impression of virgin territory, because the sand lay in drifts like newly fallen snow on which footprints were desecration. The beach itself was at low water a very wide and flat and completely desolate expanse, shining near the sea's edge with whatever gold or silver was in the air, shot with crimson bars at sunset, crinkled by the wind to a vast replica of one of its own shells, ribbed and ploughed by tempests. The daily advance or retreat of extreme high water was marked by devious lines of purple murices, by claws of seaweed and the stain of dry spume. Beyond the limit of the spring tides the sand swept up in drifts against the low cliffs that crumbled like biscuit before an attempted ascent.

This sea solitude reduced all living things to a strange equality of importance. Twittering sea-swallows whose feet printed the sand with desultory and fugitive intagliation, sea-parrots flying in profile against the sky up and down over the water, porpoises rolling out in the bay, sand-hoppers dancing to any disturbance, human beings – all became equally minute and immaterial. Inland the towans tumbled in endless irregularities of outline about a solitude equally complete. The vegetation scarcely marked the changing seasons, save where in winter the moss was a livelier golden-green, or where, beside spurges and sea-holly and yellow horned poppies, stonecrops

440

were reddened by August suns. At wide intervals, where soil had formed over the sand, there was a close fine grass starred in spring with infinitesimal squills and forget-me-nots. But mostly the glaucous rushes, neither definitely blue nor green nor grey, occupied the landscape. Close at hand they were vitreous in colour and texture, but at a distance and in the mass they seemed to have the velvety bloom of a green almond or grape. Life of a kind was always present in the scud of rabbits, in the song of larks and click of stonechats, in the dipping steel-blue of the wheatear and ruffled chestnut feathers of the whinchat. Yet as the explorer stumbled in and out of the burrows, forcing a prickly advance through the sharp rushes and often plunging ankle deep in drifts of sand, life was more apparent in the towans themselves than in the presence of the birds and beasts haunting their solitude. The sand was veritably alive in its power to extract from the atmosphere every colour and quality. Sometimes it was golden, sometimes almost snow-white. Near sunset mauve and rose and salmon-pink trembled in waves upon its surface, and as it caught fire to welcome day, so it was eager to absorb night. Moonlight there was dazzling when, in a cold world, it was possible to count the snail-shells like pearls and watch the sand trickle from rabbit-skulls like powdered silver.

Perhaps Jenny had never looked so well placed as when with May beside her in a drift of sand, she rested against the flat fawns and creams and distant blues and greys of the background. Years ago when she danced beneath the plane tree, her scarlet dress by long use had taken

441

on the soft texture of a pastel. Now she herself was a pastel, indescribably appropriate to the setting, with her rose-leaf cheeks buried in the high collar of a lavender-coloured frieze coat, with her yellow curls and deep blue eyes, deeper with the loss of their merriment. Her hands, too, were very white in the clear sea air. May sitting beside her looked dark as a pine tree against an April larch. If Jenny was coral, May was ivory. Here they sat while the sea wind lisped over the sand. Jenny marked the beauty of the country the more carefully because she disliked so intensely the country people. Every day the sisters went for long walks, and when May was tired she would sit on the beach, while Jenny wandered on by the waves' edge.

November went by with silver skies and silver sunsets, with clouds of deepest indigo and pallid effulgences of sun streaming through travelling squalls. Days of swirling rain came in with December, when Jenny would have to sit in the long room, listening to the hiss of the wind-whipped elms, watching the geranium petals lie sodden all about the paths, and the gulls, blown inland, scattered on the hill-sides like paper. The nights were terrible with their hollow moanings and flappings, with the whistle and pipe of the chimneys, with crashing of unclosed doors, with rattled lattices and scud and scream and shriek and hum and roar of the wild December storms. Every morning would break to huge shapes of rain swept up the valley, one after another until the gales of dawn died away to a steady drench of water. Then Jenny would sit in the hot room, where the slab glowed quietly into the musti-ness, and idly turn the damp-stained pages of year-old periodicals, of mildewed calendars, even of hymn-books. At last she would sally forth desperately, and after a long battle with wind or gurgling walk through mud and wet, she would return to a smell of pasties and saffron cake and sometimes the cleaner pungency of marinated pilchards.

Some time before Christmas the gales dropped; the wind veered releasing the sun, and for a fortnight there was fleckless winter weather. These were glorious mornings to wander down through the wet garden past the escallonias aromatic in the sunlight, past the mauve and blue and purple veronicas, out over the watery meadows and up the hill-sides, where the gorse was almond-scented about midday in the best of the sun. Here for a week she and May roamed delightfully; until they found themselves in a field of bullocks and, greatly terrified, went back to the seashore. 'Handsome weather,' old Mrs. Trewhella would say, watching them set out for their long walks and, after blinking once or twice at the sun, thumping back to the kitchen, back to household superintendence and the preparation of heavy meals for the farm workers. Jenny was not inclined to talk much with them. They lived a life so remote from hers that not even the bridge of common laughter could span the gulf. Dicky Rosewarne, for all his good looks, was detestably cruel with his gins and snares and cunning pursuit of goldfinches and, worse, his fish-hooks baited for wild duck. Yet he was kind enough to the great cart-horses, conversing with them all work-time in a guttural language they seemed perfectly to comprehend. Bessie Trevorrow the dairy-maid was even less approachable than Dicky. She had the shyness of a wild thing, and would fly past Jenny, gazing in the opposite direction. Once or twice under the pressure of proximity, they embarked upon a conversation; but Jenny found it difficult to talk well with a woman who answered her in ambiguous phrases of agreement or vague queries. Old Man Veal Jenny disliked since on one occasion she observed him bobbing up and down behind a hedge to watch her. Thomas was her favourite among the hands. He had grown used to bringing her curiosities newly found, and others chosen from a collection that extended back to his earliest youth. These he would present for her inspection, as a dog lays a stick at his mistress's feet. Jenny, although she was profoundly uninterested by the cannon-ball he had found wedged between two rocks, by the George III halfpenny turned up by the plough, by his strings of corks and bundles of torn nets, was nevertheless touched by his offer to strike a 'lemon' for her under a jam-jar in the spring. Nor did she listen distastefully to the long sing-song tales with which he entertained May.

The fine weather lasted right up to Christmas Day. Violets bloomed against the white stones that edged the garden paths. Wallflowers wore their brown velvet in sheltered corners and, best of all, bushes of Brompton stocks in a sweetness of pink and grey scented the rich Cornish winter. Jenny and May would wander up and down the garden with Granfa, while the old man would tell in his high chant tales as long as Thomas's of bygone Australian adventures, tales ripened in the warmth of spent sunshine, and sometimes stories of his own youth in Trewinnard with memories of maids' eyes and lads' laughter. Then

444

in January came storm on storm, dark storms that thundered up the valley, dragging night in their wake. Lambing went on out in the blackness, a dreadful experience, Jenny thought, when Zachary came in at all hours, sometimes stained with blood in the lantern light. Jenny was scarcely aware of her husband in the daytime. The volubility which had distinguished his conversation in London was not apparent here. Indeed, he scarcely spoke except in monosyllables, and spent all this time working grimly on the farm. He did not seem to notice Jenny, and never enquired into her manner of passing the day. She was his, safe and sound in Cornwall, a handsome property like a head of fine stock. He had desired her deeply and had gained his desire. Now, slim and rosy, she was still desirable; but, as Jenny herself half recognized, too securely fastened, too easily attainable for any misgiving. She certainly had no wish for a closer intimacy, and was very thankful for the apparent indifference which he felt towards her. She would have been horrified, had he suggested sharing her walks with May, had he wanted to escort them over Trewinnard Sands, or worst of all, had he invited her to sit beside him on his Sunday drives to preach at distant chapels. He did not even bother her to come and hear him preach in Trewinnard Free Church. Yet as the weeks went by, Jenny came to think that he regarded her more than she thought at first. He often seemed to know where she had been without being informed. When she complained about Old Man Veal spying on her, Zachary laughed oddly, not much annoyed presumably by his servant's indiscretion. Jenny tried sometimes to imagine what Trewinnard would have been like without her sister. The fancy made her shudder. With May, however, it was like a rather long, pleasantly dull holiday.

February brought fair days, scattered shining celandines like pieces of gold over the garden beds, set the stiff upright daffodil buds drooping and was all too soon driven out by the bleakest March that was ever known, a fierce, detestable month of withering east winds, of starved primroses, and dauntless thrushes singing to their nests in the shaken laurustinus. Jenny began to hate the country itself now, when all she could see of it was savage and forbidding as the people it bred.

In the middle of this grey and blasted month, Jenny became aware that she was going to have a baby. This discovery moved her principally by a sudden revival of self-consciousness so acute that she could scarcely compel herself to break the news even to May. It seemed such an absurd fact, when she looked across the table at Zachary sombrely munching his pasty. She could hardly bear to sit at meals, dreading every whisper and muffled giggle from the lower end of the table. Although the baby would not arrive till September, and although she tried to persuade herself that it was impossible for anyone to discern her condition, her own knowledge of it dismayed her.

'But it'll be nice to have a baby,' said May.

'What, in this unnatural house? I *don't* think. Oh, May, whatever shall I do? Can't I go away to have it?'

'Why don't you ask him?' suggested May.

'Don't be silly, how can I tell *him* anything about it?'

'He's got to know some time,' May pointed out.

446

'Yes, but not yet. And then you can tell the old woman and she can tell him, and I'll hide myself up in the bedroom for a week. Fancy all the servants knowing. What a dreadful thing. Besides, it hurts.'

'Well, it's no use for you to worry about that part of it now,' said May. 'I call it silly.'

'I hope it'll be a boy,' said Jenny. 'I love boys. I think they're such rogues.'

'I'd rather it was a girl,' said May.

'Perhaps it don't matter which after all,' Jenny decided. 'A boy would be nicest, though, if you loved the man. Because you'd see him all over again. Perhaps I'd rather have a girl. I expect she'd be more like me. Poor kid!' she added to herself, meditating.

During April the subject was put on one side by mutual consent. There was no immediate necessity for bother; but Jenny's self-consciousness made her unwilling to wander any more over the towns, for all that the weather was blue and white, and the sheltered sand-drifts pleasantly warm in the spring sun. Jenny, however, felt that every rush-crowned ridge concealed an inquisitive head. She knew already how curious the country people were, and that Old Man Veal was no exception. Once she had walked through Trewinnard Churchtown near dusk, and had been horribly aware of bobbing faces behind every curtained window, faces that bobbed and peered and followed every movement and gesture of her person.

Therefore May and Jenny determined to withdraw all opportunity from inquisitiveness by exploring the high cliffs behind Bochyn. They climbed up a steep road washed

447

very bare by the sea wind, but pleasant enough with its tufted hedges fluttering with the cowslips that flourished in a narrow streak of limestone. At the top the road ran near the cliff's edge through gorse and heather and moorland scrub. They found a spot where the cliff sloped less precipitous in a green declivity right down to the sea. This slope was gay with sea-pinks and fragrant with white sea-campion. Primroses patterned the turf, and already ferns were uncrumpling their fronds. Below them the sea was spread like a peacock's tail in every lustrous shade of blue and green. Half-way down they threw themselves full length on the resilient cushions of grass and, bathed in sunshine, listened to the perpetual screaming of the gulls and boom of the waves in caverns round the coast.

'Not so dusty after all,' said Jenny contentedly. 'It's nice. I like it here.'

'Isn't it lovely and warm?' said May.

So they buzzed idly on with their sunlit gossip and drowsy commentaries, until a bank of clouds overtook the sun and the water became leaden. Jenny shivered.

'Somebody sitting on my grave,' she said. 'But it's nice here. Nicer than anywhere we've walked, I think.'

XXXIX

Intermezzo

Circumstances made it necessary that before the end of the month May should inform old Mrs. Trewhella of Jenny's expected baby.

'What did she say?' Jenny enquired when the interview was over.

'She said she thought as much.'

'What a liberty. Why? Nobody could tell to look at me. Or I hope not.'

'Yes, but her!' commented May. 'She's done nothing all her life only make it her business to know. They're all like that down here. I noticed that very soon about country people.'

'What else did she say?' Jenny went on with – for her unusual persistence. She was not yet able to get rid of the idea that there was something remarkable in Jenny Pearl going to have a baby. Not even the universal atmosphere of fecundity which pervaded the farm could make this fact a whit more ordinary.

'She didn't say much else,' related May, not rising to the solemnity of the announcement, the revolutionary and shattering reality of it.

'But she's going to tell him?' Jenny asked.

'That made her laugh.'

'What did?'

'Her having to tell him.'

'Why?' demanded Jenny indignantly.

'Well, you know they're funny down here. I tell you they don't think nothing about having a baby. No more than picking a bunch of roses, you might say.'

This humdrum view of childbirth, although it might have relieved her self-consciousness, was not at all welcome to Jenny. She could not bring herself to believe that, when after so many years of speculation on this very subject, she herself was going to have a baby, the world at large would remain profoundly indifferent. She remembered how as a child she had played with dolls, and how in the foggy weeks before Christmas she had been wont to identify her anticipation with the emotional expectancy of young motherhood. And now it was actually in the slow process of happening, this event, happening, too, as far as could be judged, without any violent or even mildly perceptible transfiguration mental or physical. Still it must not be forgotten that Mrs. Trewhella had divined her condition. By what? Certainly not at present by her form or complexion.

'I think it's your eyes,' said May.

'What's the matter with them?'

'They look different somehow. Sort of far-away look which you didn't use to have.'

'Shut up,' scoffed Jenny, greatly embarrassed by this implication of the unusually soppy.

That evening when, after tea, Jenny leaned against the stone hedge under a sunset of rosy cumulus, Trewhella came through the garden and faced her.

'So you and me's going to have a child, missus?'

Jenny resented the assumption of his partnership and gave a cold affirmative.

'That's a good job,' he sighed, staring out into the air stained with crimson from twilight's approach. 'I feel brim pleased about that. There'll be some fine Harvest Home to Bochyn come September month.'

Then from the vagueness of such expressed aspirations Zachary turned to a practical view of the matter on hand, regarding his wife earnestly as he might from the support of a gate have looked discriminatingly at a field of young wheat.

'Is there anything you do want?' he presently enquired.

Perhaps the cool straightness of the question contained a hint of expert advice, as if for his field he would prescribe phosphates or nitrate or sulphate of ammonia. There was no suggestion of spiritual needs that might call out for nourishment under the stress of a new experience. Jenny felt that she was being sized up with a view to the best practical conduct of the agitating business.

'I wish you wouldn't talk about me,' she protested, 'like you talked about the cow the other day at dinner.'

Trewhella looked perplexed. He never seemed able to grasp whether this sharp-voiced Londoner whom he had married were laughing at him or not.

'I've always heard it spoken—' he began slowly. He always proceeded slowly with a conversation that held a warning of barbed wire, as if by disregarding the obstacle and by cautious advance any defence could be broken down, 'I've always heard it spoken that the women do dearly love something or other at such times. Mother used to tell how before I were born, she were in a terrible hurry to eat a Cornish Gillyflower. But there wasn't one tree as bore an apple that year. Irish Peaches? Ess, bushels. No, that wouldn't do for her. Tom Putts? Sweet Larks? Ess, bushels. No more wouldn't they serve. Boxers? Sops and Wines? Ess, bushels – and, darn 'ee, they made her retch to look at 'em.'

'She'd properly got the pip, hadn't she?' observed Jenny mockingly.

Trewhella saw the wire and made a circuit.

'So I was thinking you might be wanting something as I could get for 'ee on market-day to Camston.'

'No, thanks, there's nothing I want. Not even a penny pomegranate,' said Jenny, who was anxious for Zachary to go. She did not like this attempt at intimacy. She had not foreseen the alliance of sympathy he presumably wished to form on account of her child. The more she considered his claim, the more irrational and impertinent did it seem that he should dare assume any share in the unborn miracle worked by Jenny Pearl.

Trewhella pulled himself together, still progressing slowly, even painfully, but braced to snap if necessary every strand of barbed wire still between him and his object.

'What I were going to say to 'ee was, now that there's this lill baby, I'd like for 'ee to go chapel. I've said nothing so far about your not going; but I daren't run up against the dear Lord's wrath in the matter of my baby.'

'Don't be silly,' said Jenny. 'How can anything happen to *my* baby without its happening to me?'

'Well, I'd like for 'ee to come,' Trewhella persisted.

Here was Jenny in a quandary. If she refused, according to her fiery first impulse, what religious pesterings would follow her round the garden. How he would drawl in that unnatural manner of speech a lot of rubbish which had nothing to do with her. He might even take to preaching in bed. He had once frightened her by demanding in a sepulchral speculation whether she had ever reflected that the flames of hell were so hot that there a white-hot poker would be cool as ice-cream. If on the other hand she submitted to a few hours' boredom, what an amount of treasured liberty would be sacrificed and what more intrusive attempts might not be made upon her inviolable egoism.

'But I don't like church and chapel,' said Jenny. 'It doesn't interest me.'

Then she saw her husband gathering his eloquence for wearisome argument and decided to compromise – and for Jenny to compromise meant character in the melting-pot.

'I might come once and again,' she said.

Trewhella seemed relieved and, after a moment's awkwardness in which he gave her the idea that he was on the verge of thanks, departed to his business.

So, not on the following Sunday, for that would have looked like too easy a surrender, but on the Sunday after that, Jenny and May went in the wake of the household to the Free Church – a gaunt square of whitewashed stone, whose interior smelt of varnish and stale hymn-books and harmonium dust. The minister, a compound of suspicion, petty authority and deep-rooted servility, had bicycled from Camston and had in consequence a rash of mud on his coat. Without much fire, gnawing his moustache when in need of a word, he gave a dreary political address in which several modern statesmen were allotted prototypes in Israel. The pinched Staffordshire accent destroyed whatever beauty was left to his maimed excerpts from Holy Scripture.

'What a terrible man,' whispered Jenny to May.

Presently during the extempore prayers, when the congregation took up the more comfortable attitude of prayer by bending towards their laps, Jenny perceived that the eyes of each person were surreptitiously fixed on her. She could see the prying sparkle through coarse fingers – a sparkle that was instantly quenched when she faced it. Jenny prodded May.

'Come on,' she whispered fiercely. 'I'm going out of this dog's island.'

May looked alarmed by the prospect of so conspicuous an exit, but loyally followed Jenny as they picked their way over what seemed from their upright position a jumble of corpses. An official, either more indomitably curious or less anxiously self-repressive than the majority, hurried after them.

'Feeling slight, are 'ee, missus?' enquired this red-bearded farmer.

'No, thanks,' said Jenny.

'It do get very hot with that stove come May month. I believe it ought to be put out. And you're not feeling slight?'

454

'No, thanks.'

The man seemed unwilling to go back inside the chapel; but the two girls walked quickly away from him down through the deserted village.

After dinner the incident was discussed with some bitterness.

'How did 'ee go out of chapel like that?' asked Trewhella.

'Because I don't go to a chapel or a church neither to be stared at. It's a game of mine played slow, being stared at by a lot of old crows like them in there.'

Jenny defiantly surveyed Zachary, his mother and old Mr. Champion, while May murmured encouragement behind her.

''Tisn't paying any great respect to the dear Lord,' said Trewhella. 'Trooping out like a lot of great bullocks! I went so hot as lead.'

''Tisn't paying any great respect to the dear Lord, staring at two women when you belong praying,' said Granfa severely.

'Darn 'ee,' said Trewhella savagely. ''Tis nothing to do with you, a heathen old man as was once seen picking wrinkles off the rocks on a Sunday morning.'

'I believe it is then,' said Granfa stoutly. 'I believe that it's got a brae lot to do with me and, darn 'ee, if it hasn't—'

He thumped the table so that all the crockery rattled. This roused Mrs. Trewhella, who had been blinking in silence.

'Look, see what you're doing, Granfa. You'll scat all the cloam,' she cried shrilly.

Trewhella, having surveyed Jenny's defences, began his usual slow advance.

455

'What nobody here seems to understand is my feelings when I seed my missus making a mock of holy things.'

'Oh, rats!' cried Jenny, flouncing angrily from the room.

Nothing would persuade her to humour Zachary so far as to go to chapel a second time. It pleased her to contemplate his anxiety for the spiritual welfare of the unborn child. 'I wish you'd wrastle with the devil a bit more,' he said. But she would only set her lips obstinately, and perhaps under his mother's advice, Zachary gradually allowed the subject to drop.

Jenny and May went often to the cliffs in the fine weather, mostly to Crickabella (such was Granfa's name for their favourite slope), where summer marched by almost visibly. The sea-pinks turned brown, the sea-campion decayed to an untidy mat of faded leaves and flowers. Bluebells came up in asparagus-like heads that very soon broke into a blue mist of perfume. The ferns grew taller every day, and foxgloves waved right down to the water's edge. On the moorland behind the cliffs heather and burnet roses bloomed with azure scabious and white moth-mulleins, ladies' tresses and sweet purple orchids. Here and there grew solitary columbines, which Jenny thought were lovely and carried home to Granfa, who called them Blue Men's Caps. Remote from curious eyes, remote from life itself save in the progress of inanimate things towards the accomplishment of their destiny, she dreamed unceasingly day after day amid the hollow sounding of the ocean, watching idly the metallic green flight of the shags, the timorous adventures of rock pipits, and sometimes the graces of a seal.

With the advance of summer Jenny began to dread extremely the various insects and reptiles of the country. It was vain for Thomas to assure her that apple-bees did not sting without provocation, that eeriwigs were not prone to attack, that piskies were harmless flutterers and neither Johnny Jakes nor gram'ma sows actively malicious. These rural incidents of a wasp on a hat or a woodlouse in a sponge were to her horrible events which made her tremble in the recollection of them long afterwards. The state of her health did not tend to allay these terrors, and because Crickabella was comparatively free from insects, that lonely green escarpment, flung against the black ramparts of the towering coast, was more than ever dear to Jenny.

In July, however, she was not able to walk so far as Crickabella, and was forced to pass all her days in the garden, gazing at the shimmering line of the hills opposite. Granfa Champion used to spend much time in her company, and was continually having to be restrained from violent digging in the heat. During August picture post-cards often arrived from girls spending their holidays at Margate or Brighton, post-cards that gave no news beyond, 'Having a fine old time. Hope you're all right,' but inasmuch as they showed that there was still a thought of Jenny in the great world outside, very welcome.

August dragged on with parched days, and cold twilights murmurous with the first rustle of autumn. Jenny began to work herself up into a state of nervous apprehension, brooding over childbirth, its pain and secrecy of purpose and ultimate responsibilities. She could no longer tolerate the comments passed upon her by Mrs. Trewhella nor the furtive inquisitiveness of Zachary. She gave up sitting at dinner with the rest of the household, and was humoured in this fad more perhaps from policy than any consideration of affection. The only pleasure of these hot insufferable days of waiting was the knowledge that Zachary was banished from her room, that once more, as of old, May would sleep beside her. There was a new experience from the revival of the partnership because now, unlike the old theatre days, Jenny would often be the first in bed and able to lie there watching in the candlelight May's shadow glance hugely about the irregular ceiling, like Valérie's shadow long since in the Glasgow bedroom. Where was Valérie now? But where was anybody in her history? Ghosts, every one of them, where she was concerned.

XL

Harvest Home

All day long the whir of the reaper and binder had rattled from distant fields in a monotone of sound, broken at regular intervals by guttural cries when the horses at a corner turned on their tracks, and later in the afternoon by desultory gunshots, when from the golden triangle of wheat rabbits darted over the fresh stubble. All day long Jenny, obeying some deep instinct, prepared for the ordeal. The sun blazed over the spread harvest: the fields crackled with heat: the blue sky seemed to close upon the earth, and not even from the whole length of Trewinnard Sands was heard a solitary ripple of the tide. In the garden the claret-coloured dahlias hung down their tight uncomfortable flowers; geraniums, red-hot pokers, portulacas, nasturtiums and sunflowers burned in one furnace of bloom. Red admiral butterflies soared lazily up and down against the grey walls crumbling with heat, and from flower to flower of the scarlet salvias zigzagged the hummingbird-hawk moths. Granfa Champion, wiping with gaudy bandana his forehead, came out to plant daffodil bulbs stored in the garden shadows of a cool potting shed.

459

'Now, you know you mustn't go digging in this sun, Mr. Champion,' said reproving May.

'My cheeks are so hot as pies,' declared Granfa.

'Do come and sit down with us,' said Jenny.

'I believe I mustn't start tealing yet awhile,' said the old man, regretfully plunging his long Cornish spade into the baked earth, from which insufficient stability the instrument fell with a thump on to the path.

'Well, how are 'ee feeling, my dear?' asked Granfa, standing before Jenny and mopping his splendid forehead. 'None so frail, I hope?'

'She isn't feeling at all well. Not to-day,' said May.

'That's bad,' said Granfa. 'That's poor news, that is.'

'I feel frightened, Mr. Champion,' said Jenny suddenly. Somehow this old man recalled Mr. Vergoe, rousing old impulses of childish confidence and revelation.

'Feeling frightened, are 'ee? That's bad.'

'Supposing it wasn't a person at all?' said Jenny desperately. 'You know, like us?'

The old man considered for a moment this morbid fancy.

'That's a wisht old thought,' he said at last, 'and I don't see no call for it at all. When I do teal a lily root, I don't expect to see a broccolo come bursting up and annoying me.'

'But it might,' argued Jenny, determined not to be convinced out of all misgiving.

'Don't encourage her, Mr. Champion,' said May severely. 'Tell her you think she's silly.'

Jenny buried her face in her hands and began to cry.

Granfa looked at her for a moment; then, advocating silence with his right forefinger, with his thumb he indicated to May, by jabbing it rapidly backwards over his shoulder, that inside and upstairs to her bedroom was the best place for Jenny.

So presently she was lying on the tapestried bed in the tempered sunlight of her room, while through the house in whispers ran the news that it might be any time now. Up from downstairs sounded the restlessness of making ready. The sinking sun glowed in the heart of every vivid Brussels rose and bathed the dusty floor with orange lights. Jenny's great thought was that never again would she endure this agony, if but this once she were able to survive it. She vowed, tearing in savage emphasis the patchwork counterpane, that nothing should induce her to suffer like this a second time.

The afternoon faded tranquilly into dusk. No wind agitated a single dewy petal, and only the blackbirds with intermittent alarums broke the silence. The ripe round moon of harvest, floating mild and yellow and faintly luminous along the sky, was not yet above the hills. Mrs. Trewhella was not yet willing to despatch a summons to the doctor. Two more hours sank away. Out in the fields, marching full in the moon's face, the reapers went slowly homewards. Out in the fields they sang old songs of the earth and the grain; out in the waste the fox pricked his ears and the badger turned to listen. Down in the reeds the sedge-warbler lisped through the low ground vapours his little melody. The voices of the harvesters died away in purple glooms; and now, as if in a shell, the sea was heard

461

lapping the sand. Through the open lattice rose the scent of the tobacco plants. There was a murmur of voices in consultation. Jenny heard a shout for Thomas, and presently horse's hoofs trotting down the farm road.

High and small and silver was the moon, before she heard them coming back. The dewdrops were all diamonds, the wreathed vapours were damascened by moonlight, before she heard the grate of wheels and the click of the gate and another murmur of voices. Then the room was filled with black figures; entering lamplight seemed to magnify her pain, and Jenny knew little more until, recovering from chloroform, she perceived a candle, large as a column, burning with giant spearhead of flame; and beyond the blue and silver lattice Jenny apprehended a fuss of movement.

'What is it?' she asked in momentary perplexity.

''Tis a boy,' said Mrs. Trewhella. 'A grand lill chap.'

'What's all that noise?' she murmured petulantly.

''Tis me, my dear soul,' said Mrs. Trewhella, 'putting all straight as we belong.'

May leaned over her sister, squeezing her hand.

'I think I shall like having a baby,' said Jenny, 'when we can take him out for walks. You know, just you and me, young May.'

XLI

Columbine Happy

Jenny was ivory now: the baby had stolen all the coral from her cheeks. Outside, the treetops shook tremulous black lace across the silver deeps of the sky and jigged with ebony boughs upon the circle of the moon. Clear as bells sounded the slow breakers on Trewinnard beach; and in the tall room a white moth circled round the candle-flame interminably. A rat squeaked in the wall.

'Fancy,' said Jenny to May, who sat in shadow by the foot of the bed. 'I thought I shouldn't like nursing a baby, but I think it's glorious.'

A curlew cried through the October night and was answered far down the valley.

'I wish mother could have seen my baby,' sighed Jenny. 'It's *my* birthday next week. Funny if we'd both been born the same day.'

The candle spat with the moth's death, then burned with renewed brightness.

'Time the rogue went to sleep,' said May authoritatively.

'Feel his hands,' said Jenny. 'They're like velvet bows.'

'They are lovely and soft, aren't they?' May agreed.

'Won't the girls talk when they hear about my baby?'

463

'Rather,' said May reassuringly.

'I expect they'll wonder if he's like me.'

Remote winds muttered over the hill-side, and the curlews set up a chorus of chattering.

'Night's lovely with a baby,' said Jenny, and very soon fell asleep.

XLII

Shaded Sunlight

The naming of the boy caused considerable discussion in Bochyn. Indeed, at one stage of the argument a battle seemed imminent. Jenny herself went outright for Eric.

'Never heard no such name in all my life,' affirmed Trewhella.

'You must have been about a lot,' said Jenny sarcastically.

'I think Eric's nice,' urged May in support of her sister's choice.

'I never heard the name spoken so far as I do remember,' Mr. Champion put in. 'But that's nothing against it as a name. As a name I do like it very well. To be sure 'tis a bit after Hayrick, but again that's nothing against a farmer's son.'

'I don't like the name at all,' said old Mrs. Trewhella. 'To me it do sound a loose sort of a name.'

'Oh, 'tis no name at all,' Zachary decided. 'How do 'ee like it, my dear?' he asked, turning to Jenny.

'I don't know why I like it,' she answered, 'but I do.'

'There's a grand old name down Church,' said Granfa meditatively. 'A grand old rolling cut-a-piece-off-and-come-again sort of a name, but darn 'ee if I can remember it. Ess I can now. Athanacious! Now that's a name as will make your Jack or your Tom look very hungry. That's a name, that is!'

Impressive as sounded Granfa's trumpeting of it, everybody felt that nowadays such a mouthful would hamper rather than benefit the owner. As for Jenny, she declared frankly against it.

'Oh no, Granfa, not in these! Why, it would drive anyone silly to say it, let alone write it. I wish it was a girl and then she could have been called Eileen, which is nice.'

Trewhella looked anxiously at the subject of the discussion, as if he feared his wife could by some alchemy transmute the sex of the baby.

'I should dearly love to call the lill chap Matthew or Mark or Luke,' he said. 'John I don't take no account of. I do call that a poor ornary unreligious sort of name for an Evangelist.'

'I don't like John at all,' said Jenny emphatically.

'Then there's Abraham and Jacob,' Zachary continued. 'And Abel and Adam.'

'And Ikey and Moses,' Jenny scoffingly contributed.

'How not Philip?' suggested old Mrs. Trewhella.

'Or Nicholas?' said May.

'Call him Satan straight away to once!' commented the father bitterly.

'I like a surname sometimes,' said Jenny thoughtfully. 'I once knew a boy called Presland. Only we used to call him Bill Hair. Still, Eric's the nicest of all, *I* think,' she added, returning to her first choice.

The argument went on for a long while. At times it

466

would verge perilously on a dispute; and in the end, in accordance with Jenny's new development of character, a compromise was effected between Eric and Adam by the substitution of Frank for both and, lest the advantage should seem to incline to Jenny's side too far, with Abel as a second name, where its extravagance would pass unnoticed.

Winter passed away uneventfully except as regards the daily growth of young Frank. There was no particularly violent storm, nor any wreck within ten miles of the lonely farmhouse. When the warm days of spring recurred frequently it became necessary to find a pleasant place for idle hours in the sun. Crickabella was too far away for a baby to be taken there, and Jenny did not like the publicity of the front garden, exposed equally to Zachary's periodical inspections and Mrs. Trewhella's grandmotherly limps away from housekeeping. Mr. Champion, when informed of all this, cordially agreed with Jenny that the front garden was no place at all under the circumstances and promised to go into the matter of a secure retreat.

So presently, on one of those lazy mornings when April pauses to survey her handiwork, assuming in the contemplation of the proud-pied earth the warmth and maturity of midsummer, Granfa beckoned to Jenny and May and young Frank to follow his lead. He took them out at the back, past the plashy town-place, past a commotion of chickens, and up a rocky lane whose high mossy banks were blue with dog-violets and twinkling white with adder's eyes. The perambulator bumped over the loose stones, but young Frank, sleeping admirably, never stirred;

while his rosy cheeks danced with ripples of light shaken down through the young-leafed elms. Not too far up they came to a rickety gate, which Granfa dragged open to admit his guests; and almost before they knew where they were, they stood buried in the apple-blossom of a small secluded orchard cut off from the fields around by thick hedges of hawthorn.

'What a glorious place,' cried Jenny enthusiastically. 'Oh, I do think this is nice.'

Mr. Champion, his hair looking snow-white in the rosy flush of blossom, explained the fairylike existence of the close.

'This old orchard was never scat up with the others. They burnt they up in a frizz of repenitence. The Band of Hope come and scat them all abroad with great axes, shouting Hallelujah and screaming and roaring so as anyone was ashamed to be a human creature. Darn 'ee, I was so mad when I heard tell of it, I lived on nothing but cider almost for weeks, though 'tis a drink as do turn me sour all over.'

'Idiots,' said Jenny. 'But why didn't they pull this to pieces? There must be lots of apples here.'

'It got avoided somehow, and Zachary he just left it go; but 'tis a handsome place, sure enough. You'll dearly love sitting here come summertime.'

'Rather!' Jenny and May agreed.

Already in isolated petals the blossom was beginning to flutter down; but still the deserted orchard was in the perfection of its beauty. Down in the cool grass, forti-fied against insects and dampness by many rugs, Jenny and May and young Frank used to lie outstretched. They could see through the pink and white lace of blossom deep distant skies, where for unknown landscapes the cuckoos struck their notes on space like dulcimers; they could hear the goldfinch whistle to its nest in the lichened fork above and wind blown in treetops the copperfinch's burst of song. They could listen to the greenfinch calling sweetly from the hawthorn hedge, while tree-creepers ran like mice up the grey bark and woodpeckers flirted in the grass. The narcissus bloomed here very fragrant, contending wild-eyed with daisies and buttercups. There was mistletoe – marvellous in the reality of its growth, but at the same time to Jenny rather unnatural. And later, when the apple-blossom had fallen, eglantine and honeysuckle and travellers' joy flung themselves prodigally over the trees; and when the birds no longer sang, it did not matter, such an enchanted silence of infinitely minute country sounds took their place.

As for young Frank, he was to his mother and aunt a wonder. He opened his eyes very often, and very often he shut them. He kicked his legs and uncurled his fingers like a kitten and twitched ecstatically to baby visions. He cried very seldom and laughed very often, and crooned and dribbled like many other babies; but whether or not the intoxication of the sweet close urged him to unparagoned agilities and precocities, there was no doubt at all that, in the companionship of elves, he enjoyed life very much indeed.

'He looks like an apple lying there,' said Jenny. 'A great round fat rosy apple. Bless his heart.'

'He is a rogue,' said May.

'Oh, May, he is a darling! Oh, I do think he's lovely. Look at his feet just like raspberries. He isn't much like *him*, is he?'

'No, he's not,' said May emphatically. 'Not at all like.'

'I don't think he's much like anybody, I don't,' said Jenny, contemplating her son.

It might have seemed to the casual onlooker that Arcadia had recompensed Jenny for all that had gone before; and, indeed, could the whole of existence have been set in that enclosure of dappled hours, she might have attained sheer contentment. Even Jenny, with all she had longed for, all she had possessed and all she had lost, might have been permanently happy. But she was no sundial marking only the bright hours: life had to go on when twilight came and night fell. Young Frank, asleep in golden candlelight, could not mitigate the injury of her husband's presence. Even young Frank, best and most satisfying of babies, was the son of Zachary; would, when he grew out of babyhood, contain alien blood. There might then be riddles of character which his mother would never solve. Strange features would show themselves, foreign eyes perhaps, or a mouth which knew no curve of her own. Now he was adorably complete, Jenny's own against the world; and yet he was a symbol of her subjugation. Already Zachary was beginning to use their boy to consolidate his possession of herself. Already he was talking about the child's education and obviously making ready for an opportunity to thrust him into religious avarice and gloom. The arrival of young Frank had apparently increased the father's tendency to brood over the darker problems of his barbarous creed. He talked of young Frank, who would surely inherit some of the Raeburn joy of life, as if he would grow up in suspicion, demon-haunted, oppressed with the fear of God's wrath, a sour and melancholy dreamer of damnable dreams.

Zachary took to groaning aloud over the sins of his fellow-men, would groan and sweat horribly in the imagination of the unappeasable cruelty of God. These outbreaks of despair for mankind were the more obnoxious to Jenny because they were always followed by a monstrous excess of his privileges, by an utterly abhorred affectionateness. Mr. Champion, the outspoken, clear-headed old man, would often remonstrate with his nephew. Once, while Trewhella was in a spasm of misery, groaning for his own sins and the sins of the world, a sick cow died in audible agony on account of his neglect.

'You ought to be ashamed, you foolish man,' said Granfa. 'You ought to be ashamed to leave the poor animal die. Darn 'ee, I believe the devil *will* have 'ee!'

'What's a cow,' said Trewhella sombrely, 'beside my own scarlet sins?'

''Tis one of the worst of 'em,' said Granfa positively. ''Tis so scarlet as wool. Get up, and leave be all your praying and sweating, you foolish man. You do drive me plumb mad with your foolishness. How don't 'ee do your own work fitty and leave the dear Lord mind His own business? He don't want to be told at His time of life what to do. Oh, you do drive me mad.'

'Another lost lamb,' groaned Trewhella. 'Another soul

471

in the pit. Oh, I do pray wi' all my heart that my poor lill son may find favour in the Lord's eyes and become a child of grace to preach the Word and confound the Gentiles.'

'Did ever a man hark to such nonsense in his life?' exclaimed Granfa.

'I shouldn't argue with him in one of his moods,' advised Jenny, looking at her husband coldly and distastefully.

'Oh, dear Lord, give me strength to heal the blindness of my family and make my poor lill son a sword in the side of unbelievers.'

Then presently the gloom would pass; he would go out silently to the fields, and after a day's work come back in a fever of earthly desires to his wife.

There were shadows in Bochyn, for all the sunlight and birdsong and sweet peaseblossom.

XLIII

Bow Bells

Summer went by very quickly in the deserted orchard, and
in fine September weather young Frank's first birthday
was celebrated with much goodwill by everybody. Zachary
with the successful carrying of a rich harvest ceased to
brood so much on the failure of humanity. He became his
own diligent self, amassing grain and gold and zealously
expurgating for reproduction in bleak chapels that winter
a volume of sermons by an Anglican bishop. Young Frank
began to show distinct similarities of feature to Jenny,
similarities that not even the most critical observer could
demolish. He showed, too, some of her individuality, had
a temper and will of his own, and seemed like his mother
born to inherit life's intenser emotions. Jenny was not yet
inclined to sink herself in him, to transfer to the boy her
own activity of sensation. Mrs. Raeburn was thirty-three
when Jenny was born: young Frank arrived when his
mother was ten years younger than that. It was not to be
expected that she should feel the gates of youth were
closed against her. Moreover, Jenny with all the fullness of
her experience was strangely young on the eve of her
twenty-fourth birthday, still seeming, indeed, no more

473

than eighteen or nineteen. There was a divine youthfulness about her which was proof against the Furies, and, since the diverting absurdities of young Frank, laughter had come back. Those deep eyes danced again for one who from altitudes of baby ecstasies would gloriously respond. May was another triumph for affection. There was joy in regarding that little sister, once wan with Islington airs, now happy and healthy and almost as rosepink as Jenny herself. How pleased her mother would have been and, in retrospect, how sceptical must she have felt of Jenny's ability to keep that promise always to look after May.

Life was not so bad on her birthday morning as, with one eye kept continuously on young Frank, Jenny dressed herself to defy the blusterous jolly October weather. She thought how red the apples were in the orchard and with what a plump they fell and how she and May had laughed when one fell on young Frank, who had also laughed, deeming against the evidence of his surprise that it must be matter for merriment.

The postman came that morning; and Granfa, waving his arms, brought the letters up to the orchard – two letters, both for Jenny. He watched her excitement for a minute before he departed to a pleasant job of digging in the champagne of October sunlight.

'Hullo,' cried Jenny, 'here's a letter from Maudie Chapman.'

26 *Alverton Street,*
Pimlico

Dear old Jenny,

    *Suddenly remembered it was your birthday, old girl. Many
Happy Returns of The Day, and hope your in the best of pink
and going on fine the same as I am. We have got a new stage
manager who you would laugh to see all the girls think. We
have been rehearsing for months and I'm sick of it – Your well
out of the Orient I give you my word. It's a dogs' Island now
and no mistake. Walter sends his love. I have got a little girl
called Ivy. She is a love. Have you?*

        With heaps of love

             from your old chum Maudie

*Ireen's gone off with that fellow Danbie and Elsie had
twins. Her Artie was very annoyed about it. Madge Wilson as
got a most glorious set of furs. No more from Maudie – Write
us a letter old girl.*

    'Fancy,' said Jenny. 'Elsie Crauford's had twins.'

    This letter read in the open air, with a sea wind travel-
ling through the apple trees, with three hundred miles of
country between the sender and the receiver, was charged
with London sorcery. It must have been posted on the way
from the theatre. Incredible thought! Jenny visualized the
red pillar-box into which it might have slipped, a pillar-box
stationed by a crowded corner, splashed by traffic and jostled
by the town. On the flap was a round spot of London rain
and, pervading all the paper, was a faint theatre scent. The
very ink was like eye-black, and Maudie must have written
every word laboriously between two glittering ballets.

'I wonder if I could do a single beat now?' said Jenny. 'I wish I hadn't given my new ballet shoes to Gladys West.'

Then as once she danced under the tall plane tree of Hagworth Street to a sugared melody of *Cavalleria*, so now she danced in an apple orchard, keeping time to the wind and the waving boughs. Young Frank quivered and kicked with joy to see the twirling of his mother's skirts. May cried, 'You great tomboy!' but with robin's eyes and slanting head watched her sister.

Had she been a poet, Jenny would have sung of London, of the thunder and greyness, of the lamps and rain, of long irresistible rides on the top of swaying tramcars, of wild roars through the depths of the earth past the green lamps flashing to red. She danced instead about the sea-girt orchard-close all that once her heart had found in London. She danced the hopes of the many children of Apollo, who work so long for so little. She danced their disillusions, their dreams of immortality, their lives, their marriages, their little houses. She danced their fears of poverty and starvation, their work and effort and strife, their hurrying home in the darkness. She danced their middle age of growing families and all their renewed hopes and disappointments and contentments. She danced a little of the sorrow and all the joy of life. She danced old age and the breathing night of London and the sparrow-haunted dawn. She danced the silly little shillings which the children of Apollo earn. Fifteen pirouettes for fifteen shillings, fifteen pirouettes for long rehearsals and long performances, fifteen pirouettes for a week, fifteen pirouettes for no fame, fifteen pirouettes for fifteen shillings, and one high beat for the funeral of a marionette.

And all the time the gay October leaves danced with her in the grass.

'Well, I hope you've enjoyed yourself,' said May. Jenny threw herself breathless on the outspread rug and kissed young Frank.

'I don't suppose I shall ever dance again!'

'What about the other letter?' asked May.

'There, if I didn't forget all about it,' cried Jenny. 'But who's it from? What unnatural writing. Like music.'

She broke the seal.

PUMP COURT,
TEMPLE W.C.

My dear Jenny,

I think I've been very good not to worry you long before this; but I do want to write and wish you many happy returns. Will you accept my thoughts? I got your address and history from Maudie Chapman whom I met last week. I wonder if I came down to Cornwall for a few days, if you would let me call on you. If you're annoyed by this letter, just don't answer. I shall perfectly understand.

Yours ever,
Frank Castleton

'Fancy,' said Jenny. 'I never knew his name was Frank. How funny.'

'Who is this Frank?' May enquired.

477

'A friend of mine I knew once – getting on for nearly four years ago now. Where could anyone stay here?'

'There's an hotel in Trewinnard,' said May.

Jenny looked at young Frank.

'I don't see why I shouldn't,' she said.

'Shouldn't what?'

'Have a friend come and see me,' Jenny answered.

XLIV

Picking Up Threads

Castleton arrived at Bochyn under a November sunset, whose lemon glow, barred with indigo banks of cloud, was reflected with added brightness in the flooded meadows and widening stream. Jenny in the firelight was singing and rocking her baby to sleep. She jumped up to open the door to his knock.

'Why, Fuz,' she said simply.

He stood enormous against the last gleams of day, and Jenny realized with what small people she had been living so long.

'Jane,' he said, 'this is a big moment.'

He followed her into the room and waited while she lit the lamp and pointed with warning finger to the child asleep in a silence of ticking clocks.

'There's a surprise, or isn't it?'

'Rather,' said Castleton. 'It looks very well.'

'Oh, Fuz. It! You are dreadful. He's called Frank, and fancy, I never knew you were called Frank till you wrote to me last month.'

'Another disappointment,' sighed Castleton.

'What?'

479

'Why, of course I thought you altered his name to celebrate my visit.'

'You never didn't?' said Jenny, already under slow rustic influences not perfectly sure of a remark's intention. Then suddenly getting back to older and lighter forms of conversation, she laughed.

'Well, how are you, Jenny?' he enquired.

'Oh, I'm feeling grand, Where are you staying?'

'The One and All Inn.'

'Comfortable?'

'I fancy very, from a quick glance.'

'You'll stay and have tea with us and meet my husband?' Jenny invited.

'I shall be proud.'

A silence fell on these two friends.

'Well, what about dear old London?' said Jenny at last.

'It's extraordinarily the same. Let me see, had tubes and taxis been invented before you went away?' Castleton asked.

'Don't be silly. Of course,' she exclaimed, outraged by such an implication of antediluvian exile.

'Then flatly there is nothing to tell you about London. I was at the Orient the other night. I need not say the ballet was precisely the same as a dozen others I have seen, and you have helped at.'

'Any pretty new girls?' Jenny asked.

'I believe there are one or two.'

'How's Ronnie Walker?'

'He still lives more for painting than by painting, and has grown a cream-coloured beard.'

480

'Oh, he hasn't. Then he ought to get the bird.'

'So that he could say: "Four owls and a hen, two larks and a wren, have all built their nests in my beard"? It isn't big enough, Jane.'

'And Cunningham, how's he?'

'Cunningham is married. I don't know his wife, but I'm told she plays the piano a great deal better than he does. As for myself,' said Castleton quickly, 'I have chambers in the Temple, but live at home with my people, who have moved to Kensington. There, you see what alarming cataclysms have shaken the society you deserted. Now tell me about yourself.'

'Oh, I jog along,' said Jenny.

Farther reminiscence was interrupted by the entrance of Trewhella, who saluted Castleton suspiciously and from shyness somewhat brusquely.

'How do you do, sir?' said the guest, conspicuously agreeable.

'I'm very well, thank 'ee. Come far, have 'ee?'

'London.'

'That's a poor sort of place. I was there once. But I didn't take much account of it,' said Trewhella.

'You found it disappointing?'

'Ess, ess; too many Cockneys for a Cornishman. But I wasn't robbed overmuch. I believe I was too sharp for them.'

'I'm glad of that,' said the representative of cities.

'You do talk a lot of rot about London,' said Jenny contemptuously. 'As if you could know *anything* about it!'

'I found all I wanted, my dear,' said Trewhella, winking. He seemed in a mind to impress the foreigner.

'By carrying off Je— Mrs. Trewhella, eh?' said Castleton. 'Come, after that, I don't think you ought to grumble at London.'

Trewhella darted a suspicious glance, as if to demand by what right this intruder dared to comment on his behaviour.

The presence of a stranger at tea threw a munching silence over all the lower end of the table; but Castleton made a great impression on Granfa, who asked him a number of questions and sighed admiration for each new and surprising answer.

'But there's one thing I believe you can't tell me,' said Granfa. 'Or if you can, you'm a marvel.'

'And what is that?' enquired Castleton.

'I've asked scores of men this question,' said Granfa proudly. 'Hundreds, I suppose, and there wasn't one of them could give me an answer.'

'You really alarm me this time,' said Castleton.

Granfa braced himself by swallowing a large mouthful of pasty and delivered his poser almost reverently.

'Can you tell me, mister, in what county o' Scotland is John o' Groats?'

'Caithness, I think,' said Castleton.

Granfa coughed violent appreciation and thumped on the table in amazement.

'Hark, all you men and maidens down to the end of the table! I've asked that question in Cornwall, and I've asked that question in Australia. I've asked Scotchmen even, and I'm a brae old man now. But there wasn't one who could speak the answer till – till—' he paused, before the Cornish title of affection and respect – 'Cap'n Castleton here spoke it straight away to once. Wish you well, my dear old son,' he added in a voice rich with emotion, as he thrust an open hand over a bowl of cream for Castleton's grip.

Then Granfa told his old intimate tales of wrecks and famous seines of fish, and even went so far as to offer to show Castleton on the very next morning the corner of a field where with two legs and a stick he could stand in the three parishes of Trenoweth, Nancepean and Trewinnard. In fact he monopolized the guest throughout the meal, and expressed great regret when Castleton had to return to the One and All Inn.

Trewhella questioned Jenny sharply that night about the stranger, tried with all the fox in his nature to find out what part he had played in her life.

'He's a friend of mine,' she said.

'Did he ever come courting 'ee?'

'No, of course not. You don't think all men's like you?'

'What's he want to come down here-along, if he's just a friend? Look, missus, don't you go giving the village tongues a start by kicking up a rig with yon great Cockney.'

'Shut up,' said Jenny. 'Who cares about the village?'

'I do,' said Trewhella. 'I care a brae lot about it. Me and my folk have lived here some long time and we've always been looked up to for clean decent souls.'

'Get out!' scoffed Jenny. 'And don't put ideas in your own head. Village! Talking shop, I should say.'

The next morning was fine, and when Castleton called at Bochyn, Jenny entrusted May with young Frank and suggested a walk. Granfa, who was present during the discussion of the itinerary, declared the towans must be visited first of all. Jenny was rather averse from such a direction, thinking of the watchers who lay all the day in the rushes. However, when she thought how deeply it would infuriate her husband to know that she was walking over that solitude in the company of Castleton, she accepted Granfa's suggestion with a deliberate audacity.

It was pleasant to walk with Fuz, to laugh at his excitement over various birds and flowers unnoticed by her. It was pleasant to watch him trip in a rabbit's hole and roll right down to the bottom of a sand-drift. But best of all were the rests in deep dry hollows above whose edges the rushes met the sky in wind-waved, sharply cut lines. Down there, making idle patterns with snail-shells, she could listen to gossip of dear old London. She could smell in the sea air wood-pavement and hear in the scurry of rabbits passengers by the Piccadilly Tube.

And yet there was a gulf not to be spanned so readily as in the tentative conversations of a single walk. Often, in the middle of Castleton's chronicles, she would wish desperately to talk of events long buried, to set out before him her life, to argue openly the rights and wrongs of deeds that so far she had only disputed with herself. In a way it was unsatisfactory to pick up a few broken threads of a friendship, leaving the reel untouched. Perhaps it was better to let the past and the present alone. Gradually London dropped out of the conversation. She wondered if, seeing London again, she would be as much disappointed as by the tale and rumour of it borne down here by an old friend. Gradually the conversation veered to the main occupations of Jenny's mind – May and young Frank. May's future was easy to forecast. She must in these fresh airs grow stronger and healthier, and supply with the passing of every day a more complete justification of the marriage. But what of young Frank's future? Jenny could not bear the notion of him tied to the soil. She wanted his life to hold experience before he retreated here to store up the grain and the gold. There must be a great deal of her in young Frank. He could not, should not be contented with bullocks and pigs and straight furrows.

Castleton listened sympathetically to her ambitions for the baby, and promised faithfully that when the time came, he would do his best to help Jenny achieve for her son at least one prospect of humanity, one flashing opportunity to examine life.

'You see, I knew what I wanted when I was quite tiny. Of course nothing was what I thought it would be. Nothing. Only I wanted to go on the stage and I went. I shouldn't like for young Frank to want to do something and have to stick here.'

'You've a fine notion of things, Jane,' said Castleton. 'By gad, if every mother were like you, what a race we should have.'

'I'm not in a hurry for him to do anything.'

'I meant what a race of Englishmen, not bicycles,' Castleton explained.

'Oh, I see,' said Jenny vaguely. He was taking her aspirations out of their depth.

'No, but I do think it's dreadful,' she went on, 'to see kids moping just because their mothers and fathers want

485

them to stick at home. My mother wasn't like that. Yes, she used to go on at me, but she always wanted me to enjoy myself so long as she knew there was no harm in it.'

'Your mother, Jane, must have been a great woman.'

'I don't know about that, but she was a darling, and always very smart – you know, dressed very nice and had a good figure. But look at my father. He sends us a post-card sometimes with a picture of a bed or a bottle of Bass on it, which is all he thinks about. And yet he's alive, and she's dead.'

Finally Castleton promised that should young Frank display a spark of ambition, he would do his best to help him achieve it.

'Whatever it is,' said Jenny. 'Of course not if he wants to be a dustman, but anything that's all right.'

Then, the morning being nearly spent, they turned back towards Bochyn. Castleton mounted on a slope at a run to pull Jenny up from above.

'Hullo,' he cried, 'somebody's been watching us.'

'They always do on these towans,' said Jenny.

'I'll soon haul the scoundrel into daylight,' and with a shout he charged down through the rushes, almost falling over the prostrate body of Old Man Veal. Castleton set him on his feet with a jerk and demanded his business, while Jenny with curling lips stood by. The old man would not say a word, and his captor, baulked of chastisement by his evident senility, let him shamble off into the waste.

'That's one of the men on the farm,' said Jenny.

'I suppose he'll get the sack.'

'I don't think so then. I think he's edged on by someone else to follow me round.'

XLV

London Pride

Jenny and Castleton followed the course of the stream along the valley towards Bochyn. The bracken was a vivid brown upon the hillsides; the gorse was splashed with unusual gold even for Cornwall; lapwings cried, wheeling over the head of the ploughman ploughing the moist rich earth; a flight of wild duck came unerringly down the valley, settling with a great splash in the blue and green marsh.

Trewhella met them, stepping suddenly out from a grove of arbutus trees, a thunderous figure.

'What do 'ee mean?' he roared. 'What do 'ee mean by carrying my missus off for wagging tongues? Damn ye, you great overgrown Cockney, damn ye, what do 'ee mean to come sparking here-along?'

By Trewhella's side stood his dog, a coarse-coated, wall-eyed brute, half bobtail, half collie. Much alike seemed the pair of them, snarling together in the path.

Jenny whitened. She had not yet seen so much of the wolf in her husband. Castleton looked at her, asking mutely whether he should knock Trewhella backwards or whether, as the world must be truckled to, he should keep quiet.

'Shut up,' said Jenny to her husband. 'You ought to be ashamed of yourself. What do you think I am? Your servant? Mind, or I shall tell you off as you've *never* been told off yet. Let me pass, please, and what's more let my friend pass. Come on, Fuz. Take no notice of him. He's potty. He's soft. Him! Pooh!'

She gathered her skirts round her as if to negotiate mud and swept past Zachary who, all wolf now, recoiled for his spring. Castleton, however, seized his wrist, saying tranquilly:

'I'm afraid, Mr. Trewhella, you're not very well. Goodbye, Mrs. Trewhella. I'll come round this afternoon, then.'

Jenny passed on towards Bochyn and Trewhella turned to follow her at once; but Castleton still held him, and whenever Jenny looked round he was still holding him. She waited, however, at the bottom of the garden for Zachary's return, strewing the ground by her feet with spikes of veronica blooms. Presently he appeared, his dog running before him, and at the sight of Jenny shook wildly his fists.

'You witch,' he cried. 'How have 'ee the heart to make me so mad? But I deserve it. Oh, God Almighty, I deserve it. I that went a-whoring away from my own country.'

'Shut up,' Jenny commanded. 'And talk decently in front of me, even if I am your wife.'

'I took a bride from the Moabites,' he moaned. 'I forsook Thy paths, O Lord, and went lusting after the heathen.'

He fell on his knees in the shining November mud;

Jenny regarded him as people regard a man in a fit.

'Forgive me, O God, for I am a sinful man. I have gone fornicketing after lilywhite doves that turned to serpents. I have coveted the love of woman and I have forsaken Thy paths, O Lord. I ran to gaze at loose women dancing in their nakedness and——'

'Kindly shut up,' Jenny interrupted. 'And don't kneel there like a lunatic talking about me as if I hadn't got nothing on when you saw me. Don't do it, I say, because I don't like it.'

Trewhella rose and faced his wife. The drops of sweat stood on his forehead big as pebbles. His eyes were mad. She had seen eyes like them in Ashgate Asylum.

'Why were 'ee sent to tempt me? Don't 'ee know I do love you more than I do love the Kingdom of Heaven?'

'Well, I wish you wouldn't. It doesn't interest me, this love of yours as you call it. And you needn't carry on about Mr. Castleton, because he's only a friend, *which* you can't understand.'

Trewhella began to weep.

'I thought you were safe down here,' he lamented. 'I thought I held 'ee safe as carried corn, and when I brought 'ee to Bochyn, I was so happy as a piece of gold. All the time I've been preaching, I've wished to be home-along, thinking of 'ee and wishing I held 'ee in my arms right through the black old night, as I belong.'

Jenny shuddered.

'And 'tis a lawful thought,' he cried defiant. 'You're my wife, you're mine by the power of the Lord; you're mine by the right of the flesh.'

'I'm going indoors,' said Jenny coldly, and she left him raging at temptation. Then she sat down and wrote to Castleton.

Dear Fuz,

Perhaps you hadn't better come and see me again – I expect you'll think I'm mad – but it isn't any good to have rows because I've got to live here any old way.

I liked seeing you dear Fuz and I'm sorry he made a fool of himself and I'll write someday about young Frank – No more news from your little friend

Jenny

Who cares?

She gave the letter to Thomas, who took it down to the One and All. It was Jenny's inherent breeding that made her send it. All her pride bade her insist on Castleton's company, begged her to defy Trewhella and, notwithstanding scenes the most outrageous, to establish her own will. But there was Fuz to be considered. It would not be fair to implicate him in the miserable muddle which she had created for herself. He belonged to another life where farmers did not grovel in the mud before Heaven's wrath, where husbands did not swear foully at wives, asking forgiveness from above before the filthy echo had died away. Fuz was better out of it. Yet she wished she could see him again. There were many questions not yet asked.

Trewhella was foxy when next he discussed Castleton with Jenny.

'He wasn't too careful about calling of 'ee Mrs. Trewhella,' he began.

'Don't be silly. He always knew me as Jenny in the old days.'

'Oh, I do hate to hear 'ee tell of they old days. I do hate every day before I took you for my own.'

'I can't help your troubles that way,' said Jenny. 'Perhaps you'd like to have married me in the cradle?'

'I'd like to have kept 'ee locked up from the time you were a frothy maiden,' he admitted. 'I do sweat when I think of men's eyes staring at your lovely lill body.'

Jenny stamped her rage at the allusion.

'Yes, you ought to have known my mother's aunts,' she said. 'They'd have suited you, I think. They wanted to shut me up and make me religious.'

The emphasis with which she armed her reminiscence gave the verbs an undue value, as if the aunts had intended actually to lock her in a larder of hymn-books.

'I wish with all my heart they had done so,' said Trewhella. 'Better that than the devil's palace of light where you belonged to dance. Oh, I wish that Cockney were in Hell!'

'I can't do more than ask him to go away, so don't keep on being rude about my friends,' said Jenny.

'Ess, and I wish now I'd never kicked up such a rig and frightened the pair of 'ee. I was too quick. That's where it's to.'

'What *are* you talking about?'

'Why, if I hadn't been so straight out, I might have trapped you both fitty. If I'd waited and watched awhile.'

Trewhella sighed regretfully.

'You are a sneak,' said Jenny.

'Oh, I wish I could see your heart, missus. Look, I've never asked 'ee this before. How many men have loved 'ee before I did?'

'Hundreds,' said Jenny mockingly.

'Kissed your lips and hugged your body and bent your fingers as I belong?'

'Oh, shut up, and don't talk about me like that. Thousands, if you want to know.'

'Kissed 'ee?' shrieked Trewhella.

'Of course. Why not?'

The —s!' he swore.

Veins wrote themselves across his forehead, veins livid as the vipers of Medusa.

'Witch,' he groaned. ''Tis well I'm a saved man or I might murder 'ee. Hark, listen! Murder 'ee, you Jezebel! I do know now what Jehu did feel when he cried, "Throw her down and call up they dogs and tear the whore to pieces." '

He ran from the room, raving.

After this new fit when the wolf drove out the fox, Trewhella settled down to steady cunning. Jenny became conscious of being watched more closely. Not even the orchard was safe. There was no tree trunk that might not conceal a wormlike form, no white mound of sand that was not alive with curiosity, no wind even that was not fraught with whispered commentaries upon her simplest actions.

Bochyn could no longer have been endured without

young Frank and May and Granfa. These three could strip the most secretive landscape of terrors, could heal the wildest imaginations. All the winter through, Trewhella never relaxed his efforts to trip her up over her relations with Castleton and to compel an admission of the bygone love-affair that would not necessarily, as he pointed out, involve her in a present intrigue.

'How did 'ee send him away, if there was nothing at all?'

'Because I'm ashamed for any of my friends to see what sort of a man I've married. That's why.'

'I'll catch you out one day,' vowed Trewhella. 'You do think I'm just a fool, but I'm more, missus; I'm brae cunning. I can snare a wild thing wi' any man in Cornwall.'

'Fancy,' Jenny mocked.

And round the dark farmhouse the winter storms howled and roared, beating against the windows and ravening by the latches.

XLVI

May Morning

Young Frank had always been from his birth an excitement; but as he neared, reached and passed his eighteenth month, the geometrical progression of his personality far exceeded the mere arithmetical progression of his age. He could now salute with smiles those whom he loved, was empurpled by rage at any repression, and was able to crawl about with a blusterous energy that seemed inspired by the equinoctial gales of March. Jenny's fingers would dive into his mouth to discover teeth that were indeed pearls in their whiteness and rarity. Exquisite adumbrations of herself were traceable in his countenance, and so far, at any rate, his hair was curled and silvery as hers was once famed to be. His cheeks were rose-fired; his eyes were deep and gay. Only his ears seemed, whatever way they were judged, to follow his father's shape; but even they at present merely gave him a pleasant elfin look. Jenny was proud of young Frank.

Trewhella, with the lapse of time, and after another violent outbreak on account of the arrival of a letter from Castleton, ceased to importune his wife with jealous denunciations of the old glittering days before they met.

The farm prospered: he took to counting his money more than ever, since an heir had given him a pledge for the commemoration of his thrift. During the winter Jenny drove once or twice in the high cart to Camston and, with May to help her, scornfully turned out the contents of the drapery shops. On these occasions Granfa was made responsible for young Frank, and when they came back he had to give a very full account of his regency. Other winter events included a visit from Mr. Corin, who had opened a dairy away up in the east of the Duchy. He annoyed Jenny by his exaggerated congratulations, embracing as they did himself as much as Zachary and her. Mrs. Trewhella would from time to time announce her surrender of the household keys; but Jenny was not anxious to control anything except her son, and the old woman, manifestly pleased, continued to superintend with blink and cackle maid Emily. Jenny lost her fear of bullocks, dreaded insects no longer, and might have been a Cornish maid all her life, save for her clear-cut Cockney to which not a single Western burr adhered. She no longer pined for London; was never sentimental towards eight o'clock; and certainly could not be supposed to exist in an atmosphere of regret. At the same time, she could not be said to have settled down, because her husband was perpetually an intrusion on any final serenity. She could not bear the way he ate, the grit and soil and raggedness of his face; she loathed the grimy scars upon his hands, the smell of corduroy. She hated his mental outlook, his preoccupation with Hell, his narrow pride and lack of humour, his pricking avarice and mean vanity, his moral cowardice and religious bravery, his grossness and cunning and boastfulness and cruelty to animals. She feared the struggles that would one day arise between him and his son. She felt even now the clashing of the two hostile temperaments: already there were signs of future storms, and it was not just a fancy that young Frank was always peevish at his father's approach.

The equinox sank asleep to an April lullaby. Lambs bleated on the storm-washed air. The ocean plumed itself like a mating bird. Then followed three weeks of grey weather and much restlessness on the part of young Frank, who cried and fumed and was very naughty indeed. What with Frank and the South-east wind and the cold rain, Jenny's nerves suffered, and when May morning broke in a dazzle, she thought it would be a good plan to leave young Frank with Granfa, and in her sister's company to go for a long walk. May was delighted and together they set out.

They followed the path of the valley past the groves of arbutus, past the emerald meadows down into the sandy waste over which the stream carried little pebbles to the sea, flowing over the wide shallows like a diamonded lattice. They plunged into the towans that never seemed to change with the seasons. They rested in the warm hollows under larksong. They climbed precipices and ran along ridges, until at last they raced gloriously down a virgin drift out on to the virgin sands on which, a long way off, the waves were breaking in slow curves, above them a film of spray tossed backwards by the breeze blowing from the shore.

Jenny sat in the solitude, threading a necklace of

wine-stained shells. She was dressed in some shade of fawn that seemed to be absorbed by these wide flat sands, so that she became smaller and slighter. She wore a silver-grey bonnet set closely round her cheeks in a ruching of ivory. May was in scarlet and looked, as she lay there in the vastness, not much bigger than Jenny's cap of scarlet stockinet left long ago on the beach at Clacton.

'Hullo, there's somebody coming along the sands. Can you see them?' asked Jenny.

'A long way off?' enquired May, peering.

'Yes, just a speck – now – where those rocks are. No, you're looking in the wrong place. Much further along,' directed Jenny.

'You *can* see a way,' said May.

The figure drew nearer, but was still too far off for them to determine the quality or sex, as they watched the sea-swallows keep ever their distance ahead, swift-circling companies.

'I wonder who it is,' said Jenny.

'I can't ever remember seeing anyone on the beach before,' said May.

'Nor can I. It's a man.'

'Is it?'

'Or I think so,' Jenny added.

'What a line of footmarks there'll be when he's gone past,' said May.

'It is a man,' Jenny asserted.

Suddenly she went dead white, flushed crimson, whitened again and dropped the half-strung necklace of shells.

'I believe I know him, too,' she murmured.

497

'Shut up,' scoffed May. 'Unless it's Fuz?'

'No, it's not him. May, I'd like to be alone when he comes along. Or I don't think I'll stay. Yes, I will. And no, don't go. You stay too. It *is* him. It is.'

Maurice approached them. He gave much the same impression as on the first night of the ballet of Cupid, when at the end of the court he raised his hat to Jenny and Irene.

'I – I wondered if I should meet you,' he said.

His presence was less disturbing to Jenny than the slow advance. She greeted him casually as if she were saluting an acquaintance passed every morning:

'Hullo.'

Maurice was silent.

'Isn't it a lovely morning?' said Jenny. 'This is my sister May.' Maurice raised his cap a second time.

'I wonder,' he said, looking intently at Jenny, 'I wonder if – if—' he plunged into the rest of the sentence. 'Can I speak to you alone a minute?'

'Whatever for?' asked Jenny.

'Oh, I wanted to ask you something.'

Jenny debated with herself a moment. Why not? He had no power to move her now. She was able coldly to regard him standing there on the seashore, a stranger, no more to her than a piece of driftwood left by the tide.

'I'll catch you up in a minute,' she told May.

'All right, I'll go on. Pleased to have met you,' said May, shaking hands shyly with Maurice.

He and Jenny watched her going towards the towans. When she was out of earshot, Maurice burst forth:

'Jenny, Jenny, I've longed for this moment.'

'You must have treated yourself very badly then,' she answered.

'I did. I—'

'Look,' said Jenny sharply. 'It's no good for you to start off, because I don't want to listen to *anything* you say. I don't *want* to.'

'I don't deserve you should,' Maurice humbly agreed. 'All the same I wish you would.'

It may have been that in his voice some vibrant echo of past pleading touched her, so that across a gulf of four years the old Jenny asked:

'Why should I?'

He seemed on fire to seize the chance of explanation and would no doubt have plunged forthwith into a wilderness of emotions, had not Jenny seen May signalling from the towans.

'She wants me to go over to her.'

'But you'll come out here again?'

'I might — I might come out on the cliffs over there.' She pointed towards Crickabella. 'I don't know. I don't think I shall. But don't try and see me at home, because I wouldn't know you there.'

She ran from him suddenly across the sands back to May.

'Why did you wave like that?' she asked.

'I think there's been somebody watching you,' said May, looking pale and anxious.

499

XLVII

Nightlight Time

Trewhella gave no sign that he knew anything of the event on the sands: yet Jenny's instinct was to avoid a meeting with Maurice. Once or twice, indeed, she was on the point of starting out; but she never brought herself to the actual effort, and the May days went by without her leaving the precincts of Bochyn. Maurice had made but a small impression upon her emotion; had raised not a single heartbeat after the first shock of his approach over the long sands. She had no curiosity to discover why he had come down here, with what end in view, with what impulse. She cared not to know what his life had been in those four years, what seas or shores he had adventured, what women he had known. Yet somehow she felt, through a kind of belated sympathy, that every morning he was out on the cliffs by Crickabella, watching for a sight of her coming up the hill. Should she go? Should she finally dismiss him, speaking coldly, contemptuously, lashing him with her scorn and wounded pride and dead love? June was in view, and still she paused. June came in, royally azure. Yet she hesitated: while young Frank waved to the butterflies and grew daily in the sun like a peach.

'He do look so happy as the King of Spain,' said old Mr. Champion. 'Grand lill chap, he is sure enough. Do 'ee hear what I'm speaking, my young handsome?'

Granfa bent down and tickled the boy.

'Bless his heart,' said Jenny.

'I were down to Trewinnard yesterday,' said Granfa, 'and I were talking about him to a gentleman, or I should say an artist, who belongs painting down-along. Says he's in a mind to bide here all the summertime. He do like it very well, I believe.'

'What's he like?' Jenny asked.

'This artist? Oh, he's a decent-looking young chap. Nothing anyone could dislike about him. Very quiet, they're telling, and a bit melancholy. But I believe that's a common case with artists. And I'm not surprised, for it must be a brim melancholy job painting an old cliff that any ornary man wouldn't want to look at twice, leave alone days at a stretch. But he told me he didn't properly belong to paint at all. He said his own trade was writing.'

Unquestionably this was Maurice. All day Jenny thought of him out on the cliffs. The idea began to oppress her, and she felt haunted by his presence: it would be better to meet him and forbid his long stay. To-morrow would offer a fine opportunity, because Zachary was going to Plymouth to arrange about the purchase of some farm implements and would not only be away to-night, but was unlikely to be back till late the next day. Not that it mattered whether he went away or not; yet somehow she would like to lie awake thinking of what she would say to Maurice, and to lie awake beside her husband was inconceivable to Jenny. How much better to be alone with young Frank. She would certainly go to-morrow. Maurice might not be there: if he were not, she would be glad and there would be an end of the dismay caused by his presence, for she would not move a step from Bochyn till she heard of his departure.

Trewhella now came out into the garden where they were sitting. He was equipped for Plymouth, and looked just the same as on the afternoon Jenny met him at Hagworth Street. He was wearing the same ill-fitting suit of broadcloth and the same gleaming tie of red satin.

'Well, I'm going Plymouth,' he announced.

'You're staying the night?' she asked.

'Ess, I think.'

'Well, are you?'

'Ess, I believe.'

He never would commit himself to a definite statement.

'What time are you coming back to-morrow?'

'In the afternoon, I suppose.'

'In the afternoon?' she repeated.

Trewhella looked at her quickly.

'Kiss me goodbye, my dear.'

'No, I don't want to,' said Jenny, freezing.

He looked harder at her and pulled his moustache; then he leaned down to prod a farewell into his son's ribs. Young Frank immediately began to yell. The father chuckled sardonically and strode off to the cart, calling loudly as he went for Old Man Veal. He paused, with his foot on the step, to impress something on the stealthy old man. Then he told Thomas to get down and Veal to take his place. There was a sound of wheels, and everybody sighed with relief.

The long drowsy June day buzzed on. They all lay about in the shade, wishing they could splash through the stream like the cattle.

'I can't think why we don't all go paddling, I can't,' said May.

'Oh, whyever not – with young Frank?' cried Jenny, clapping her hands.

'Of course.'

'And Granfa must come,' Jenny insisted.

'Oh no, no, no,' declared Granfa, smiling very proudly at the suggestion. 'No, no, no! But I might go along with 'ee and pick a few wrinkles off the rocks.'

Jenny thought how imperative it was for Maurice to be out of these planned allurements of summer. She would never enjoy herself if all the time she felt he were close by, liable to appear suddenly. Certainly she would see him to-morrow.

'We might even bathe,' said May dauntlessly.

'Well, don't 'ee tell Zack then,' Granfa advised. 'For I suppose he can see the devil in the deep sea so clear as anywhere else. That man's got a nose for evil, I believe.'

The sun was now hanging over the marsh in a dazzling haze of gold where the midges danced innumerable. Long shadows threw themselves across the hills. The stream of light dried up as the sun went down into the sea. Cool scented airs, heralds of night, travelled up the valley; travelled swiftly like the spray of fountains.

Jenny went to bed soon after half-past nine. It was

scarcely dark. Along her sill were great crimson roses like cups of cool wine, and from every ghostly white border of the garden came up the delicious odour of pinks in full June bloom. Moths were dancing, fluttering, hovering: a large white owl swept past in a soundless curve. And while she brooded upon this perfumed silence, away in London the girls were trooping down for the second ballet, were giving the last touch with a haresfoot to their carmine beauty, were dabbing the last powder on their cheeks or rubbing the liquid-white upon their wrists and hands. How hot it must be in the theatre. She heard quite plainly the tinkle of the sequins and spangles as the girls came trooping down the stone stairs into the wings to wait there for the curtain's rise. Then she perceived in the dim light Old Man Veal diligently cleaning his master's gun. Wishing he would not sit there underneath her window, she turned back into the tall shadowy room and lit the candle. Soon she heard his retreating footsteps, and watched him go down the garden path with the slim and wicked gun beneath his arm. Young Frank, rose-misted with dreams of butterflies and painted rubber balls, lay in his hooded cot. Shading him with her hand, which the candlelight made lucent as a shell, she watched him lying there, his fingers clasped tightly round a coral hung with silver bells, his woolly lamb beside his cheek. Jenny wondered whether, had she been a boy, she would have looked exactly like young Frank. Then she fell to speculating whether, had he belonged to her and Maurice, he would have been the same dear rogue as now. Oh, he was hers, hers only, and whatever man were his father, he would be nothing more than hers!

She went to see how May was getting on, and in company they undressed, as they used to undress before Jenny joined the Ballet. Soon both of them in long white nightgowns, each with a golden candle, pattered in once more to marvel at young Frank.

'Oh, I must have him in bed with me, May.'

'Well, why don't you?'

Carefully they lifted him and, warm with sun-dyed sleep, laid him in Jenny's cool bed.

'Light the nightlight, there's a love,' said Jenny. 'Good night.'

'Good night,' whispered May, fading like a ghost through the black doorway, leaving the tall room to Jenny and Frank. Tree shadows, conjured by the moon, waved on the walls, but very faintly, for the nightlight burned with steady flame in the opalescent saucer. Jenny settled herself to think what she should say to Maurice next morning. But soon she forgot all about Maurice, and 'I'd rather like to have a little girl,' was her last thought before she went dreaming.

XLVIII

Carni Vale

Jenny woke up the next morning in a grey land of mist. A sea-fog had come in to obliterate Trewinnard and even the sparkling month of June, evoking a new and impalpable world, a strange undated season. Above the elm trees and the hill-tops the fog floated and swayed in vaporous eddies. Jenny's first impulse was to postpone the meeting on the cliffs, and yet the day somehow suited the enterprise. Shrouded fittingly, she would face whatever ghosts Maurice had power to raise.

'I'm going for a walk,' she told May. 'By myself. I want to tell Maurice not to hang about here any more because it gets on my nerves.'

'I'll look after Frank when you're gone,' said May.

'Don't let him eat any more wool off that lamb of his, will you?'

'All right.'

'I shan't be long. Or I don't expect so.'

'If he gets back from Plymouth before you come in, where shall I say you've gone?' May asked.

'Oh, tell him "Rats!" I can't help his troubles. So long,' said Jenny emphatically.

'Say "ta-ta" nicely to your mother, young Frank,' commanded Aunt May.

As Jenny faded into the mist, the boy hammered his farewells upon the window-pane; and for a while in the colourless air she saw his rosy cheeks burning like lamps, or like the love for him in her own heart. Before she turned up the drive she waited to listen for the click and tinkle of Granfa's horticulture, but there was no sound of his spade. Farther along she met Thomas.

'Morning! Mrs. Trewhella!'

'Morning, young Thomas.'

'Going for a walk, are 'ee?'

'On the cliffs,' Jenny nodded.

'You be careful how you do walk there. I wouldn't like for 'ee to fall over.'

'Don't you worry. I'll take jolly good care I don't do that.'

'Well, anybody ought to be careful on they cliffs. Nasty old place that is on a foggy morning.' Then as she became in a few steps a wraith, he chanted in farewell courtesy, 'Mrs. Trewhella!'

Along the farm road Jenny found herself continually turning round to detect in her wake an unseen follower. She had a feeling of pursuit through the shifting vagueness all around, and stopped to listen. There was no footstep: only the drip-drip, drip-drip of the fog from the elm boughs. Before she knew that she had gone so far, the noise of the sea sounded from the greyness ahead, and beyond there was the groan of a siren from some uncertain ship. Again she paused for footsteps, and there was nothing but the drip-drip, drip-drip of the fog in the quickset hedge. On the steep road that ran up towards Crickabella, the fog lifted from her immediate neighbourhood, and she could see the washed-out sky and silver sun with vapours curling across the strange luminousness. On either side, thicker by contrast, the mist hung in curtains dreary and impenetrable. Very soon the transparency in which she walked was veiled again, and through an annihilation of shape and colour and scent and sound Jenny pressed forward to the summit.

On the plateau, although the fog was dense enough to mask the edge of the cliff at a distance of fity yards and to merge in a grey confusion sky and sea beyond, the fresher atmosphere lightened the general effect. She could watch the fog sweeping up and down in diaphanous forms and winged nonentities. The silence in the hedgeless, treeless country was profound. The sea, oily calm in such weather, gave very seldom a low sob in some cavern beneath the cliff. Far out a solitary gull cried occasionally.

How absurd, thought Jenny suddenly, to expect Maurice on such a day. What painting was possible in so elusive a landscape, so immaterial a scene? He was not at all likely to be there. She stood for a moment listening, and was violently startled by the sight of some animal richly hued even in such a negation of colour. The fox slipped by her with lowered brush and ears laid back, vanishing presently over the side of the cliff. She had thought for a second that it was Trewhella's dog and her heart beat very quickly in the eerie imagination of herself and his master alone in this greyness. She walked on over the cushions of heather, pricking her ankles in the low bushes of gorse. Burnet roses were in bloom, lying like shells on the ground. Ahead of her she saw a lonely flower tremulous in the damp mist. It was a blue columbine, a solitary plant full blown. Jenny thought how beautiful it looked and was stooping to pluck it, when she drew back conscious that it would be a shame not to let it live, this lovely deep blue flower, nodding faintly.

Jenny stood once more fronting the vapours on each side in turn, and was on the point of going home, when she perceived a shadow upon the mist that with approach acquired the outlines of a man and very soon proved to be Maurice. She noticed how pale he was and anxious, very unlike the old Maurice, even unlike himself of five or six weeks ago.

'You've come at last,' he said.

'Yes, I've come to say you mustn't stay here no more. It worries me.'

'Jenny,' he said, 'I knew I'd been a fool before I saw you again last first of May. I've known for four years what a fool and knave I'd been; but, oh God, I never knew so clearly till the other day, till I'd hung about these cliffs waiting for you to come.'

'Where was the good?' she asked. 'It's years too late now.'

'When I heard from Castleton where you were, I tried not to come. He told me I should make things worse. He said it would be a crime. And I tried not to all this winter. But you haunted me. I could not rest, and in April the desire to see you became a madness. I had to come.'

'I think you acted very silly. It isn't as if you could do anything by coming. I never used to think about you.'

'You didn't?' he repeated, agonized.

'Never. Never once,' she stabbed. 'I'd forgotten you.'

'I deserve it.'

'Of course you do. You can't mess up a girl's life and then come and say you're sorry the same as if you'd trod on her toe.'

They were walking along involuntarily, and through the mist Jenny's words of sense, hardened to adamantine sharpness by suffering, cut clear and cruel and true. She did not like, however, to prosecute the close encounter in such a profusion of space. She fancied her words were lost in the great fog, and sought for some familiar outline that should point the way to Crickabella. Presently a narrow serpentine path gave her the direction.

'This way,' she said, 'I can't talk up here. I feel as if there must be listeners in this fog. I wish it would get bright.'

'It's like my life has been without you,' said Maurice.

'Shut up,' she stabbed again, 'and don't talk silly. Your life's been quite all right till you took a sudden fancy to see me again.'

'Walk carefully,' said Maurice humbly. 'We're very near the cliff's edge.'

Land and air met in a wreathed obscurity.

'Down here,' said Jenny.

They scrambled down into Crickabella, slipping on the pulpy leaves of withered bluebells, stumbling over clumps of fern and drenching themselves in the foxgloves, whose woolly leaves held the dripping fog.

'This is where I often used to sit,' said Jenny. 'Only it's too wet in the grass now. There's a rock here that's fairly dry, though it does look rather like a gravestone sticking up out of the ground.'

They were now about half-way down the escarpment from the top of which the rampart of black cliff, sheer on either side of the path, ran up for twenty feet, so far as could be judged in the deceptive atmosphere. Jenny leaned against the stone outcrop and faced Maurice.

'Jenny,' he began. 'When I didn't turn up at Waterloo that first of May, I must have been mad. I don't want to make excuses, but I must have been mad.'

'Yes, we can all say that, when we've done anything we shouldn't have.'

'I know it's not an excuse. But I went away in a jangle of nerves. I set my heart on you coming out to Spain, and when you wouldn't and I was there and thought of the strain of a passionate love that seemed never likely to come to anything vital, I gave up all of a sudden. I can't explain. It was like that statue. I had to break it, and I broke my heart in the same way.'

'If you'd come back,' said Jenny, determined he should know all his folly, 'I'd have done anything, anything you asked. I'd have come to live with you for ever.'

'Oh, don't torture me with the irony of it all. Why were you so uncertain then?'

'That's my business,' she said coolly.

'But I never really was out of love with you. I was always madly in love,' Maurice cried. 'I travelled all over Europe, thinking I'd finished with love. I tried to be happy without you and couldn't because I hadn't got you. I adored you the first moment I saw you. I adore you now and for ever. Oh, believe me, my heart of hearts, my life, my soul, I love you now more, more than ever.'

'Only because I'm someone else's,' said Jenny.

'No,' he cried. 'No! no! The passion and impetuousness and unrestraint is all gone. I love you now – it sounds like cant – for yourself, for your character, your invincible joyousness, your glory in life, your perfection of form. Words! What are they? See how this fog destroys the world, making it ghostly. My mere passion for you is gone like the world. It's there, it must be there always, but your spirit, your personality can destroy it in a moment. Oh, what a tangle of nonsense. Forgive me. I want forgiveness, and once you said "Bless you." I want that.'

'I don't hate you now,' Jenny said. 'I did for a time. But not now. Now you're nothing. You just aren't at all. I've got a boy who I love – such a rogue, bless him – and what are you any more?'

'I deserve all this. But once you were sorry when I – when I—'

'Ah, once,' she said. 'Once I was mad, too. I nearly died. I didn't care for nothing, not for *any*thing. You was the first man that made me feel things like love. You! And I gave you more than I'd ever given anyone, even my mother. And you threw it all back in my face – because you are a man, I suppose, and can't understand. And when I was mad to do something that would change me from ever ever being soppy again, from ever loving anyone again, ever, ever – I went and gave myself to a rotter. A real dirty rotter. Just nothing but that – if you know what I mean. And that was your fault, you started me off by teaching me love. I wanted to be loved. Yes! But I gave too much of myself to you as it was, and I gave nothing to him really – only anyone would say I did. And then my mother went mad, because she thought I was gone gay: and she died: and I got married to what's nothing more than an animal. But they're all animals. All men. Some are nicer sorts of animal than others, but they're all the same. And that's me since you left me. Only now I've got a boy, and he's like *me*. He's got my eyes and I'm going to teach him so as he isn't an animal, see? And I've got my little sister May, who I promised I'd look after, and I have . . . Go away, Maurice, leave me. I don't want you. I can't forgive you. I can only just not care whether you're there or not. But go away, because I don't want to be worried by other people.'

Maurice bowed his head.

'I see, I see that I have suffered nothing,' he said. 'Superficial fool that I am. Shallow, shallow ass, incompetent, dull and unimaginative block! I'm glad I've seen you. I'm glad I've heard you say all that. You taught me something – perhaps in time. I'm only twenty-eight now – and fancy, you're only twenty-four – so I can go and think what might have been and, better, what I may be – through you, what I will be. I won't say I'm sorry. That would be an impertinence . . . As you said, I simply am not at all.'

The mist closed round them thicker for a moment; then seemed to lighten very slowly. Jenny was staring at the cliff's top.

'Is that a bush blowing up and down or a man's head bobbing?'

'I don't see any man,' he answered.

'Goodbye,' Jenny said.

'Goodbye.'

She turned to the upward path, pulling herself up the quicker by grasping handfuls of fern-fronds. Suddenly there was a shout through the fog.

'Snared, my lill wild thing!'

There came a report. Jenny fell backwards into the ferns and foxgloves and withered bluebells.

'Good God!' cried Maurice. 'You're hurt!'

'Something funny's happened. Oh! Oh! It's burning,' she shrieked. 'Oh, my throat! my throat! . . . my throat!'

The sea-birds wheeled about the mist, screaming dismay.